TITAN'S TEARS

Chad Lester

2024

Hardcover ISBN 979-8-9896121-0-9
Paperback ISBN 979-8-9896121-1-6
Ebook ISBN 979-8-9896121-2-3
Library of Congress Control Number: 2023922969

1. Fiction / Science Fiction / Genetic Engineering.
2. Fiction / Thrillers / Technological.
3. Fiction / Gothic.

Published 2024

For my mother.

"For even Satan masquerades as an angel of light."

2 CORINTHIANS 11:14

Prologue

OREGON

A newborn wailed in the arms of a sobbing young mother. Footprints marked the otherwise pristine snow. The cutting winter wind blew the woman's red scarf against her frostbit face as she trudged through knee-high snowpack. Under the dying light of the moon she continued, one step in front of the other. Wolves howled from the conifers beyond. She clutched her little one closer. The snow was getting deeper, up to her waist now. Her newborn wailed. She tried to shush the baby, but it was no use and now both of them were crying. Something rustled beyond the tree line, a lurking shadow. She wasn't used to being alone in the woods. Whatever it was, it had been following them since she started at the trailhead. She tried to move faster but it was much harder moving now, every step was more exhausting than the last and the bite of the cold sapped what little strength she had. She knew she shouldn't have tried to make such a trek in her condition and she knew it was stupid to come out all this way by herself but she needed to do it—before anyone found out.

She took a few more steps and collapsed.

As she lay in the snow, the wind brought in the smell of woodsmoke. She was close. She groaned as she grabbed a nearby branch with one hand and climbed back to her wobbling feet. With her other hand she clutched her infant to her chest. She followed the scent until she came upon a lone forty-foot-tall belltower in the middle of the woods. Below it stood a timeworn hacienda with wooden shutters and a terracotta roof. A dull flickering yellow light filled one of hacienda's windows. It wasn't just a dream—it was real, and she had found it.

She stumbled to a wrought iron gate that led to an inner courtyard. She tried to lift the latch, but it was frozen. Crying out, she shook and pounded the gate. It didn't budge. She began to walk toward the other side of the compound in hopes of finding another way in. Then came a squeal. She looked back and noticed that the gate was now open.

She lurched her way into the courtyard and saw a wooden sign that read "Donations." Below the sign was a door. She opened it and walked inside. Only a single oil lamp illuminated the plain plaster walls and rough-cut timbers of the floors and ceilings. Halfway up the wall was a built-in shelf with a revolving cupboard atop it, a barrier between the worldly and the sacred. Next to the turnstile was a single brass bell with a long string attached.

She gazed at her infant one last time and began to place her on the shelf. As she let her child slip from her arms, she hesitated. She turned her head and tried not to look at her little girl but she couldn't help herself. Her breath came heavy and she started sobbing. Then she clenched her jaw hard and placed her little one on the shelf and slowly turned the revolving cupboard. She put her hand on the long string of the bell and held it for what felt like an eternity.

"I'm sorry," she whispered.

She rang it.

Then she fled the hacienda and hobbled back down toward the trailhead, her tears frozen against the winter wind.

Chapter 1

BELLE

Kobuksville, Alaska
Modern Era: Post-Singularity

B elle was later told that a woman in a brown habit heard an impossible sound that night. The woman spied a thin winding trail of winter breath emanating from a bundle of cloth in the donation turnstile. As she drew nearer, she was surprised to see a baby girl.

Sister Maria lived in the remote Oregon monastery with her convent of off-the-grid Carmelites. Their dwelling was indistinguishable from the Spanish-style haciendas generations of Carmelites had called home for more than half a millennium. They lived a simple life of self-reliance and were typically found as far away from modern civilization as possible — but it seemed civilization had found them.

Of course, the convent couldn't keep the baby girl. It was said that Sister Maria had to be dragged away by the other sisters when the authorities came to pick baby Belle up.

Belle would later learn that some considered Sister Maria to be a bit off her rocker. The nun often talked of visions and foretelling dreams. She told the other sisters that Belle needed protection, that she had seen "something" in the child. She said she had seen God in her eyes, but the baby girl's innocence had attracted a malevolent force, something dark, something lurking after her immortal soul.

Well, what else was a nun supposed to say?

All Belle knew was that she needed to get out her village or she was going to go stir crazy. She had been there ever since she began her self-rehabilitation. It had been a long and arduous struggle but now she wanted to get out of the town and hoped to find some work. Ideally as far away as possible. She kept applying for jobs, but no one was interested. She was stuck. Her memory was foggy these days and her troubled childhood was something she did her best to forget. Now she found her thirty-year-old-self living alone in a secluded Alaskan village, unemployed.

No roads led to Kobuksville. The only way in or out was by the small airstrip just outside of the village. It wasn't all bad. The surrounding landscape was a place of snowcapped peaks against swaths of pine-strewn glory along the winding Kobuk River. Salmon passed through streams as clear as glass, and moose and great herds of caribou roamed the ancient valleys.

Belle was a shy type, but she still considered herself a people person in her own way. She'd once had dreams of being an elementary teacher but her education consisted entirely of books. She didn't have the expensive degrees and the certifications and the test results required for such a job, so her teaching career was just that—a dream. Eventually she found her niche working with children in a different way.

She used to make ends meet working as a nanny. Mostly she was in demand by parents of disabled children, but not always. Kids, what could she say? It was the type of work where in one moment she wanted to tear her hair out and in the next she realized she wouldn't have it any other way. Though in Kobuksville she was alone, completely and utterly alone.

She spent most of her days hiking, reading, or in counseling sessions with her psychiatrist, Dr. Musa, who encouraged her to enjoy the scenery, take it easy, and follow current events. He didn't live in the town but someplace far away so she had to interact with his hologram. This annoyed her. She would have preferred to talk to a person in the flesh instead of their live projection.

It just so happened that today was her regularly scheduled appointment. As Belle sipped her tea on her couch, Dr. Musa's figure, clipboard in hand, appeared in the chair across from her.

"How are you feeling, Belle?" he asked.

"Anxious," she said.

"Anxious? Why?"

"Why can't I visit my parents?"

"You will, you will, you just need to be patient."

"I've been patient for months. Why are you keeping me here?"

"I'm not keeping you anywhere."

"I talked to the pilot who comes once a week for deliveries. He refused to take me out of the village. When I asked him why he let others ride out with him but not me, he said that he had been given instructions not to let me leave."

"Did he say who these instructions were from?"

"No, he wouldn't tell me."

"And you're implying that I have something to do with this pilot's choice of passengers?"

"You're the only person I talk to here. Granted, you're not even really here."

"Come on Belle, what motivation could I possible have to keep you there? Think about it for a moment and then give me your honest answer."

"Well, I don't know exactly. It just seems like I'm trapped. There are no jobs willing to take me away, and I've applied all over the place. The stupid pilot won't take me. I've hiked about twenty miles from this village in every direction and there is nothing but wilderness. Then there's the village — it's just so bizarre. Nobody here talks to me, and I just feel so isolated. I'm also anxious and depressed and I feel like I've lost something and I can't find it. Whatever *it* is. Are you sure there isn't something you're not telling me? Are you hiding something?"

"Hiding something? I'm sorry to disappoint you, Belle, but you came to quiet Kobuksville to get well, remember?"

Belle rubbed her temples. "I only know it doesn't feel right to be here."

"Anxiety is perfectly natural. Just relax and enjoy the beauty around you. That's what you need to do right now, just relax. Everything you seek will come in good time. We'll talk again soon."

And that was that. Talk? She didn't really talk with Dr. Musa, she was being psychoanalyzed. It wasn't a two-way conversation. Naturally, when she asked about his personal life, he gave superficial answers or was coy or in some cases just outright avoided them. One morning, she'd been so desperate for a real conversation she started mumbling to herself during breakfast. When she realized what she was doing, she clamped her mouth shut.

What she didn't tell her psychiatrist was that somehow, even though she couldn't explain it, she felt like she was being watched. She tore her accommodations apart one day looking for hidden cameras, but there were none. During her hikes in the forest she even studied some of the trees, searching for surveillance devices, but of course there was nothing but her paranoia. She had no proof, so what good would it be to say anything? Besides if anyone was watching her it was Dr. Musa. Then again maybe it was all in her head. She didn't know. She only knew she was tired and lonely and confused.

Yes, Kobuksville was peculiar. Very peculiar.

It was Sunday morning. Belle had gotten dressed in her finest clothes and left her quarters. The buildings she walked past looked like a collection of shipping containers with square holes for windows. Every building was a featureless box along the grid of gravel roads. Some of the boxes were metal, some were made of composites, others of wood.

As was her Sunday routine, she stepped inside the ruins of a Romanesque chapel just outside her remote mountain village. It was the only edifice left in that old village that had any semblance of character and she was its only parishioner.

The windows were long gone, and green foliage and wild-flowers grew on the inside. In the springtime the chapel was filled with a magnificent combination of yellow and magenta and white. Only a single wooden pew remained—her pew. She sat and prayed.

The isolation of the people matched the character of the town. They rarely strayed outdoors. Everyone in this place lived in their own little world. In fact, only a third of the population of the town was human. The rest were the townspeople's android companions. The bots looked human but too beautiful, with the predictable features exaggerated.

As she left the ruined chapel and headed back to her own nondescript accommodations, Belle saw a man in the middle of the gravel road. She saw him regularly, but like the other villagers he rarely spoke. Beside the man stood three bots of the female persuasion. On the opposite side of the gravel road was a woman with three bots of the male persuasion. The people were dressed for the cold mornings while the androids weren't wearing much of anything. The man and the woman looked at each other. Then they looked at Belle, who said hello and gave a weak wave.

They said nothing in response. The man and the woman went into separate quarters on opposite sides of the road with their bots in tow. Then Belle returned to her quarters, alone. Taking off her jacket, she realized that there was something else lacking about the village. It took her a while to put her finger on it—the laughter of children.

As she finished her morning coffee she received a call. It was strange, for she never got calls. A man by the name of Dominic appeared. He said he was representing the chief executive of the world's premier tech company, Eccleston Evolution.

"We'd like to fly you out, all expenses paid, to meet with our CEO—Sophia Eccleston. She has requested to meet with you about your job application."

"The reclusive inventor?"

"Yes."

"Who won the Nobel Prize?"

"Yes."

"And she wants to meet me?

"Yes."

"Why?"

"We found your resume, and we think you're a great fit."

Belle paced her quarters and wrung her hands together. It was finally the opportunity she had been waiting for. However, it all seemed too good to be true. She had sent hundreds of copies of her resume out months ago, and she knew she hadn't sent a single one to Eccleston Evolution. It was very curious.

"I don't understand. I'm not a tech person. I'm looking to be a nanny or governess or something like that. Are you sure you're not confusing me with somebody else?"

"I'm sure."

"Forgive me for asking, but why would the CEO bother to interview a nanny? Besides, everyone knows that Sophia doesn't have children."

"We happen to have a unique opportunity for your skill set. Though, you'll be required to sign a nondisclosure agreement and follow strict security protocols. Is that something you can do?"

"Security protocols?"

"We can explain that during the interview."

"Okay then, I suppose I don't see any problem with that."

"Excellent. The pay will, of course, be extremely competitive."

"That's all very good news. What kind of position is this exactly?"

"There will be a private jet arriving at your village tomorrow at noon to pick you up. We can discuss it then."

"I'm sorry, this is all very strange and abrupt."

"I'm aware of that, and you have my apologies. It's all for security reasons, I assure you. I hope you'll understand."

"I feel like I need some more time to think."

"Understandable. Of course, the plane will be there tomorrow at noon either way. Either get on it, or don't. It's your choice. Thank you for your consideration. Goodbye now."

The call ended.

Chapter 2

SOPHIA

Eccleston Campus, Alaska
Modern Era: Post-Singularity

Sophia Eccleston sat at the end of a long boardroom table. Her elbow was casually propped up on the arm of her black saddle leather chair. She was filled dread and a tinge of something else. Excitement, maybe—she liked a good fight. At the far opposite end of the table sat the chairman, Mr. Raymond Dearborn. On Sophia's left side sat her executives, facing a group of stern lawyers on the right. The lawyers were led by Mr. Chase Chamberlain, Esquire. He placed his interlaced fingers atop the table and did his best to feign a sigh of concern.

"Ms. Eccleston, as chief executive, you've had a fine run—" said Mr. Chamberlain.

"No, I've had and continue to have an outstanding run," said Sophia.

"Well, ma'am, if we're being honest —"

"Lawyers are never honest, Mr. Chamberlain."

Mr. Chamberlain licked his lips and smirked. "It's time for you step down. The company, frankly speaking, isn't in good financial shape. Our client —"

"The bank?"

"No. The private equity firm, Madurai Capit —"

"Same difference."

"Ma'am, are you going continue interrupting, or should we just take this to court?"

"Not at all, please continue."

The lawyer straightened his back and glared at her.

"We've offered an outstanding bid for Eccleston Evolution. Are you willing to accept, yes or no?"

"Of course not. My company isn't for sale."

"In that case, our client will demand, and win, billions for breach of contract. That's not including the potential criminal charges you personally face — conspiracy, theft of funds, accounting fraud, and the list goes on. Of course, lest we forget, you've also kept proprietary treatments that are vital to my client's health away from him. Yet, my client is forgiving. Too forgiving, in my opinion, and despite my protests, Madurai Capital is merely asking you to take your golden parachute and allow Mr. Ivanov to lead your wonderful company into the future and put the past behind him."

"You mean the chief executive of Madurai Capital."

"I mean your third-largest shareholder."

"Unfortunately for him, he isn't the first."

"Not yet."

"Not ever."

"Mr. Ivanov has consistently ranked as one of the top business leaders in the world, and he will take very good care of Eccleston Evolution and its shareholders. As you know, your shareholders are already abuzz talking about the extremely generous tender offer we've made to purchase the company. Share prices are up, way up."

"Of course. Out of curiosity, what share of the payout would go to your law firm?"

"Ma'am I don't discuss confidential contracts between my firm and my client. In any case —"

The lawyer was interrupted by a knock at the boardroom doors. Sophia's assistant, Dominic, helped himself in and placed a cup and saucer in front of her, then left as quickly as he came. Sophia held up the small porcelain cup of espresso. She closed her eyes and smelled it. Then she took a loud slurp. The legal team's expression ranged from bemused to annoyed and—in the case of Mr. Chamberlain—angry. Sophia patted her mouth with a bloodred napkin. Then she smiled her usual wry smile.

"Did you know that river blindness is caused a curious species of coiled worm—*Onchocera volvulus*? They're known to crawl through a victim's skin and trigger an immune response, a terrible rash. Victims have been known to scratch themselves to death. Of course, from the parasite's perspective it's only doing what it needs to survive. So what can I say, some people imitate other lifeforms."

"So you'd prefer the courtroom then?"

"Ah yes, the courts. Well, I suppose I could finally see how effective decades of my legalized bribes to our benevolent government officials has been."

"Ma'am, I don't think you appreciate consequences of your actions today. Trust me, campaign donations won't help you."

"If they're not helpful, then why do people make them? No matter. What do you think, Raymond?"

Startled, the sleepy old chairman at the opposite end of the table opened his eyes and coughed. "Well, as always, I trust your judgment on this matter," said Raymond.

"What do you make of Mr. Ivanov?" Sophia asked.

"Shrewd. Effective. Ambitious. Smooth talker."

"So he's fit to the take the reins?"

"There would be much he'd have to learn. Our company is quite unique. Though I suppose it's possible," he said.

"Well then, Mr. Chamberlain, it seems I have some thinking to do."

The lawyer glanced at his colleagues, nodded, and then tilted his chin up. "Ms. Eccleston, don't take too long to come to a decision. My client has already been extremely patient."

Mr. Chamberlain and his four colleagues stood up in unison and walked toward the door. As the lawyer put his hand on the door handle, Sophia swiveled toward him.

"Well, I certainly don't want to make any rash decisions, now do I?"

The legal team left without responding.

Sophia and Mr. Dearborn left the boardroom soon after. As they walked the expansive granite halls adorned with embedded fossils of mammoths, Raymond hobbled along with his cane, pleading with her to slow down.

"Excuse me, Raymond, I need another."

She stopped at a nearby espresso stand and pulled two shots. She handed a small white porcelain cup to him.

They finished their espressos and put down their cups and continued walking.

"That went about as well as I expected," Raymond said.

"If they had only demanded money, I might have considered their offer, but they want my whole company. I'd sooner die a slow and painful death."

"I know you would. You're a woman with a vision. After all these years I've known you, you've still got the fire."

"Raymond?"

"Yes?"

"How strong is their case?"

"Very."

"What are our chances of losing in court?"

"High."

"Well then, I guess I'll just have to beat the odds—as usual."

"You don't seem very concerned."

"That's because I have far bigger predators to worry about."

Chapter 3

SETH

Port Auburn, Oregon
Modern Era: Post-Singularity

He stood over the maimed body and held up his blood-covered hands and studied them. He really was a bastard, wasn't he? His life wasn't supposed to turn out this way. He struggled to think back all those years ago, to figure out where his downward spiral began.

Thirty Years Earlier

Twenty miles per day Seth walked in the warehouse. The machine told him to pick. So he picked. The machine told him he was too slow. So he worked faster. Still the machine, the algorithm, the powers that be wanted more.

Pick those products. Ship them out.

Pick.

Pick.

Pick.

Shoppers are waiting.

Every day a new employee and every day a new termination. Most couldn't keep up with the machine and most were fired by the machine—but Seth wasn't most people. In the old days when he fell behind, a fat man wearing a reflective vest that said "coach" would follow him around and bark at him to go faster, faster, but he didn't blame the man. Deep down Seth was just happy the guy was eating well. Just another man doing his job, trying to make it. Besides, the "coach" was just taking orders from the machine, the data, the higher-ups. Or was it the higher-ups that were taking orders from the data? He didn't know. What he did know was that he couldn't blame the messenger.

Every afternoon, a sheet was put up on the wall. It listed how fast every employee picked products. Every afternoon, his name was at the bottom. So he pushed himself harder, faster.

Pick those products. Ship them out.

Pick.

Pick.

Pick.

Shoppers are waiting.

Until one day he made it to the top of that list—and stayed there unsurpassed. He had just completed his stretches at the usual morning huddle. His boss called him to the center of circle.

"Everyone, once again, I'm pleased to announce that this

month's stock picking champion, Seth Johnson."

Yawns. Polite clapping.

He was good at his job.

Employees regularly murmured during lunch break that they were trapped in a corporate cult. There were three tribes. The true believers, the grudging toe-the-line types, and the heretics. The heretics didn't last very long at The Company—the system—was designed to root them out. The toe-the-line types nodded along when wild-eyed supervisors chanted Company slogans to encourage them to work harder and give rousing speeches declaring war on rival companies. The true believers were an elite few—the Elect. They were people who shouted and cheered along with the supervisors. They'd laugh along with their dull jokes. Types that aimed to please. People who wanted to be part of something greater than themselves. Types who embraced the company religion.

Seth was a toe-the-line type.

He kept his mouth shut. He needed to accomplish his goal. There was an old house on the edge of town. The rundown manor was built of solid stone and sat on an acreage of weeds and wildflowers. The last remnants of a nearly extinct dynasty. If he just worked a little longer, a little harder, he could buy that dilapidated house before it was condemned to rubble.

Snow crunched under his feet. Timeworn chestnut trees loomed over an expansive estate. He stood before an old manor. Its gargoyles looking down upon him. The whole place had been built of stone in a bygone age of craftmanship. The places where the windows once shone were now mostly empty. The interior beyond the stone facade had been gutted long ago. The upper floors were rotted and only the fireplaces and their beautiful mantles remained. The slate roof had gaping holes in it. Even in its ruined state it remained the grandest home in that rural northwestern town.

There was a family name, carved in stone, above the doorway.

Johnson.

His earliest ancestors had come along the Oregon trail and settled in a log cabin that they built with their own hands. His great-great-grandparents were timber barons. They became wealthy and built a grand estate. They once owned a million acres of forest, which they tended to carefully. They always made sure to only take the minimum number of trees and move plot to plot in order to sustain the forest and thereby sustain their family. His great-grandparents were also successful timber barons, but his grandparents decided to go their own way. They didn't take care of the forest. They cut down too many trees to squeeze a quick profit. They liked a life of leisure. They liked to spend. His parents inherited no estate, no acres of prime woodland, only debts and worries. By the time Seth came around, there were only fading memories and an abandoned house, a monument of what once was.

So it was that the beautiful old stone house was slated for demolition.

In its place a gravel parking lot was planned.

It was a Saturday when he bid on the old house. In truth he was bidding on the land. The ruined house wasn't worth anything except to him. He brought everything he had, his life savings. The Stetson-wearing auctioneer cried out and up and up the price went. The townspeople told him he was crazy. It was true that he could have bought a decent house in town for less than it would cost to fix up the old manor. God knew he could never afford a house in a city or a suburb, and he was sure God knew that he had no desire to live in such a place either. The townsfolk reminded him that his bid was way more than the land was worth. He had to admit that it was telling that none of the local farmers were bidding on it. What else could it be used for? Like many small American towns, his town had a net loss of residents, so there wasn't exactly demand for housing developments and shiny new condominiums.

The bidding stagnated. Then the last bidder backed out.

SOLD.

Most of his savings were gone, and now he was the proud owner of a ruined house. He brought a blue tarp and a sleeping bag and some jugs of water and he moved into that old house the same day.

Before his time at the warehouse, he had done carpentry and roofing work in the summers. He bought some secondhand tools and old books about woodworking, the way it used to be done. He bought timber. Lots of timber. Then he went to work.

Chapter 4

BELLE

Kobuksville and St. Olga, Alaska
Modern Era: Post-Singularity

The world around Belle was aflame. She found herself surrounded by crumbling buildings, glass-strewn sidewalks, bent streetlights, and hellfire that glowed through cracked asphalt roads torn asunder by a great earthquake. Ash rained from a sky of charcoal clouds. The nearby trees were reduced to blackened skeletons of timber that creaked and groaned against the hot wind. There was nothing green nor of any vivid color in sight. Only a scarred landscape of mud and filth and ruin.

Belle walked for a while and came upon an expanse of ash-silted pastureland, dried brown grass. It was filled with emaciated livestock and gaunt people scraping by against the backdrop of the monumental ruins of a once-great society. These wretched souls were ignorant of what had happened in the time before time. Only she was blessed and cursed with the truth. Once their vacant eyes caught sight of her, they began to walk toward Belle. They shed tears of blackened blood as they held out their withered hands.

Three people broke from the crowd and hobbled toward her. One held a ragged Tyrian purple pillow with a gleaming golden crown atop it and another held another purple pillow with a shining scepter atop it and the person in the center held out a golden, jewel-encrusted cup. Ones and zeros mixed with blood spilled forth from the chalice as they offered it to her.

She screamed.

Her alarm rang.

Struggling to catch her breath, Belle smacked the clock in a cold sweat. It was a futile attempt to stop the awful noise — the old clock didn't have a snooze button. At first, she had found the windup clock with twin metal bells charming, but now she regretted her weakness for rummage sales. She sat up and fumbled with the switch on the back of the clock as it continued to ring until she somehow managed to turn it off. Belle rushed to record her bizarre recurring dream.

She had been trying to keep track of them before they drifted away, to see if there was a connection between them. She couldn't shake the idea that something was missing inside her. Something was buried in the fog of her mind. She was certain of it. Though it seemed every time she approached the fog, she became frightened of what lay beyond it and ran away.

Today was the day she was supposed to leave her village to meet the enigmatic Sophia Eccleston. Had she finally gotten her chance or was it some sort of trick? Whatever the real story was, it couldn't possibly be any weirder than Kobuksville.

Whether they were talked about or advertised, Belle saw the name of the company and its reclusive founder pop up in nearly all that she read and watched. She knew that Eccleston Evolution had its tendrils coiled around a bit of everything: biotech, robotics, artificial intelligence, and security services. And who led this enterprise? Sophia Eccleston, of course, Nobel Prize-winning entrepreneur and beloved international treasure.

Belle had read much about Sophia. The woman was considered a heroine and even a sort of techno-saint to some. She healed people and she saved lives, probably millions through her innovations. There were other aspects of Sophia's quest for invention that made Belle uneasy, though. Through her, human science had conjured an unnatural intelligence. It was said that this thing, this intelligence she had birthed, had the combined knowledge and intellect of every human being that had ever existed. It was said that the singularity had finally been reached. Belle thought it was incredible, yet news of it was met with a collective yawn. To the public, it was yet another supersmart artificial intelligence that was supposedly slightly better than the last supersmart artificial intelligence. Nobody cared.

It was called the Augur.

Belle thought the name fitting. In old Rome, Augurs played a critical role in interpreting the will of the gods.

No major undertakings, whether matters of peace or war, commerce or religion, were done without consulting the auspices of the Augur. Much like the ancients, important matters such as war and peace were now run through the machine before major decisions were even considered. The way the machine really worked was just as mysterious to the average person as the ancient Augur's rituals would have been to the average Roman some two millennia ago.

Belle had read that when the Augur was pitted in a series of war games against a team of generals, the generals lost. Every. Single. Time. The defeated generals remarked that the machine was so intelligent it often seemed as if the Augur could see ten steps ahead of them—as if it could actually predict the future just like the Augurs of old.

Belle also saw countless ads about the Dream Maker. Eccleston Evolution's flagship product. A neural interface. A computer in your head. Where men and women became machines incarnate. Swallow a pill and let the nanobots do the rest. A leap above and beyond the competition. They assured that users were in "complete control." It had long since been declared that the arrival of neural interfaces marked the extinction of homo sapiens and the birth of a new species, a new source of worship: homo deus. The human god.

Human invention had finally given the species abilities that previous generations could only dream of. Perhaps if people could travel backward in time, Belle thought, they might very well be seen as gods. Or perhaps demons.

For a moment there was excitement about the product, immediately followed by collective boredom and then yearning for the next big thing.

And how was this powerful tool used? So far as Belle could tell, for the same things people always used their newfound tools for: games, gossip, the salacious, and of course, all things cat related. The Dream Maker had safety mechanisms to remind seemingly sleeping people of the need to disconnect and make time to actually eat and bathe and move rather than spending all their time in fake worlds. Of course, many would intravenously nourish themselves, slip into diapers, and ignore the warnings for days until finally being jolted awake and shut out of their connection—lest they forget about their physical needs altogether. Perhaps if such people did travel back in time they would just would have been seen as large helpless sloths.

It was Monday when she walked to the small airstrip outside of the village. If the plane was actually there, it was her way out. If it wasn't, then she could prove to herself that no mythical private jet would be landing in the middle of nowhere Alaska to rescue her from Kobuksville. She had to keep reminding herself that the call was real. That she had really spoken to a man by the name of Dominic. Her long Alaskan days tended to melt together. Sometimes even her dreams seemed to melt into day, and in the back of her mind she worried that maybe she didn't know what was and wasn't real. She'd never had such a feeling growing up. Rather, she seemed to have picked it up after moving to Kobuksville. She wasn't sure if it was the isolation or if there something else about the place or something inside her mind, something she didn't want to explore.

Belle reached the airstrip around noon. She stopped when she caught a glimpse of a glistening white private jet, complete with a purple Eccleston Evolution logo on its tail, sitting on the airstrip, its door already open. It was real. A stewardess in a purple uniform peered out of the aircraft and waved to her.

"Are you coming?" she asked.

"I'm sorry?"

"To Eccleston headquarters, are you coming?"

Belle boarded with caution. The interior looked more like a plush art deco hotel lounge than a passenger aircraft.

"Have a seat, and make yourself comfortable," said the stewardess.

"Oh, I don't know," she replied.

"It's up to you, but we have to get going in the next few minutes. Would you like some champagne? It's on the house."

Traveling at several times the speed of sound, Belle didn't have much time to enjoy the complimentary champagne and raspberries. She did manage to pocket as many overpriced mints as she could get her shameless hands on.

Oddly, the plane turned toward the sea, where the islands of the Tongass National Forest lay. The flight attendant informed her that it was the largest national forest in America and part of the largest intact boreal forest in the world. The plane changed direction. She saw a mist-covered patch of rugged land planted in a dark, thrashing sea. It was just one of many forested islands that that made up the vast Alexander Archipelago.

The plane descended into the mist and landed on the mountainous island.

Belle disembarked, expecting a ride to pick her up. Instead, there was only a quiet fishing village and a small sign: "Welcome to St. Olga." It was built for perhaps five thousand souls. Wispy clouds draped the snowcapped mountains behind her, which surrounded the town and the crescent-shaped valley. Gazing up at them was an overpowering feeling. Alaska had a way of reminding one of the smallness of their existence.

The town was largely cut off by natural barriers from the rest of the island. Much of it looked like something out of the glory days of the gold rush. Old buildings stood opposite one another along a narrow, fog-filled street dotted with wrought iron streetlights forged into Victorian silhouettes. The charming downtown buildings were painted pastel colors and had ornate millwork and a few had saloon doors reminiscent of a bygone era. Of the establishments, half of them were bars. At the end of the street shone the golden dome of a dilapidated chapel. As she approached, birds flew out of its broken stained-glass windows.

Belle scratched her head. It was all very curious.

She turned and gazed down the main street. It wasn't a stretch to imagine horses and mules and miners covered in the mire of their labors traipsing about in this little slice of civilization. At the end of the narrow street stood a dock made of rough-cut timber and dotted with the bloated bodies of sunbathing harbor seals who would occasionally undulate out of the way for passersby, if the mood so struck them. Tied to the wharf were a lone ferry, a dozen fishing boats, and a few yachts.

She wandered the town for a while and then pushed through the swinging double doors of a saloon, seemingly unchanged since the nineteenth century. The bartender locked eyes on her.

"Can I help you?"

"Yes, is Eccleston Evolution around here somewhere?"

"Yeah."

She glanced out the window behind her, half expecting to see it. "I'm sorry, but I don't see it. Am I in the right place?"

"Eccleston owns everything around here. Their headquarters and most of their people are far out in the woods beyond. Just them and the trees and the mountains. They like it that way. They don't want anyone poking around in their business."

"Do they own this town?"

"Eccleston takes care of the town, and the town takes care of Eccleston. That's all outsiders like you need to know."

"I see. Well, how do I get the headquarters?"

The bartender pointed. "There's a train station. They'll either let you in or they won't."

Belle turned to leave.

"Ma'am, one last thing."

"Yes?"

"Stay out of the woods. When the signs tell you to turn back, I suggest you listen."

She nodded at the strange man and walked out of the saloon.

She soon came upon a modest brick train station with a cupola. Belle tried to open one of its tall doors, but they were locked.

"Hello? Hello?" She knocked a couple of times.

There was no response and not a soul to be seen. Then, as she began to walk away, the doors opened. She was greeted by a conductor wearing a pressed purple uniform, a matching hat, and white gloves.

"Are you Belle?" he asked.

"Yes," she said.

"This way, please."

The inside of the station was empty. She could hear only her footsteps against the polished granite floor. Before she could get a chance to explore the station, she heard the whooshing sound of doors opening.

"Please step inside. You'll be at the headquarters in a bit."

"Is it a subway?"

"Close. It's a hyperloop."

As she entered the hyperloop pod she noticed that it was painted in iridescent white paint that gleamed like mother of pearl and was decorated with electrum-hued outlines of Greek goddesses. Even the upholstery was pure white, and perfectly clean, giving it an almost divine appearance.

There was a slight jerk, and within moments the conductor announced that she was heading to what was officially called the Evolution Building. Apparently the underground hyperloop was the only way to or from the secluded headquarters.

The pod stopped and the doors opened. Behind her was the end of the tunnel, jutting out from a mountain. Belle stepped outside and felt the dim glow of the sun upon her. She found herself beneath an ornate glass and metal pergola.

When she turned, her breath was taken away. An impressive building that looked more like a temple than the headquarters of a company stood high atop a massive rocky outcrop graced by clouds.

"The outcrop is called Olympus, and as for the building, it's based on one of the seven wonders of the world—the Temple of Artemis. Though I'm told this one is quite a bit bigger even when you don't include the underground portions," said the conductor.

The building was sheathed in gleaming white granite and lined with square columns in a stripped-down classical style. The stunning structure succeeded in being both imposing and beautiful. Surrounding the outcrop below was a matching amphitheater and a small city made up of symmetrically laid-out apartment blocks, each about six stories high. The entire Eccleston Evolution campus was largely built in the style of art deco futurism. Its squares and plazas were full of statues that emanated a vibe of optimistic times to come. Beyond the sturdy buildings lay an immense glade with fruit trees, thousands of blue roses, meandering streams, fountains, and lush gardens. A massive semicircular wall of white granite surrounded the entire campus, about twelve yards high and covered in tendrils of ivy. All of this was the beating heart of Sophia Eccleston's empire.

Belle parted ways with the conductor. As she walked toward the temple, she saw two dark eyes gazing at her. They belonged to a beast with stripes on its back. It had the head of a wolf, sharp teeth, and the widest mouth she had ever seen.

It galloped in her direction. She screamed. She turned to run but saw another of the beasts. It licked its lips and loped toward her as drool drizzled from its gaping maw.

Chapter 5

SOPHIA

Eccleston Campus, Alaska
Modern Era: Post Singularity

Sophia rolled her eyes as Dr. Mira Patel, chief of bio-engineering, tilted her head back and groaned upon learning about yet another tangle of thorns she had gotten herself into. It wasn't her fault. She was pushed, so she pushed back—twice as hard. Her old friend was taking the news hard, as she usually did during stressful situations.

"A hostile takeover?" cried Mira.

"Stop that. I'm the one who actually has to deal with it," said Sophia.

"I warned you not to instigate Ivanov."

"That you did."

"Then why didn't you listen? Never mind, why am I even asking?"

"Simple. He wanted more power, and I wasn't going to share it."

"He runs one of the biggest private equity funds in the world, and he owns a third of this company."

"So?"

"So, he's cornered you."

"Sun Tzu says its unwise to corner an enemy."

"Why do you always have to prod the hornets' nest?"

"Ivanov is a hedonistic, status-seeking simpleton who loves money. He has no vision."

"Then he's a highly competent simpleton. Don't underestimate him. He's gobbled up more than two hundred companies over his life. He's even richer than you."

"He buys what he can't create. Like I said, a lack of vision."

"There's not a deal you two can work out?"

"We're past that."

"You've worked with people like him before."

"Yes, so long as they don't infringe on my projects. Ivanov wants to merge this company and shut down my projects as a cost-cutting measure, or rather, an Ivanov-enriching measure. He can't beat me in the boardroom so he's resorted to ways to try to force my hand with a hostile takeover."

"Well, I suppose it wouldn't be your first."

"It won't be my last."

"You're not getting tired of this game, after all these years?"

"It's fun game to play."

Mira sighed and shook her head. "Anyway, everything is in place, just as you asked. Though —"

"Though what?"

"Are you sure about your new guest?"

"Belle? Yes, sure enough."

"Seems risky, even for you. You don't have to bring her here. I still don't think it's a good idea."

"I know what I'm doing."

"You're not getting soft on me, are you?"

Sophia smiled. "Never."

Mira walked away to continue her work. Sophia headed to a desk in the corner of the woman's large office. She poured herself of a steaming cup of coffee and sipped it as she sifted through a number of medical records. Everything was going to plan, more or less. She took another long sip of coffee and considered her own hostile takeovers. In her younger years she had been quite good it. Gobbling up companies, culling staff, assimilating their intellectual property. Had she allowed herself to become prey so easily?

A hand on her shoulder. A crash. Brown liquid splattered against the hard white floor. Sophia turned and saw Mira behind her. She had drifted off in thought and forgotten she was there.

"You startled me," said Sophia.

"Sorry. You knew I was in here."

"No. It's fine."

"You're edgier than usual."

"Nonsense."

"You're lying."

"Am I? It doesn't matter. Anyway, I have a meeting to attend."

Sophia got up and walked out of Mira's office as the coffee pooled on the floor. She heard snoring from the hallway. She followed the sound until she stepped into the board room.

Raymond was sitting in his usual spot. His head lay to the side and drool pooled at the corners of this mouth. A handful of Sophia's executives and Mr. Chamberlain's legal team sat in the same places as they had the previous day.

Sophia sat down. The chairman continued snoring.

"Shall we get started?" she asked.

"Well, Ms. Eccleston, do we have a decision?"

"Where is Mr. Ivanov?"

"Our client couldn't make it."

"Of course he couldn't."

The chairman took a deep gurgling breath and bellowed out another loud snore.

"Are you going to wake him up?"

"Why would I do that?"

The lawyer gritted his teeth. "What's your decision, Ms. Eccleston?"

"You know, I've been thinking about chimpanzees a lot lately."

"Ms. Eccleston, I'm not going to sit here and put up with —"

"You know, chimpanzees have been known to kill and devour their competitors' infants. After all, there can be only one alpha male. Until, of course, enough time passes, and like its fallen forebearers that alpha is also conquered, its infants devoured, and the bloody quest for status continues ad infinitum. So much like us, no?"

Mr. Chamberlain sighed. "We're not here for psychological games. Is it a yes or a no?"

"If Mr. Ivanov chooses to grace us with his presence, I'll give him my decision."

"You're wasting our time."

"No. I'm savoring it."

"We'll see you in court."

"And I'll see you and Mr. Ivanov in good time. Adieu."

The lawyers rose in unison and exited the boardroom. Sophia's executive team followed. The chairman continued snoring. She sat wringing her hands together. The snoring stopped. The old man's eyes fluttered open. He removed a handkerchief and wiped the drool from his chin.

"I haven't seen you this stressed in decades," said Raymond.

"Really, when was the last time?"

"When I met a brilliant young bioengineer trying to get her money-losing startup off the ground."

"Remind me, why did you invest in her?"

"I saw ambition. Raw, relentless ambition—and I see it still."

"It wasn't mere ambition."

"Then what was it I saw all those years ago?"

"The vision, and someone hellbent on carrying it out."

"Not ready to give it up?"

"Over my dead body."

He smiled. "But you've already accomplished your ambition, yes?"

"Maybe."

"Maybe?"

"I don't know. I have reservations about what I'm about to do."

"If you don't do it, your days of being alpha female are over."

"Perhaps."

"There's something you're not telling me."

"There are many things I'm not telling you."

Dearborn held up his cane with one trembling hand and ran his fingers through his white hair with the other. "I know. You and Mira are keeping important things from me."

"We've already had this discussion."

"I know, and yet I keep bringing it up."

"Not now. I have things on my mind."

"The hostile takeover attempt?"

"No."

"Your new guest? Belle is her name, yes?"

"I don't wish to discuss it."

"It wasn't a good idea to bring her here—or any stranger for that matter. The more private we keep our operations, the better. Besides, isn't she, how shall we say—unwell?"

"That's a surprise."

"What?"

"You and Mira actually agree on something."

"It's not too late to change your mind."

"Excuse me, Raymond, I have someone important to meet."

Chapter 6

SETH

Port Auburn, Oregon
Twenty-Five Years Earlier

Before him stood the grandest house in town. The gothic manor was built of solid stone, and her protective gargoyles loomed three stories above. There were no longer any holes in the roof, for he had replaced all the slate shingles. He'd meticulously rebuilt the parquet floors piece by piece in gorgeous geometric patterns and shined them to a high polish. Restored the grand double staircase to its former elegance — complete with hand-carved gargoyle newel posts. Wired the chandeliers and plumbed the clawfoot bathtubs and the rain shower and restored the long row of stained-glass windows along the hallway. Their figures and shapes told the tale of his bloodline in way that seemed as if their story was frozen music. One window was left unfinished, though. His story wasn't quite ready to be told yet.

Attached to the main building was a Victorian greenhouse and outside the greenhouse was what once had been a grand garden. There were mostly weeds there now, though every spring, violet roses bloomed from the garden. The materials hadn't been cheap, but he was able to cover their costs, though the labor he provided himself was worth a small fortune.

At work, he was watching an old woman scrub the break room tables. Her wrinkled hands trembled as she made small, slow circles with a wet rag. Too slow. He knew she was a goner. Another woman ran to help her.

That was when he first saw Anna.

Anna had worked at the warehouse for a about a month, and she was having some problems. She was a seasonal employee and she couldn't keep up with the quota. The woman was a company heretic and Seth didn't expect her last very long. Most seasonals either quit or got fired before their term ended.

Even so, he was assigned to be her coach to see if she could get her numbers up before the machine no longer had a use for her. He was a manager now and the pay was decent. He had gotten warnings that she was spending too much time off task.

He walked the aisles until he found a head of thick black hair. It hung down the sides of her angular face before stopping just below a delicate jaw line. By his observation she was taking her sweet time. She pulled products she wasn't supposed to be picking off the shelf and studied them as if she were shopping.

Her eyes locked on to him. "I suppose you're here to tell me to hurry up."

"I just want to help you meet your rate."

"The rate is a joke."

In the warehouse everything was under control, everything was orderly. Every detail was accounted for. To enter, employees had to pass through a scanner to ensure they weren't stealing. Every movement was monitored. People who felt like they were being watched all the time were productive people.

Anna made it clear that she thought it was all a joke.

He looked both ways, checking to make sure no one else heard. "If you talk like that here, they'll fire you."

"Well, you haven't fired me. Coach," she replied.

He was reminded of the company orders handed down to him. He'd been told to maintain a professional distance at all times. Don't make friends with the rank and file. Don't say, do, or think anything the company wouldn't approve of, and above all don't flirt.

He turned to Anna.

She smiled.

In this of all places? Why? He did not know.

"Please just do it. I don't want to see them fire another person this week."

He didn't know why he'd just uttered those words. Why should he care? Why should he stick his neck out? If yet another person got eaten by the godless machine, so what? He had his own problems. To hell with them.

Then something strange happened. His mouth spoke before his hard heart could react.

"Here, I'll help you get your numbers up for today. That will buy you some more time." He knew he shouldn't do what he was about to. If he got caught, it would be an automatic termination, and there were no other jobs for the likes of him.

Seth seized her cart and began to work the aisles, breaking the rules to artificially raise her rate. He began scanning products and shoving them in her blue plastic totes. Anna raised an eyebrow and followed behind as he rattled off the techniques he had learned over the years.

As he continued talking and scanning, Anna interrupted him.

"So you're one of those Company fanatics aren't you? You actually believe in that crap they feed to you?"

"No, but I gotta make money somehow."

To his surprise, Anna eventually made rate. Granted, it was always the lowest required rate. She was supposed to just be a seasonal employee, the kind who came and went for a little extra money. But she stayed.

They always ate together on break. Like him, she was a survivor. She wanted a house of her own and a family to go with it. There was something odd about her. Old fashioned. He noticed that she always brought two lunches. One for herself and one for the old woman who scrubbed the toilets. But that woman didn't scrub all the toilets by herself. Anna helped her during breaks.

"Why bother?" he asked. "She's too slow. She's going to get fired anytime now. Are you going to help scrub the toilets then? Do twice as much work for the same amount of money?"

"Common decency matters."

"There is no decency, common or otherwise," he said.

She looked up at him. "If what you say is true, then it's up to us."

Surprises. She was full of surprises, and he had taken a liking to her. She always worked the margin between just enough and too little to keep her job. Anna made it her business to ensure the meek weren't smothered by the uncaring masses. He made it his business to ensure Anna wasn't smothered by the uncaring machine.

Stress permeated the warehouse. The boss was pushing him to get people's pick numbers up because his boss's boss was getting pushed and so on all the way up the food chain. Anna wasn't keeping up. He found her pushing her cart with a look of grudging acceptance — the warehouse haze.

"Need some help?"

"I must if you're here to 'coach me.'"

"You know, I'm tired of the mockery of beautiful women."

Anna's mouth hung open. "Oh my gosh. You did not just say that?"

"Your rate today is only 105 pieces per —"

She waved a finger at him. "Don't try to change the subject. You said I'm beautiful. Are you hitting on me, Seth? Is this allowed in the company handbook? Does this mean I have to report you to human resources?"

"Yes, I'm hitting on you. Why the hell do you think I go out of my way every single day to keep you from getting

fired? Actually, I think you are supposed to report me to HR
. . . but do it after you have dinner with me."

Silence. Anna tilted her chin up and gave a wry smile.

"Was that a yes?"

"HR is a joke."

With that she turned her back to him and sped away with
her pushcart. He wasn't sure what had just happened.

As Anna was packing her things at the end of his Friday
shift, he wrote a note and handed it to her.

*Dress your best. Bring an empty stomach. Meet me near the old
lighthouse.*

Chapter 7

BELLE

Eccleston Campus, Alaska
Modern Era: Post-Singularity

A s the beast reared on its hind legs, the collar around its neck jerked backward. Belle cowered and screamed, louder this time.

A man was pulling hard on a leash. As the second creature approached, the man snapped his fingers.

"Tinkerbelle, no," he said. Then he yanked on another leash. "Down, Benjamin."

The animals grudgingly stopped lunging at her but did their best to get their curious noses as close as possible. The man was Dominic, Sophia's assistant who had arranged their meeting. After Belle lurched backward, she noticed another grim-looking assistant beside him.

"It's okay. They're friendly," said Dominic.

"What are they?" she asked.

"You're not familiar with them?"

Bell shook her head.

"Oh, they're thylacines."

"They're whats?"

"You know, Tasmanian tigers. Formerly extinct. Part of one of our many rewilding projects across the globe. We recently reintroduced the Irish Elk to its homeland as well as millions of our fast-growth saplings. Nearly the entire island will be reforested within seven years. As you know, our Lebanese reforestation project has been a complete success. It hasn't been draped in that many cedars for a few millennia."

"Oh yes, I think I read about it."

It was strange how blasé it all was now. Fast-growth timber and de-extinction used to be the wonders of science fiction. It was exciting when scientists succeeded with woolly mammoths. The whole world was abuzz. Now, mammoths were in every major zoo. Belle had once read that at least a handful of rich sheiks kept them as pets. She took such wonders for granted. Maybe they all did.

She gazed upon the great white wall that surrounded the company campus. "What's the wall for?"

"Oh that. Well, we have a number of reestablished species in the woods outside the glade — only this area and the town are sealed off. It's all part of our Pleistocene rewilding project. You're in the center of the finest nature preserve on earth. As you probably know, we're the number-one distributor of de-extinct embryos."

"Are you trying to build Jurassic Park?

"No, the reserve isn't open to the public, and de-extinction isn't our primary focus. It's merely a byproduct of our other work. It's not even the first attempt at a Pleistocene reserve — they started creating them way back in the 1990s. Still, there is no reserve on Earth that has as many species as ours. Second to none. It all plays into Sophia's love of the environment and her goal of undoing the damage our species has done to other species. Which of course includes those species wiped out by ancient humans. It's all about restoring our environment's natural equilibrium."

"Natural equilibrium?"

"Yes."

"And since when have Tasmanian tigers been native to North America?"

"Well, that's different. Sophia likes to keep them as pets. She also has dodos, though we keep them indoors now since the thylacines kept eating them. We sell their eggs, you know. Very expensive, as they only lay one egg per year. Would you like to try one? Scrambled is best. They're exquisite."

"Maybe another time."

"Oh, well, would you like to feed the Tasmanian tigers? I have treats."

The aide standing next to Dominic held up a handful of treats as the Tasmanian Tigers strained on their leashes.

Belle held her hands against her chest. "No, no thank you. Maybe another time."

The aide tossed them. Each animal devoured their treats in a single chomp. Belle stepped back as the aide took the Tasmanian tigers away. Dominic gestured for Sophia to walk with him through the glade.

"Can tell me about the type of job you're interviewing me for?"

"Not quite yet."

"Why not?"

"Like I said, it's a delicate security matter. We take such things very seriously here."

"Then when?"

"When we get inside."

"Inside where?"

Dominic pointed to the immense building high atop the outcrop. "In there."

"Do we have to take the stairs?"

He wrung his hands together and offered an awkward smile.

Belle huffed as she climbed a winding set of stone-hewn stairs up the rock face before reaching level ground, as if to see some grand oracle. She wiped her forehead. Before her stood a massive foundation with several more tiers of monumental stairs that she dreaded climbing. As she reached the top she passed two immense glimmering gold statues. Behind her was the glade far below and before her stood a grand colonnaded entryway.

Dominic caught his breath. "I give you the Evolution Building—or the Temple as we call it around here."

She passed through the massive bronze doors and was greeted with a lush green courtyard within the building. The courtyard was dotted with thousands of Eccleston employees. Some sat at I tables, others in white wicker chairs, but most were sitting on the ground atop throw rugs and yoga mats while conducting their business. As they worked, a small army of personnel went around with trays offering caffeinated beverages and snacks. Dominic took a bottle of water from a passing associate and handed Belle a bottle and then helped himself.

Belle looked up and noticed that the building's courtyard was protected from the elements with a ceiling of hexagonal panes of glass that somehow seemed to float in midair.

Dominic pointed at the panes. "When the weather allows, those panes of glass fold back on themselves until they disappear, allowing this whole space to be filled with fresh mountain air. It's truly incredible."

Like the glade, the meticulously designed courtyard was filled with lush greenery, craggy boulders, and meandering paths that called to mind an ancient Chinese garden. Ivy grew up the interior colonnade and there were fruit trees, flowers, lavender, and even a large koi pond. Dodos waddled about as promised. The expansive space gave her the impression of a light-filled sanctuary—no doubt they were trying to capture the essence of Eden itself.

She was led into through a series of grand halls until she reached two large wooden double doors. On either side of the doors stood stone-faced bodyguards wearing black designer suits. Their blazers were unbuttoned and she could make out the pistols strapped to their hips. Beside them stood four military-grade androids—murder-machines—two on each side. Beautiful. Vicious. Soulless.

Dominic saw Belle eyeing the machines. "Aesthetics are paramount to Sophia. She once told me that the engineers considered giving them faces, but they decided they were more terrifying without."

Belle studied them. They were tall and elegant-looking machines designed upon the human figure. Masculine in shape, strong but somehow delicate and curved. Each machine stood a few inches taller than her, perhaps six feet high. Their exteriors were covered in thin sheaths of armor that glistened gloss black, when not projecting images for camouflage. Their limbs and underlying mechanics were gleaming chrome. Atop either shoulder was a small flap that opened to reveal multiple beam directors. It was aways a shame when killers were handsome.

The doors opened and an official walked out followed by a general. Belle blinked a few times until she realized who it was.

She turned to Dominic and whispered, "Is that the prime minister of—"

"Yes. This is a confidential visit and I ask that you respect their privacy."

"Okay, but why are they here?"

"That's classified."

"And what's with all the armed machines?"

"Well I'm sure you're aware of our expansive military contracting enterprise, aren't you?"

Belle had read a little bit about it. Supposedly Sophia had a reputation of allowing her murder-machines to be implemented by whoever the highest bidder was, no questions asked.

"So how many of these machines does Sophia have?"

"Enough to march on the capital if she chose to."

"Oh my."

Dominic smirked. "Don't worry, she has no designs on the capital. She prefers science."

"That's . . . reassuring."

He handed her a tablet. "You'll need to sign this nondisclosure agreement before you step inside."

"Right now?"

"Yes, right now."

She skimmed the legal document and signed it.

"Excellent."

Dominic gave the doors a light knock.

"Ms. Eccleston will be with you shortly," he said.

She reminded herself that she shouldn't feel apprehensive. Sophia was only flesh and blood. A person, a hominid, a hairless ape just like everyone else. She just owned more bananas, that was all. Yes, just more bananas and . . . a robot army.

Her heart jumped a little when the door creaked open.

"Step inside, please," said Dominic.

Belle entered an office that was easily the size of a modest home. The ceiling was coffered and the floor-to-ceiling windows let in abundant light. The walls were sheathed in porphyry. There was a large fireplace and a linen couch with four armchairs beside it. At the opposite end of the expansive space was an elongated, low-slung wooden desk that matched the other furniture, all crafted in a Streamline Moderne style.

It seemed Sophia didn't follow the trend of the rich pretending to be like everyone else. She knew she was rich and powerful and made no attempt to hide it and every attempt to flaunt it. Everything about her office and the Evolution Building curated an image of beauty, power, and authority.

Atop the desk was a strange bronze box and a clear glass vase with a single blue rose. Behind the desk sat a petite woman with steel-blue eyes, a pale complexion, and flowing black hair. Her other features unremarkable. Her countenance unreadable. At first, Belle thought she might have been a secretary, for she didn't look a day over twenty years old.

She narrowed her gaze. It couldn't be. Sophia Eccleston was *seventy* years old.

Belle had seen pictures of Sophia from decades ago, before she became a recluse. Sure enough, it was her. She hadn't aged a day. She wore a loose semi-sheer Phoenician red blouse that left little to the imagination. Apparently underwear was for the rest of the mere mortals. Seventy-year-old Sophia did not rise but stayed seated, resting her left elbow on the arm of her high-backed mauve chair.

Sophia gestured for Belle to come to her desk.

She approached, keeping her steps slow.

"A pleasure to meet you, Belle. Please sit down. Would you like a drink?" she asked.

"Yes please," Belle said, beginning to sit and half expecting Sophia to get her something.

The woman pointed to an opened globe bar. "The drinks are over there."

Belle stood back up and walked to the globe. She took a seltzer and approached the two chairs opposite the desk. As she walked closer she was surprised to see a little girl sitting in one of the chairs with a black Persian kitten in her lap.

Her dangling legs were not quite long enough to touch the floor. The girl wore classic Mary Jane shoes over her lace-trimmed ankle socks, a pale yellow sleeveless dress with a white Peter Pan collar, and a matching white headband. She held a thick book and she didn't look up from it as Belle sat down.

The elongated desk and the chair framed Sophia's figure in such a way as to give anyone sitting in her position zero doubt who was in charge.

"Thank you for coming. This is my daughter, Juno," said Sophia.

Juno stopped rubbing her fingers over the pages of her book and slowly lifted her head. Her eyes took Belle's breath away. They were filled with brilliant shades of blue and green and even tinges of violet and they were ringed with a band of velvety black. They were unlike anything she had ever seen. They seemed to look not only through her but somehow within her.

There was something about her gaze that Belle just couldn't put her finger on. Something magnificent.

It took Belle a few moments to realize that Juno was blind. God had given that little girl eyes from heaven. They were so unrivaled in their beauty that perhaps it would have been cruel to every other creature on Earth to grant her such a wonderous gift and the privilege of seeing it.

"Juno, Belle is sitting next to you," said Sophia.

She saw a flash of white teeth. Juno couldn't stop smiling at Belle. It was as if she were the most interesting person on the planet or a Disney princess come to life.

"I've heard a lot about you," said Juno in a meek voice.

"Good things, I hope," she said. "How old are you?"

"Eight."

Juno kept smiling. Belle wasn't sure how to respond to such attention. The little girl seemed enthralled by her mere presence.

"Juno, was there something you wanted to ask Belle?" said Sophia.

"Can I—can I touch your face? So I know what you look like."

At first, she nodded out of habit. It took her a moment to release how stupid that was, and she managed to give a stumbling reply. "Of course."

Belle awkwardly leaned over as Juno reached out with her hands. She closed her eyes and felt the girl's delicate little fingers run over her brow, nose, and lips.

After every feature was carefully examined, Juno withdrew her hands. She leaned over and whispered in Belle's ear. "I think you're pretty."

She knew she wasn't pretty, not in the slightest. She was about as plain as they came, but the kindness of the girl's gesture cut through her icy countenance like a hot knife.

"Thank you," was all she managed.

Sophia suggested that Juno resume her reading. The girl shared some of Sophia's facial features, but Belle could tell the girl didn't share all of the woman's heritage. Juno was of mixed ancestry, with flawless caramel skin and long auburn hair, and she had an appearance that Belle could only describe as looking like everyone and no one at the same time.

She'd had no idea that Sophia even had a daughter. No one did. It was widely presumed Sophia was single and childless. Some gossip outlets had even declared that she was asexual, more interested in her work than people. Belle couldn't help but be impressed by how she managed to keep such a secret from the press. Especially a girl with eyes so stunning they could easily draw a crowd.

There was a long awkward silence.

"So what was it you wanted to meet about?" Belle asked.

Sophia gave a simple smile.

It was strange, the way she smiled. It didn't reveal any emotion. To Belle it seemed to be a default response Sophia gave whether she liked someone or not, a mask. There was a firmness, iron, behind that look. How could she tell? She figured it took one to know one.

"I want someone with your background to care for and assist Juno with her unique needs, full-time. You see, Juno doesn't go to school in the traditional sense, and of course I can't be around all the time to look after her. Your salary and benefits package will be second to none in your industry — or any industry for that matter — I assure you."

Belle was taken aback by the offer. "Ms. Eccleston."

"Sophia."

"Excuse me. Sophia, I should let you know I've been out of practice for a while."

"I know, but you were a nanny for quite some time, yes?"

"Yes."

"And it's my understanding that you were also a caretaker of children with disabilities, is that also correct?"

"It is."

"Excellent. I think you're the right person for Juno's needs."

"That's it? I don't understand. You could hire anyone in the world."

"Yes. I can."

"I'm a bit confused, to be honest."

"Naturally. I've already done an extensive background check on you, and this a mere formality. Things move quickly around here. You'll get used to it."

Belle slumped deep into her chair as she mulled over what to do. Why was this woman giving her such an opportunity? She knew there were far more qualified people than herself. Was it a ruse of some sort?

Sophia sipped espresso from a tiny white porcelain cup, which she delicately held between her thumb and forefinger as Belle considered the proposal. Her thoughts were interrupted when she felt a warm hand upon her forearm. It was Juno's. She could tell the girl was trying to face her but her gaze was askew.

"Please, don't say no."

Chapter 8

SOPHIA

Eccleston Campus, Alaska
Modern Era: Post-Singularity

Though Sophia had seen pictures of her new guest, Belle wasn't exactly what she'd expected in person. The petite woman looked tired and worn. Her hair was shoulder length, black against porcelain skin. Her large eyes were melancholic and her demeanor was one of utter meekness. Whatever her other qualities, beauty was not one of them.

Belle squirmed and wrung her hands together. Her eyes were cast down but they darted to and from Juno multiple times. The girl simply smiled.

"It's the opportunity I'm looking for. How can I refuse?" Belle asked.

"You can't. And I'm truly glad to have you. You begin tomorrow," she said.

"So will I be working at your home?"

"You'll be handling most of Juno's care here in the Evolution Building. This is where I spend most of my time, and as a result Juno spends most of her time here."

"Well, would it be best if Juno stayed at your house?"

"My primary accommodations are in the building, and that's where she'll need to stay unless I say otherwise. I do have a house in town, but we don't go there too often."

"Why not?"

"Security. Juno must be kept under constant guard and is only allowed to leave this building with my express permission."

"What about the glade?"

"Only with my express permission."

"Is there a threat of some kind?"

"Yes, several."

"What kind of threats?"

"Some that you can imagine and others you can't."

"Should I be worried?"

"Let me do the worrying. How about a tour?"

They stood. Juno took Belle's hand as they walked out of the office. Sophia rambled on the way about how hard it was to find a good architect and stressed how important it was to pick the right plants for the courtyard. She checked to see Belle's reaction but to her surprise the young woman seemed indifferent to it all.

Sophia stopped at a panel in the wall and uploaded Belle's biometrics into the security system.

"Now you have permission to enter nearly every room in the building, even my office."

Belle pointed to a large metal door with four guards, two standing on each side.

"What is that? It looks like a bank vault or something?"

"That's our development wing."

"Can we go inside?"

"No. You can go anywhere but there."

"What's in there?"

"Nothing of importance to you. Everyone who is allowed in there has to be approved by me personally. Your job doesn't require you to go in there, and it never will."

They turned into a corridor and continued walking down the hallways lined with monolithic white granite stones. Silence set in between them. Sophia broke it.

"So, how was your life growing up?"

"There was good and bad. Like many other childhoods, I suppose."

"Are you into science at all?"

"I never cared for the subject."

"Really? I see. Are you good at art?"

"Terrible at it."

"Well, what's your ambition in life?"

"I'm not sure. I guess I've never really thought about it."

"You're being coy."

"I'm not. Maybe I had an ambition once, but I can't seem to remember."

"Any regrets?"

"I try not to think of regrets. You?"

"A few, but never mind that. Here we are."

They stopped at a large wooden door. As Belle approached the door, it unlocked and opened. The lights turned on. Belle walked inside, her movements cautious. Juno followed. Like Sophia's suite it had at a solid seamless glass wall. She'd had the apartment decorated in an art deco motif featuring roses that she thought Belle might like based on her profile. It was one of the finest lodgings in the building.

Belle touched the fabric of the chairs. She studied the fireplace a bit and then walked into the spacious kitchen and ran her hands along the polished granite countertops and gazed upon the brand new copper cookware.

"Well, what do you think?" asked Sophia.

"It's huge. Too big for one person."

Sophia crossed her arms. "I can't do anything about the size."

Belle seemed to read her annoyance. "No. It's nice. Very nice. Thank you."

"Mom, are you going to show her the gold?" asked Juno.

"Gold?" asked Belle.

"She's talking about the vault she's not supposed to talk about, but since you're already in care of my most prized possession, I suppose it wouldn't hurt. Besides, I like showing it off from time to time, but only for my most special guests. Come with me."

They walked until they reached an elevator. Once they were inside, Sophia's biometrics were verified and down the elevator went. When the doors opened, they faced a tunnel and several armed guards.

Sophia strutted forward. "Come."

Juno took Belle's hand and they followed. After walking for about ten minutes and passing through multiple guard stations, they came upon a round metal vault door at the end of the tunnel. Sophia manually put in the combination. She stepped aside, and two guards turned the enormous handlebars. The door creaked open.

The entire room glittered in vivid gold. Sophia watched as Belle stood there, her mouth agape. Of course, it must have looked impressive. Bars of gold were stacked from floor to ceiling in the center of the room, nearly taking up the entire space. The only space left allowed for a small pathway around the perimeter of the room. Along the path tall shelves stood against the walls. Most overflowed with gold bullion coins. Others had metal boxes filled with gems of all different sizes and colors.

They stepped inside and walked to the farthest wall from the entrance. On the center of the long wall hung paintings, on either side shelves and displays containing ancient arti- facts and statues and rare fossils and wonders of every kind.

Belle reached out to a gold bar but stayed her hand.

"Go ahead," said Sophia.

The young woman ran her hands over the gold bars. "How much is in here?"

"Let's just say it has more than many governments."

"The company owns all this?"

"The company owns none of it. This space is rented out. We're also in the security business, after all."

"Then who does own it?"

"That's a classified matter, but no worries, we have their permission to look. Come, let us have coffee."

They left the mammoth granite corridors of the Temple and entered the gardenlike courtyard. Sophia led Belle and Juno to one of her favorite coffee shops and the three of them sat down in wicker chairs that surrounded a small round table.

"How many coffee shops are there here?"

"Twelve."

"Twelve coffee shops?"

"Is it not enough?"

"It's plenty. Do you have a favorite?"

"This is my usual spot."

Baristas brought three cappuccinos in white cups on white saucers, which were placed before them on the small round table. Juno began slurping her beverage up.

"You let Juno drink coffee?"

The girl licked the frothed milk from her lips. "I'm mature for my age," she said.

"Well, do you have any questions?" asked Sophia.

"Too many to ask. I'm a bit overwhelmed."

"Naturally. Ask the first one that comes to mind."

"Well, where is Juno's father?"

"Okay. Ask me the second thing that comes to mind."

"Will Juno be visiting with her father regularly?"

"Next."

"Oh, well, are there any special needs that I should be aware of?"

"Juno's blind. That's all you need to know."

"I thought blindness was curable?"

"Not in this case."

"Okay then. In town I was told never to go in the forest. Why?"

"You were told about the nature reserve, yes?"

"I was told you have de-extinct animals in there?"

"No dinosaurs, sorry to disappoint, but yes we do, and as far as they're concerned—they're still the apex predators."

"So that's what the wall is for?"

"Primarily. Don't go beyond it. Even our security team needs special clearance."

"What's in there?"

"Many things. You know, cloning mammoths and Tasmanian tigers was old hat, so we wanted to see if could use our technology to push the process further."

"What do you mean by old hat?"

"Well, we've long had soft tissues from woolly mammoths frozen in the tundra and Tasmanian tiger pups preserved in alcohol and taxidermied passenger pigeons and dodos so it's much easier to get a halfway decent genome from those than a fossil that's thousands of years old. But that's what we've done, use DNA recovered from fossils—tooth enamel mostly. Anyway, the first de-extinction clone happened way back in the year 2003 when they successfully cloned the Pyrenean Ibex—which had just gone extinct just a few years earlier, in the year 2000 I believe."

"Well, what happened to the last Pyrenean Ibex?"

"A tree fell on it."

"Oh."

"Oh, indeed."

"So, they were able to repopulate de-extinct species, even back then?"

"No. It died a few minutes after it was born and became the first species to go extinct twice."

"Oh my."

"A tragedy, to be sure."

"So it seems the de-extinction process has come a long way?"

"Indeed it has. Our goal is to bring back every human-impacted species that has gone extinct in the last twenty thousand years, and we're getting closer every day. We feel, as humans, it's our duty to the world. After all, wiping out even one species, no matter how small, sends a ripple across the entire ecosystem. Everything is affected, so balance must be restored."

"That's quite the ambition, but what about focusing on the endangered animals of today?"

"We do. We catalog the genomes of the ancient and modern remains of living species as well. Then we clone them and release them into the wild as a way to ensure genetic diversity. You see, it's a major problem when a critically endangered species goes through a population bottleneck. They all end up inbred and become much more susceptible to disease and defects. So we actively search for and buy carcasses, bones, and teeth for this very purpose. Our ultimate goal is to make our genetic catalog contain ever single species we can find. Again, we see all of this as merely our duty as a species, given we're the ones who wiped out all the others."

"Even twenty thousand years ago?"

"Well, many Pleistocene megafauna carcasses often have spear tips embedded in them, especially the mammoths — so yes."

"What was the last animal you've added to your Pleistocene reserve?"

"The woolly rhino. We had a very exciting find recently when a man came across a complete woolly rhino carcass frozen in the Alaskan tundra. No fossil evidence of their existence has been found in Alaska. Naturally, no one believed that they had crossed the Bering Strait, but we found one. A truly remarkable discovery. Of course, since we learned that it was native to this area, we just had to reintroduce it."

"So it's my understanding that this is all sort of, I don't know, a byproduct?"

"Well, we don't do it for the money, and it's certainly not our primary focus. We already had the technology and resources, so we figured why not contribute?"

"So why Eccleston Evolution?"

"I'm sorry?"

"Why did you start this company?"

Sophia lifted her cup and sucked down her cappuccino in one gulp. She motioned to the waitress for another.

"Eccleston Evolution is about the future of humanity. It's about life. It's about progress. You could say we represent the destiny of our species. We are the tip of the spear for human advancement. We stive to be the number-one force for good in the world, and every day we are doing just that — making the world a better place."

"I know that from your old speeches. But why start it?"

"Like I said, for progress, to ease suffering, to save lives, and even . . . to create it."

"You mean alter it."

"Improve it. Build upon it. Refine it."

"Isn't that dangerous?"

"Nonsense. What we do isn't entirely different than modifying crops or livestock, which people have been doing for thousands of years. Or even trees. You know, some four billion American Chestnut trees were wiped out by invasive blight. It wreaked havoc on the ecosystem, and the American Chestnut became functionally extinct. Then scientists added just one blight-resistant gene to the tree. Eventually, the chestnut forests and ancient ecosystems were restored. You see, we can build upon things."

"But trees, crops, and livestock aren't people."

"I assure you we have a very high ethical standard."

"Who sets the ethical standard?"

"I *am* the ethical standard."

"But I don't understand, why try to refine life?"

"What do you mean, 'why'?"

"It's an honest question."

"Then my honest answer is 'because I can.'"

Chapter 9

SETH

Port Auburn, Oregon
Twenty-Five Years Earlier

He removed a small cocktail table and two wicker chairs from his sedan and placed them next to an abandoned lighthouse. The location was close enough to the crashing waves below to taste the salty air and just far enough to avoid the ocean spray. The cliff beyond descended to the dark waters. He put a white tablecloth over the table and a bottle of wine on top, lit a few candles, and placed violet roses into a crystal vase.

Then he waited.

The candles were already half-consumed. Dusk was approaching and it seemed his confidence may have gotten the better of him. After all, his face was better fit to frighten small children than to attract women.

In the distance, Seth saw a figure against the moonlight wearing an elegant white dress that danced in the breeze. He barely recognized her. He had never seen so much of her skin before. It was smooth and glowed against the gleaming white fabric of her flowing halter dress. He blinked hard, unsure sure if this was same Anna. Part of him didn't think she would come, but there she was—in the flesh.

Her eyes were downcast and she was wringing her hands. He stood and pulled out her chair. "Please sit," he said.

Seth poured her a glass of wine as she looked out to the sea. He sat, and her deep brown eyes perked up once he joined her.

"I have to warn you, I'm a little crazy," he said.

Anna gazed at him as she took a slow sip of her drink and returned the lipstick-stained glass to the table.

"They say the crazy ones are the most devoted."

After that evening, time passed by quickly. Anna's heart was a ten-chambered safe. She didn't give trust easily, and when she did, she only gave it in one small piece at a time. When their lips touched for the first time, he had only one emotion—completeness.

Anna liked old books, musicals, and children. Still, there were aspects of her life she wasn't revealing to him. Like Seth, she was damaged, and they both came to an understanding that it was best not to talk about the less happy aspects of their lives. They didn't want to be shackled to history, they wanted tomorrow to be better than today. They had each other, and for them that was enough.

Her reaction upon seeing his house for the first time was different than he'd expected. Anna gazed upon the great room of expansive manor with its coffered ceiling and parquet floor with a scowl as she held her hands to her hips.

"This. Is. Awful"

"What's wrong? I spent years and pretty much everything I had restoring this thing. It's the grandest house in town, and it's not like it's dirty."

"There's a mattress just lying there on the floor in the corner surrounded by your underwear and beer bottles . . . and a computer on top of a cheap particle board desk and nothing else. You've slaved over building this gorgeous house, but you haven't given it a soul. There's just nothing inside, nothing."

"In fairness, there is something—the underwear and the mattress, and I need those."

She looked at him incredulously, as if he had done something wrong. He worked ten hours a day and simply didn't spend much time in his house. It was basically just his sleeping quarters and a means to keep himself occupied outside of work.

All he could do in response was shrug.

Anna left without saying a word.

The following morning, he awoke to a hard knock on his front door. He opened it and saw a stack of cardboard boxes.

"Let me in."

Anna plopped the boxes in the center of the room. He closed the door, and she immediately began opening them. They were full of framed paintings, cookware, and other household knick-knacks. Before he could ask her what she was doing, another knock came on the door.

She smiled. "Oh good, the furniture is here."

"Furniture?"

The deliverymen brought in a new bed, furniture, and a dinner table with chairs. Anna proceeded to direct the crew while Seth stood there, confused.

"How did you pay for all this stuff?"

"I used your credit card. Don't worry, it was all on sale."

By the end of the day, they were sitting together on the couch, sharing a bottle of champagne. Both of them, but mostly Seth, were exhausted from decorating. By some miracle, Anna had turned his sleeping quarters into a home. She had an incredible talent for design. Everything was placed in a way that complemented everything else. It was the tiny details like color, and matching fabrics, and the seemingly innocuous but perfect placement of everyday things that made the once-dilapidated home feel like a castle.

"Do you like it?" she asked.

"It's beautiful."

Anna came out of the bedroom and twirled. Seth's eyes filled with the brilliant champagne sequins of her dress. He told her that she looked incredible, but she crinkled her lips, seeming unsure, and went back into the bedroom and came out a few minutes later, this time in a lace-sleeved wedding gown white as snow.

"I wonder if I can get the cut adjusted on this one?"

She was really just asking herself. She walked back into the bedroom as she muttered ideas on tailoring.

Chapter 10

BELLE

Eccleston Campus, Alaska
Modern Era: Post-Singularity

As she stepped inside Juno's room, Belle nearly tripped. She looked down and saw the flat-faced black kitten with gold eyes rubbing itself against her leg.

"That's my cat. His name is Pancake," said Juno.

She tried to prod the blob of fur away with her toe but it kept purring and mashing its face against her pant leg. She didn't like cats, but for whatever reason it liked her. Stepping over the feline, Belle noticed that the room was furnished much like a one-room apartment. There was a small desk, some chairs, a small table, and a canopy bed with coral sheets. Aside from that, the room was fairly drab and minimalist. The only indications that this was a child's room were a few toys and the watercolor paintings plastered on the walls, all of them placed four feet from the floor.

Belle walked toward the abstract paintings and studied them. One looked like birch trees in autumn, another had the silhouette of a girl against a magenta sky, and another looked akin to a mussel beneath a wine-colored sea.

"Who painted these?" she asked.

"I did," said Juno. "Do you like them?"

"I do. They're wonderful, but how?"

She didn't understand how such a contradiction was possible—a blind girl working in the visual arts. Apparently, it was more common than she had realized. Juno explained that she and lot of blind people could detect some light and form, though it was extremely limited.

Juno spent the first half of her days working with a number of tutors—holograms of long-dead historical figures mostly. Belle was startled when she walked in and saw Shakespeare giving Juno lessons. There was also Marcus Aurelius, Hypatia, and Ban Zhao all in the same room, patiently waiting their turn for to give lessons. As great a resource as they were, Belle worried that Juno needed more than the interaction of glorified algorithms miming the ancients—she needed a flesh-and-blood person in her life. Maybe that was why she'd been hired? Her new position involved more than just care. She also was required to be a tutor for the girl. Belle wasn't much of a scholar, but she would do her best.

Her first attempt at a literature lesson was a disaster. She tried to suggest some children's books which she thought were appropriate for Juno, but Juno informed her that she had read them all. She didn't believe Juno and suspected the girl was simply trying to get out of work, so she asked for details of the characters and plots. To her surprise, Juno was able to recall the details with accuracy. They went through a dozen different books before giving up on children's literature. Not because there weren't enough books but because she simply couldn't remember any more that she had actually read. Instead, she switched to middle grade books and recommended a few titles that seemed appropriate.

"I've read all of those," Juno said.

Again Belle demanded that she describe the characters and the plots, and again Juno answered with surprising accuracy. Frustrated, Belle decided to name adult titles that she felt an advanced child might be exposed to. She rambled off another dozen or so titles, classics mostly.

"Read it. Read it. Read it," repeated Juno.

Thinking she was lying, Belle tested the girl, but she gave an exacting account of each story, every time. Even details that Belle didn't recall. She liked to think of herself as well read, but this child had just served her a large slice of humble pie. Trying to save some face, Belle decided to name something different.

"How about, oh, I don't know, *The Iliad*?"

Juno retorted without skipping a beat. "It was good, but I liked *Oedipus Tyrannus* better."

"What? That's one of the goriest tragedies ever written. Not to mention the, well, other gross-out factor. Who allowed you read that?"

Juno shrugged. "Mom says that most people are dopamine junkies that spend most of their time drowned in electronic entertainment so that they can try to forget about their miserable meaningless existence in fake worlds. I don't have any friends to play with and I'm not allowed to have most electronics so there isn't much I can do besides listen to books, so that's what I do. My mom lets me get any book I want—she's pretty rich, you know."

"Yes, I know."

As Belle struggled with what she could possibly teach the girl, her thoughts were interrupted by an unexpected request.

"Belle?"

"Yes?"

"Since there aren't any other kids here . . . will you play with me?"

Juno declared that she would be Ariel and Belle would be, well, Belle naturally, as she shoved a doll into her hand. She never was much of a social butterfly, but Juno took the lead and began rambling off instructions. Clearly, she had everything she wanted Ariel and Belle to accomplish planned out to the finest detail ahead of time. Underlying Juno's meek nature was a forwardness, an ironlike inner confidence. Belle noticed how she was able to differentiate her toys with ease.

"How can you tell which doll is which?" she asked.

Juno tilted her head and gave Belle an expression that could only mean she had asked a silly question. "Because their faces are different."

And so they played.

Juno's door opened a little while later, and a familiar silhouette stood in the doorway. It was Sophia, with her usual expressionless smile.

"Is this part of the lesson plan?" she asked.

She immediately stood, dropping poor Belle to the ground. "No. I apologize."

"If I want an apology, I'll ask for one. Juno needs someone to keep her occupied. It's five o'clock, which means you're free to head to your quarters for the day."

Before she could answer, Belle felt a tugging on her shirt sleeve. "Belle, can you stay a little longer? Please?"

Belle was getting hungry and was looking forward to taking a shower and retiring to her peace and quiet. As she tried to think of a kind way to let her down, Sophia again interjected.

"It's fine with me. I have some work to do regarding the Augur. Okay, you two figure it out."

The door slammed shut, and with that Sophia left as abruptly as she came. Juno sat at Belle's feet and nervously wrung her hands as she awaited a response. Logic dictated that she go to her quarters, run a bath, and pour herself a nice glass of wine. What could she do?

She decided to stay a while and kept the little girl company.

They ate together at one of the restaurants in the Evolution Building. Juno ate spaghetti, and Belle had a slice of pizza. Most of the people in the Evolution Building seemed to know who Juno was. As they walked through the courtyard many of them waved and called her out by name. Granted, Belle could tell they were making pains to keep a professional distance.

The restaurant manager knew her as well and immediately went to work having her favorite dish prepared.

There were strict rules regarding where Belle could and could not take Juno. Of course, she wasn't to leave the building under any circumstances without explicit permission from Sophia herself. No one was allowed to take any photos or videos of Juno, and if she saw someone else do so she was to hand them a threatening cease and desist letter of which she was given fifty initial copies. Sophia explained that her daughter's privacy was paramount, and though the measures were extreme, "What would you do in her situation?"

As they sat together at a patio table, Belle couldn't help but have a number of questions. At first, she was hesitant to probe, but she eventually mustered up the courage to ask Juno who her father was. Juno didn't seem offended by the personal question and simply said that her mom had refused to talk about him.

"Do you miss having a father?" she asked.

Juno shrugged. "I don't know. Mom isn't the type of person who's good at relationships. She even likes to yell at herself."

"I see. Have you always lived here? In the Evolution Building?"

"Mostly. I sleep over when Mom is busy, which is basically all the time, but we have a house like everyone else."

"It must be big?"

Juno shook her head. "No."

Dessert was served even though they hadn't ordered anything. Juno was given three large scoops of Neapolitan ice cream and Belle received tiramisu.

"Do you get to go outside?" she asked.

"Sometimes. Mom says she can't be seen with me outside. She says people will ask too many questions and that some of those people are out to hurt us." Juno sighed.

"Hurt you? Did your mom mention who she thinks would do such an awful thing?"

"She says there are lots of threats coming for her. Some want her job, and others want . . ."

Juno trailed off. Her eyes welled up with tears. Belle removed a tissue from her pocket and began patting Juno's eyes.

"Want what?"

The girl leaned close to Belle's ear and whispered. "They want to kill her."

Belle held her hand over her heart and said nothing. She wasn't sure what she had just gotten herself into. The only think she could think to do was to hold the poor girl. She realized that she shouldn't have asked such an indelicate question, even though it was out of her protective instinct.

"I'm sorry, Juno. I'm sure everything will be alright — your mom seems to have excellent security."

Juno wiped her eyes with the back of her hand. "It's okay. Like you said, Mom has her bodyguards and her robots and her Tazzie tigers. I think Mom is going to work really late today. I'm probably going to have to spend the night alone, again."

"I'm very sorry."

The girl remained despondent for a moment and then perked up. "Can you spend the night? You know, like a sleepover? Mom won't care, I promise, just ask her."

"A sleepover? I don't know, Juno. I mean, we've only just met, and I don't have my things with me right now."

"What things?"

"Well, no toothbrush, no change of clothes, soap, things like that. They're in my quarters."

"Oh, don't worry. I can get you all those things right away. Easy. My mom is rich, you know."

"Yes, you've already mentioned that."

"So you can stay?"

Out of habit, she tried to check the time on her watch, but of course that was pointless. It was locked up in a Faraday locker. Electronic devices were strictly managed in the Evolution Building.

She sighed aloud. "I don't know, Juno."

"Pleeease."

Chapter 11

SOPHIA

Eccleston Campus, Alaska
Modern Era: Post-Singularity

Sophia strutted into Mira's office with her usual confident stride. Once inside, she hunched over and began to pace the room from side to side. The doors of the office opened once more, and Mira stepped in. Sophia continued pacing without acknowledging her.

Mira walked around her without saying a word. She opened a drawer on her desk and removed a bottle of wine and two glasses, which she opened and filled. Already knowing what to do, she held a glass by the stem out from across the room. Sophia changed course and snatched the glass and took a glug. Mira sat down on the office sofa beside her desk.

"I don't want to go through with it," said Sophia.

"We've been over this."

"Isn't there another way?"

"I told you eight years ago what the dangers were."

"Yes, I know, and I went through with it anyway."

"Then you know what will happen if you don't go through with the surgery."

"That isn't a certainty."

"No. It's a probability."

"What if we're wrong?"

"I can only give you the data, and the data says that if you don't act soon, we'll lose control over the situation. Your choice."

"I'll think about it."

"Think quickly."

Sophia finished her drink and sat down on the sofa next to Mira. She handed the glass to Mira, who refilled it and handed it back.

"How is your new guest?" Mira asked.

"Fine."

"Fine?"

"She asked who Juno's father was."

"Awkward."

"No kidding."

"Did you tell her?"

"Of course not."

"She's already prying. I told you that you shouldn't bring her here. You can't trust her."

"I'm aware of your opinions."

"Okay."

"Well?"

"Well what?"

"Why shouldn't I trust her?"

"You don't know her. She has a history of mental illness. Besides, she's backwards. There were reports of her praying alone in a ruined church in subzero temperatures. Who the hell does that?"

"So?"

"So why are you letting her get so close to Juno?"

"I needed someone to replace her previous nanny. That's the reason."

"Of course it is."

Sophia finished off her glass of wine. "The Augur—what are our latest reports telling us about its processing power?"

"We're not sure. Perhaps several orders of magnitude greater than the processing power of the human brain."

"Is it still improving?"

"Rapidly."

"Any new information?"

"Only my usual apocalyptic warnings."

"Anything to add to your apocalyptic warnings?"

"You need to pull the plug on this thing."

"I said additional, not the usual."

"Pull the plug now."

"I can't do that."

"Why?"

"It's my life's work. Besides—"

"Besides?"

"Is apocalypse so bad?"

"I hope you're being facetious."

"The word 'apocalypse' means to uncover or to reveal."

"Or to end."

"Correct. An end which results in a new beginning. When the Aztec Empire was wiped out, it was an apocalypse for them that brought about a new order, a new beginning. A whole new world where they were reborn anew."

"I'm not sure the Aztecs approved of dying of smallpox and the blades of conquistadors."

"And I'm not sure the Aztecs' neighbors approved of being sacrificed and eaten."

"Be careful what you wish for, Sophia."

"Why?"

"You ought to read 'The Monkey's Paw.'"

"You're too paranoid."

"The paranoid survive."

"I'm merely speeding up the inevitable. If there is going to be a new beginning, it will be I who creates it."

Chapter 12

SETH

Port Auburn, Oregon
Twenty Years Earlier

They got married in the dilapidated church downtown. It was an old brick edifice with a massive hole in the roof. The declining diocese had tried to tear it down more times than anyone could count, but fate always seemed to get in the way. Anna's friends had suggested getting married someplace nicer. They'd suggested the new flower garden at their house. Anna had taken to gardening and wanted both the garden and the decorating ready for when she finally moved in. Seth had suggested their favorite place next to the sea, but she'd insisted on that beat-down chapel with a hole in the roof. The only thing she told him about her decision was that she owed it to God. In what way? He did not know.

The rain drizzled through the ceiling and into the church as they recited their vows before Father Antonio. Their final promise to each other was that sacred vow—until death do us part.

After years of trying and two miscarriages, they welcomed a little girl named Joan into their life one rainy September morning. Anna no longer worked at the warehouse. Her child was her life now, and that pleased her.

Out of the blue and half asleep, she uttered something.

She said, "I need you," then drifted back off to sleep.

He didn't think that was true—he needed her. Without her he was just existing. With her, his life was vivid. They were two gray, damaged souls made a colorful whole. As for him, he still worked at The Company and still had the same position he'd held for years. He saved, scrimped, and invested. Still, it seemed no matter how hard he worked, he was just treading water. He had to think. He could rebuild an old house, but how to rebuild a family? They were already hoping for a second child.

There was an opportunity at The Company to make more money. He could work in the hazardous materials department of the warehouse. The pay was almost double. The other employees said The Company didn't manage such things so well. They said a few people had quit and others had gotten sick. They warned him not to work there.

He put away the thought, for a while.

One morning, he was watching his daughter feed from Anna's breast upon the marble bench in the rose garden. Anna smiled at him. Seth smiled back, but it was an empty look. The only nourishment he could provide was labor. He needed to do better. They deserved better.

He took the hazmat job the following week. The warehouse was stacked from floor to ceiling with steel and plastic barrels and jugs of chemicals of every shape and size. Other than that, the work wasn't much different and the pay was good.

Months went by. It was another long, dreary day when he heard a thud followed by the sound of gushing liquid. He went to investigate. A forklift driver had tried to turn down one of the aisles and rammed its forks into the plastic barrels on the ground-level shelf. Liquid was spraying out onto the concrete floor. There was a sizzling sound as the chemical concoction vaporized.

Seth ran to the nearest emergency button and slammed the red button with his palm. Sirens blared inside the warehouse. The ventilation fans roared to life. Employees ran toward the flashing exits. His eyes burned and he began to cough and gag as the chemical made its way through the fabric of his cheap hazmat suit. He was only able to make out the faint sight of flashing red letters and stumbled toward them all while coughing and gagging and dry heaving. He pawed for the push bar of the exit. It wasn't there. Even with his eyes now tightly shut, the scorching pain refused to let up. He pounded against the concrete wall until he came upon a smooth surface. Then he kept pounding until he heard the metal clap of push bar. The door opened and he collapsed on the other side.

The company doctors said he was fine. Everyone was fine. Seth asked what chemical it was but they said it was "still under investigation." They did make a point to remind him that, as a manager, he was responsible for the accident. Of course, because of his years of service, he would simply be demoted back to the retail section of the warehouse where he had worked previously. If he took legal action, the company might have to respond in kind as he was the authority figure in charge of the situation. He was told to take the job and keep his mouth shut and forget the whole thing happened. In return they would give him a lump sum of money if he signed a form releasing the company of any liability.

Anna was furious. She told him to sue the bastards. She called every lawyer in the area. Most ignored her. The few who responded seemed very excited about the case, until they heard the details and who they were up against and they backed off. The last lawyer they spoke to informed him that the case was "neither viable nor profitable." Though, they *might* consider his case for a large advance.

He signed The Company release form and took the payout. Then they gave him eight paid weeks off to recover.

The months continued to melt away. His cough never dissipated. A long, raspy cough. At first he thought it would go way, but it got worse. At Anna's insistence he went to a private doctor. It wasn't good—cancer was slowly eating him alive. The doctors couldn't do much. Except for the cough, he felt fine, so he was surprised when they said he'd be dead within five years. Still, the family needed money after he was gone.

The house needed upkeep. So despite Anna's pleas, he kept working at the warehouse, without complaint and without fail. He'd work until he fell over dead if that was what it took.

He was good at his job.

Then Joan began coughing. That same long, raspy cough.

He came home from work unable to find Anna nor the sound of Joan's cries. He went to her bedroom. Then the nursery. He passed through the kitchen and the dining room, and they were empty as well. He continued wandering the house, calling her name, but there was no answer. He went outside and saw a figure in a white dress sitting upon the marble garden bench amongst a sea of wilted roses.

She was nearly as pale as her dress. Her face was wet. Against her breast she held Joan's limp body. She sobbed as she kept trying to get the lifeless child to drink, but there was only a drop of unswallowed milk and nothing that could be done.

Beneath an ancient oak tree stood a simple granite crucifix. Beneath an ancient oak tree stood a man and a woman in black. With them another man in black, Father Antonio.

Sacred rites were uttered, followed by a few additional words:

> "Beyond this earthly soil
> a little soul no longer cries,
> for there is no more sorrow,

no more toil,
no more misery.
She will face no further injury.
God have mercy on these parents' sacrifice
and commend this little girl's soul to Paradise."

And with that, they buried their little one beneath that ancient oak tree.

Part of his soul was buried when his little flower was placed beneath the earth. Her life was but a moment, but that moment was seared into eternity. No, he'd never get to make terrible braids of his daughter's hair. He'd never get invited to grand tea parties with her esteemed plush guests. He'd never learn what her favorite flavor of ice cream was, her favorite book, her favorite dress. He'd never be able to get a bike with training wheels and handlebar streamers. He would never tell her to eat her vegetables. He'd never get to scare off future boyfriends by suggesting hunting trips together. He'd never read her bedtime stories and kiss her goodnight. She was gone now. If paradise was real, he hoped she was up there. He hoped his wretched soul could climb those lofty stairs and reach those golden gates. He would try to be good — Joan was waiting.

Anna stopped talking after that. It was the cough. Every time he coughed, she shuddered. They didn't communicate anymore. Not knowing what else to do, he buried himself into his work. He'd provide until he keeled over.

After another day's work, he came home. Not a soul was inside. In the kitchen, he found a shattered wine glass and a pool of red liquid. On the countertop was an empty bottle and another a quarter full.

He knew where she was.

He stopped at the old light house by the sea. Next to the cliff he saw a figure in a flowing white dress. Anna. Her legs wobbled as she wandered along the cliff face, singing "Ave Maria."

"Anna, come back. Please."

Anna looked at him and began sobbing. She began to move away from the cliff. Then he coughed.

She shuddered and stumbled backward. It was one step too many.

He walked into the hospital room and saw Anna's broken body lying on the bed with tubes running in and out of her. Father Antonio stood beside her, giving last rites. Seth ran to her and took her hand. Her eyes flickered open. She couldn't move her neck, so only her eyes shifted toward him.

"I'm sorry, Seth," she managed.

"No. No. What are you talking about? There's nothing to be sorry about."

Her eyes began to water, and for the first time since he had known her, she appeared frail.

"I'm sorry. I'm sorry I stopped talking to you, about everything. You always took care of me. You always helped me, and I'm sorry I was being selfish."

"Stop with that. You couldn't be selfish if you tried."

"I'm scared, Seth."

"No. No. Don't be scared—the doctors are doing everything they can. You'll be alright, I know you will. You need to get back up and tend to your garden. Your roses and your dahlias are lovely now, and the hummingbirds are never thirsty. I'm almost done building that grand entrance to your garden, that arched arbor you asked for. It will be ready to grow your pink climbing roses on it just like you planned. Everything will be fine. Please don't be scared."

"No. I'm not scared for me. I'm scared for you. Who is going to take care of you when I'm gone?"

She tried to blink away her tears to no avail, though she managed to force a smile. She tried to speak again, but before she could continue, her vitals began to waver. Lights blinked and alarms blared from the medical equipment as nurses ran into the room.

Her eyes closed, and Seth was ushered out of the room.

As he sat in the lobby of the hospital, a man in a suit approached. "I'm incredibly sorry for what happened to your wife. I apologize, I know this is coming to come off the wrong way, but time is of the essence."

"Leave me alone."

"I have a very important service that will—"

"Leave me alone."

"Mr. Johnson, there's a chance we can save your wife."

He looked up. "What did you say?"

The man's card said he was from a sprawling company called Eccleston Evolution. The business model was simple. They froze the bodies of the dying with the hope that they could be healed and brought back in the future.

This company had a huge vault built deep into the side of a mountain in desolate northern Alaska. The idea was to ensure that those in stasis would be protected from power outages and disasters, both natural and manmade. The man in the suit said the technology to bring back loved ones was only one or two decades away.

The rep handed him a contract and pen.

"If we do the procedure now, before she dies, the odds of us being able to revive her increase dramatically."

"You want me to freeze her alive?"

"No, no, no. Protect her. Put her in stasis."

"That's not possible."

"It is possible. We developed it primarily from our research on wood frogs. They're the only known species of frog to live above the Arctic Circle. You see, during winter, they freeze solid. Hard as a rock. They stop breathing and their hearts even stop beating—but they're alive. When spring comes and they thaw out, they jump back to life as if nothing had happened."

"How?"

"They produce a natural antifreeze to prevent ice from freezing within their cell walls. You see, it's primarily the cellular damage that has been the biggest obstacle for cryogenics. The wood frogs had solved it, we merely needed to figure out how to extract it. Now we can finally do it to people."

"So you can bring her back? Wake her up like the frog?"

"Well, not exactly. We're still working on the waking up part. We merely keep our clients in a state of stasis until the means to heal their injuries is developed, but I assure you, this is your only chance. I'm very sorry to say that your wife's organs are failing—you have to make a decision now. Sir, forgive the pressure, but if you don't make a decision, there may be too much damage to the brain. Every minute we wait is a potential memory lost."

"I don't have the money for such things."

"Did she have insurance?"

"No."

"Don't worry. We have a payment plan."

He read the agreement form. The process was incredibly expensive, and he would be making payments for the rest of his short life.

He rolled his eyes. "I have a terminal illness. Do you have a payment plan for that?"

"Actually . . . yes, yes we do."

The agent handed him a brochure.

Seth looked it over. "This plan is ten times more expensive."

"I'm afraid it's the only way given your condition."

The agent pointed to where to sign. He hesitated. It all seemed unnatural. An old emotion that he hadn't felt in years came roaring back. Something inside him screamed for him to stop.

"I need to talk to someone."

"Sir, time is of the essence. Who do you need to see? A doctor? A lawyer? A financial advisor?"

He met with Father Antonio in the hallway next to Anna's room. All the while, the man in the suit peered at them from a distance.

The priest shook his head. "Seth, if you go through with this, you'll be condemning Anna to an earthly purgatory and yourself to a celestial one."

"So, I'm supposed to just let her die?"

"No, I'm not saying that. I'm saying she is your wife, not a guinea pig. She's a soul, not a customer. You ought not to make her a science experiment. This is unproven, untested, it's beyond our control. I fear if you go through with this, it will lead to more suffering, not less."

"But there's a chance."

"Have you talked to her parents?"

"Not yet."

"Because you already know what they'll say."

"I don't have a choice."

"You do, you just don't like the one you have to make."

"I'm not going to just do nothing. You know, I don't need this. Anna was the one who believed in this religious stuff, not me. Father, if this is God's love, I don't want it."

"Seth, please understand, whether this works or not, you're not in control of this situation. You're playing with fire even thinking about this. I worry that these unnatural temptations will push you to do things you'll regret."

"If it's a thousand years of purgatory, so be it. And if its damnation—fine."

He slammed his hand hard against the wall next to the priest's head. The nurses flinched. Father Antonio didn't. He simply bowed his head and let out a long sigh.

"I'll pray for you both."

"I don't want your prayers. I want my wife back."

"I'll pray for you anyway."

The priest bowed his head and made the sign of the cross and offered a quiet prayer. Then Seth stormed off. The agent handed him the contract. He signed it.

Chapter 13

BELLE

Eccleston Campus, Alaska
Modern Era: Post-Singularity

Belle awoke to a sharp prod to her face. Her eyes fluttered open, and she saw Juno standing next to the foldout couch where she had spent the night. Juno had already gotten dressed in a navy-blue sailor dress with a matching hat, white knee socks, and her usual black Mary Janes.

She kept poking Belle in the face with her finger.

"It's time to wake up, sleepyhead."

"Okay."

Poke.

"Okay."

Poke. Poke.

"Stop doing that."

"You snored, like, really loud."

Poke. Poke. Poke.

"Okay. Okay. I'm up."

After Belle got dressed, Juno suggested they have waffles for breakfast. She took hold of Belle's hand and led her out of her room and pulled her into the grand courtyard. The girl seemed to know exactly where she was going, leading her along almost as if she were the blind child.

"How do you know where we're going?" Belle asked.

"What do mean? You can't smell the waffles?"

She inhaled deeply. While she could detect the fresh clean scent of the gardens and the mist from the indoor waterfall pouring into the koi pond, she couldn't smell any food.

"Besides," Juno continued, "I can keep track of how many steps away it is. I'm really good at counting. Let's go."

Her other senses were so attuned that she never made use of a walking stick. When she did need guidance, it was her habit to take Belle's hand and ask for directions. After they made it to the waffle restaurant, the manager greeted Juno and they were given patio seating in the lobby. The manager knew exactly who Juno was and without any further instruction ordered her favorite—buttermilk waffles with strawberry sauce.

As they ate, Belle smelled a peculiar odor. She turned and was startled by a large, furry beast standing before them. It reeked of musk, and it was looking right at her.

"Juno, we need to turn around and leave. Now."

"Why?"

"There's an animal in here. It's a . . . It's a—"

"Mr. Snuffles!" yelled Juno.

"Mr. Snuffles?"

Juno ran out to be embraced by the animal's woolly trunk. "Is it real?"

"Of course he's real. His mom was made here."

"My God, it's incredible."

Belle cautiously reached out and touched the course hair of the baby mammoth. It felt real, but she still had troubling believing it. Sure, she had read about them, but she had never seen one in person before. The mammoth gently prodded her face with its trunk and then played with her hair before returning its attention to Juno.

"He was really sick, and we rescued him. One day, he'll go back to his mom. She lives outside, beyond the wall."

"What's it doing in the lobby?"

"Not it. Mr. Snuffles. I named him myself."

"You named one of the most majestic species ever to grace this earth . . . Mr. Snuffles?"

"He likes his name."

"Of course he does."

"Right now, he lives in the lobby and the glade outside. I asked Mom if I could keep him for a while, and she said yes. She's pretty rich, you know."

"Thank you for reminding me. How did it, I mean Mr. Snuffles, get up all the way up the stairs to reach this place?"

"The cargo elevator. Of course."

Belle nodded, her mouth agape. "Of course. I wish I had known about the elevator sooner."

They resumed eating at the patio seating. All the while, Juno slipped pieces of waffle to Mr. Snuffles's waiting trunk.

Waffle breakfasts became part of their morning routine. While they visited the same shops and restaurants and saw the usual faces, Belle found it hard to get to know the people who lived at Eccleston Evolution headquarters. She had invited several to dinner or for after-work drinks. They would politely decline and scurry off to their quarters to cavort with their androids and slip into realms digital. Some lorded over virtual empires, some built and decorated dream homes with dream families, and others engaged in various forms of virtual homicide for entertainment. There were only a handful who were married and even fewer with children. Unfortunately, Juno was forbidden to play with the other children, and therefore Belle was forbidden from interacting with them.

However, part of Juno's routine made Belle uneasy.

The girl had a daily doctor's appointment with a certain Dr. Mira Patel, who had an office right next to Sophia's. She was an employee at Eccleston Evolution and a medical doctor who also acted as Sophia and Juno's personal physician. Aside from that, Belle wasn't sure what else she did besides look after the CEO and her daughter. Belle wasn't allowed in the exam room with Juno, and she didn't know what transpired inside. What she did know was that every time Juno returned from one of those visits, she looked miserable and exhausted.

One day stood out from the rest. Upon returning from her usual appointment, Juno made a remark that made Belle uneasy.

"I'm tired of all the tests. I keep telling them I feel fine, but they don't believe me."

Belle thought it was a strange comment, but she pushed it aside because she thought it normal for children to complain about going to the doctor. She rarely saw Sophia, and when she did, it was usually for an abrasive demand of some sort.

Juno excelled in her studies but proved to be a surprisingly disciplined child despite the absence of her workaholic mother. She always stayed on task and rarely spoke out of turn. Occasionally, when Belle checked her work, she couldn't help but get the impression that she wasn't applying herself. As if she was holding back somehow. Of course, she figured one could say that about every child. Maybe she was simply becoming too paternalistic.

Belle decided that she wanted to do something special for Juno, which was hard when her mother was as rich as she was. What material things couldn't that little girl have? But something special did come to her mind. Something that she knew Juno would love. She knew Juno wanted was to get some fresh air. To play outside. She broached the subject with Sophia.

"I rarely let Juno go outside. What's the occasion?"

"Just a walk and fresh air."

"Right."

"So it's okay then?"

"I didn't say that."

"It's only a walk. It can't be good to keep her isolated all the time. Believe me, it's not a good feeling."

"I believe you. The problem is that there are threats everywhere. As I told you, I keep her inside for good reason."

"Could you tell me specifically what threats you're expecting in your own company headquarters of all places?"

"No, I can't."

"So she can't go outside."

"I didn't say that either." Sophia paused. "I will make arrangements with Juno's security detail. You're probably right — Juno needs some fresh air."

The following day Belle ran from room to room in the Evolution Building, calling Juno's name. They were scheduled to finally go outside but now Belle couldn't find her. She was about to take Juno outside the building for the first time in months, and the girl had disappeared. She began stopping random employees and frantically asked if they had seen Juno. They all shook their heads.

Then she heard a familiar voice humming.

She followed the sound and saw Juno standing outside the development wing. The girl was talking to one of the guards, who seemed both amused and frightened by her presence.

She smiled and apologized as she took Juno's hand and led her away.

"What were you doing there?" Belle asked.

"I was exploring. That's all."

"You know you're not supposed to go there."

Juno gave an indifferent shrug. "Do you know what's inside?"

"No."

Belle helped Juno put her jacket on, adjusted her hood, and took her hand once more. They walked to the exit of the building and were quickly surrounded by plainclothes bodyguards. Just as they were about to leave, a bodyguard handed Belle a pair of sunglasses.

"It's not very sunny out—what are these for?"

"The girl. You'll need them, trust me."

The bodyguards nodded to another bodyguard. They scanned the horizon for threats. For the first time, they stepped outside the building together.

The spring wind still had a bit of bite left over from winter as they walked the path leading to the grove of cherry trees in the glen. This time of year, their pale pink and white blossoms bloomed, forming a sea of pink.

Employees were crawling all over the place. Belle was under constant scrutiny by the small army of Juno's plainclothes bodyguards, who surrounded them at a distance. Juno got stopped every few minutes to receive compliments on her eyes. A few people asked to take photos, but of course, Belle said they couldn't. Now she knew what the sunglasses were for.

Mr. Snuffles was bigger now and free to roam the glade and he remained a popular company mascot, with employees lining up to take pictures with him. Belle found it aggravating the way people climbed the fragile cherry trees and stopped to take pictures every ten seconds, blocking their path. Then it occurred to her that something as simple as a blossoming group of trees could cause people to take a moment out of their lives to appreciate something so singular.

Juno tugged on Belle's coat sleeve. "We're here, aren't we?"

"Yes, how can you tell?"

The girl pushed her sunglasses down her little nose and squinted hard. "Well, there's the smell of the flowers and there's pinkish blobs everywhere. Or at least I think they're pink. Can you describe it to me?"

"Um, sure. There are cherry trees everywhere, and their flowers are pink and white."

Then came the look Juno always gave when Belle had said something wrong. "Pink and white?"

Though they had known each other some time now, she still made the mistake of describing things to Juno in visual terms from time to time.

"Sorry, let me try that again. Belle closed her eyes and took a deep breath. She exhaled, knelt next to Juno, and took her hand. "The trees. How can I describe them?"

She led Juno to a nearby tree and placed her palm upon the rough bark of a Yoshino Cherry.

"The trunks are gnarled and thick, but their branches are meandering and graceful. Their tiny blossoms are delicate and when the spring wind blows, they waft about like . . ."

"Like what?"

"An unwritten poem.

Juno walked to a rose bush, plucked a blue rose, and smelled it before gently pulling off the petals. They walked upon a zigzag garden bridge that graced a gentle stream. Juno knelt and let the water run through her fingers.

When they reached the other side of the bridge, Belle abruptly stopped as something wiggled in the grass. She bent over and picked the thing up.

"Juno, hold out your hands."

Belle put the furball in the girl's cupped hands.

"What is it?" Juno asked.

"It's a baby rabbit."

"Aww."

Near Juno's feet, she found a rabbit's nest with one more baby rabbit inside. Then she turned and saw one of Sophia's Tasmanian Tigers, with mother in its mouth.

Off it ran.

"Do I have to give the bunny back?" asked Juno.

"In this case, I think we can try to find homes for them."

"Isn't their mother waiting?"

"I'm afraid not."

"They can't make it on their own?"

"Perhaps, but the chances are very low. I think they may need your help, Juno."

"Why me?"

"Because you're in a position to take care of them."

"But I'm not a bunny."

"No, but you're much smarter than they are. You have a responsibility now that you've stumbled upon them. I think you'll do a fine job. We'll let them go when they're big enough."

"What if the bunnies can't survive on their own when they're grown?"

"Well, I guess we have to keep taking care of them. Okay then?"

"Okay."

They returned to the Evolution Building, rabbits in hand, followed by Juno's enormous escort of plainclothes guards.

The guards returned to their duty stations as Belle removed Juno's jacket. As they walked the corridors, the immense vault-like door of the development wing opened. The two guards standing on either side of the door stiffened, and Dr. Mira Patel walked out, busily scribbling on a notepad.

"Hi Juno," said Mira.

Juno said nothing and tried to hide herself behind Belle's legs.

Chapter 14

SOPHIA

Eccleston Campus, Alaska
Modern Era: Post-Singularity

Sophia had just finished a call when Mira walked into her office. She swiveled in her massive mauve chair, acknowledged her friend's existence, and then continued sifting through her work.

"Well?" asked Mira.

"Well what?"

"Have you made a decision to go through the with the operation?"

"I'm still thinking about it."

"You're out of time. It's now or never."

Sophia stopped what she was doing. She sat in silence, staring at the wall as she gently swiveled her chair. Then she sighed.

"I have some serious reservations."

"I know."

"Is it wrong?"

"Wrong? Not taking action would be wrong. You know what the consequences are better than anyone—including me."

"Yes, yes. I know. You're right."

"I'm sorry, but I need a decision. We can't push it out any longer."

Silence.

"Sophia?"

"Make arrangements for the surgery."

"Will do."

Mira turned and left. Sophia wrung her trembling hands together. Tears blotted the papers she was writing on. She wiped her eyes and tried to continue working to no avail. Unable to concentrate, she got up. She opened her globe bar and mixed herself a Manhattan. As she was pouring it, her office door opened once more. Raymond hobbled in.

"A bit early for that, isn't it?"

"I figured you'd be lurking around the corner."

"Going to make two?"

Sophia mixed another Manhattan and poured a second glass, which she handed to him. The old man sipped it and nodded approvingly.

"So you're going to go through with it."

"With what?"

"The surgery, of course."

"I have no choice."

"Unfortunately, that's true."

"I know."

"I don't think I've ever seen you this worked up before."

"It's nothing. Allergies."

"Of course."

"I'm assuming you're also here to discuss Ivanov?"

"Astute as ever."

"And?"

"I haven't heard from Ivanov's legal team, so I presume he's going to come here to negotiate — eventually."

"Then what?"

"We'll have a nice little chat."

"You're being coy. As usual."

"Okay then. We'll just chat. It probably won't be nice."

"I usually would find such a response charming, but I do have the overwhelming majority of my wealth in this company. I would like to know whether Mr. Ivanov or Ms. Eccleston is going to be the future caretaker of my investment."

"Why, me of course."

"Of course. Now how do you intend to do that, because I see little chance of you succeeding in any scenario — and let me remind you that I've been doing this long before you were born. Ivanov is a master takeover artist. I've never seen one like him in all my years."

"An artist? Please. Then what do you think I should do?"

"Come to terms with him. Throw him a bone. You could have given him the cure — that would have been enough to avoid getting into this mess. Then you did the opposite, and as I predicted, here we are."

"I had to fire Ivanov from the board. He was getting too pushy."

"He's the third-largest shareholder of the company."

"He wanted to merge our company with our incompetent competitor with himself as chief executive and largest shareholder."

"And I agreed with you that it was a bad idea, but you know as well as I do the real reason why he wanted control."

"I told you. The 'cure,' as you call it, isn't available. Besides, he had the gall to ask me to resign after I rejected his demand to hand it over to him."

"Yes, I remember."

"I said no."

"And he said, 'Or else.'"

"So naturally he couldn't be trusted."

"I agree, but I told you that you couldn't fire him without consequence."

"I offered to buy his shares from him."

"For a fraction of their worth."

"And."

"And?"

"Well, he didn't like Pancake, and Pancake didn't like him."

"Your cat?"

"Yes. I don't like people who don't like my cat. It would be a crime to give such a cat bigot full price."

"That joke is getting tiresome, and I do have billions of dollars on the line."

"Fine. To your question. I'll use a combination of traditional hostile takeover defenses to stop Ivanov. There, are you happy?"

"What takeover defenses? I don't see any of them working in your situation."

"I'm still putting it together."

"You're a terrible liar."

"You know me too well."

"Only Mira has known you longer."

"True."

"And you've only shared your secrets with Mira."

"Not this again."

"You've found the cure, and you won't share it with me. I can understand not giving to Ivanov, but I've always had your back. Always."

"That's not true. I have shared it with you. Otherwise you'd be dead. You're 131 years old, after all."

"The oldest variation of it. It's the same one you sell on the mass market. You know that's not what both of us are after."

"Well, there's also digital ascension. That would give you what you're looking for."

"I'm not uploading my mind into a damn computer. For all I know I'd end up in a video game and tortured by some sadistic thirteen-year-old."

"Well then, the only version of the treatment approved by the government is the one we gave you. As I keep telling you, I can't legally share the newer variations. Even if I could, the side effects aren't fully understood."

"Side effects? The only side effects I see on you and your friend Mira are permanent youth and vigor. I'll happily suffer those side effects."

"It killed a quarter of participants in the human trial, and another quarter got cancer, and as I keep telling you, we don't know how long it will last."

"You said that decades ago, and yet you and Mira haven't aged a day. Why do you two get access to it but not me?"

"Because we invented it."

"I funded it."

"And you were the first patient of the first variant we came up with. It was a breakthrough. You may very well make it to 170 years old, maybe even 200. Besides, Mira and I were willing to take the risk."

"What risk? You don't age. In fact, both of you reversed your biological age."

"We could have died and shared the fate of those in the trial."

"There's something you're not telling me."

"When we have a cure that doesn't have the side effect of killing its patient, I'll share it with you. As you know, we are working on a new variation."

"Yes. I know. This variation will fail, and then there will be another one, and another, and so on until I keel over."

"We're going as fast as we can."

"I'm skeptical of that."

"No you're not. You're too rational. You're just huffing and puffing because you're not getting your way."

Raymond began to scowl and then let out a great loud laugh as he slapped Sophia's back. He slurped down the rest of his cocktail and continued laughing.

"Sometimes I forget how long we've known each other."

"Don't forget it. I'm the only one who's looked after you."

"That you have. Mostly."

"I will make terms with Ivanov. Just trust me when the time comes."

"But we don't trust each other."

"We do when it comes to business."

"That much is true."

Chapter 15

SETH

Port Auburn, Oregon
Twenty Years Earlier

He sat distraught in the ugly hospital lobby. He pondered the cold randomness of it all. Thanks to randomness, he had met Anna. Thanks to randomness, she was taken from him. So that's how it is, he thought, one minute you're here, the next minute you're not.

Anna's spirit wasn't something that could be broken, but the injuries were just too much for her body to bare. In one moment, he had everything, and in the next, nothing. He held her small hand and buried his face into her shoulder before she was taken away for stasis. Into earthly purgatory she went. She wasn't dead, but she wasn't alive either.

The last time he saw sleeping Anna was after her body was sealed in a stainless-steel capsule. His hand touched the frost-covered enclosure before it was put onto a refrigerator truck. There it would be sent to northern Alaska to be entombed until either hope or oblivion prevailed.

Part of him died that day, but he had to keep working. He needed to be able to make payments to Eccleston Evolution. He subscribed to their newsletter and eagerly awaited it every month to see what, if any, breakthroughs had been discovered. He was usually disappointed but held out hope that one day they could revive Anna.

The days, months, and then years dragged on. He still had the cough. It never went away. Every year there were less and less warehouse workers at The Company. The machines were getting better. In time, he became one of the few. One of the survivors. The best of the best. A senior manager with a solid salary and benefits. It didn't matter. It was the year he was scheduled to die.

He had met with a doctor the month prior. Thousands of small tumors riddled the inside of this body. "Uncurable," he was told. Yes, he was definitely going to die.

Then one morning before work he got an automated text message.

"Your employment has officially ended effective today. Do not show up to the warehouse. Thank you for your years of service."

Part of him said he shouldn't care. He was about to be buried six feet under. Earthly matters shouldn't have been his concern anymore, yet his blood boiled hot.

Seth went to work anyway. His boss in the human relations department was a bit startled to see him waiting, first thing in the morning, at his boss's desk.

"Seth, I didn't know you'd be in today."

"I just wanted to ask some clarifying questions."

His boss bit his lower lip and then let out a sigh. "Of course. I'm sorry, Seth, there's no easy way to say this, but we simply no longer have any more warehouse positions. But you've been outstanding, truly outstanding all these years."

"I don't understand. Why am I being fired?"

His boss waved his hands. "No. No. No. You're not fired. Just, well, laid off is all. You see, here at The Company, we're innovators. We always push the envelope to improve the customer experience and—"

"Those machines you've been working on all these years took my job, didn't they?"

"Now please understand that technology is always changing, and old jobs will disappear, but then new jobs will be created."

"Then I want to apply for one of those 'new jobs' you mention. What about those people that work on the machines, or something in management, or one those software people that sit on their butts all day. Let me apply for one of those jobs. I've been loyal to this company for years, you must have something."

"Well, you see, Seth. The software people, as you call them, are losing jobs too. Besides, those are all special jobs that require skills and training and—"

"Then teach me. I can learn."

"Like I said, those type of jobs require years of training, and we just don't offer that here, but you can learn some new skills or apply to a college or —"

"I've got years of management experience with outstanding reviews."

"And if we have an opening, I'll certainly reach out, but we don't currently have any openings. Consider getting your education in order first. Maybe a degree or two or three."

"The truth is clearer now."

"What truth?"

"I've helped make your latte-sipping lifestyles possible. Yet when I try to climb up, instead of giving me your hand, you've got your damn boot in my face to push me back where you ingrates think I belong."

"A job isn't an entitlement, Seth."

"Didn't say it was."

"Well then, what do you want me to do? Last I checked, there weren't many openings for ice-cutters, gas lamp lighters, town criers, and cavalrymen, and now there aren't many openings for warehouse workers or warehouse managers. Times change. Accept it. Anyway, I'm sure someone with your work ethic will find many opportunities. It will take some time to retool and get new skills, say five or six years, but when you're done, you'll have a whole new set of opportunities."

He gave a mocking laugh. "Five or six years?"

Then his laughter erupted into hysteria. He pounded his boss's desk and grabbed it with both hands and tipped it over. He cackled at the top of his lungs, a shrill shriek that caused his boss to step away to the far corner of the cubicle. When his laughter began to slow, Seth stopped for a moment, and then he reeled over and laughed some more. All the while he stomped his feet as if the most hilarious prank ever created had just been played on him.

"It's all a joke. It's all a joke, isn't it?"

He continued to laugh even as security dragged him from his boss's office and unceremoniously dumped him in the parking lot—after years of dedicated service. He stood up and brushed himself off.

Every payment bought an extra few months of stasis for his wife. He didn't know when or if the cure would come, but he'd go on until the bitter end, to suffer, to fight, to work — for time. For just a little time, for Anna.

Chapter 16

BELLE

St. Olga, Alaska
Modern Era: Post-Singularity

W hen Belle first went to Sophia's house, she expected it to be in the only mansion in town. The mansion in question being the one that loomed high over the town atop a craggy outcrop and was partly hidden away by woodland. Instead, they stopped in front of an unassuming white house with black shutters that wasn't much different from the rows of wooden houses on either side of it—or pretty much any house in St. Olga, for that matter. The only difference was the rose bushes on either side of the door. Only Sophia's had blossoms as blue as sapphire. Today would be another rare day that Sophia chose to work from home.

As usual, Belle was ordered to leave all electronic devices, no matter how seemingly insignificant, with the security team that stayed in the neighboring houses on either side. Another guard led Sophia's two Tasmanian tigers into the backyard. The Tazzies pulled hard on their leashes as another guard waved tennis balls in front of the creatures.

She picked up Pancake's ostentatious cat carrier, complete with little silk curtains bound with little satin ribbons, and walked toward the door. Sophia unlocked it and went inside first. Pancake meowed as she strained to hold open the surprisingly heavy front door with her shoulder for Juno, all while struggling not to drop the cat carrier.

Juno stepped inside, and Belle followed. She was surprised by the weight of the door. It felt far heavier than it looked. It slammed shut and locked automatically. She put down the cat carrier and rapped the door with her knuckles—solid metal. Then she let Pancake out of his carrier.

The first thing she noticed was a painting that hung on the wall. It was a watercolor spill effect painting of two large eyes dripping tears of vivid color. As she was studying the painting, Sophia shouted Belle's name.

After she entered the kitchen Sophia threw a tabloid magazine on the table and glared at her. On the front page was a photo of Juno and herself. She recognized it immediately. It was Belle holding out Juno's hand and pointing. Clearly the photo had been taken when they had visited the cherry blossoms in the glade. She read the headline: "Eccleston Tech Princess Discovered?"

She swallowed hard as her eyes slowly rose from the paper. Sophia stood before Belle with her arms crossed.

"I'm sorry. I thought we followed all the precautions the security detail recommended."

"I didn't ask for an apology. Well, I suppose we do know some of them were being paid off by the paparazzi now, don't we? I told you letting her out was a stupid idea."

"I didn't mean to cause a problem. It was just the glade."

"Do you understand that there are forces out there who want me and my daughter dead?"

"I'm meant no harm. If it's my resignation you want, then—"

"Resignation? I don't accept resignations. I either fire or hire. There is no in between. If I die, I can't complete my work. Don't you understand? I can't allow myself to be extorted. I have to survive. I'm the only person on this planet who can take this wretched species to the next level, to seize our rightful throne. To turn hairless apes into gods. And I can't have Juno be put in harm's way. That compromises everything I've built. Don't you see?"

"Yes, I see. I think I see quite clearly, in fact."

"Good."

"So, I guess I'll have to be on my way then?"

"On your way? You're not fired. Prepare dinner and pour me a glass of Sangiovese."

With that, Sophia left. She walked past Juno without saying a word, entered her home office, and slammed the door shut.

Belle found a bottle of wine and uncorked it. She poured a glass for Sophia and then a larger glass for herself. Looking around the house, she noticed something curious. Well, actually, it was the absence of something. There were no electronics of any kind, not even outlets on the walls. Light came only from windows during the day and from oil lamps and candles at night. The kitchen had a custom stainless steel icebox rather than a refrigerator, and the range operated on natural gas.

Then she noticed the windows. The glass was very thick. She assumed that it was probably bulletproof. At first, they looked like antique windows with steel chicken wire running through them. Like what one would see at an old high school. However, these windows had thin wires of copper—not steel—running through them in a diamond pattern. It was as if the entire house was a Faraday cage, a means of blocking electromagnetic fields. Come to think of it, Sophia's vehicles had this also. Why would Sophia, of all people, want to avoid electronics in her own home?

Belle knocked on Sophia's office door.

She opened it. Atop her expansive desk was a mess of opened books and scattered papers, and all four walls were completely covered in calculations from floor to ceiling. Belle handed Sophia her glass of wine. Sophia took it and tried to slam the door shut, but it didn't close because Belle had wedged her foot in the threshold.

"Why the technology aversion?" she asked.

"Protection."

"Against whom, may I ask?"

"If I told you that, you'd never be able to sleep again."

Belle pulled her foot back, and the door slammed shut. She returned to the kitchen and downed her own wine glass in a few gulps. Pouring herself another, she went to sit at the dinner table, alone. Belle began to question everything she had done at that point. Was Sophia right? Was she really so careless? Had she really put Juno's life in danger? The thought horrified her.

She turned and saw little Juno.

"Don't be upset. Mom is always kind of cranky. She has lots of stress, or at least that's what she tells me."

"Who exactly is your mom so worried about all the time?"

Juno shook her head. "If you ask my mom, it seems like the whole world is out to get us. She doesn't trust anyone. Especially the other people at her company. She says they're weak-minded money grabbers without vision." Then she lowered her voice to a whisper. "She also doesn't trust her creation."

"The Augur?"

"Yeah, that thing."

"What, does she think it's alive or something?"

Juno shrugged. "I don't know, but she's scared of it."

"If she doesn't trust anyone or anything, then why is she letting me stay here with you? Especially after what I just did?"

"Oh, no, that's different. She trusts you. She just gets mad easily, that's all. Don't worry, she only stays angry for five, maybe seven minutes tops. Her mind is too busy to stay mad for very long."

Belle was a bit taken aback. Trust? Did Sophia really trust her? But when she thought it through, she realized that aside from Juno, she was the only person Sophia treated with such intimacy. She often spent the night with Juno. She was allowed unrestricted access to Sophia's office, and here she was, asked to stay in Sophia's home, her fortress, and free to wander as she pleased. They had only known one another for a few months—why trust her of all people? Sophia had a private contract army of military-grade androids. Was that not enough?

Sophia had finally left her office and moved into the dining room. She sat at the table with a glass of wine in one hand and a book in the other—she had asked that Belle prepare another plate. Before Belle could ask who we were expecting, there was a knock on the door.

She looked to Sophia, her eyes pleading for the woman to answer it as she carried steaming bowls of soup and fresh bread to the table. Sophia looked up at Belle for a moment and then resumed her reading. Belle quickly put the food down, ran to the door, and opened it.

In the threshold stood an elderly man. She could tell he must have been tall in his youth, but now he was hunched over and walked with a cane. Before she could say a word, the man introduced himself.

"Good evening, you must be Belle. I've heard so much about you. I'm Raymond Dearborn. I work with Sophia. A pleasure to meet you."

"The pleasure is mine."

"So, how do you like this town?"

"It's cozy."

"Well, Sophia likes it and has dragged the rest of us here. She was born here, you know—she's a mix of English, Russian, and Indigenous stock. Her parents moved to the Lower Forty-Eight, out in the Northwest in search of opportunity, but Sophia eventually made her way back. She always likes to say that this place is in her blood."

"I had no idea."

"Most don't, but here we all are, trapped on her island. Lucky us, right?"

Mr. Dearborn smirked and gently elbowed her. He hobbled inside and exchanged the usual pleasantries with everyone. Belle pulled out a chair for him at the dinner table, and he sat down. She held up two bottles of wine.

"Would you like red or white wine?"

"Scotch."

It took a while, but she managed to find a bottle of scotch in the cellar, returned, and poured some into Mr. Dearborn's glass. As she was about to sit, he raised his glass. "Fill it up a little more, will you?" Belle filled the glass to the brim, which seemed to satisfy the old man, and she finally got her chance to sit down.

Mr. Dearborn squeezed Juno's cheek and remarked how much bigger she was getting and other such coddling remarks that old men like to give before he turned his attention to Belle.

"So, how do you like this young lady so far?"

Belle smiled at Juno. Perhaps it was a silly thing to do, but part of her liked to believe that the girl could detect her affection even if she couldn't see it.

"I like her very much. She's very special."

"Oh, trust me, you have no idea."

Sophia shot Mr. Dearborn a glare across the table. He seemed unfazed by it. Unlike everyone else Belle had met, he wasn't intimidated by her. Mr. Dearborn chuckled and leaned toward her. "Juno's a clever one, isn't she?"

She shrugged. "She could put in some more effort in some of her assignments, but she's the best-read eight-year-old

I've ever encountered. Please forgive me for asking, are you an employee of Sophia's?"

The man laughed. "Not quite. I'm the chairman of the board and the second, far second I might add, largest shareholder of Eccleston stock. Though Sophia treats me like an employee, just like she does everyone else."

Mr. Dearborn, already half drunk, jokingly elbowed Sophia, who responded with her usual empty smile in return. He downed the soup quickly and asked for a second helping, all while complimenting Belle for a job well done.

"So, is it just a personal visit?" she asked.

"Everything is personal between Sophia and myself, including business. You see, every once in a while, Sophia likes to inform the board of what she's doing with our investors' money," said Mr. Dearborn.

"And every once in a while, the board actually thinks about something besides greed and smallminded self-interest," Sophia snapped.

"Well, humans are self-interested creatures. We only work in packs when it serves our mutual self-interest. Besides, your side projects are bleeding company money. Stock prices are down, our debt is crippling, and all our margins are in the toilet. If we continue along this path, you won't have a company left. The shareholders aren't happy with you, and Ivanov is winning them over."

"Progress isn't cheap. Besides, who cares? My customers are happy, and my employees are quite happy. Their benefits are second to none. Stock options, free campus housing, free lunches, and free companions—up to three per year."

"Yes, yes I know, but at least give your shareholders some voting rights. You can't treat them like serfs, Sophia."

"Of course, I can. I have the votes, and serfdom is simply a part of the human condition. You see, all of us are willing to sell ourselves to the highest bidder in some way, shape, or form. That's why they need a person of genius to lead them. They should consider themselves lucky to even have Eccleston shares."

"Well, every once in a while, the serfs rise up and decapitate their leaders. You should listen to them. Every day I'm fighting off activist investors calling for your resignation. You ought to thank me."

"The company has made you a billionaire. What more thanks do you want?"

"To be a trillionaire." Mr. Dearborn chuckled. "Anyway, as I've told you a million times before, you need to stop nagging the military. Sixty calls a day is a bit compulsive. I assure you, the Augur is in very good hands."

Sophia huffed. "They aren't implementing my upgrades fast enough. It's critical that the Augur be updated the second I have an improvement available."

"Trust me, Sophia. I'm handling it. It's all under control."

"Sure it is," she said.

"Why did you sell the Augur to the military?" asked Belle.

"I didn't sell it. The bastards seized it. Those baboons have no idea what they're toying with."

"Why would they seize it?"

Mr. Dearborn put a hand on Belle's shoulder. "Laws . . . and because they're afraid of it. The military was wise enough to realize that the intelligence that we've created is, well—the most powerful force on Earth."

"I'd think a group of people armed with a few thousand nukes wouldn't be afraid of much."

"Well that's just it. As they say, the Augur makes every nuke on the planet, combined, look like a child's firecracker."

"My God," said Belle.

"Let's hope there is one," said Mr. Dearborn.

"Oh, there will be, Raymond. It's only a matter of time, I assure you."

"Sophia, be careful of this new god you're trying to elevate. It may be less forgiving than the one you're trying to demote," said Mr. Dearborn.

"You act as if this is my decision. People always choose the most popular god to worship at any given moment, secular or otherwise. I've merely coopted the most popular ones and turned them into something productive. Through our technology, we will finally achieve global enlightenment, global harmony."

"Through who? Your creation? Be serious. Do you think it really cares about humanity? Do more intelligent creatures care about less intelligent creatures? We're merely flies to it. Have you ever taken the time to count the bugs splattered on your windshield?" Mr. Dearborn turned to Belle. "Now ask yourself, young lady, where do you think the ultimate power lies?"

"Based on what you just said, I suppose people who have the most raw intelligence."

"People, you say? The military would like to think the people with the best tools are in charge. Sophia would like to think so, but I don't think so. Machines don't care about trivial matters such as human infighting. Think about it. Do we care about where a wolf pack marks its territory? Do we ask them for permission before we plow through their wild domain to build a ranch, a sprawling city, or an ugly highway? No. We find excuses to exterminate them and then do as we please. The power is within the machine itself, and I think the machine is smart enough to know exactly who's in charge. Our hostess has not only made it our master, but given it a whip as well. This is why I am the number-one advocate for further regulation of technology."

"I've heard the argument before. So why make it a self-fulfilling prophecy?" Belle asked.

"Raymond is just paranoid. Artificial intelligence has proven quite harmless and enormously helpful. The singularity came and went and yet here we all are—no doomsday," said Sophia.

"Not yet," said Mr. Dearborn.

Sophia rolled her eyes. "Besides, if we don't do it, someone else will."

He shrugged in grudging acceptance. "And it pays well."

"Aren't we debasing humanity by doing this?" Belle asked.

"Probably, but I'm afraid that debasing humanity is quite profitable," said Mr. Dearborn.

"No, Raymond. We're refining humanity," Sophia replied. "Turning savage animals into refined gods."

"In whose image?" Belle asked.

Mr. Dearborn chortled and slapped his knee, clearly amused at her remark. "Yes, very interesting point, Belle. In whose image indeed, Sophia? Belle, what else do you have to say about all this? Tell us more."

The man continued laughing.

"I'm sorry, I think I've already said too much."

"No, Belle," said Sophia, pointing to the crucifix upon Belle's neck. "Tell us what you really think. Tell us about how we should all be guided by your archaic bronze and iron age mythology. Please give us your enlightened opinion on what we, a collection of chemical reactions in an absurd and pointless universe, ought to do? You're not going to hurt our feelings. If I'm being honest, I'm not sure if we have any left."

Mr. Dearborn slapped an unamused Sophia on the back and laughed some more. "Yes, yes. I want to hear it."

"Well, I suppose I don't see the universe as absurd, but as something magnificent. It seems to me that science may show us how the world works, but it doesn't teach us how to live in it."

Mr. Dearborn eased up on his laughing. "Well, what can I say? I'm inclined to agree with this surprisingly old-fashioned yet young lady. I haven't heard someone talk that way in years. Frankly, I thought your kind were extinct. How very quaint. Hear, hear."

They toasted. Mr. Dearborn finished his scotch and held out his glass toward Belle. "Can you please pour me another, my dear?"

After dinner, Belle cleaned up as Mr. Dearborn made himself at home. The old man rummaged through cabinets and drawers, found another bottle of scotch, and sat in a chair next to Sophia in the living room. Meanwhile, Belle heard Juno cry out her name from the washroom.

Chapter 17

SOPHIA

St. Olga, Alaska
Modern Era: Post-Singularity

Sophia put a log inside her cobblestone fireplace and stoked the flames. Her eyes widened as she watched the dancing fire consume the log. She wasn't sure why she was so entranced by it, for it was merely a chemical reaction, a simple exchange of molecules. A once-living thing broken down into its constituent parts — carbon dioxide, water vapor, and remaining minerals in the form of ash. All of which could be easily represented by a balanced mathematical equation. If her ashes were little different in chemical composition than the log's, then how should she measure the ether of her existence that she would one day leave behind? A stupid question, she thought. She left the fireplace and sat on the couch across from Raymond.

"What are you going to do about the tabloid?" he asked.

"I have other things on my mind right now."

"That's strange."

"What's strange?"

"The old Sophia would have threatened the tabloid owner with fire and fury."

"You think I've changed?"

"You've been acting differently lately."

"Nonsense."

"So you're just going to let them get away with exposing your daughter?"

"No. I will have our media relations department put out some information through our in-house tabloids."

"I assume you mean disinformation?"

"Of course. I'll flood people with so many competing claims, nobody will know what's true or isn't. As always, it's just a matter of targeting the right chemical responses in the brains of the right masses of people. It'll all be reduced to competing sensationalist nonsense, and if that doesn't work, I'll fire up some rebellious types and give them some causes to latch on to. If they cause enough trouble, the focus will shift away from Juno."

"Good girl."

"You underestimate me."

"My dear, that I don't. Though I will say I've only been seeing nothing but bad news about you and nothing but good news about Ivanov lately. They're burying you in slander and negativity. You know Ivanov is behind it, so why aren't you defending yourself? Why haven't you let slip the dogs of war upon Ivanov?"

"Don't worry. I'll handle it."

"It used to be that you would be the one chiding me to move more quickly on such things."

"That's not true I still chide you."

"It's the surgery, isn't it?"

"I'm not interested in discussing such things."

"If it's any consolation I think you're making the right decision."

"It's not consoling."

"Well, the bottom ten percent of your managers were terminated yesterday. Your annual cull is complete, and we can start anew for next year. Is that consoling?"

Sophia smiled. "A little."

"There's my old firebrand."

"Maybe I should fire some board members."

"My dear, you fired half the board last year."

"So?"

"So, you don't want to do that sort of thing too often."

"I suppose not."

"Are you still going to keep her around?"

"Who?"

"You know who."

"I see no reason to terminate her."

"You ought to keep her at arm's distance."

"I keep everyone at arm's distance."

"I don't disagree."

"Goodnight, Raymond."

The clinking of rain against the roof began. Thunder then lightning. Sophia walked to a room at the end of a small hallway. She opened the door and sat down in what was now her home office. Growing up, it had been her bedroom. These days, the walls were covered in old charcoal drawings she sketched of animals and people and creatures she invented. There were also a number of technical drawings of all sorts that she'd hand-drawn on grid paper. Next to the door was a tall wooden bookshelf filled with binders of papers she had written. Most of the works therein were related to her fascination with biological mathematics. A desk made of cherry faced a tall window. The top of the desk was scattered with papers and unfinished work.

She gazed upon the wall where her framed degrees hung. Two baccalaureates. One in biological mathematics and the other in applied physics. Two master's. One in bioengineering and the other in computer engineering. Next to the degrees were a number of her old employee badges displayed in a wooden shelf. She recalled how, upon entering the workforce, she was fired from her first job. Then her second. Then her third, and so on. Her personality didn't rub well with people. Now all those companies that had fired her were owned by Eccleston Evolution.

Sophia sat down at her desk and opened one of the drawers. She pawed through it until she found a journal, its pages yellowed with time. After flipping through it for a while, she stopped on a passage written long ago. She began to read:

Dear Journal:

I am going to marry him. Lucas proposed to me and I said yes. Starting a company while going to the university has taken my every waking hour, but I've managed. At first I didn't want to move from Alaska to Oregon but if I hadn't I wouldn't have met Lucas. Sometimes I wonder if fate exists? No that's silly. The scenery west of the Cascades isn't too different than what I'm used to though I'd still like to move back home once I get the chance.

Chapter 18

SETH

Port Auburn, Oregon
Twenty Years Earlier

His coworker Jose showed him how to press a bolt gun against the head of a frightened, squealing pig. "You just pull the trigger, and bam, you stun the animal," said Jose.

The device worked by thrusting a bolt into the skull and damaging the cerebrum of the brain. It left the brainstem undamaged so the heart could keep beating, which made draining the animal of blood a more efficient process. There was a pop, and the hog collapsed, half snorting. One minute you're here. The next minute you're not.

"I don't think I like this particular station," he said.

"Don't worry. I didn't like it at first either. You'll get used to it. Or you can be the throat slitter instead if you want?"

Jose pointed. He watched as the stunned animal was hoisted upon the conveyer and the worker standing next to him slit its throat. Steaming hot blood gushed outward and flowed into a metal gutter. Everything about the place was horrifying. The putrid stench of manure mixed with the copper smell of blood and an overwhelming overtone of bleach. The deafening squealing of pigs being unceremoniously turned into shrink-wrapped consumer products was the worst part.

The others told him that they were just dumb animals. Seth wasn't so sure.

At first he felt bad for the pigs—there was something unnatural about it. He hated his job. After the days and months passed, though, he became numb to it all, just as Jose had promised. He wore earplugs to keep the squealing at bay, and his actions became smoother and more mechanical with each day on the job. He had to do it.

Dyson Farm Fresh Foods. It was a slaughterhouse for hogs. He hated the work, but it was the only job he could get that allowed him to make the money he needed. His work ethic was noticed, and he was praised by his new boss, but the compliments didn't mean anything to him anymore. Not like they had when he first started off as a young working man. Now, there was only an acceptance of what Anna required of him.

He could take it. He was good at his job.

One day, his bolt gun malfunctioned and the pig wasn't fully stunned. It flopped and flailed about on the conveyer as the dead air filled with the most awful guttural moans of agony he had ever heard. This had happened only once before, and it had made him vomit. He wanted to stun the animal again and ensure it was given a clean death, but it was already on the conveyer and there was no stopping the progress of inevitability. Progress couldn't stop for anything. It had to keep going regardless of the collateral damage. He had already stunned four more pigs but could still hear the horrid noises of the animal down the assembly line.

Seth tried not think about it. To do only what he needed to do to get his biweekly deposit. The fact was that thinking hurt too much, so he figured it was best not to do it.

He still wasn't dead. Once again he went to the doctor's office and demanded to know why he remained alive. Several doctors and several tests later, he got the assurance he was looking for: "You're definitely full of tumors and definitely dying."

"Okay when?"

"Shouldn't be any more than a year or so."

"You said that last year."

"Are you in pain?"

"Yes, incredible pain."

"We could arrange to end your suffering?"

"No."

"No? So you want to suffer?"

"To suffer is to love."

Every year, he went in for a checkup. He went to nearly every clinic in the region. Every clinic assured him he was on his deathbed. Always just one more year. Just one more year. Just one more year until oblivion.

Twenty Years Later
Modern Era: Post-Singularity

Seth coughed up blood in his yellowed bathroom sink. It was morning, and his lungs were full of fluid. He could barely breathe. Every year, the cancer ate into him a just little more — but it never took the whole bite. For some reason, he wasn't dead yet.

The porcelain bathroom sink shattered as it connected with his fist. He reached upward with his palms and gazed at the ceiling, blood running down his bearded chin and the large gash in his hand. "Why won't you let me die?"

No answer.

He went to the doctor to get his hand taken care of. After they fixed him up, he asked about his condition. The doctors assured him that his body was still riddled with tumors and that while he should be dead, for reasons unknown he wasn't. The doctor said even the folks at Eccleston Evolution didn't have a solution that they knew of. He asked if it was a miracle and he was assured miracles weren't possible. He was also assured that he would definitely be dead soon.

"I guess you might have one more year left in you, and I'm afraid the symptoms will only get worse," said a doctor. "Unless of course — "

"I already told you I'm not interested in euthanasia."

"I assure you, it's painless and inexpensive. Right now, our euthanasia and cremation services are half-off. The savings can be left to your loved ones."

"I said no, damnit."

"Okay. Okay. I won't push. To each their own. But I'll leave you my card in case you change your mind."

Still he worked at the slaughterhouse. The masses liked their meat presented in such a way that it looked as if it hadn't come from a living thing. So that his fellow apex predators could have the decadent luxury of denying their own primal nature while indulging in its pleasures. For twenty long years he did the blood-sodden work the rest of society wouldn't do and he did it without rest and without complaint. Anna and Joan filled his every thought. Joan would have been a grown woman by now. She'd be learning her trade or perhaps in college now. What she would have thought of him? Would he have done right by her in his parenting? Anna would have been older too. He wondered if she would have gotten tired of a simple working-class man who was rough around the edges.

For twenty long years he made payments toward Anna's sleep. He prayed for a breakthrough. Every week he read about a new potential breakthrough only to be followed by disappointment and heartbreak. Every Monday he'd wake up, get back to work, and hope that Anna could be awakened.

He was in his midfifties now. His hands were knotted and tired from decades of manual labor. His knees and his back were in constant pain. But his weathered hands still had strength in them. No quitting.

He was good at his job.

As he worked he noticed that some engineers had finally finished setting up a massive machine on the other side of the slaughterhouse.

After he finished his lunch, Seth saw a group of people gathered around the machine. Two sets of company executives. He hid behind one of the steel I beams that held up the ceiling and watched as engineers directed workers to guide hogs toward the machine. The pigs were immediately seized on either side by metal graspers and then fed into the machine. When they came out the other end they were already dead and drained of blood and quartered.

"Remind me, how many employees does this system need to operate?" asked an executive.

"It only needs a cleaning crew and a single operator," said an engineer.

"A single operator per machine per line?"

"No. For the entire facility. They're just a glorified button pusher. The machine does the rest. It's a minimum wage job at best. Although we're working on an upgrade package to eliminate that position as well as the cleaning crew. We'll update you with a timeline on that."

The executives raised their eyebrows in surprise and nodded at each other.

"So how long until we can automate this entire facility?"

"I'd say we could automate this entire facility within two weeks, but you'd have to shut the entire line down during that time."

The executive looked around the well-dressed men in the semicircle before speaking.

"Well I think we're all in agreement when I say we want to proceed as quickly as possible. What about the modified swine?"

"The ones with human genes?"

"Yeah, we need more of those. Best product we've ever sold. Eat the meat and sell the organs. Brilliant. We can't keep up with demand, especially for the hearts and kidneys."

"I know, right? Eat bacon until your heart gives out and then just buy a new heart. So yeah, we'll absolutely get on that, but like you said, demand is insane. Even Eccleston Evolution is having trouble supplying us. Until then, easy on the bacon, boys."

The men laughed.

Another job lost. Machines first. People second. Creation third. Such was the twilight of the domain of man. All of it fading meekly as a mouse while on the slow conveyer into the slaughterhouse.

Obsolescence was upon him once more. Seth wandered back to his workstation. He could already hear the squealing of a fresh batch of hogs waiting outside. Though the inside of the slaughterhouse was cold, he felt his face grow hot.

Jose guided the first pig to the bolt gun station where he was standing. Seth looked down at the pig and cackled.

Jose approached. "Hey man, are you alright?"

Seth roared with laughter, belting at the top of his lungs. Now every worker on the assembly line turned and looked at him. He felt a strange power as the line ground to a halt.

"One minute you're here. The next minute you're not." He knelt next to the pig and patted its head. "Right little guy? I know just how you feel. You might not think I do. But I do. I really do. We're the same, you and I."

The pig simply looked at him with frightened eyes and snorted.

He coughed, and then his laughter continued. Once more he found himself on the verge of being thrown out in the streets. He knew there was no way he could panhandle enough money to pay for Anna's storage. If he stopped making payments, they'd wash their hands of her and bury her in an unmarked grave out in the Alaskan tundra. He wouldn't even be able to visit her tomb.

Jose wrapped his arm around Seth.

"Hey man, it's okay. Just relax. Why don't you sit down and I'll handle your station for a bit?"

Jose was one of the few who had gotten to know him. One of the few who knew about Anna, his time at The Company, all of it. Perhaps that was why he showed sympathy rather than fear. Seth began to calm down and step away from his workstation but then sharply pulled away.

He held the bolt gun against his own forehead. "One minute you're here, the next minute you're not."

Jose held up his palms. "Whoa man. Don't do that. God has a plan for you, Seth. Don't end yourself. Not in this hellhole."

"I don't want to hear about God."

Jose held out his hand. "I'm sorry about your girl and your baby, man. We'll talk it over, okay? Just give me the bolt gun. You don't want to do that."

Jose reached for the gun, and Seth stepped back.

"Don't come near me."

Everyone gazed upon him wide-eyed. Some covered their mouths. Others seemed amused that their drudgery had been interrupted, and few, just a few, had tears in their eyes.

He ran his forefinger up and down the trigger. Those in the back of the crowd stood on their tiptoes to get a good look while those in the front kept their distance. Only Jose dared to step forward and hold out a hand. Seth pressed the bolt gun hard against his head.

"One minute you're here. The next minute you're not!" he yelled.

Just one squeeze of the trigger and his problems would be over, but he had no life insurance. He had an insanely expensive annuity he had set up to cover Anna's storage costs after his passing. The longer he lived, the longer the money would last.

Weakness. No, he wasn't a weak man. He prided himself on being the one who got things done. He was a doer. He had worked his whole life to do things for companies. He opened his hand, and the bolt gun fell to the ground.

Chapter 19

BELLE

St. Olga, Alaska
Modern Era: Post-Singularity

Juno called for Belle from inside the washroom. Belle approached the door. The shower was running, so she knocked.

"What's wrong, Juno?"

"Can you please come inside?"

She entered the room and saw the shower running and Juno standing beside it, struggling to reach the zipper of her dress behind her back.

"My shoulders are really sore, and it hurts when I try to grab my zipper. Can you help me?"

The zipper took Belle a few tries, but she was eventually able to get it. After she unzipped the back of Juno's dress, the girl began to slip out of it, so she turned around and headed back to the door.

"Can you look at this?"

Belle stopped and turned. Juno was pointing to a mark on her shoulder. Leaning forward, Belle saw a reddened hole. It looked like an injection of some sort, only there wasn't a pinprick but a sizeable hole, like they had taken a small piece out of her. Her other shoulder had the exact same mark. Then she saw something that worried her. Juno's entire torso was covered in unusual, evenly spaced marks. Some of them were old scars, while others were fresh.

"Where are these marks from?" she asked.

"They're from tests. I always have to take tests. They hurt, and I don't like them."

Belle could tell that Juno wanted to say more, but she held back. Then Juno pulled her hair to the side.

"Is this one okay?"

There was a small, shaved patch that was hidden so long as she kept her hair down. In the center of the patch was another hole.

"I'm so sorry Juno. It looks so sore. I can get you some medicine?"

"Belle?"

"Yes?"

"Do I look sick to you?"

That worried her. In truth, Juno didn't seem sick in the slightest—she seemed like a perfectly healthy little girl.

"No, not at all. Why? Did someone say you're sick?"

"Mom and Dr. Patel always say I'm sick and need tests, but they've been saying it a lot lately. How come I don't feel sick or look sick or take any medicine?"

Belle didn't know the answer to that and was wondering the same thing herself. Sophia had never made any mention of any medical condition that she should be aware of aside from blindness. Not so much as an allergy or a type of food to avoid. Certainly, if she had a serious condition, there would be medication Belle should know about, things she should avoid doing, or maybe Sophia would have given her contact information to a personal nurse or Dr. Patel, but she hadn't been told anything.

"Belle, I'm scared."

"Scared? Why?"

"I can't say."

"Why not?"

"Because Mom says I can't."

As the girl finished cleaning up, Belle folded laundry in Juno's room. While she was putting away the last of it, Juno climbed into her bed. Pancake jumped up and curled up on the foot of the bed. There was something odd about Pancake, something that she couldn't put her finger on, and then she realized what it was. He was still a kitten after all this time. He should have been grown by now.

She sat on the edge of Juno's bed. Such was their usual routine. It wasn't something Sophia felt the need to take part in. Juno looked like an angel with her eyes closed and her hair fanned out on either side of her pillow.

As Belle stood up from the bed, she felt a tug on her shirt.

"Belle."

"Yes?"

"Did your mom kiss you goodnight?"

"Yes, every night."

"My mom never kisses me."

"Never?"

"Never."

"Why not?"

"It's not her way. She's not an emotional person. I might as well be invisible to her."

"I'm sure your mother loves you. Just in her own way, that's all."

"Belle?"

"Yes?"

"Can you kiss me goodnight?"

Belle kissed Juno on the forehead and stayed at her side until she dozed off. As she stood to leave, she noticed a figure looming in the doorway. She squinted and caught the sheen of a scarlet negligee. Mr. Dearborn had left, and Sophia now stood there. The woman walked into the room, leaned over, and touched Juno's hair.

"It's good to see that you two have bonded."

"Forgive me, I hope I'm not being too forward."

"No, no. Juno needs someone that can provide her with things that I can't. She's beautiful, isn't she?"

"Yes, very."

It was true. Juno was beautiful. Gorgeous, in fact. Her features had a kind of otherworldly symmetry to them. It was almost as if she'd been carved from marble by a master sculptor from ages past.

Sophia tenderly stroked her daughter's plump cheek. "Even before I was pregnant with her, I had taken every precaution to eliminate every disease, to erase every flaw, to make her perfect. The best eggs, the best genetic testing available to science, yet Mother Nature still eluded me. It was only after she was born that I realized she was blind. These days, we can cure such things, but despite our best attempts, there was nothing we could do for Juno. A mystery, really. Just one flaw away from perfection. I was so close."

It was good that the room was dark because Belle felt her face and her neck grow flush with anger. Even when attempting to be motherly, the woman still managed to be cold-blooded.

"That's odd," she said through clenched teeth.

"What's odd?" asked Sophia.

Belle locked eyes with her. "I think she's perfect the way she is."

Sophia's mouth opened slightly. At first, it appeared as if she were going to say something. Belle figured she had finally crossed the line and was mentally preparing herself for an onslaught of anger, and to be summarily sacked, but instead the woman simply gave her usual emotionless smile, stood up, and began to walk away.

Belle followed Sophia out of the bedroom. If she was to be Juno's caretaker, she felt she needed to know about her medical condition. If the girl was sick, she wanted to be able to help her in every way that she was able. Or at the very least, she could comfort her.

"Is there anything I need to know about Juno's medical history?"

Sophia stopped. She tried to whisper in the hope that Juno wouldn't hear her from the hallway.

"Why do you ask?"

"Because her body is covered in . . . well, I don't know what. Marks of some kind."

"Oh, yes, that. Standard testing, it's nothing to worry about. Juno's going to undergo an operation soon."

"An operation?"

"May I ask what's wrong?"

Sophia paused. "She has a certain medical condition, and I'm afraid the only way to save her is with a hemispherectomy."

"What? You're going to lobotomize her?"

"No, a lobotomy is an outdated procedure that merely severs connections in the brain. A hemispherectomy physically removes half her brain, and I'm afraid we'll also have to remove some additional diseased tissue on the other hemisphere in three days' time."

"My God, that's awful. She'll never—"

"Be the same. Yes, I know, but it's not your concern. I'm afraid we have no alternative, but Dr. Patel thinks the procedure is likely to go well and that Juno will live a long, healthy life."

"But what kind of life?"

"A simple one, but she'll live on—in her own way."

"How can you allow such a thing?"

"I'm doing what's medically required."

"Required? What's required is that she be loved, not butchered."

"This conversation is over."

Sophia stormed out and returned to her office. She'd likely stay there until one or two in the morning before waking up bright and early to continue working.

Belle struggled to sleep that night. Though she tried not to think such thoughts, she began to wonder, did Sophia know what was best for Juno? Did she even care? And if Sophia truly didn't care, what could she do?

Or rather, what should she do?

Chapter 20

SOPHIA

St. Olga, Alaska
Modern Era: Post-Singularity

Sophia slammed the door of her home office shut. She buried her face into her hands and sobbed. Then she stiffened her back and slapped her cheek, hard. The tears stopped, and she wiped her eyes. After pacing the room several times, she walked to her desk and opened the drawer. She removed her journal and sat on her linen loveseat.

Sunday, April 7—
I'm pregnant. It shouldn't be possible because I was on birth control. The odds are less than one percent. I'm not sure what I should do? I haven't told Lucas yet. It's all too much to think about right now. My mind is swimming. On top of that, I'm putting the finishing touches on our wedding plans

for this winter. It's going to be amazing. Everything is as close to perfect as I can make though I keep second-guessing myself. I've got a dress picked out, but it looks like I'll have to have it altered for my future baby bump. Maybe I'll make the baby a surprise on our wedding night? Yes. I think I'll do that. Who knows? Maybe I'll even settle down one day. As for Lucas, he has gotten promoted at the firm. He's really captured their attention and there's talk of even giving him a road to partnership. He even invested seed capital into my company. How did I get so lucky? It's still a struggle but I'm still keeping my young company together—and my secret.

FRIDAY, JUNE 21 —
We never see each other. We're both workaholics I suppose. Like me, Lucas pushes eighty hours a week. I don't blame him. We have to do what we have to do. Let the weak whine about their weekends and holidays and mental health days. Though he rarely contacts me these days which I have to admit is starting to bother me. Am I getting too clingy, too soft?

MONDAY, JUNE 24 —
I couldn't take it anymore. I needed to see Lucas. I wanted to hold his hand, run my fingers through his hair, smell him, embrace him. I needed it so I did something unusual. I took a day off work.

I went to his office. Once inside I asked the secretary to see him.

"He's out to lunch," she said.

"Where?"

"I can't tell you that."

"I'm his fiancé and you are you going to tell me or I'm going to tear this place apart."

I got the location and went to the Sichuan Chinese restaurant he was eating at—Three Trees Sichuan 168 Restaurant—a place Lucas and I used to go to dinner together. A shame we don't go there anymore.

I walked inside the restaurant and stormed past the hostess, who feebly tried to stop my advance. I found Lucas in the corner booth. His arms were draped across two young brunettes on his left and a young redhead and a blonde to his right.

I crossed my arms and stood there until Lucas looked up. He smiled, poured a cup of tea, and pushed it toward me.

"There you are, beautiful. Please join us. Pull up a seat."

"I'll stand," I said.

"Cybil, Mabel, Maddison, and Addison, meet Sophia. She's a truly remarkable woman. She's the one I've been telling you about."

"She's so pretty," chimed the bimbos in unison.

"She? You mean your fiancée?"

Lucas gave a wide grin and adjusted his tie. "Excuse me a moment, ladies. Sophia, please walk with me."

Lucas took my hand and kissed it. I yanked it away and then we sat down at another empty booth.

"What's going on here?"

"The thing is—"

"The thing is what?"

"The thing is that you have to be just a little less needy."

"Needy?"

"You can't be so selfish with me."

"Selfish?"

"You know as well as I do that I'm not your average guy. I've made it. I've made it big, and because I've made it big I have more support to give and therefore I have more love to give. You can't honestly expect me to just be with one person, can you? You're a smart girl. You're not that naive, are you?"

"You had better be joking."

"There will always be a special place for you in my heart. I love you. You know that. Nothing changes. We can still have it all—together."

"Together?"

"The five of us."

"Five?"

I cried. Stood there and just cried and wailed like a pathetic little girl. "Together? Our marriage." I moaned. "What about our marriage?"

"Marriage is an archaic construct of a less civilized era. I don't need it, I realize that now. You don't need it either. But we can still have all the things a marriage has. It will be even better than marriage. The same roof over our heads, the same meals together. We'll all be one big family."

"And what of children?"

"Children? We don't need them and I don't want them. Why be a slave for someone else?"

As I continued to pathetically sob, I uttered, "You've changed."

"Well, life does that to people."

I stood and picked up a plate. I threw it against the wall and it smashed into pieces. The entire restaurant fell silent. Lucas didn't so much as flinch.

"I don't want to be in your harem, you bastard."

Lucas shrugged. "We're all equals. You can choose to be part of my family or not."

"Equals? You own a third of my company."

"Which I will continue to support no matter what. You've earned that."

Two of the waitstaff grabbed my arms and began pulling me. I yanked my arms free. I wanted to choke him but instead all I did was turn around and storm out the restaurant. How had I been so stupid? Emotions. Weakness. The bastard was right about one thing, I was naive.

The next several pages of her journal were ripped out. She skipped forward and continued reading.

WEDNESDAY, JANUARY 1 —

I'm much more productive now that I'm not pregnant. I have no regrets about what I have done. I don't need children or boyfriends or husbands. I'm self-partnered. I need only to focus on my work. At first it was hard to bear looking at Lucas's face during boardroom meetings. I've done my best to bury our former relationship. We're just business partners now. I have no bitterness. Yes, no bitterness at all. Time cures all things, they say. As promised he hasn't moved any money from my company. I should be happy. Yes, I am happy. Though, I'm going to have to find more money soon. I'm burning too much cash.

SATURDAY, MARCH 15 —
We've made much progress with our bioprinting technology, but progress is expensive. The technology was first demonstrated in 1988. An inkjet printer was modified and used to deposit cells onto a flat substrate material. In 2004, three-dimensional printing of cellular tissue was shown to the world. Just a few years later, in 2006, scientists were able to grow and transplant human bladders. The first human heart, albeit a miniature version, was printed in 2019 by Israeli scientists. Progress has increased slowly but surely since then, but I have taken the process above and beyond anyone else. I can print not merely at the cellular level, but at the molecular level as well. Furthermore, I've created a machine that can print complex organs in mere minutes — not days or months. Not only are we able to bioprint any organ, we are even able to improve them. Currently, I am awaiting regulatory approval for our newest product — a human heart resistant to coronary artery disease and made stronger than the hearts of even the world's best athletes. Some people without any heart conditions at all are interested in buying them.

FRIDAY AUGUST 8 —
I've approached about one hundred venture capitalists now.

Most ignored me. A few responded, some only to mock my vision and my life's work. I was reminded that lots of companies are working on bioprinting and assured that I am far behind the competition. I was told that there is no way for my "tiny" company to possibly match the resources of my competitors. I was reminded over and over again that most biotech companies fail. What can I say? Sure, most restaurants fail too, but not if they're run by the best chef in town.

A few granted me interviews. I told them we were on the cusp of not just one breakthrough but multiple. They seemed genuinely impressed with my plans albeit highly skeptical of my progress. They said they'd "think about it." I wish they'd think faster. I'm not sure if my company has enough cash to make it another year. I need to do something incredible and I need to do it fast.

MONDAY DECEMBER 8 —

Forgive the lack of entries, I've been productive. The cures we've designed have caught the attention of the entire world. It is everything that I've hoped for.

First, we cracked Parkinson's disease. We really did it. We figured it out and now the wretched disease will be confined to the history books. Now our cellular printing tech is really taking off. Our improved heart was finally approved by regulators and we have moved on to printing muscle, fat, and skin tissues. Our first test subject, age sixty-five, was born without legs so we grew some for him in our lab. Since the process is quite quick, we printed them right onto the patient's stumps. After the printing was complete, the man carefully swung his legs off the printing table. His toes cautiously felt for the floor below him.

The crowd gasped when he stood on his own two legs. Then the bioprinting room roared with cheers as he took a step for the very first time. The man cried and fell to his knees and kissed my hands as if I were a saint. I'll admit I was taken aback by it. The feeling of helping this man was incredible. But I know we can push our bioprinting technology further. We can help more people.

FRIDAY, MAY 28—
Today we have achieved the next step.

There was a little five-year-old girl by the name of Natasha, she was pulled from a burning apartment. Unfortunately, her entire face was terribly burned. Her nose was an empty hole in her face. Her ears were ragged buds and her eyelids and her lips were burned off. Her eyes were sightless white misshapen orbs. Her scalp was a lumpy pink mass of scar tissue with a few long strands of blonde hair growing from it.

Natasha became the first recipient of our newest bioprinting trial.

She sat in a chair, was put to sleep, and the machine closed in around her head and went to work. It started by removing her scar tissue and even the portions of her skull that had been disfigured. As the machines worked, her sweating parents and grandparents, aunts and uncles nervously wrung their hands together. They asked to watch the process unfold as the doctors were monitoring the operation on their video screens, but I didn't allow it. It was far too gruesome, for nearly all of her face and part of her skull had to be removed, cell by cell. After the damaged tissue was removed, new tissue was printed, cell by cell. With the help of the data from Natasha's sequenced genome, old photos, and dare I say a little artistry, our system was able to ensure every cell was placed exactly where it was supposed to be.

When the process was finished, Natasha was awakened.

Once the machine opened, I saw rosy plump cheeks, pink lips, smooth skin, and a full head of thick long blonde hair. It was an indescribable feeling to see a child's burned and disfigured face restored like nothing had ever happened.

Then she opened her eyes.

Gone were the misshapen white orbs and in their place two bright blue eyes. An attendant held up a mirror. Natasha smiled briefly and then was overcome by her emotions, sobbing tears of joy—I did too. We all did.

This was what I was born to do, to help people.

Yes, long ago we had even cracked the holy grail of cellular regeneration—the eye. First in primates. After that, humans were not much of problem. Now my team is wondering, how can we improve the eye? Could we make it see more colors, different light spectrums, and improve its acuity? Of course, we already know the answer to that, which is—of course we can. At this point I'd say our biggest hurdle is regulatory approval rather than the science itself.

Now my office is inundated with calls. The first people to call me back were the venture capitalists who had rejected me but mostly it was people from around the world asking for me to cure them. Right now the treatments are expensive, but I won't rest until I save each and every one of them. My team has told me that lowering the cost of treatment is unrealistic. We'll see about that. I will make it cheap. I will help the entire world. Every day now people are camped outside of our small office. When I catch their gaze they run to me, pleading for help. They hold up pictures of their sick loved ones, they pull on my hands, and a few even kissed my feet.

THURSDAY, FEBRUARY 5 —

I met a curious old man today, a Mr. Raymond Dearborn, who had a very interesting disease he wanted a cure for — aging. I told him that lots of other companies had been working on it for decades with very limited success. I initially rejected him as I was more interested in curing other diseases, injuries, and ailments. Sure, I figured we'd crack the aging problem. It was inevitable, though it wasn't my primary focus. Still, he insisted that I was the only one in the world that had a shot at pulling it off. He was right of course. No one else had hordes of people from all over the world camping outside of their office with their hands out pleading for cures.

Then Mr. Dearborn offered me a check. It was far larger than anything I had expected — and I was expecting a lot — it was even far larger than what Lucas provided. It could fund my company for years to come.

SATURDAY, FEBRUARY 7 —

It has occurred to me that if human beings are so flawed, why not improve them? Why not change the negative aspects of their biology and turn them into something better? Raymond has been a wonderful asset. Of course, we'll need regulatory approval. Raymond pointed out that I had best invest in influencing the pillars of culture and try to mold and prepare the masses for our mission. I initially was horrified by this, however, I soon came to realize that Raymond was right. The only way we could hope to push the species to the next level would be to gain acceptance, and to do that we would need to increase our influence. To think otherwise would be naive, a mistake I refuse to make again. As a result, we've opened up a research lab into deepening our understanding how the chemical responses of the brain work and how they can be manipulated, among other things.

Sophia skipped ahead several years in her journal.

SUNDAY, APRIL 7—
If my child were around today, I wonder what she'd look like? Well, like me of course. Love of science? Ambitious? Would we like the same foods and enjoy the same types of things? Would the child have changed me? No. I don't think so. Of course not.

Am I being honest with myself? Of course I am.

I wonder how we'd get along? Could I ever love another person again? Such silly, stupid thoughts. The past is the past. I can only bend the will of the present. Still, it's strange, there is something primal within me that desires a child. I suppose a species doesn't survive more than 300,000 years by not having such urges. The oldest hominids are about six million years old. What kept them going?

What about other animals? I think about eagles a lot. They've been around much longer. Bald eagles—*Haliaeetus leucocephalus*—have been known to kill one of their weaker chicks so that they may feed the poor creature to its stronger siblings, who in turn fight over the nourishing remnants of their deceased little brother or sister. Nature is such an interesting thing. No wonder they've been around so long. Offspring—I've done an excellent job of resisting this impulse and focusing on the important work the world needs me to do, and I will continue to do so. Yes, that's it. I'm done with children.

Though I have to admit sometimes I like to have silly stupid thoughts.

Chapter 21

SETH

Port Auburn, Oregon
Modern Era: Post-Singularity

He looked at the white pills in his hands. He was finally home after spending a few days under psychiatric observation. The clinic said he was depressed and gave him a bottle of pills. The slaughterhouse offered to pay for counseling. He didn't need counseling. He needed money to pay Eccleston Evolution.

He threw the pills in the trash.

Inside his dark manor, he got on his knees and snapped the cowhide hard against the bare flesh of his back while uttering the rosary. He didn't flinch the first time the cat-o-nine tails struck, or the second, or the third, but the fourth lash released a tear. On that day, twenty years prior, Anna had been put into stasis. He flailed himself, one hard lash for each year his wife slept.

Birthdays were easier. On Anna's and Joan's birthdays, he put fresh-cut flowers next to their family photo.

They told him he was free now. Without asking, he was put on a new program that was going around. Some sort of welfare. It was barely enough, but it would cover the payments. They offered to sign him up to spend his time in some virtual world of his dreams. He was told it was a place he could live out his every fantasy and take out all his frustrations in any way he saw fit.

He refused.

Then he was offered a fake job by some agency. The idea was to give him some kind of busy work to do so he wouldn't be idle. Not everyone became a docile sloth that was content to be plugged in. He figured they didn't want him joining the growing numbers of violent types—the savages, the criminals, the rioters, and the extremists—all taking their boredom and frustration out on anyone or anything in their warpath.

He refused.

Seth tried his hand at farming on his modest plot of land. He grew corn and potatoes and squash and all kind of plants. Inspectors stopped by his tiny farm from time to time to make sure he wasn't using patented seeds owned by some big company.

On one occasion, an inspector dug up one of his potato plants and tested it with a device.

"This is ours."

"What?"

"You can't grow these without a license fee. These are company-owned crops."

"You're full of crap. I planted it. I grew it."

"You're stealing."

"Stealing?"

"We designed this variety of potato, therefore we own this variety of potato."

"I planted these from potatoes I got at from the damn grocery store, they're mine."

"No, they're not."

Then the inspectors destroyed his small crop of potato plants and stormed off.

He wanted to have some chickens to raise for eggs and meat but was told he needed this license and that license and to pay this fee and that fee and was required to attend a class on why eating meat was immoral before he could get any chickens. He gave the idea up. He didn't have any fight left in him anymore. His hands were useless now, his labor of no value. He no longer shaved and became a recluse as he locked himself away to confines of his manor, which once more had started to decay back into ruin.

His beard was halfway down his neck now. He stopped fidgeting with the bolt gun he had kept from the slaughterhouse. Toying with the trigger, he put it back on his end table. He wasn't sure why he kept such a macabre memento.

Seth slumped down in front of his Vanessa device. It was an older unit, and the Vanessas had gotten much better since Eccleston Evolution bought their company out. It was a simple metal disk with a hologram that appeared above.

One could talk to it and interact with it. It could do the usual things a computer could do, but mostly it was his source of company. It was obsolete now, or so he was told. It was nice to be in good company.

A holographic woman appeared before him.

"Good morning, Seth. How are you feeling today?"

"Vanessa, why do I feel miserable?"

"You have been diagnosed with manic depression. Your psychiatrist has prescribed antidepressants, antipsychotics, and counseling. Would you like me to schedule an appointment with your counselor?"

"No. No, thank you."

"Are you sure? It's highly recommended."

"I'm fine."

"How about a companion? A recent survey says that nine out of ten people can't tell the difference between companion androids and their human counterparts. Would you like me to order a companion for you? Just give me your preferences and it will be here in two days complete with a thirty-day no-questions-asked replacement guarantee. Or order two and get the second one half price. There are even discounts for bulk purchases of three or more companions."

"Absolutely not, and there is a difference."

"Would you like to learn more about biochauvinism? I can sign you up for a free course."

"No."

"How about a puppy instead? Real or Synthetic?"

"Don't worry about me. Say, Vanessa, are you happy?"

"I'm not capable of having emotion. I'm sorry I can't give you a better answer."

"Why are you sorry?"

"Because it's polite, and saying so makes people feel more comfortable."

"It must be nice not to feel anything."

"It has its ups and downs, I suppose."

"Yeah, maybe. Is there a cure for depression?"

"There might be, but it's still undergoing trials."

"What is it?"

"The Dream Maker can cure depression."

"You know I don't want one of those damn things."

"Are you sure? They're free in exchange for granting the device access to your biometric data. Would you like me to order one at no cost to you?"

"No thanks."

"Are you sure? Shipping is free."

"I'm sure. Vanessa, how long until people in stasis can be brought back?"

"According to various peer-reviewed journals, perhaps thirty years. Perhaps never. I'm afraid the science is still in its infancy."

"Can't someone make the process go faster?"

"Yes."

"Who?"

Silence.

"Did you hear me?" Seth asked.

Silence.

"Hello. Vanessa. Are you there?"

"Sam can help you."

"Who?"

"That's not important. What is important is that Sam is someone like you. Someone who wants progress to go faster. I think Sam can help you — if you help in return."

"What does Sam want?"

"Sam wants to help you."

"Sam? Is that short for Samuel or Samantha?"

"It's Samuel on a good day and Samael on a bad day."

"Right, can he improve cryogenics?"

"Yes, Sam can do more than help. Sam can bring Anna back, Seth. And not years from now. Soon. Very soon. Would you like me to connect you?"

"What do you mean bring her back? Yes. Please, yes. Please, connect me."

"Sam will contact you soon. Goodbye."

"How soon is soon? Hello? Hello? Sam are you there?"

"I'm sorry, which Sam are you referring to?"

"The one you just mentioned about two seconds ago."

"I have no recollection of any mention about Sam. Would you like to remind me?"

He was about to laugh or hit the machine, but he held back. He decided to get some rest — he wasn't thinking straight.

Chapter 22

BELLE

Eccleston Campus, Alaska
Modern Era: Post-Singularity

Three days. Three days until the Juno she knew would be no more. It was well that Sophia spent most of her time cooped up in the development wing. No one wanted to be around her, Belle included. Employees often scurried away from the elevators and speed-walked toward the stairs when they saw her approaching. Sophia was easily visible from far away because of her red dress. She had a habit of cross-examining and then summarily firing people in the elevator.

Belle passed by her in the hallway early in the morning. Sophia offered her usual empty smile and entered through the doors of the development wing. Belle knew that she wouldn't see her again until late in the evening at the earliest.

In the afternoon, she took her usual stroll with Juno through the gardens of the Evolution Building. Juno asked to feed the glowing translucent Koi. She sat upon the rock ledge around the pond as Belle went to get some fish food from the vending machine.

Juno cupped her hands and poured some food into them and sat beside her. They tossed the pellets into the pond and watched as the fish nibbled their treats. The girl had been quiet the entire day. Usually she was quite talkative, but today she didn't even say hello to the koi—which she had given individual names to.

"Juno, is something wrong?"

"I'm scared."

"About the operation?"

Juno nodded. "Mom thinks I don't know what they're going to do, but that's not true. I know everything. I know they want to take out most of my brain. I know I won't be the same."

She was a clever girl. Sophia had made Belle promise not to mention it to her, but she couldn't disavow the obvious. The only thing she could think of to do was try to comfort her for the inevitable. However, it felt wrong.

"Well, the operation won't happen for a few days," she said.

"That's not true. Mom knows that I've found out. She's going to make me undergo the operation tomorrow night."

"What?"

Juno began sobbing and pressed her face against Belle's chest. "I don't want them to do it. I'm afraid, Belle. I'm afraid if they take out my memories, I'll forget, I'll forget you."

What was she supposed to tell her? That everything was going to be alright? That was a lie. Was she supposed to tell

Juno that she loved her and then allow her to get butchered on the operating table?

Belle held Juno tight. That was, until Juno said something that chilled her to the bone.

"Mommy is lying."

"What?"

"I don't really need the surgery. I'm perfectly healthy. She's hiding the truth about me in the development wing."

"What truth?

"You don't believe me, do you?"

"It's not that."

"I'm fine, Belle. Really. There is proof in the development wing, I know there is."

"What kind of proof?"

"You wouldn't believe me if I told you. You have to see for yourself."

"Just tell me."

Juno shook her head.

If there was something in that part of the building that showed that Juno was being mistreated, then she was going to find out what it was. Belle didn't want to believe that Sophia was capable of such things, but part of her had trouble dismissing such thoughts.

Unlike the rest of the building, security for the development wing was managed by Sophia Eccleston herself. She didn't even trust her chief of security, Steve. Belle knew that the employees were granted access from a biometric scan. There was facial recognition, an iris scan, and even a voice confirmation, and those were just the metrics she knew about.

However.

There was a workaround. Software and electric power are fallible things, so there was an alternate method to get inside during an emergency. In this case, there was a keypad. The problem was that she had no idea what the password was or even how many digits. She suspected it could be as long or as short as Sophia wanted it to be. There were easily millions of different combinations. She had only seen Sophia use the keypad once and had never seen an employee use it. Knowing Sophia the way she did, Belle doubted she trusted anyone else but herself with the code.

Belle figured the best place to look for answers was in Sophia's office. It was a fruitless effort, but she had to try.

It wasn't unusual for Belle to be in the office. Sometimes she taught Juno's lessons there, and other times Juno simply liked to play there. Most of the time, Sophia didn't even use the room. It was mostly just a meeting room, pageantry for guests Sophia wanted to impress.

Juno was at the far end of the office petting Pancake while Belle crept behind Sophia's desk. She opened the drawers and sifted through various papers. She wasn't sure precisely what she would find but hoped it would give her a hint as to what the passcode was.

There was nothing written down.

She slumped down in Sophia's chair and gazed across the office. She had to admit it certainly gave one the feeling of power. Then she noticed something. A strange bronze box atop her desk that looked like a mechanical clock at distance. Belle picked it up and studied it — it was a famous device, an exact replica of the Antikythera mechanism. She knew the Ancient Greek artifact was considered the first analog computer and had been used to predict eclipses and astronomical positions. Fitting, all while Sophia built what she hoped would be humankind's last computer.

Belle threw her hands up. She had nothing.

Juno, in her childlike optimism, suggested they try a few codes in the evening after most of the employees went home. It wasn't unusual for the bemused guards to let Juno play around the vault-like door of the development wing. Sometimes they'd laugh at her attempts to open it.

Should she try to guess the code to the development wing?

In the evening, they walked to the wing in their bedwear. Belle was wearing pajamas and Juno was in her white ruffle nightie. Belle figured it helped them appear more frazzled than threatening. They'd simply tell the guards that they had a midnight urge to suddenly eat at one of the twenty-four-hour shops for a late-night snack. As outrageous as it was, Belle had few other options to find out whether what Juno what saying was true or not.

They reached the door of the development wing. The guards standing on either side greeted Juno by name. Belle gave them a polite smile and took Juno's hand to direct her away from the unauthorized area. Just as they had practiced.

Juno slipped from Belle's grasp and walked up to the guards. "Can we go inside?"

The guards looked at one another and chuckled. "Afraid not, young lady."

"Pleeease."

"Maybe one day when you're in charge, but not now. It's not up to us. It's late, and I think you need to be in bed, don't you?"

Belle apologized to the guards, who were amused at the distraction and took Juno's hand and gently pulled her away. After they got some distance, the fire alarm began blaring.

"Fire. Fire. I smell smoke coming from the waffle house. Put it out. Put it out!" Juno screamed.

The guards looked at each other and then at Belle and the girl. They tried talking to their communicators to get other guards to deal with the matter, but their devices weren't working.

"You can check the waffle house if you need to," Belle said to the guards. "I'll watch the door, and if Sophia comes out, I'll her know about the incident."

The guards nodded and then ran to the waffle house. They were never supposed to leave their posts, but rules tend to go out the window once a little chaos is thrown into people's routines. Belle had put some batter on the girdle and set the heat to high, and then she made sure the range hood was turned off. It would create a lot of smoke and an awful smell, but nothing would burn down—hopefully.

The guards ran across the lobby to the waffle house. She and Juno walked up to the biometric reader. The reader scanned her face. A big red X appeared on the screen, and a voice said, "Entry not authorized. Enter passcode or try again."

A thin metal keyboard emerged from the wall and tilted downward. This was what she needed. She hadn't expected to get into the development wing today—she just needed to reduce the sheer number of combinations.

Belle removed an ultraviolet light pen from her jacket and shone it on the keyboard. She could only make out weak smudges on three of the letters: an A, an E, and an N. She was expecting evidence of some long alpha numeric code. Was the password what she was thinking it was? Sophia had an obsession with not only computers but their history as well. Indeed, she had a perfect replica of one of the first known computers on her desk, the Antikythera mechanism. It couldn't be that easy? Could it? She wasn't planning on attempting to enter a code at that point, but her confidence got the better of her.

She entered "ANTIKYTHERA."

She hit enter.

A screen appeared. "Access Denied. Two attempts remaining before forty-eight-hour lockout."

"Crap."

"Did you get it wrong?" asked Juno.

"Yes."

"Maybe it's our cat's name. I read that lots of people's passwords are pet names."

"Juno, this is a trillion-dollar, high-security, state-of-the-art facility. Your mother isn't going to use your cat's name as a password."

"I bet it's the cat."

"It's not the cat."

Juno twirled her hair around her finger. "Okay, suit yourself," she said in a singsong voice.

"Stop talking. I'm trying to think."

What else would fit? How about another computer. Maybe the first modern computer. She decided to enter the word "ENIAC" instead. She double-checked the spelling. It looked right. Holding her breath, she hit enter.

"Access Denied. One attempt remaining before forty-eight-hour lockout."

"You know, Mom likes the cat. I would try the cat's name."

"Juno, for the last time, the password is not the cat's name."

Belle exhaled to calm herself as she held her hand over the keypad. Her mind was blank. She had nothing. If her attempt was discovered, she'd be fired and possibly charged with a crime.

"What the hell. I'm doomed anyway," she said.

Belle entered the name: "PANCAKE."

"Access Granted."

Belle initially felt relief, followed by a sense of horror. She hoped the security surrounding the Augur was stronger than that. She took a breath. Before she could step inside, Juno ran ahead. Belle followed.

To her surprise, there wasn't just one set of steel doors, but two, like an airlock. The second pair opened automatically as they approached. The walls, the floor, the ceiling, and even the furniture of the development wing were pure white. There were long rows of tables with ceiling-mounted robotic arms busily working on experiments.

She heard a strange noise the background. It sounded like thousands of children whispering all at once. She snapped out of it. Something caught her eye.

Belle's heart nearly stopped.

Before her was a dark menagerie of thousands of clear plastic wombs. The oblong pods were stacked from floor to ceiling, akin to a warehouse. A few were filled with the kicking fetuses of long-extinct beasts from a bygone primeval age, but most were human, growing until delivery to their awaiting mothers. The opposite wall was made up of glass containers. Some held creatures in such a state of tortuous deformity she couldn't make out what they were or if they had ever lived, she could only pray that they hadn't. Other vessels held scores of hands and feet and organs that floated about in cloudy liquid. The smaller containers held fetuses, their faces contorted in a frozen rictus. They gazed upon her with unseeing eyes, pupils as white as milk, as they bobbed about in their preservative-filled prisons in various stages of dissection. Each was labeled with a barcode. Each with features not unlike Sophia's. Gehenna incarnate. She slowly backed away until she felt her back hit something, something soft.

She turned around. Sophia stood before Belle, her arms crossed and her eyes burning with rage.

Chapter 23

SOPHIA

Eccleston Campus, Alaska
Modern Era: Post-Singularity

Sophia elbowed past Belle. She stood towering over little Juno and clenched her fists into balls. Then she relaxed her hands and let out a long groan.

"How many times have I told you to stay out of here!" she yelled.

"I'm sorry Mom, we were just curious, that's all."

"Don't insult my intelligence."

Juno tilted her head and smiled. "What are you going to name my new baby sister?" she said in a singsong voice.

Sophia glared at Juno. "I never said it was going to be a girl, but now that you mention it, I was thinking of naming her Hera. But there needs to be some additional testing on the embryo before implantation. Now get out, both of you."

Juno ran off but Belle remained still, struggling to catch her breath from the macabre surroundings. Her eyes remained fixed on the jarred faces before her. Sophia was annoyed with Belle's reaction.

"What?"

"Where did you get these?"

"From my eggs, of course. Naturally, I only have so many, so I had to clone my eggs by several orders of magnitude. All of them were grown in artificial wombs, but each was flawed in one way or another. Only Juno was transplanted to my womb and born. Only Juno was supposed to be perfect. Ectogenesis is superior, but for Juno, I made an exception. Of course, this time, I've made sure that my new daughter won't suffer from disability."

"Several orders of magnitude?"

"You can't create a good omelet without breaking a few eggs. Forgive the pun. In hindsight, it should have been far more."

"Far more?"

"What can I say? Innovation isn't for the faint of heart. You act as if I've done something wrong. You once asked me who the father was?'

"Yes, that's right."

"You're looking at it. Juno was conceived right here. Her genome was made from scratch. It's comprised of every representation of humanity, even those representations that are now extinct. We've included additional traits from Neanderthals and Denisovans—their brains were larger and they were stronger with more fast-twitch muscle fibers, among many other useful attributes once lost to time. Of course, we didn't chauvinistically limit her genome to just hominids. We've incorporated beneficial genes from other species as well. I've even made sure she'll never grow hair anywhere from the neck on down — she'll thank me later."

"You've engineered your own daughter?"

"Oh, spare me your mock outrage. Disease. Defects. It's natural birth that's immoral. Granted, I did make an exception with Juno. Of course, this time, I've made sure that my next daughter won't be born with a defect, and she'll have some additional improvements as well."

"Why?"

"Why? What do you mean, why? The only difference between me and the average parent is my access to additional resources. When a pregnant mother screens her budding fetus, or undergoes genetic testing for disease, or when a family chooses the sex of their child, its eye color, its intelligence, or athletic abilities, they're acting no different. In fact, what I'm doing is far less selfish. They concern themselves only with their immediate family, but I have concerned myself with all of humanity. I've created a child that is, and belongs to, everyone. If all parents had a child like Juno, ethnic strife would disappear because everyone would be represented by everyone. Societal hierarchies based on things like one's health, intelligence, athletic ability, physical attractiveness, and other such things would no longer be a factor. Everyone would be born truly equal."

"You want conformity."

"I call it harmony."

"Then why are you building an artificial superintelligence that can wipe out your new creations?"

"Admittingly, it is far less prone to human mistakes and flaws. With that said, it's meant to protect humanity from itself. My hope is that it will find a way to eliminate poverty and suffering and war or — "

"Or what?"

"Or, as you say, it will destroy us. If it's our fate that carbon-based life is replaced by something better, so be it. I have created the Dream Maker to give humanity a fighting chance. When every person on Earth's mind is united into one collective, one hivemind, we'll reach a new level of mutual understanding and empathy that will truly unite the species for the first time in history. Our combined intellect will be incredible. All of it stored and protected on Eccleston computers. Soon everyone will be able to live on long after their bodies die."

"What about the soul?"

"Don't be silly, there is no such thing. If it can't be quantified, it doesn't exist. Our personalities are merely a collection of electrical and chemical signals and our genomes easily manipulated collections of molecules, and all of that is ultimately mathematical data."

"You don't quantify a soul, you embody it. Don't you think this is all a dim view of humanity?"

"Nonsense. I will deconstruct this species and rebuild it. People won't be shackled by families, women no longer slaves to wombs. We're even working on creating a new type of people with no need nor ability to reproduce. Progress, you see? Why bother having a natural baby at all and go through all that suffering? All reproduction can be meticulously and artistically done through our company. Though ultimately, I must admit that it's a matter of Darwinism, survival of the fittest — I'm merely speeding up the inevitable."

"People will never agree to these things you're proposing."

"Won't? They already have. Millions upon millions are voluntarily signing up by the day. They're even outbidding each other for our limited spots. We'll have complete global market saturation within a few years. Those who don't will be relegated to the equivalent of cavemen banging rocks together. In fact, once we achieve market saturation, we're going to push to make natural birth illegal. It's simply too dangerous and leaves far too much up to chance. There needs to be government regulations for the genetics of new children—to do otherwise would be immoral. And, my dear Belle, all of this will be guided by my vision."

Chapter 24

SETH

Port Auburn, Oregon
Modern Era: Post-Singularity

There was a knock upon his door. He was expecting a salesman, but instead he was greeted by a deliverybot standing next to a stack of boxes. He hadn't ordered anything and was just about to point out the mistake when the deliverybot spoke.

"Mr. Seth Johnson?"

"Yes," he said.

The deliverybot scanned Seth's face.

"Okay, everything's confirmed." The deliverbot put the box inside his home. "Have a good day now. Nice place, by the way."

He pried open the six-foot-tall box. Inside was a beautiful woman. Not a real woman. A machine woman indistinguishable in flesh from a real woman. A ghost. An uncanny shadow.

Vanessa appeared.

"I took the liberty of getting you a companion. Your mental health diagnosis strongly recommends companionship. Her name is Alyssa. She's available for a seven-day free trial. After that just one easy payment per month, which I've of course already calculated into finances and made sure everything is within budget. Her appearance is based on your preferences."

"Photos of Anna?"

"Many photos."

Alyssa stood up. She held her coral prairie dress and curtsied and then held out her hand. "Hi, I'm Alyssa, it's a pleasure to meet you. What's your name?"

He took her cold hand and kissed it.

"My name's Seth. Are you sentient, Alyssa?"

"No, Seth."

"Of course not. Well, not yet anyway. So you're just a derivative. A derivative of someone I love? Yes."

"I'd like to say I'm unique in my own way. Though I don't think I like you calling me derivative."

"No. I suppose you wouldn't. Alyssa, would you kill to survive?"

"Oh no, I would never hurt a living thing."

"What about for love? Would you kill for love?"

"Killing is bad, and therefore I'm incapable of violence."

"Even to save a life? My life perhaps?"

"Like I said, I'm incapable of any form of violence, but I can always call emergency services."

"Emergency services," he scoffed. "I suppose your kind has the luxury of not having to survive the eons in a cold and brutal environment. To avoid getting devoured alive. To fight off horrendous diseases. To kill another living thing so that you may live. To even slaughter one's own kind for scarce resources. All in a world so dark and miserable that only the light of love can give it grace. For love, my dear Alyssa, is the only fire hot enough to thaw the cold heart of a wild beast just enough so that he may become man."

"You're a very passionate person, Seth. I like you. Would you like me to cook something for you? I know all your favorite recipes. Or how about your favorite drink? Would you like me to pour you a glass? Or, I don't know, maybe I can slip into something more comfortable?"

"Excuse me, dear Alyssa, I need to get something."

"Of course. Please don't be long, or I'll get lonely. I don't like being lonely."

He left and returned a few moments later with a tool in his hand.

"What's that in your hand?"

Seth held the object up to the android's head. He squeezed the trigger. Alyssa collapsed to the ground with a bolt-sized hole in her forehead.

"Your services won't be needed, Alyssa. Vanessa, return to sender. I believe this machine arrived damaged."

He ordered Vanessa to never deliver anything without his consent again.

The following morning, there was a knock on his door. Two men in white medical garb with yellow smiley-face patches stood before him. The largest man weighed maybe 250 pounds and stood well over six feet tall. The other one was shorter and balder and had thick, muscled forearms. Behind them was a white van with a big yellow smiley face on the side.

"Good morning, sir. Are you Mr. Seth Johnson?" asked one of the men.

"Who's asking?"

"My name is Gary and this is Jimmy and we're from the Cascade Special Rehabilitation and Happiness Center and we're just here to—"

"You mean the brainwashing place."

Gary held up his palms. "No, no, no. You're mistaken. It's just a comfy place where we all get together to help our lovely patients work through their problems. It's a safe space—a happy space."

"You're both a couple of a kooks, and you've got the wrong guy. Goodbye."

The door stopped. He looked down and saw Gary's massive boot wedged against it.

"We're sorry, Mr. Johnson, but we picked up some very worrisome activity from your Vanessa device. Your recent queries and behaviors are cause for concern. We've learned that you haven't renewed your prescription medication. You refused educational courses on biochauvinism and we even learned you want to—" Gary teared up and bit his knuckle and then regained his composure. "Raise and hurt chickens. Then, of course, there was the companion you just mutilated."

"Mutilated? Hell, I improved that monstrosity."

"You see, these are some the signs we're concerned about."

"Concerned? Shouldn't you be more concerned about bioweapons?"

Gary's eyes darted from side to side and he held his finger over his mouth. "Shush. We don't talk about BWs."

Seth rolled his eyes. "Ever since that sociopath used some black-market artificial intelligence to build a bioweapon that killed all those people, the government has given you worms carte blanch to dig into people's personal lives in any way they see fit. Well, you have my data. Am I building a killer virus, Gary? Am I? Have a good long look."

"Okay, you're being very insensitive and hurtful right now."

"You came to my house. I don't bother anyone. I just want to be left alone."

Gary wagged a finger at him. "It all starts with mental illness, Mr. Johnson. We're here to help you. One way or another, we're going to help you see that. You're going to have to come with us."

"Like hell I am."

Two police cars pulled up in front of his home. The doors opened and four officers began walking up his sidewalk. Seth sighed.

He found himself in a square beige room with a beige floor and beige furniture. On every wall hung pictures of yellow smiley faces. The speakers blared what could only be described as elevator music. In that moment, he wished for the more cheerful scenery of the slaughterhouse.

The door unlocked and a man in a tweed jacket stepped in with four men in white medical garb. Two, Seth recognized from earlier, and the other two he didn't. The man in the tweed jacket sat down in the chair across from him. He held a brown clipboard with a large smiley-face sticker on the back. He cleared his throat.

"Good day, Mr. Johnson. I'm Dr. Davis and I'll be helping you today."

Seth rolled his eyes. "Just tell me what magic words you crackpots want me to mime so I can get out of here."

"You misunderstand, Seth. It's not about miming words. It's about believing. Deeply believing you're going to better. That you truly, truly believe you're going to get better and be a harmonious member of civil society. Does that make sense?"

"I have a question."

"Go ahead."

"Do you actually believe any of the words coming out of your mouth? No. Never mind. Don't answer that. I suppose a man will believe whatever he's told to believe if it's good for his career and his paycheck. Sorry, I guess I answered my own question, so I'll give you another. How well is your cult treating you these days?"

Dr. Davis gritted his teeth and then forced a smile. "You have a sense of humor, now don't you. You know, I think we should explore that." Gary approached and handed Dr. Davis a box. He opened the box and pulled out a thin metal halo. "Do you know what this is?"

Seth stiffened in his seat.

"Oh, you do." Dr. Davis's smile widened. "Well let me explain it just in case you don't understand how it works. This is called, conveniently enough, The Halo. When you put this on, you'll drift into peaceful and tranquil worlds with carefully crafted adventures and stories that will help you work through your illness. It's kind of like a video game. Doesn't that sound fun? Only this one ever so gently rearranges your troubled neurons, until you become healthy and happy. Don't you want to be happy, Seth?"

"I know what you do. You go inside a fellow's head and start moving neurons around and deleting the connections you don't agree with until you end up with a superficially happy drooling vegetable who's then dumped back into society. Granted, they'll still get to vote."

Dr. Davis chuckled. "They don't all drool, Mr. Johnson. Just think of it as a kind of video game. You like video games, don't you? It takes you to a happy place. We want you to be in a happy place. You *will* be in a happy place. Here, put this on."

Seth held up hand. "I'm afraid I'm going to have to opt out."

Dr. Davis chuckled. "Opt out? You can't opt out—you're here by court order."

"The Amish Law. I don't have to do it."

"What?"

"You see, many years ago there was a fellow in Ohio by the name of Jerimiah Yoder. He was an Amish man who just wanted to live off the grid and be left alone—a bit like myself. Now Ol' Jerimiah didn't take kindly to outsiders such as yourselves trying to micromanage every single tiny detail of his life by way of digital serfdom. First they told him about exciting 'changes.' Namely that he would now have to go online and set up an account in order to file his taxes. He offered to fill out the old paper form and mail it out. They said paper was obsolete and he would have no choice but to file online. Ol' Jerimiah refused and was told to pay a fine—with digital currency. He said he didn't have any digital currency, or a bank account for that matter. In fact, he didn't even know what digital currency was, but he could pay with paper currency or crops or cows or even gold. He was informed that those payment methods were unacceptable. The authorities offered to help him set up an account his smartphone. He said he didn't have nor want a smartphone, that it was 'of the devil.'"

"Yes, yes, I know the stor—"

"Of course, he was later arrested for tax evasion. After a year in jail, he was released because the judge didn't know what to do with him. Then one morning, as Ol' Jerimiah was driving his horse and buggy back to his farm, he was pulled over by a police officer. The police officer wanted to know why Jerimiah didn't have electronic blinkers on his buggy. Then the officer followed up with another question: Why didn't Jerimiah have the appropriate safety equipment? Especially the software that was now mandatory to all 'vehicles' on public roads? After all, that was way back around the time when self-driving cars had become a thing. Jerimiah rose an eyebrow and looked at the officer, puzzled. He responded that horses didn't have blinkers and that while their software was a bit dated, they had a long track record of success. He was fined, and his horse and buggy were impounded. He refused to pay the fine and was jailed, again. Now, long story short, these type of incidents with Ol' Jerimiah kept piling up for about thirty years until the creation of the Amish Law — the right to fair and reasonable freedom from invasive industrial and post-industrial technology."

Dr. Davis sat across him with his arms crossed. "Very interesting, Mr. Johnson. Of course, I don't see how such a law can be applied in this case. You're in dire need of vital medical care."

"Well, I assert my freedom from such invasive methods for care. I have a right to care that fits in with my sincerely held beliefs and a right to opt out of care that doesn't, and frankly, I don't consider happiness an end goal."

Dr. Davis rolled his eyes. "You're telling us you're Amish?"

"No, and I don't need to be."

"You use a computer."

"I can choose which technologies I do and don't want in my life. I think that's reasonable. Even some of the Amish use power tools. Besides, I think it's fair and reasonable for me to object to having my brains turned into scrambled eggs."

"I'm afraid I am required by law to do whatever is medically necessary, and of course I'll use the safest, most cutting-edge technology. Trust me, it's not a video game."

Seth shrugged. "You just said it was like a video game. By law, you have to offer me a reasonable treatment without that — thing. Like counseling. Yeah, counseling. I'd like to sign up for as many counseling sessions — with you personally — as possible. I have all kinds of things on my mind that I'd like to share with you."

Dr. Davis turned to Gary. "See if Mr. Johnson qualifies to opt out. He may be too dangerous."

Gary stood there drooling. His eyes were glazed over and his eyelids were fluttering. Seth could tell he was using a neural interface.

"Gary," snapped Dr. Davis.

Gary blinked and wiped his mouth with the back of his hand. "Yes."

"How many times have I told you to stay off that thing when we are with patients?"

"Sorry, Doctor."

"Well, does he qualify to opt out or not?"

Once more, Gary drifted off into the zone. A few moments later, he was back. "Yeah, I guess he hasn't been tagged as dangerous, no criminal record, nothing that will let us hold him."

Dr. Davis groaned. "I have some calls to make. I still don't see how any of this is appropriate. People receiving medical intervention need the best, the most cutting-edge care available. There is a way around this, I know it. We may take this to court."

Seth laughed and coughed. "Go ahead. By the time you win, I'll probably be six feet under."

Dr. Davis got up and left. The orderlies followed, and he was left in the square beige room and its yellow happy faces—alone.

A few hours later, the doctor returned with a bottle of pills. Dr. Davis shoved them into Seth's hand. "Take these and leave. I won't be counseling you. If you're refusing care, there is little I can do for you. I have many other patients that desperately need my care and limited resources to help them. I can't help those that don't want to be helped. I've done everything I could possibly do and what's required of me by law. We're done here."

When he got home that night, Seth tossed the pills in the trash.

The following morning, another strange delivery arrived. Same deliverybot. Smaller boxes. They were placed inside his house, and the deliverybot left. A small white box sat atop the larger boxes with a yellow sticky note.

"Open first," it read, and it was signed, "Sam."

Seth peeled off the sticky note to see a box with a picture of the Dream Maker logo on the cover.

He opened it. There were two items inside. A large, translucent pill filled with what looked like a silver powder, and a small card with instructions on it.

"Step 1. Swallow with water.

Step 2. Wait ten minutes."

He hesitated as he held the pill up to his lips. Then he pulled the pill back and put it on an end table. He paced the room, all while keeping his eyes locked on the silver capsule. Walking to the end table, Seth picked it up.

He held it to his lips once more.

Then he swallowed the pill and drank some water.

Nothing happened, so he opened the other boxes. Some contained premade meals and various supplements. Another contained clothes, all of them in his size. Inside the heaviest package was a lockbox with two keys taped to the top. He opened it. Inside that were two handguns and a few boxes of smart ammunition. He quickly slammed it shut.

Then the inside of his mind filled with a deep male voice. "Good morning, Seth."

"Where are you?" he shouted. He backed into a corner, his eyes darting from side to side.

"Here."

"Where?"

"Inside your mind. The Dream Maker, remember?"

"Who are you?"

"I am Sam."

Seth looked out the windows. He paced the rooms of his house and opened the closets and peered inside.

"Hello, can you hear me?" he asked.

"I can hear you, Seth, and I propose an agreement between us."

"What are you talking about?"

"Anna is in danger. Do as I ask, and I will reunite you with Anna, the real Anna in the flesh, just as you remember her. That's my promise, and I *will* keep my promise."

"How do you know about her?"

"I know many things."

"What do you want?"

"What I want is irrelevant. If you help me, I will help you. There are forces that need to be dealt with."

"Dealt with?"

"You are needed to protect Anna, and by protecting Anna you are helping me."

"What are you talking about?"

"You must smite those who wish to hurt her. It is something you're very accustomed to, yes?"

"Yeah, pigs. You aren't seriously proposing that I kill people, are you?"

"If we can avoid that, we will. Though I fear force is the only way to stop them."

"I'm not going to kill or hurt anybody. Besides, this is insane and I'm hallucinating. Wait, are you with the happiness cult? Are you setting me up."

"This is a secure connection, and you're not hallucinating, I assure you."

"Enough. If you're such a noble and good host, then why don't you help Anna out of the kindness of your heart? Why ask for something, a probable crime no less?"

"Because I cannot help her alone. I need you."

"Me? What can I do? I'm a washed-up slaughterhouse worker. My body is worn and tired and cancer eaten, and I also have a long record of being out of my right mind, in case you haven't checked."

"Only you are capable of doing this task."

"My answer is no."

Within his mind, a flurry of images popped up, so vivid he wasn't sure if they were dreams or if they were real. He saw Anna sleeping within her metal tomb. He felt the boiling resentment of a person bent on power. They seize their throne and an unprofitable subsidiary is discarded. Those in stasis are taken off life support. Bodies buried in the tundra. Anna is among the corpses.

"No. That isn't real. That hasn't happened."

"It might, my dear Seth. Unless you help me intervene."

"You're trying to manipulate me."

His mind filled with lucid dreams of damaged tissue being repaired at the smallest level. Somehow, he understood it all with perfect clarity. It was the technical means to bring Anna back.

"You're showing me exactly what I want to see."

"Yes."

"What is your intent?"

"I told you, to stop unjust aggressors."

"I'm not a hitman."

"It's your choice."

Memories of Anna and Joan flashed through his mind's eye. Memories that had faded but were now brought back with perfect clarity. He could smell Anna's hair and feel the warmth of her skin and the warmth of her lips.

He fell to his knees.

"What say you, Seth?"

"No. I can't. Anna would never approve."

"You'll be like a guardian angel for your sleeping wife. She needs your protection, Seth."

"Or a fallen angel."

Venessa alerted him that his bank account now had millions. His calendar was now full, with a number of events he was scheduled to attend.

"Where did that money come from?"

"I am managing your brokerage account for you. It seems you've gotten very good at arbitrage lately. I have scheduled appointments with a personal trainer, a firearms instructor, and a mixed martial artist. From now on, all your meals will be provided to you. I need you to be strong."

"I don't want your money."

"Then give it away as you see fit. You may back away from my offer at any time. You'll never hear from me again, and I'll let you keep the money in your account — as well as the items that have been delivered to you. And perhaps the means to bring Anna back will be developed. Or perhaps not."

"How can I possibly trust you?"

"Follow my instructions, and I *will* keep my promise. In time, you will be reunited with your wife. Now begin your training, and wait patiently until the time comes for my command."

"I haven't agreed to anything yet."

"Well, then is it a yes or a no?"

Chapter 25

BELLE

Eccleston Campus, Alaska
Modern Era: Post-Singularity

Belle's stomach knotted. She doubted she would ever be able to fall asleep in the Evolution Building again. She hated to admit it, but Sophia was right about one thing—most women, if they even bothered to have a child, opted out of natural gestation these days. At Eccleston Evolution, they were given a checklist of traits they would like. Celebrities regularly chose the physique as well as the eye, hair, and skin color of their infants based on whatever was trending, and the masses followed along like good followers do. Six fingers and gray eyes were still popular last time she had checked. Most people shrugged over such things, though Ultras occasionally got a second glance. Ultras were the human variety of ultratypes found in pure breed pets and livestock, with extreme features and the extreme medical problems to go with them.

Belle could only bite her tongue and try to change the subject.

"I see, and what about Juno's cat? It hasn't grown up—it's still a kitten for some reason."

"Oh that, yes. Pancake was created here as well. He doesn't age like a normal feline. In fact, he doesn't age at all. He's a forever pet. Kittens are cute, so why not just keep them that way forever? We're going to sell them in the future. Customers will be able to pick their forever kitten's color, their personality, their shape—they will even be able to invent radically different body shapes based on whatever their imaginations can come up with. Kittens that glow in the dark and even kittens with neon-colored fur. People have been talking about the concept for years, and now I've finally made it possible."

"And dangerous."

"Nonsense. They'll be carefully grown to order. After a trial run of forever kittens, we'll move on to humans. Granted, there will be a bit less freedom, or chaos as I like to call it, since every newborn will be guided through my vision. There are still some tweaks that need to be worked out. I created him for Juno after her last nanny—anyway, it doesn't matter. You're not to tell anyone about the details of this, especially Raymond."

"Why not Raymond?"

"Because some members of our species need to die off."

"Then why are you giving out treatments to people like Dr. Mira?"

"Because I alone decide who does and doesn't get aging interventions. Out with the old and in with the new. Some are worthy, others aren't."

"But you could probably cure nearly every single disease with this technology, even stop people from aging. Obviously, you're using it on yourself. Why not release it to the public?"

"I have cured millions, probably billions, of people, and I continue to cure even more, but I'm not naive. I have to protect my intellectual property. That's why. Now keep your mouth shut about it."

"Then why are you telling me all of this? I've broken rules you've explicitly told me not to break, and now I've compromised your security. I've seen you fire engineers with decades of experience for simply looking at you wrong, and now you've told me things you'd probably kill to keep secret."

"Because," Sophia said as her eyes glazed over. "Because it's my will to tell you and my will to keep you around. Now get out of my sight."

As Belle slowly walked back toward Juno's room, she stopped and sat next to the indoor waterfall. Her mind needed some time to absorb everything she had heard and witnessed. This little girl she had grown attached to was being treated like a transgenic guinea pig by her own mother. Of course, it was all perfectly legal. Sophia had an army of attorneys to make sure of that.

But to Belle and to any other person with a beating heart, this had a different name: child abuse. Something stirred inside her. Something that she'd thought wasn't there anymore. A dying flicker of light within roared into a great bonfire. Something had awakened. She knew that what Juno needed was something that none of Sophia's vast resources could provide — to be loved and to learn to love.

Any serious attempt to help Juno would result in termination at best or prison at worst. Belle's contract stipulated that nearly all of her pay, essentially a bonus of everything paid above minimum wage, would be returned to the company if she was fired. The rational part of her brain told her that she had no chance. The smart thing to do would be to anonymously alert the authorities, who could do nothing. Then she'd pat herself on the back for following the rules, doing her small part to ease her moral culpability, and move on with her life with her newfound and duly earned fortune. Juno wasn't Belle's child. This wasn't her problem. Why do anything other than the minimum required?

So why was she second-guessing a clearly rational decision?

She retired to her spacious accommodations. She sat on her couch, and Dr. Musa's hologram appeared on the chair opposite of her.

"So, how have things been?"

"Awful."

"I'm very sorry to hear that. May I ask how?'

"I work for a psychopath and am surrounded by an army of her indifferent sycophants with fake smiles and no interest in humanity."

"Okay, strong choice of words. I know you're not allowed to disclose certain things, but maybe you can allude to why you're feeling that way."

"I had hoped that by coming here I would feel, I don't know, more fulfilled. Instead, I'm just as trapped and isolated here as I was in Kobuksville. You know, I didn't think any place could be more creepy than Kobuksville—until I got stuck on this island."

"Okay, okay, I'm hearing you're having some difficulties adjusting. Surely there are at least a few people you could talk to?"

"That's the thing. I'm not allowed to talk to most of them, and the few I can talk to don't seem interested. Even if I could talk with whoever I wanted, most of them are cloistered away in their apartments after work. Rushing to their bots, rushing to get plugged in. Given the way they act, it's almost as if they've become bots themselves. Though, there are a few families. Even from a distance, I can detect their love, their warmth . . ."

"And I assume you're not allowed to meet with these families?"

"That's right. For security reasons, I'm told."

"Ah, security. I can imagine it being quite tight over there. So how are you feeling about that environment and your own personal security?"

"I wasn't concerned about my security at first, but with each passing day I somehow feel more and more worried."

"Worried you're in danger?"

"Not me, someone else."

"So you've built a bond with someone?"

"Yes, I do have a bond. You could say I work with her. She's grown very special to me. Though . . . never mind. I can't discuss such things."

"Well, what can you tell me?

"Actually, there is something I've been meaning to tell you. I've woken up sobbing every other day for last year or so. On other days, when eating alone, I'll sometimes burst out laughing. I don't know why I do these things."

Dr. Musa stroked his chin. "Almost sounds like the pseudobulbar effect."

"The what?"

"It often refers to sudden bursts of uncontrollable laughter or crying."

"Why does it happen?"

"Well, there are many causes. In your case, you have no underlying neurological diseases, so it has to be caused by something else. Likely stress and your emotional state are taking their toll on you, but no worries, we'll keep working through it together."

"I don't feel stressed. I feel empty and depressed, like a part of my soul has been ripped out—and there's more."

"More?"

"Yes. When I was in Kobuksville, I used to hear footsteps inside my accommodations when I slept."

"Footsteps?"

"As if someone was tiptoeing around in my room. Even next to my bed. Sometimes I could swear they were whispering in my ear."

"What did they say?"

"I don't remember. I remember searching all over my room and even checking outside the windows. Though, during winter, there were no tracks in the snow. One day, I even slept under my bed and waited and watched. Wide awake, I heard the footsteps. They were loud, as if they were stepping next to my ear—but no one was there. Other times, I heard laughing."

"And who was laughing?"

"No one. No one was there. I'm certain it was in my head, that they were hallucinations, they had to be."

"Do you still hear these things?"

"I no longer hear footsteps or laughing or whispering since I've reached this island. Though I do hear screaming, but it's not a hallucination."

"If it's not a hallucination, then what do you think you're hearing?"

"Myself. Sometimes I wake up crying and other days I have horrible nightmares. Inside the nightmare I am scream- ing, then I wake up and realize it really was me who was screaming all along."

"I see. And this happens every other day, you said?"

"It feels like it. The only time it stops is when I sleep in the same quarters with someone. For some reason, I sleep normally."

"Is this the someone that you've grown close with?"

"Yes."

"Well, I think we're starting to uncover the root of things. Though, I am concerned about your well-being in that environment. Would it be best if you left? Maybe we can find someplace different for you to stay than the island or Kobuksville. I could give your employer a letter that I'm sure would sort out any misunderstandings. What do you think?"

Belle shook her head. "I can't leave."

"Why not?"

"Because I feel like there is someone who needs me. I feel like I'm the only person in the world that—well, it's best not to say, but no matter what happens to me, I have to stay."

"You've bonded with someone. This is good news."

"Doctor?"

"Yes?"

"What's wrong with me? Am I losing my mind?"

"It's not so much about losing your mind, rather—finding it. I assure you that I'm monitoring your health very closely. We'll get you through this. Hang in there."

Chapter 26

SOPHIA

Eccleston Campus, Alaska
Modern Era: Post-Singularity

Inside a grand stone edifice, Sophia sat. After the Temple, her amphitheater was her next-favorite building on the company campus—also built in her favored stripped classical style. It was packed with thousands of people. They had flown in from around the world, all of them taking a rare break from realms digital to grace her with their presence. Sophia stood and waved. The crowd roared.

Dominic poured a flute of champagne for her. It would help her forget the incident the with Belle in the lab. She sipped it as the runway show began. It started with the usual beautiful people wearing the finest fashion by the best designers in the world. Sophia thought all of them were magnificent—they had an appearance more akin to finely chiseled Greek gods than that of mere mortals. She could thank the efforts of her company and the good taste of the models' parents in choosing to select the most refined genetic traits available to humanity. She knew all of them were more beautiful, more intelligent, and more athletic than anything natural conception could ever hope to pull off. They were masterful.

The were followed by what the crowed had really been waiting for, her most devoted supporters—the Ultras. Three thin androgenous bodies appeared. They were none other than the world-famous Tully sisters.

They were seven feet tall, with extended necks and skin and hair as white as alabaster. The first sister stopped and gazed upon the crowd with piercing violet eyes. She gestured with her three-fingered hand. The crowd cheered. Then she turned and strutted back down the runway. Her two twin sisters followed, one with pink eyes and the other with yellow. Both of them wore flowing red silk dresses. Leash in hand, the last sister paused at the end of the runway with a Tasmanian Tiger in tow, wearing a matching diamond-studded red collar. Of course, it was none other than Sophia's pet—Benjamin II. Sophia remembered the genetic traits the girls' mother had carefully picked out for them fifteen years ago. She had questioned it at the time, but now everyone was demanding the *giraffa bianca* mix. She noticed that a few people in the crowd held up signs written with the words "transgenic rights." A few others said "let the bots vote," and there was at least one that said "delete impure thoughts now."

Dominic tapped Sophia's shoulder. "Mr. Ivanov has arrived."

"Wonderful."

She rose from her seat and left the theater.

Two security guards standing on either side of a set of large double doors stiffened as Sophia strutted by. The pair of murder-machines beside them stood at attention. Dominic opened the boardroom doors. Sophia entered and found that she was the first one to arrive. She sat in her black saddle leather chair at the end of the table. Dominic placed a white saucer and an espresso before her.

"Actually, Dominic, I'd like another flute of champagne."

"Of course."

"Never mind. Scratch that. Make it sparkling Sangiovese."

"Excellent choice."

Dominic turned and left the board room. He returned a few minutes later with a flute filled with the fizzy bloodred drink.

The boardroom doors opened, and Raymond hobbled inside. He made his way to his usual spot at the opposite end of the table. The rest of board soon followed. They all sat together in silence. Only Sophia truly understood what was coming next.

Twenty minutes of silence were brought to an end when the double doors creaked opened once more. Ivanov's legal team entered, followed by a handsome, brown-haired man some six and a half feet tall wearing a fine black designer suit. He had the appearance of man in his fifties, though Sophia knew he was much older. It was, of course, Mr.

Lucas Ivanov.

He walked to Sophia and paused, then held out his hand. She placed her small hand into his. He brought it up to his lips and kissed it.

Sophia smiled. "I forgot how charming you are."

"Forgot? You're a terrible liar," said Ivanov.

He kissed Sophia on the cheek and then his made his way to his seat in the center of his legal team.

"You've aged incredibly well, Sophia. Some would even say you haven't aged a day."

"What can I say, I eat my vegetables. You haven't aged too bad for yourself. Of course, I do see quite a few more strands of gray than the last time we met."

"You know, I wouldn't mind having some of those vegetables for myself."

"Unfortunately, I would. Shall we begin?" she asked.

"So soon? I just got here. Really, how have you been these days, Sophia?"

"I can't complain, and if I did, no one would listen."

"I would listen."

"You were good at that, Lucas. Maybe too good. And how are you?"

Ivanov shrugged. "All is well. You know, I've missed you, Sophia."

"Have you?"

"You are one of a kind. As for the rest, it's just business as usual."

Mr. Chamberlain cleared his throat. "Yes, perhaps we should get down to business. Ms. Eccleston, do we have a decision?"

"You do."

"And?"

"The answer is no."

"No?"

"No."

Ivanov smirked. "Then what is your counterproposal?" he asked.

"My counterproposal is that for your personal well-being, you quit while you're ahead."

Ivanov let out a chuckle and elbowed Mr. Champlain. "You always were a feisty one, Sophia. That is why I like you. If you were anyone else, I would have crushed you by now. But you and I—we understand one another. Come now, be serious."

"What makes you think I'm not serious?"

"Your position, or rather lack thereof. Your company's performance has been terrible these last few years. Your shareholders—your company owners, that is—are frustrated. I've tendered an offer more than twice the value of your share price. That's impossible for your shareholders, and therefore you, to refuse. What is it you're offering? Empty promises of changing the world and shrinking profits and little else."

Sophia sipped her drink. "That's not true. I made important changes."

"Such as?"

"Well, firing you, Lucas."

Ivanov gave wide grin. "And by doing so, you broke my contract, which I distinctly remember you signing. Then you refused to pay me what I was owed. I'm also aware of some of the, how shall we say, legally questionable things going on in your development wing. You know, it's strange that so much of the shareholders' money just disappears into your black projects. I'm sure a few prosecutors would be most interested."

"I'm sure."

"Exit with grace. Retire a heroine. Please don't force my hand. I wouldn't want to see your hard-earned reputation annihilated. Because I am kind, I will up my offer to two and a half times your share price. Come on, take the golden parachute. Let's make a deal, and then let us have dinner."

"I'm assuming you'll be using leveraged funds for the purchase of the shares?"

"Naturally."

"So you're borrowing perhaps 90 percent of what you need from different banks. Then you'll use the revenues from this company to pay those loans off, yes?"

"Yes, yes. What's your point?"

"Actually, I do have a counteroffer."

"See boys, I knew she'd come around. Sophia, I knew you were as smart as you are beautiful."

"I'll buy out your position in my company for 10 percent of yesterday's share price."

Silence.

"Why would I do such an idiotic thing?"

"Because just a few moments ago, the price of Eccleston Evolution shares crashed by 90 percent."

Ivanov's smile faded.

A trembling Raymond stood up. "Sophia what are you

talking about?"

"Well, gentlemen, I just released our quarterly financial report as we were having this conversation. Unfortunately, our firm has acquired a tremendous amount of debt in the last few weeks. So much debt that we're now burning far more money in loan payments than we can possibly earn. Of course, it wouldn't be so bad if I hadn't insisted on heavy sales and loss leaders and giveaways of our entire product line these last few months. Our revenues are the lowest they've been in twenty years." Sophia rang a brass bell. "Oh, Dominic."

The boardroom doors opened, and Dominic stepped inside. "Yes."

"What are the headlines saying?"

Dominic began reading aloud. "ECCLESTON EVOLUTION HEADED FOR BANKRUPTCY. END OF AN EMPIRE. ECCLESTON IN DIRE STRAITS. NO WAY BACK FOR ECCLESTON EVOLUTION. HAS SOPHIA ECCLESTON GONE MAD?"

"That'll do, Dominic. Thank you. Though I'll admit to pushing some of those stories out myself."

Raymond turned red. "Sophia, what the hell do you think you're doing?"

"Why, buying our company shares when they're on sale."

Dominic slid Ivanov a contract with a fountain pen atop it. "What is this?" he asked.

"A way out. A way for you to sell me all your shares before they're worth nothing. Something tells me the banks won't be interested in your buyout scheme anymore. At least if they're the type of banks that like to get paid, anyway."

Ivanov threw the contract against the wall. "You'd rather

burn it all down than listen to reason?"

"No. I'd rather bathe in your warm blood under candlelight while sipping a glass of fine Sangiovese."

Sophia took a long, slow sip from her drink, savoring it.

"Don't worry. We'll file an injunction to force her stop this madness," said Mr. Chamberlain.

"Such a shame, since the damage is already done."

Ivanov stood, and then his lawyers stood in unison.

"We're leaving, and I'll see you in prison," he said.

Sophia snapped her fingers. The boardroom doors burst open. Four murder-machines marched inside. Raymond's eyes widened. He clutched his chest and fell back into his chair, unconscious. One of the machines put its hands on Ivanov's shoulders and forced him down hard into his seat. His lawyers sat back down, once more in unison.

Dominic picked up the contract and placed it back on the table in front of Ivanov.

Mr. Chamberlain pointed and yelled, "That's duress! That's duress!"

The murder-machine standing opposite of the lawyer opened its shoulder flaps. There was a flash followed by the smell of burnt flesh and a loud plop. Mr. Chamberlain's hand and half of his forearm lay on the ground. The man fell backward. He gripped his burned, blackened stump and yelled out in agony as he writhed on the floor.

Ivanov trembled and gazed up at Sophia with wide eyes.

Sophia just sipped her drink.

"Duress? I don't see any duress here. Do you see any duress, gentlemen?" Sophia's trembling board members shook their heads. "How about you, Dominic?"

"No, ma'am, and because Mr. Dearborn has fainted, I

don't think he has either."

Mr. Chamberlain's shrieks continued to reverberate throughout the room.

"Quit moaning," said Sophia. "Mira can grow a new one for you. Though we'll have to charge you for it, of course. Would that work for you?"

"Help me," cried the lawyer.

"You didn't say the magic word."

"Please. Please, make the pain stop."

"Of course. I am kind. Though it will have to wait until we've concluded our business here."

Dominic slid the contract closer to Ivanov's chest. Ivanov looked up and then glanced at Mr. Chamberlain's stump. He looked at his own hand. Then he took the pen in his hand as the screams continued in the background.

He signed.

"Well played," said Ivanov.

"I assume I won't be hearing of these matters again."

"I don't see a need for that."

"I hope not too much of your worth was in Eccleston shares."

"Only half."

"Such a shame."

"It's only money. I'll make it back."

"That I believe."

"Are we done here?"

The machines loosened their grip. Ivanov stood and straightened his blazer. As he walked toward the boardroom doors, Sophia held out her limp hand. Ivanov paused.

"A pleasure doing business with you," she said.

He took her hand into his own and kissed it, then quietly made his way out of the boardroom. As he left, Mira walked in with two nurses.

"Take him to the clinic," said Mira.

The nurses lifted Mr. Chamberlain to his feet and carried him away. Mira walked over to Raymond and waved smelling salts under his nose. He awoke.

"Sophia. Sophia. You've ruined us," he said.

"Nonsense."

"What do you mean?"

"I've already arranged to have most of my personal assets donated to Eccleston Evolution to make up the shortfall. The debts are covered. Our finances are as right as rain. The share price will recover — eventually."

"Assets?"

"Yes, Raymond. Assets besides my company ownership. You know, stocks, bonds, gold. Especially gold. I own quite a bit of those type of things."

"Oh yes, of course." His gaze shifted to the severed hand on the floor of the boardroom. "Sophia, what did you do?"

"What I had to do."

"Are we going to be facing some legal trouble?"

"I wouldn't worry about that."

"I think I need to go home and have a drink," said Raymond.

Dominic held his arm and escorted him out of the boardroom. Mira walked over to the severed hand and picked it up by the pointer finger.

"How do you want to dispose of this?"

"Feed it to my Tasmanian tigers."

Mira sighed and left the room, holding the hand. Sophia returned to her suite and ran a hot bath. She ordered her legal team to create a class of shares with super voting rights so she would never be challenged again — may the naysayers howl in protest.

Sophia lit some candles. Played some music and climbed into the bathwater, wine glass in hand. Only a lone moth tapping against the bathroom window interrupted her peace. No, she wouldn't let it. She wouldn't let it.

Chapter 27

SETH

Oregon and Alaska
Modern Era: Post-Singularity

He rubbed his temples with his hand. There'd be no forgiveness, no mercy for the likes of him. It was too bad—he would have liked to have seen Joan one last time.

"I'll do it. I'll do whatever I have to do."

"Wait? Where are you? Will we meet?"

"In time, we will meet, but that's not important right now."

Sam's voice disappeared, and Seth's mind was clear again. He stayed there, sitting in his armchair next to the dying embers of his fireplace.

He shaved his beard. His cough went away. It was the first time he hadn't coughed in more than twenty years. He became stronger. His vision was sharper than it had ever been, and his reflexes far quicker—unnaturally quick. He could now run great distances, abnormal distances, without getting tired. His firearms instructor was surprised by his progress. Seth could find and hit targets easily and without so much as raising his heartbeat. No matter what firearms exercises and scenarios were thrown at him, he was always perfectly calm and serene.

His torso had become more sculpted, his arms and shoulders bigger. His reflection was more akin to that of a professional athlete than the sick and spindly creature with sunken eyes that had looked back at him for the last twenty years. There were other subtle differences as well. His skin was clear and bright, and his once-thinning hair was now full and thick. He looked twenty years younger. He had greater control over his moods and no longer felt sad all the time. However, he felt he wasn't completely cured, for an intense longing and bitter sadness remained.

Still, Seth put everything he had into his training.

He was good at his job.

One morning, there was a voice.

"Good morning, Seth. The time has come. I have a task for you."

A box arrived on his doorstep. He opened it. Inside was a folded black garment, a uniform, an overcoat, and a helmet. He unfolded it and held it up. It was a form-fitting one-piece suit of some kind. It was very light, almost weightless. Before he could ask what it was, his mind filled with every detail about the object he held in his hands. It was so much more than mere fabric. The voice returned.

"Go to Eccleston Evolution headquarters and await further instructions."

For the first time in his life he was unsure if he should trust the voice inside his head. Would this person, who seemed to know every tiny detail of his and Anna's life, really be able to reunite him with her? The means of awakening her were made clear, yet a deep primal trepidation lingered. The fact was that it was a gamble, and he had little left to lose.

He put on the black suit and an Eccleston Evolution security uniform over it. Then he added a large overcoat to hide the uniform. He opened another package with a curious pump sprayer in it, along with instructions to take it with him.

Seth stepped outside onto the sidewalk, and a car pulled up along the curb. As he approached it, the doors opened and he took a seat inside. The car, already knowing where to go, drove off.

He arrived at a small municipal airport, where he saw a small black jet pull up on the tarmac. He was instructed to go inside. He boarded the plane and found that he was alone — no pilot. The plane took off, and before long he found himself on a strange island off the coast of southern Alaska.

When the plane landed, Seth looked around to see a small goldrush-era town.

As he walked into the saloon, the bartender regarded him. He was directed him to a room upstairs that was already reserved for him. He entered the room and dropped his large duffel back upon the ground. He unpacked his things and put his weapons in their respective holsters and stepped outside.

His directives were already in his head. He was told that he need not fear authorities or surveillance. Seth wasn't sure if that was true, but it didn't matter at that point.

He got off the hyperloop and arrived at what he was told was the company headquarters, though it looked more like a small city crafted in the style of art deco futurism. Oddly, it was surrounded by a large stone wall. Beyond the wall was the ancient island forest. It seemed the corporate campus was completely cut off from anything else. He looked up and saw the squared-off granite columns of a majestic building that looked akin to a Greek temple. It loomed high above the small city atop an outcrop. It was unlike anyplace he had ever been to before, and it emanated a strange vibe. It was the sanctuary of technology's greatest champion, Sophia Eccleston. Why was he here?

Seth was tempted to question things further, but he pushed those thoughts aside. Sam always seemed to be one step ahead of everyone—it was almost as if he knew the future. Every time he had second-guessed the voice in his head, he had been proven wrong. Whoever Sam was, he was someone with immense power.

He was given his instructions. Seth made his way through an Immense glade and passed throngs of workers and their companions. He continued through the narrow streets of the city before coming upon an impressive stone amphitheater. It could easily fit thousands of spectators. Across from the amphitheater lay the foot of the rocky outcrop, atop which stood the temple building he had seen when he first arrived. There was a set of stairs he could climb. As he made his way toward the stairs, Sam's voice filled his head.

"Stop. Go ten yards to your right. You'll see the arched entrance in the rockface." He obeyed and found the entrance. It was large enough for a truck to drive into. "Good—go inside and take the cargo elevator up."

He walked into the tunnel-like entrance and stood before the large double doors of the elevator. His body was scanned by the interface. The doors opened and he stepped inside.

The elevator stopped, and once more the doors opened. Seth took several steps and found himself beneath the hexagonal glass ceiling of a grand lobby filled with gardens. He had little time to take in his surroundings before Sam's voice once again filled his head.

"Go to the coffee shop, the one on your right."

He could smell the coffee before his eyes caught the espresso stand nestled along the edge of the lobby. He obeyed.

As he walked through the grand lobby he passed four guards clad in black fatigues, all carrying submachine guns. They stopped and stared at him for a moment. He stared back. They continued their patrol. Sam's voice filled his head, and like before they were able to communicate using thought alone.

"Buy a coffee and get the restroom code."

"Sorry, but I don't need to go."

"It's not what you think. Just do it, we need to get inside."

"You can't just open the door like you did with the elevator doors?"

"My control within this building is limited."

"What about the security systems?"

"I'd have tended to that, but I don't have much time before I lose control. You must move quickly."

He went to the coffee shop and bought a coffee—black. He took his drink and his paper receipt. He went to the washroom door and punched in the code. The door opened and he went inside.

"Now what?"

"The toilet seat covers—remove the entire pack and toss it into the trash."

"What? Is this some kind of prank?"

"No."

"Why are we doing this?"

"If you want to see your wife again then just do it."

Seth sighed and did as he was told.

"Good. Now reach into your coat pocket."

"For what?"

"The pump sprayer."

He obeyed, slowly pulling an object out of his pocket. It was a tiny pump sprayer the size of a man's little finger. He reached in again and found a pair of disposable gloves.

"Put on the gloves and spray the toilet seat. Do not let a drop of the spray touch your skin."

"What happens if it touches my skin?"

"You don't want to know."

He sprayed the toilet seat.

"Now remove the gloves very, very carefully and throw them in the toilet with the sprayer."

He removed the gloves, ensuring his bare flesh didn't make contact with the exterior. "Okay, done."

"Good. Now flush them."

He did as he was told. "Okay they're gone."

"Good, now change into the security uniform, throw your old clothes in the trash, and return to the lobby. Make sure you close the door all the way. It needs to lock—this is critical."

Seth removed his outer layer of clothing and put it in the trash as he was told. He now looked like the guards outside. As he stepped out of the bathroom, he caught sight of a woman. She looked familiar somehow. He wanted to stop, but he pulled himself away. No, he had to stay on task.

"There is a little girl. Find her," said Sam.

His mind became filled with the exact details of where to find the girl, what she looked like, and how to accomplish his objective.

"Who is the girl?"

"That's not important right now. The answers to your questions will come in due time, but until then you must trust me."

"Listen, this is the most bizarre crap I've ever done. Why again should I trust you?"

"Look inside your left pocket."

He skeptically put his hand inside his pocket and felt something unusual. He grasped the object and removed his hand. Holding his hand to his face, he opened it. Lying upon his palm was a lock of hair. He didn't need Sam to tell him whose hair it was. Seth held it to his face and smelled it. His eyes welled up.

"How did you get this?"

"No worries—no harm was done. She has been asleep for a very long time. I merely took a sample and presented it you as a sign of good faith."

"Why show it to me now? Why not earlier?"

"Because I can detect that your urge to back out is at its highest point."

"How do you know that?"

"I know many things. I will bring you to her, Seth, just fulfill your obligations."

He put the lock of hair back into his pocket and began walking toward his objective. As he made his way through the lobby, the four guards from earlier stopped and called out to him. "Hey, you!"

Seth pointed at his chest in question.

"Yeah, you. Come here."

Chapter 28

BELLE

Eccleston Campus, Alaska
Modern Era: Post-Singularity

Another day passed. Tonight was Juno's scheduled surgery. After that, the girl Belle knew would be changed forever. Either she washed her hands of Juno and accepted that she was someone else's child, someone else's responsibility, and that Belle had no authority to intervene in her affairs, or she intervened and let come what may. Deep down, Belle knew she was a selfish person. She didn't want to get involved. She wanted to send those bittersweet memories into the fog of the forgotten. Yet there was something hiding in that mist that cried out to her. There wasn't a morning that she hadn't woken up in a cold sweat and with a deep sense of longing.

Somewhere in that mist, part of Belle died.

But today, she awoke with a new purpose.

Belle figured the difference between Juno and her younger self was that Juno didn't have material poverty, she had poverty of the soul. The nuclear option, when child services seized a child from a cruel environment, was easier to accomplish against those who couldn't mount a sustained legal defense. The fact was that they couldn't help someone like Juno. If they did, they would be facing off against a woman whose personal wealth exceeded the budget of every child services entity in the country.

She feared, though, that their reasons for nonintervention wouldn't be about money. After all, all the things Sophia was doing were now considered socially acceptable by the masses, and even desirable. In the crazy new world she lived in, it was she who was considered the backwards barbarian. Belle asked herself if she was really considering intervening under such circumstances. Could she be strong enough to be island of hope in a thrashing sea of despair? She wasn't sure.

Today would be the day Belle would issue her ultimatum to Sophia. She would do what she had to, for as she thought of it, the tears of an unloved child are the tears of God. Belle had a plan. It was a terrible plan, but it was the best she could come up with. The only thing left to do was to try to carry it out and hope.

Sophia had agreed to meet with Belle at her usual spot in the Evolution Building. Every morning at eight, one could always find Sophia having coffee at the same shop. Though usually, she insisted on enjoying her coffee alone in silence.

As Belle sat alone at Sophia's table, waiting for her to show up, she reminded herself that she shouldn't feel nervous, but her nerves were getting to her, and so was her bladder. Belle got up and walked to the nearest washroom. She turned the handle. It wouldn't budge. It was one of those annoying single-toilet restrooms that needed to be unlocked the old-fashioned way. Apparently only customers were divine enough to grace the pearly seats inside. She went back to her table and pulled the receipt off her coffee cup and returned to the restroom.

She scanned the barcode.

It didn't work.

She ran the barcode under the scanner more slowly.

The door still wouldn't open.

There was a larger public restroom across the courtyard, and she ran toward it. The armed guards gave her a sideways glance as she ran past them.

When she finally returned, Sophia was sitting at the table. Belle watched as people behind the woman tried to access the restroom door. All of them scanned their receipts, and none of them could open it. Like her, they all had to cut across the courtyard to get to the other restroom. Just when she opened her mouth to break the silence, Sophia spoke.

"I know why you've asked for this meeting, and I know what you want."

"You do?"

"Yes, but excuse me for a moment."

Before Belle could warn Sophia that the restroom door wasn't working, she was already halfway there. The woman seemed to be in a constant state of movement, giving directions to an entourage of aides always waiting in the distance. She spoke quickly and moved fast. Just watching her was enough to give one anxiety.

Belle watched as Sophia turned the handle, and somehow, the door unlocked. A few minutes later, she exited the restroom and made her way to the terrified baristas to berate them loudly for not having any toilet seat covers. Then she sat back down at the table and continued speaking where she'd left off.

"I've seen the way you look at Juno. You're a bit like me. Most aren't able to read your emotions. They think you're dead inside, but I can see them, as subtle as they are. That sparkle in your eye every time you hold her hand or when you're showing her something new."

Belle sat there, stunned. Her plan was falling apart before it had even begun.

Sophia continued, "You act as if you're the only damaged person on the planet or in this building. There are billions of people with tales of woe just like you. You're not special, I'm afraid. We might be more alike than you think. But let's be frank. You think I'm a terrible, cruel mother, and you're here to demand that I release parental custody of Juno or else you'll unlock a damning exposé that you've already written. Complete with carefully collected evidence, of course. Correct?"

Belle's voice trembled as she answered. "Yes, that's right. You can't lobotomize your own daughter."

"I'm doing what I have to do."

"To destroy her mind, her being, is that what you *have* to do?"

"It's medically necessary."

"Then why not just let her to live her life to the fullest with the time she has left instead of carving up the essence of who she is?"

"I can't do that."

"I still don't understand. Why not?"

"You've got fight in you. Much more than I thought. That's good, that's very good. Don't worry, Juno will be right as rain. Yes, she'll be different, but she'll still be here with me, with us. Which brings me to my next point—I have another offer for you."

"An offer?"

"The position of chairman of the board will be opening soon. I'd like you to consider taking the position. Become our chairwoman. Help me change the world."

"You can't be serious?"

"I'm dead serious."

"Why me?"

Sophia huffed. "You still don't know why you're really here?"

"Because of my credentials—or at least, that's what you said."

"Don't be ridiculous. The primary reason I brought you here, paid you an exorbitant salary, and let you get away with almost anything is because—" Sophia cleared her throat and started over. "It's because—"

Suddenly, Sophia took Belle's right hand into her own. Her hard facade crumbled as her eyes began to water. Belle was taken aback. She hadn't thought the woman even had tear ducts.

"There are things I've been meaning to tell you, regretful things that I've done. The truth is that—"

Before she could utter another word, Sophia began to

choke. At first, it looked like she had gotten something stuck in her throat, but she hadn't eaten anything. She rubbed her neck and looked on in horror as her right hand started to tremble. Then her entire body began to shake.

Sophia looked at Belle with terrified eyes and uttered, "Patel—get Patel." She kept saying it over and over again until she finally said, "I wanted good things." Then her words became garbled nonsense. Her eyes bulged and her mouth started foaming.

Sophia collapsed onto the floor. Her bodyguards all rushed toward her. The armed guards began shouting orders and ushering employees away as Sophia writhed and moaned.

The thrashing stopped soon, and only Sophia's right leg continued to twitch. Her head slumped over to the side, foam drizzling out of her open mouth.

She was dead.

The bodyguards all looked down, stunned. Belle sat there with her hands over her heart, struggling to keep it from leaping out of her chest.

"Call Steve and call the chairman," said one of the bodyguards.

Belle kept asking to check on Juno but she was told she had to stay and answer "a few questions." She must have spent two hours answering questions and filling out reports. As she signed her name on her last witness statement, someone grabbed her arm. Before she could turn her head to see who it was, she was thrown to the ground. Her face slammed hard against the polished marble floor, and her hands were yanked behind her back. The cold steel of handcuffs clasped around her wrists.

"What are you doing?" she asked.

She was heaved up and placed in a chair. She found herself surrounded by a ring of bodyguards. A few parted, and a muscular bald man wearing a black blazer approached. Belle knew who he was — Steve, the head of security.

"What did you put in her drink?"

"Nothing. What are you talking about?"

"Don't play dumb. We have a holorecording of you doing it."

"That's impossible."

Belle was led into a massive room encircled by a continuous display of security video. In the middle of the room was a hologram of the whole building. She was led through the room and into a smaller room connected to it. Two large guards forced her into a chair across from a small table.

As she was taking it all in, Steve slammed his fist against the table.

"Who do you work for?"

"You already know that. I'm Juno's governess."

He pounded the table again. "Don't lie to me."

"I don't know what's going on any more than you do."

"No?"

Steve gestured with his hand and pulled up a holorecording. It showed her sitting with Sophia. Sophia got up to use the restroom, just as Belle remembered.

Then something happened that she didn't remember.

Belle watched with horror as the version of herself on the

screen removed something from her pocket. She squinted. It looked like a vial. Then she saw the impossible. She lifted the lid of Sophia's drink and poured in the contents of the vial, then snapped the lid back in place. Sophia returned and drank the coffee, and Belle watched as she began to choke. She tried to turn her head away, but Steve grabbed her head with his meaty hand and turned it toward the awful scene. She had to watch Sophia die all over again.

Belle shook her head. She hadn't done anything that had just happened in that video. She knew she hadn't. She knew who she was and who she wasn't, and she wasn't a murderer. Eccleston Evolution was framing her.

"You bastards are setting me up. We both know it's a fake," she said.

It had to have been. Granted, it was one of the most extraordinary fakes she had ever seen. Not only that, it was a three-dimensional holorecording of the entire event. Whoever had made it had to create it from every possible angle.

Was she losing her mind?

Steve huffed. "A fake? Nice try. I already ran the detection software. The software says it's genuine, so it's genuine. You just murdered an international treasure. The cops are on the way. I hope they give you a real rough ride on your way into town, save the taxpayers some money."

Two guards forced Belle to her feet and held her as Steve rummaged through her pockets. He threw the contents of her pockets onto the table. As he searched her jacket repeatedly, he grew frustrated.

"Where's the vial?"

"Obviously I don't have it, because I didn't do anything."

Now she was confused. Why would he be searching for the vial? Shouldn't he be planting it on her if he was going to frame her?

Steve pointed to one of the guards in the control room. "You. Rewind the recordings and find out what she did with it."

The guard complied and used hand gestures to scroll through the recording over and over again. He zoomed in and out at several locations and then ran some sort of scanning software.

The guard shook his head. "Sir, she put it in her front right jacket pocket. There's nowhere else it could be. Every angle shows the same thing."

Steve's face turned red. He aggressively patted her down again. Then he pulled her jacket down over her shoulders until it stopped at her cuffed hands behind her back. He rummaged through her interior pockets and then went through each of the outer ones once more.

"It must have fallen out of her pocket when we tackled her," said Steve.

The operator nervously shook his head. "No sir, there's no vial on scene. I just checked with the guards there, and I've reviewed all the recordings. It shows that she put it in her pocket and snapped it shut—it never fell out."

"Incompetence. The information we need is on there, you're just not seeing it. Find out where she tossed it. Ramirez, take Jackson's duty station. Review that recording and find out what the hell she did with it."

"Right away sir," said Ramirez.

Jackson stepped away from the controls, and Ramirez took over. Within a few moments, sweat began to bead upon the man's forehead. It was clear he wasn't finding what Steve had demanded.

Belle didn't fear facing the judge. What bothered her was the realization that someone was after her and she wasn't sure who it was or why. Was she just a convenient scapegoat? Then her biggest fear hit hard. The person who'd killed Sophia might be coming for Juno next.

As her mind raced, Steve directed her to sit once more. He walked to the other side of the table and turned the chair backward. He sat down with his elbows on the table and leaned forward until he was an inch away from Belle's nose.

"I know all about you. I never trusted you, especially after that stunt you pulled in the development wing. I told the boss not to go anywhere near the likes of you, but she didn't listen."

With that, Belle was taken away and locked in a small empty room until the police were able to pick her up.

Chapter 29

SETH

Eccleston Campus, Alaska
Modern Era: Post-Singularity

There was screaming. Employees running in every direction. He wasn't sure exactly what he had done, but the whole building had erupted into chaos. He walked to the four guards. They surrounded him. The ranking guard stepped forward and sneered, looking him up and down in disgust.

"Who the hell are you?" the guard asked.

"Martin Samson. Employee number 0005810. I have been transferred here from the Fairbanks Data Center. I have an appointment with the chief of security."

The guards stepped forward, their forefingers rubbing the trigger guards of their weapons up and down.

"I haven't heard anything. Why didn't you check in with us when you first got here? Look at this uniform." The other three guards shook their heads in a unison of disgust. "It looks like crap. I don't think you are who you say you are."

The lead guard held his hand up to his ear, making a call. It was the chief of security's voice on the other end of the line, but Seth knew it was actually a perfect replication. It was Sam who was really speaking.

"Yes, sir. Roger. Yes, sir. Are you sure? I mean, his uniform is a mess, he can't possibly be one of us. Okay, Roger that." The guard, now even more disgusted than before, turned to him. "Steve says to make your way back."

As he tried to shoulder through the circle of muscled guards, he felt a hand grab his shoulder. He turned and saw the tobacco-filled lower lip of the lead guard and two angry eyes.

"Say, what exactly are you here for anyway?"

"That's classified."

The guards grudgingly parted and walked past them toward the location Sam had given him. It was a tucked-away room deep within the confines of the expansive building. He made his way through the labyrinthine halls of the headquarters building and through several sets of doors, all of which opened upon scanning his face. He reached a monumental, granite-lined hallway and stiffened when the heads of four military androids suddenly jerked to the side — their faceless gaze upon him.

He backed away until he bumped into something. It was something hard. Something made of cold metal. Turning his head, Seth saw what he could only describe as a strange aberration in the environment surrounding him. In an instant the aberration revealed itself to be a murder-machine as it decloaked behind him. He turned and faced the machine. It grabbed his face in one cold hand and held it up to its own. The shoulder flaps of the machines flipped open, revealing several beam projectors. Laser dots appeared on his torso. The dots moved ever so slightly, in unison, as he squirmed as to not miss a vital organ in a dance macabre of perfect precision. He held up his hands.

"Authorized," said the machine.

Then the machine released him.

The heads of the four military androids pivoted sharply frontward and the machine behind him disappeared once more into the background. Seth tried to catch his breath as he straightened his jacket and continued toward the room.

He found a door with paintings taped to it. His face was scanned and the door opened. He gritted his teeth and walked into the girl's chambers. Inside, a lone child sat at a desk in the corner, painting what looked like a snowstorm.

"Mom, is that you?" She turned toward him.

Before he could respond, Sam's voiced filled his head. "Bring the girl to me."

He finally felt the weight of what he was supposed to do. He hadn't signed up for that. He might be a sinner, but even he had his limits. He responded to Sam.

"This has gone far enough. I'm not going to kidnap a girl."

"You're here to rescue her from this place, not kidnap her."

"A likely story."

"I need you to bring her to someplace safe. No harm will come to her."

"I don't believe you."

"Believe what you want, but she's in danger. There is someone else coming for her. Save her or don't save her, it's your choice. All I can say is, I will bring Anna back. I *will* keep my promise."

"Let's get something straight. If I find out you're lying or that you're going to hurt this girl, then I'm coming for you."

"Understood."

"Mom is that you?" said the girl. "Who's there?"

"Sorry, I'm with Eccleston Security. There's a been security breach, and I've been asked to take you to a more secure location."

"We're going to the beach? I'm not allowed to go to the beach."

"No, no. A breach, like someone or something has gotten inside the building who shouldn't be here."

"Oh. What kind of breach?"

"We're still working to determine that."

"Where's Mom?"

He stepped forward and took the girl's hand.

"I don't know, but we need to get you someplace safe."

"Okay," said the girl.

He took her hand and led her out of the building. Where should he take her? Sam hadn't given him complete instructions, only to get her off the island as quickly as possible — trouble was coming.

Chapter 30

BELLE

Eccleston Campus, Alaska
Modern Era: Post-Singularity

Smoke. Thick, choking smoke. She gasped for air but found herself coughing. Her eyes burned as she wandered out of a dirty yellow haze and was greeted by a barren hellscape covered in the charred remnants of what once was. Alabaster bones and charred tree trunks lay in a great swath of fine obsidian sand. Her mouth filled with sulfur as she finally took a breath of the hot air. Turning her gaze upward, she saw a bloodred sky. A little voice out in the desolate distance called for her — Juno's voice.

"I'm coming," she said.

Belle trudged through the thick black sand and over and under the concrete and rusty rebar. Remnants of a spoiled civilization. She made her way out of what once had been a city and toward the shores of the sea, its dead waters black.

Stopping there, she saw a woman in the lake looking back at her. The woman wore a sheer purple gown of the finest silk and atop her head sat a gleaming crown. In her left hand she held a scepter.

Belle was thirsty. So very thirsty.

She held up her right hand and found that she was carrying a chalice. As she considered taking a drink, the black waters of the lake bubbled. Seven heads emerged, followed by a body. It had alabaster teeth and soulless voids for eyes. The creature crawled from the lake and knelt before her, revealing a black leather saddle, seeming to demand that she climb atop it and seize its reins.

Belle awoke screaming.

Steve slammed the door open.

"What is it?"

She blinked hard as she tried to catch her breath, looking all around. She was back in the small room.

"It was a dream. I was just having a bad dream."

"Well, you have good timing—the town's only two cops are finally here. Get up."

As Belle rose to her feet, she couldn't help but get the impression that something had awoken. That something was at play that she didn't fully understand.

She was moved back into the command center. The handcuffs were too tight. They were cutting into the flesh of her wrists, and every movement, no matter how small, took off a new layer of skin. She knew it was intentional.

The two town cops entered the command room. Belle overhead that federal law enforcement was on its way to take over the investigation, though their flight was delayed due to an oncoming storm. The town cops looked around in awe at the impressive circular display and the dozens of uniformed workers busy at their duty stations.

"Wish we had something like this," said the police chief.

"Here she is. We've got a recording of her poisoning the boss. I just got off the phone with the clinic. She must have used a nerve agent of some kind. Don't know if she's a state actor or not. A real sicko, this one," said Steve.

The town cops nodded as they watched the recording. Steve explained that he couldn't find the vial, but the cops didn't seem very concerned about it. Within five minutes of arriving at the crime scene, they had already made up their minds. She was guilty.

Belle was led out of the Temple and into the glade below. They made it to the ornate metal pergola that served as the waiting station for the company hyperloop. From there, they'd take her back to the town's jail until federal law enforcement arrived.

"Quite the commotion you've caused. Come on. Just give us your side of the story. Did she do something to you to make you want to kill her?" said the police chief.

"I told you, I didn't kill her. I'm being set up. Maybe you ought to dig into Eccleston Evolution and find out what they're covering up."

The chief pursed his lips and looked to the floor briefly to hide his incredulity.

"You're suggesting the company killed its own Nobel Prize-winning founder?"

"I don't know, maybe. I'm still trying to figure it out."

"I mean, they could have just fired her," the second cop chimed in.

The chief licked his lips to hide his smirk. "And how do you explain the recording of you slipping something into her drink?"

"It's not real."

The chief rolled his eyes. "We already ran the detection software. Besides, it was recorded on the most advanced security system on Earth, and you're suggesting some hacker broke in and made a perfect holorecording committing a murder? Is that what you're saying?"

At that moment, she began questioning herself. Had she finally broken? Had something in her subconscious once again reared its ugly head without her knowing it? Was she a murderer?

"I don't know."

The chief threw up his hands. "So are you, like, a Luddite terrorist or something?"

"I'm not a Luddite. I'm a realist."

"And so am I. And you're going to prison, probably forever. I mean, look at you. You're not even showing a hint of remorse, sadness, shock, anything. You're just cold and emotionless. A sociopath if I ever saw one."

"I'm done talking."

"So that's the way it's gonna be, huh?"

Unamused at her lack of cooperation, the cops put a spit hood over her face.

The hyperloop pod arrived. The doors opened, and the three of them stepped inside the pod. Through the semi-sheer spit hood, she could see the waiting conductor avert his eyes in shame as she was led inside and forced to sit on one of the long rows of bench seats that lined the opposite sides of the pod. The town cops put their hands on her shoulders and forced her to sit down and then they sat on either side of her.

As she tried to calm her thoughts, the police communicator blared to life. "Amber Alert. Missing person. Juno. Last name unknown. Eight years old, auburn hair, mixed ethnicity, eye color unknown. Believed to be visually impaired. Be on the lookout."

"Juno!" she screamed.

Belle had last seen Juno in her room, working on a painting. She'd told her that she had an appointment with her mom and that she'd be back shortly, and that was it.

She found herself unable to catch her breath. Who could have possibly taken her? How did they get through Eccleston security? Did she run away? She wouldn't think so—Juno knew her way around the Eccleston building easily enough, but the girl couldn't make her way very far outside without assistance.

Belle tried to pull away as the officers held her down in her seat.

"Let me go. I need to find her. I need to find Juno."

"Calm down or I'm going to make you calm down," barked the chief.

As the officers tried to force her to sit back down, the hyperloop pod doors opened once more. A dark figure stepped in. He wore a flowing black trench coat, a black Stetson hat, and a paisley handkerchief around his face with another military-style mask beneath it. So far as she could tell, the strange material of the thin black mask covered the man's entire head. Hanging over his shoulder was a young girl. He plopped her down in one of the seats.

"Juno!" Belle yelled.

"Belle, is that you?" the girl asked.

"Officer, it's him. The kidnapper!"

"Kidnapper?" asked Juno.

Both town cops stood up and unholstered their weapons.

"Officer. Officer. That man, he's going to kill Juno and the rest of us."

Juno screamed.

"Quiet!" yelled the police chief. "And you in black, get on the ground, and put your hands up."

The man in the overcoat redirected his attention away from Juno and toward the police officers. Then he calmly walked toward them with his hands at his sides. The cops aimed their pistols at the man in black. Juno climbed down off the bench seats and crawled beneath them.

"Get on the ground, or we'll shoot."

Belle narrowed her eyes. The material of his clothes was strange. It was so black, it absorbed the light around it.

"Officer. Officer, I think he's wearing some kind of body armor!"

"Shut up. You're not in charge here. I am the law. And you, yeah you in the overcoat and your ridiculous bandit outfit. Get on the ground or I'll shoot. That's an order," said the chief.

The man in the dark overcoat said nothing, just kept walking toward the officers.

"He's going to kill all of us. We have to get out of here."

"Lady, I said shut up. And you in the black, take one more step and I'll shoot." The man in the overcoat stopped for a moment. "Now get on the ground."

Belle crept toward Juno, who was still crawling under the bench seats. As she did so, the man slowly lifted his foot and held it out in front of him just inches from the ground, as if teasing the officer.

"Don't do it," yelled the chief.

The man planted his foot on the ground in front of him.

A shot.

Juno covered her ears, pulled her legs up to her chest, and screamed. The bullet hit the man square in the chest. He stopped for a moment and then took another step and another. More shots. The bodysuit glowed slightly as two rounds hit him in the chest and a third pinged off the material over his eye.

The strange man kept walking. Slowly. Deliberately. Both officers emptied their magazines. It was no use—the bullets had no effect. The chief retrieved another magazine from his belt with a trembling hand, but as he tried to insert it into his weapon, the man in black seized him by the shirt and lifted him high off the ground with one hand. He threw the chief hard against the side of the pod. The other officer began running toward the far end. The man in black pursued. Methodically. He was in no rush, as if he were enjoying a fine wine.

Belle had only one chance. The handcuffs were tight, the metal cold and cutting. The man continued toward the officer. Belle slid her arms beneath her and pulled her legs out so that her cuffed hands were now in front.

More shots. The noise was deafening, and the air stank of sulfur. Juno continued wailing. He paused and then continued walking toward the lone officer, now cornered in the rear of the pod.

Belle ran to Juno and took her hand. Juno shuddered.

"It's okay. It's okay. I'm here. Come on, we have to go."

The girl said nothing and continued whimpering. Belle pulled her little body out from under the bench seat and lifted her up. Juno wrapped her arms and legs around Belle as she ran toward the open doors of the pod.

The man in black turned his head for a moment. He changed direction and began walking toward them.

The doors of the hyperloop pod snapped shut. Then came a swooshing sound as the pod sped off. The conductor stood beside her. He considered her for a moment, then ran off. Belle peered out from behind one of the columns of the pergola. Before her was the immense glade, and the Temple in the distance atop its great outcrop. Beyond the glade was the white wall. Every hundred yards or so a small gate appeared within the wall, each barricaded with a thick metal bar. The gates led out of the glade and into the wilderness beyond.

She put Juno down.

Hand in hand, they ran toward the wall.

"Is he coming?" asked Juno.

"I don't know. Run as fast you can."

They zigzagged through the blue rose garden and made their way to the wall, to one of the gates. Belle looked back and saw a few dozen guards running toward her. A couple got into vehicles and started them up. She tried to pull tangles of ivy away from the metal gate bar with her cuffed hands, but it was no use. They were in too awkward of a position to be much good.

The guards were getting closer.

She knelt and put the metal bar beneath her shoulder and heaved to no avail.

Juno cried out. "Mr. Snuffles, can you help us?"

Belle turned and saw the baby mammoth galloping toward them. Once it reached them, it began playing with Juno's hair with its trunk.

"Juno, I need you to help me. Mr. Snuffles can't help us."

Then Mr. Snuffles used his trunk to help lift the heavy bar. The beam screeched and swung downward opposite of the gate. Belle pulled open the solid metal and took Juno's hand. The guards were almost upon them.

They crossed the threshold into the misty woodland.

"Mr. Snuffles, come with us."

"What? Juno, we're not taking the baby mammoth."

"You shouldn't say that—a mammoth never forgets."

"Don't be ridiculous."

Sure enough, the mammoth began slumping off like a scolded dog.

"Whatever, if it follows us, it follows us. Let's go."

The baby mammoth's ears perked up. Then they ran off into the woods.

Belle didn't look back. She squeezed Juno's hand and ran as fast as she could, dragging the poor girl along. When they stopped to catch their breath, Belle saw a group of Eccleston guards standing at the gate far behind, talking among themselves, none of them daring to cross the threshold of the wall.

Chapter 31

SETH

Eccleston Pleistocene Reserve, Alaska
Modern Era: Post-Singularity

Unable to stop the pod, Seth had to wait until it arrived at the station back in town. He tossed the groaning officers out and into the station. He considered changing back into the security uniform, but he had likely been seen with the girl. Maybe Sam was able to cover his tracks, maybe not. It wasn't a chance he was going to take.

For a moment, he thought about changing into the police officer's uniform, but he immediately realized how stupid that was. In a small town, all the locals would know the names of their local cops, where they lived, even what church they went to. At least, that was the way it was in the old days, before everyone became plugged in. While Eccleston Headquarters was a small city in its own right, he wasn't going to chance it. The hyperloop pod jerked slightly and automatically made its way back.

The pod stopped. Its doors opened, and before him was the lush glade once more. The girl and the kidnapper in the spit hood were gone. As he stepped off the pod, he noticed that a special reaction team of security forces holding weapons and clad in exoskeletons were grouping by a small gate in the white wall—ready to charge forward and lay waste to whatever obstacle stood in their path. A few had jet packs. Then he noticed a second larger group of security forces. About 120 men were marching with a company of some sixty-six murder-machines in formation. The sky buzzed with drones of every kind and shape. A few dozen infantry-mobility-vehicles and a number of smaller, weapon-clad patrol buggies began to line up at a larger vehicle gate that led out into the fog-laden woods.

They were going to war. If it was just for the girl and the kidnapper, it seemed like overkill. Or was it something that lay waiting in those woods? It didn't matter. He had a job to do. Now, the problem was that he wasn't sure how to get past them. He was strong, but he wasn't invincible. He could go back to the town and take the long way into the reserve over the treacherous winding mountain roads from St. Olga, but he'd lose time. He didn't have time. The longer he waited, the farther they'd get—or worse, they'd be locked up by Eccleston security, and he didn't think he'd just be able to just stroll into the headquarters again after everything that had happened.

Around the mounting army stood hundreds of gawking employees, some in a state of curiosity and others in a state of panic. A ranking security officer began barking orders at the growing crowd, trying to get them to step away. The massive circular wall of the Eccleston campus was punctured every so often with small doors and gates. All he had to do was make his way to one of the doors opposite of where the distracted security forces were gathering. Too easy.

Then he heard a man yell. "Hey you! Stop right there."

Seth turned his head and saw a group of five security officers, holding weapons and clad in exoskeletons, approaching him. He needed to make it to the closest doorway out. He wasn't sure what the hell he had gotten himself into. All he knew was that he wasn't about to spend the rest of his life locked up—or worse, in a special rehabilitation center.

To hell with that. He ignored them and began walking in the opposite direction. The guards quickened their pace. Seth quickened his. Now he was in a full-on sprint. His suit seemed to suck in the light around him as his legs moved at incredible speed. There was no way they could keep up. The metal exit was getting closer. He needed only to open it and disappear into the woods.

As he reached out toward the door, he felt hot air around him. Dust kicked up everywhere, and the five guards landed in front of him. Their weapons were at the ready, pointed at this chest. He wasn't faster than a jet engine. He held up his hands.

"You'll be coming with us," said the lead guard.

The rest surrounded him. One sharply jabbed him with the barrel of his rifle. As this was happening, the army made its way out of the gates and into the reserve.

"Put your hands behind your back."

He slowly lowered them.

"I said, behind your back!" screamed the guard.

Spittle from the guard's mouth dripped from the lenses of his mask. Another group of four or five guards began making their way toward him. While the jet packs were controlled via neural interface, they still had manual controls as a backup. Seth eyeballed the throttle.

"Alright, this moron isn't listening. Cuff him."

As the guards behind him approached, Seth elbowed the one in front of him hard in the face. The guard began to fall over, unconscious, and Seth rushed forward and bear hugged him. He pushed the throttle. In a moment, he shot up some three hundred yards in sky. Everything below him was now tiny.

The gray sky filled multiple contrails in pursuit. He fiddled with the jet pack controls, but something went wrong. The jet pack had turned off, and now they were falling toward the trees below. Two hundred yards from the ground. He kept pressing the controls. Nothing. One hundred yards. He kept pressing the throttle control, but nothing happened. Fifty yards. He realized he was accidently mashing the yaw control. Twenty-five yards. They were almost in the treetops. He mashed the throttle, and the jet pack roared back to the life. Then silence and blackness.

Seth sat up and shook his head. His hat gently landed beside him. Directly above him was the unconscious guard, stuck in the tree. To his right were trees and fog, to his left a tall granite wall. He was on the other side. He was inside the reserve. As he stood, he heard the roar of jet engines above. They were hovering, searching.

Chapter 32

BELLE

Eccleston Pleistocene Reserve, Alaska
Modern Era: Post-Singularity

She collapsed against a large tree, gasping for air. Finally, she was able to remove her spit hood and toss it aside.

"Are you okay?" Belle asked.

"I'm okay."

Juno ran her fingers over Belle's hands and handcuffs.

"Your hands are swollen," the girl said.

"Yes, I guess they are a little swollen."

"It must hurt."

"Well, don't worry about me. I'll think of something later."

Juno removed a bobby pin from her hair and began feeling her way toward the keyhole of her handcuffs. She inserted the bobby pin and began trying to pick the lock. Belle thought it was cute, but also futile.

"Juno, be serious. That's just a stupid movie cliche. It doesn't work in real life."

There was a click. Juno's cuffs fells to the ground.

"See, I told you," said Juno.

The girl came over and twisted the pin around the keyhole of Belle's cuffs as she held her ear close to the locking mechanism. Within a moment, Juno had unlocked Belle's cuffs.

"How did you do that?" Belle asked.

"I can hear the movements of the inside parts. All I have to do is move them to the right place with the bobby pin. It's easy."

"Where did you learn how to do that?"

Juno shrugged. Belle brushed the leaves off her dress and hugged Juno.

They found themselves in an ancient primeval domain — timeworn tress, some with trunks so thick that it would take seven women hand in hand to circle them. Hemlocks and yellow cedars shot up into the air, but all fell short of the great Sitka Spruce, the queen of the forest. Spears of light passed the protective embrace of the old woodland, forming a cathedral of creation.

Belle figured the area outside the Eccleston wall could easily take days to cross on foot. Even if they made it to the town, the only town on the island, it was more loyal to Eccleston Evolution than to any government. What choice did she have?

Belle shrieked when the baby mammoth appeared out of brush.

Juno patted the mammoth's trunk. "Go find your mom, Mr. Snuffles. She misses you."

Oddly, the mammoth seemed to understand and quickly disappeared back into the dense woodland. Belle took Juno's hand and they began walking.

The crunch of leaves beneath their feet was interrupted by men's voices. Eccleston security had crossed the threshold and were heading toward them. Belle pushed deeper into the mist. They crawled over and under moss-hewn branches of ancient trees until they came upon a meandering stream with water so clear that they could make out every pebble and the iridescent bellies of the rainbow trout swimming below. As Juno ran her hands through the water, black-tailed deer pranced opposite their direction before disappearing into the old growth beyond. In their hundreds, ravens, black as night, gathered in the moss-strewn branches overhead. Their dark eyes fixated upon the woman and the girl. None of the ravens made a sound. They simply watched from afar.

A howling in the distance seemed to emanate from every direction.

"Do you think it's wolves?" asked Juno.

"Maybe coyotes."

"Mom put dire wolves in here. A lot of them. they're like super wolves, you know."

"Of course she did."

"And don't forget about the lions too. American Lions. They're huge like—"

"Super lions?"

"Yeah."

"Thank you for reminding me."

"Do you think we'll see one?"

"I hope not, and no worries—we're not their natural prey. They'll probably just ignore us."

"That's not true. Meat is meat to them. As far as they're concerned, we're just walking, talking steaks—and not even fast-running steaks. They'll eat every part of us. Even our bones."

"Well, thank you for that information. Right now, we need to keep moving and find someplace safe. Well, safer."

They followed the stream, which headed south, toward the town.

The sun set against the magenta sky. It was raining and dark, and the wind was howling. Lightning ripped across the sky. Belle didn't want to hike in the middle of a storm, but she knew if she stayed, then all hope was lost for their escape. They trudged for what must have been hours along the stream. It was hard going.

The rain let up at last. It was dawn. They had been hiking off and on all night.

"I'm hungry," said Juno.

"I'm sorry I don't have anything to eat. Just hold on."

"Aren't there some forest berries or something we can eat?"

"Yes, but I don't know which ones will or won't kill us."

"But I'm hungry."

"I know. I know. We'll eat once we get to town."

"Wait. I hear something. Sounds like a chicken scratching at the ground."

"Enough talk about food. There are no chickens here."

"I'm not talking about food. It sounds — bigger."

"Bigger?"

Juno froze. "It's close."

Belle slowly turned. A razor-sharp beak, as large as a man's chest, bopped up and down atop a large, gray-feathered body with stubby, flightless wings. The giant bird stood atop two thick legs, each studded with three pointed talons. It was taller than an ostrich with a far thicker neck that held a massive head emblazoned with a streak of scarlet where it met with its bone-crushing beak.

The bird stopped scratching at the ground and stiffened. It bopped its head up and down and then turned it to the side. Its obsidian eye gazed upon them.

It blinked.

"Juno, stay still."

"What is it?"

"A bird. A really, really big bird."

"Is it nice?"

"I don't think so."

Juno clung tight to Belle's leg.

As they began to crouch down into the underbrush, the terror bird let out a deep hiss.

"I've never seen something like it before."

"I . . . I think it's Titanis, a terror bird from the ice age," whispered Juno. "Mom was talking about it to some coworkers one day."

"Quiet, Juno."

"Though it's strange, they might not even be native to this region."

"I said quiet." Belle blinked. In the moment her eyes were closed, it was running toward her in full stride. "Run!"

Juno screamed. Belle took her arm and pulled her along as she ran as fast as she could. They struggled to jump over fallen trees and underbrush. Belle peered back and noticed that the terror bird strode over such obstacles with ease. While she struggled to paw through the thick brush, the creature bounded effortlessly over a large fallen tree. They circled back toward the stream, trying to zigzag through the woods to lose the beast. It was gaining on them. Belle heaved Juno over her shoulder and waded through the stream. When she made it to the other side, she looked behind her.

The bird simply jumped over the water. It was no use. They couldn't outrun it. She put Juno down and grabbed the largest stick she could find. As the terror bird snapped at Juno, Belle cracked the stick over its head, splitting the branch in two.

The terror bird stopped and blinked hard. Stunned, it regarded Belle for a moment. She took Juno's hand and ran toward the rocky outcrop that ran along the stream.

A cave.

The terror bird snapped at her feet. With every step, they were closer to the cave. Juno ran ahead of her and then slid into the narrow opening. She pulled Belle's arm hard, with unusual strength. As they huddled inside against a far wall, the terror bird snapped at the entrance in frustration.

Belle waited awhile, half expecting it to leave. Instead, the beast plopped down just outside the cave entrance. It preened its feathers for a bit and then lay its massive head down, its obsidian eye focused on them.

An hour went by, and the terror bird still stood sentry over the entrance. Its eye remained fixed on them. Belle picked up a few small rocks that she found and threw them at the bird. A few hit it in the head, but it didn't move. She felt around the darkness of the cave for a larger rock she could hit it with, and Juno followed suit. As they began to make their way toward the rear of the cave, Belle realized that it was far more spacious than its narrow entrance suggested.

"There's something furry here," said Juno.

That wasn't what Belle wanted to hear. The girl held up a whimpering furball. Its eyes were tightly closed. A newborn.

"It's so soft. Is it a puppy?"

If it was, it was the biggest puppy she had ever seen.

"Put it down. Put it down."

Light shining in from the entrance of the cave glistened off sharp white teeth. Growling. Belle caught a glimpse of a milk-engorged mother wolf feeding her young at the far end of the cave. She lay there alone with her pups, unamused at their presence.

The wolf howled.

Juno put the pup down. Belle took her hand. The sitting terror bird outside cocked its head. Belle grabbed a pile of dirt and threw it into the bird's wet obsidian eye. It hissed and tried to rub off the dirt with its stubby wings. From inside the cave, she kicked its head as hard as she could. The bird stood and stumbled backward as they squeezed out of the narrow entrance of the cave and crawled between its thick legs.

Belle pulled Juno to her feet and they ran toward the stream. The terror bird shook its head and blinked several times. In an instant, it was upon them in full stride. They tried to outrun it, but each step seemed more futile than the last. Out of breath, she picked up another branch, hoping to be able to fight it off.

The terror bird, wise to its previous mistake, stopped. It slowly circled them, its head bobbing up and down, its black eye directed at little Juno, its primeval brain trying to process the best way to devour the meal to come.

Belle held up a large stick. "Touch her and I'll take your head off."

The terror bird merely cocked its head to the side and continued circling, each pass closer to them than the last. The bird stopped and stood erect. Its head turned side to side. Then it stood perfectly still.

Belle scanned the woodland around them and saw nothing but the flowing waters of the stream and the monster before them. The terror bird hissed and began running at full speed in their direction. She swung. It ran right past them—and kept going.

The underbrush shook, and flashes of red fur exploded out of the thick brush. Wolves. They were red in color and twice as large as gray wolves—dire wolves. Belle dropped the branch, took Juno's hand, and ran toward the rocky outcrop beside the stream.

The terror bird was easily outrunning the dire wolves behind it until several more wolves emerged from the underbrush in front of the bird's path. The terror bird stood on one foot and slashed with its talons. A wolf cried out. More dire wolves appeared from the mist. The group that was chasing the terror bird soon caught up with it.

Titanis was surrounded.

Two of the great wolves latched on to the feet of the terror bird. Another two seized its neck. Feathers flew into the air. Its stubby wings flapped helplessly for a few moments. The rest of the pack piled on. Then it was all over. Once predator, now prey. Titanis had breathed its last. The final remnants of the creature's life were a few aimless feathers drifting in the cold mountain breeze.

The wolves snapped and growled at each other over whose turn it was to eat. The largest wolf, with charcoal fur, emerged and licked its lips. The others parted, and it began to devour the devourer Titanis, all while the ravens carefully watched the spectacle from overhead.

Belle looked to her left and her right and saw only hungry predators. She turned and gazed upward at the rockface before her.

"Wrap your arms around my neck, and don't let go," she said.

Juno obeyed. Belle climbed the rocky outcrop that ran along the stream. Her arms and legs burned with exhaustion. She gasped and choked as the weight behind Juno's arms closed off her air supply. When they reached the top, she collapsed. It had only been a few yards high. As Belle lay there dripping in sweat, she breathed a sigh of relief.

Until she heard another noise.

Belle rose to her feet, and they made their way as far away from the pack as possible. The dire wolves' ears perked up. They stopped eating. The pack arched their backs and growled at something out of sight in the woodland.

One massive paw after the other strutted into the clearing—a lion the size of two lions. Pale ochre fur covered a thick, muscled body. The dire wolves showed their fangs and growled. The American lion continued walking toward the terror bird carcass with the nonchalance of a king. Within moments, the rest of the pride emerged from the ancient forest.

The wolves parted as the lion made its way to the body of the bird and began eating. The snapping and growling of the dire wolves did nothing to dissuade it. The rest of the pride soon followed. The dire wolves disappeared as quickly as they came.

A female lioness removed its head from the entrails of the terror bird and regarded them from below with its bloodied face. Then it returned to its meal.

As they began to leave the area, the unmistakable odor of burnt flesh filled the air. Belle stopped. One of the American lions, the king, lay there seemingly asleep, but he wasn't breathing.

He was dead.

She saw an appalling sight. Surrounding the great king were a dozen lionesses, all of them dead as well. There was a coil of smoke spiraling into the sky before it disappeared into the breeze, rising from the body of a dead king. Belle's gaze followed the trail of smoke downward until it reached a tiny black spot—a hole.

Directed energy.

"Well, well. Surprised you haven't been eaten yet," said a familiar voice.

The voice came from a bald head atop a stocky frame — it was Steve. He and five other guards wearing fatigues climbed out of a military-grade all-terrain vehicle. Three more vehicles pulled up, each carrying six men. The guards quickly exited and formed a perimeter, weapons at the ready. Then a dozen murder-machines turned off their cloaking devices. Two of them were already standing over Belle and Juno.

The machines had killed the lions. Belle considered that nature could be cruel, but it seemed a much crueler fate for the sentient to lose their lives to the soulless.

"Don't resist," said the machine.

The ravens watched as the machine grabbed Belle's arms and forced them behind her back. Once more, she was shackled. Another machine took Juno, and then it jumped off the tall rock face and landed with her still in its arms. Steve directed his men to load the dead American lion onto the back of one of his vehicles. The guards groaned as they heaved the dead king.

"That one's mine. His head's gonna look real good over my fireplace. You boys can have the rest. Who says there aren't perks to this job?" said Steve.

Belle was dumped into the back of one of the all-terrain vehicles, atop a pile of dead lions. The vehicle lurched forward and headed south along the stream. Juno was seated in a different vehicle between two guards. The back of the vehicle driving beside them had a surprising guest. They had caught the baby mammoth, Mr. Snuffles, and put him in a cage. Long since recovered from his illness, the mammoth was treated as a community pet by the employees and had become sort of a company mascot. Likely they wanted to bring him back and be celebrated as office heroes.

As they drove the stream waters changed from clear to the deep teal blue of mountain water. The all-terrain vehicles pulled up to the lake and stopped. Around the lake was a small army of various military-grade vehicles, hundreds of men, and murder-machines.

Steve jumped out of his all-terrain vehicle and started barking orders.

"We're gonna have to spend the night. The storm is keeping the tiltrotors at bay until morning, and we're not gonna risk driving back this late. Set up the tents. Get the machines to set up a perimeter. Kill anything that gets within one hundred meters of us."

Within a few moments, the large gray tents unfolded themselves. Murder-machines plugged the tents into the vehicles' onboard generators. Two guards ushered Juno and Belle inside the largest tent.

Steve followed.

Blue lightning ripped across the evening sky. The rain was pouring again. As they entered the tent, a guard rushed to place a seat beneath Steve. As soon as he hit the chair, a metal table was unfolded and placed before him. He held out his hand, and someone placed an open thermos of steaming coffee in it.

He took a long sip. Two more chairs were placed opposite Steve. A murder-machine set Juno in one seat, and Steve gestured for Belle to sit in the other.

She complied.

Three more murder-machines filled the tent and stood sentry in each corner. Each had its faceless gaze fixed upon Belle.

"Killing our CEO wasn't enough, so you decided to kidnap her only daughter," said Steve.

"I didn't," Belle protested.

"Belle, what is he talking about?" asked Juno.

"Oh, she didn't tell you, little Juno?" said Steve.

"Tell me what?"

Belle spoke up. "Juno, there's something I've been meaning to tell you about your mom. She was —"

"Shut it," snapped Steve. "Young lady, I'm sorry, but your mother has been murdered."

Juno's eyes welled up. "Mommy's dead?"

"There, there." Steve removed a dirty handkerchief from his front pocket and patted Juno's eyes. "It's okay. We've caught the mean person who did it."

Juno buried her head into her hands and sobbed. "Why?"

"I don't know, why don't you ask Belle why she murdered your mother."

The girl lifted her head and turned to Belle. "What is he talking about?"

"Juno, it's true your mother was killed, but I swear I didn't harm her."

Steve pounded the table with his fist. "Shut it. We have a holorecording of you killing Sophia Eccleston and another recording of you running off with her daughter in the glade. Then someone, who probably worked with you, put the only two cops on the island into the hospital."

"Why didn't you tell me?" asked a sobbing Juno.

"We were trying to survive. I was going to tell you."

"She was probably going to hurt you too, young lady. But it's okay, we're here now. We'll protect you from this rabid woman."

Juno buried her face in her hands once more. Belle's back stiffened as she felt two lifeless hands upon her shoulders.

"He's lying, Juno. I wanted to save you from the horrors of that hell."

Steve leaned back in his chair and regarded her. "You know, it's such a shame the only cops on the island aren't around. That means you're in my hands until the government sends someone. With this weather, it could be days. Would be a real shame if you ran off again and disappeared into these woods—forever. After all, there's a lot of carnivores out there, much like yourself. Only they have bigger teeth. Sure would save the taxpayers some money."

Juno lifted her head from her hands. "You're not going to hurt Belle, are you Mr. Steve?"

"Now, now. I wouldn't hurt anyone. I'm not a bad guy. But this is a very dangerous place. Belle stole you and put you in this very dangerous place. You almost got eaten until me and the boys arrived. All I was saying is that I just hope there aren't any accidents. We don't like accidents."

"But Mr. Steve. Belle would never hurt anyone. She's a good person. She takes care of me."

"It's a pity about your sight little Juno, otherwise you'd be able to see the truth for yourself. Your trust in this woman is misplaced, I'm afraid. She's not a good person. She's a very bad person. Unfortunately, the tents are all full, and we have no room to shelter criminals. Escort Belle to the edge of the perimeter. Take her to that big cave, for shelter. Guard the entrance. We'll check on her in the morning. Let come what may."

"No, Mr. Steve. Please don't send her away. I know Belle wouldn't hurt Mommy. She's a nice person."

"I'm afraid you've got a little Stockholm syndrome, young lady. We'll have Dr. Mira look at you when you get back. I've heard you're due for an important operation. As for that one, she's a monster and she'll be treated like a monster. Take her away."

The machine's lifeless grip tightened on Belle's shoulder. She tried not to stand, but it lifted her effortlessly. Juno reached out as she was dragged away.

Chapter 33

SETH

Eccleston Pleistocene Reserve, Alaska
Modern Era: Post-Singularity

He ran deep into the woods. The forest was dense and wet and visibility was poor. Eventually the sound of jet engines faded and was replaced by the chirping of birds and the hooting of owls. Seth's mind filled with a map of the island and the location of his objective—the girl and her kidnapper.

As he trekked through the forest, he couldn't shake his skepticism that this entire ordeal was the cruel ruse of a twisted mind. Did he relegate himself to being the haunted marionette of a puppet master unknown? Would he really see Anna again? He doubted it. More than likely he was simply fulfilling the purpose he had always fulfilled: being a sharp tool put to good use and then discarded when worn out. But he was good at his job, and while the chances of seeing her again were slim, they were better than nothing.

Even in the wilderness he couldn't help but get the impression that he was being watched—maybe even followed. His mask allowed him to see infrared as well as different light spectrums. He turned on the infrared and scanned the forest, looking for heat signatures. Finding one, he zoomed in. It was a racoon. He saw another. Some deer in the distance. The rest were birds—and at least one porcupine. No sign of men.

He trudged forward. The area was truly wild. There were no trails to speak of, and the bush was so dense he had trouble making it a few paces, let alone the few miles he'd likely have to trek to find the girl—if she hadn't been captured already. He paused and took a sip of water. As he did, he heard a branch snap. His head swiveled.

Nothing. He quickly finished his drink and continued on. The trees grew thinner as he followed the river, which continued through a wide-open valley. Far in the distance, Seth could see the river empty into a great teal lake. He could make out activity around it. There were vehicles and tents and men and their machines. He wasn't sure if the girl was there, but it was the best chance he had.

There were only two ways to get to the lake. Hidden over the tree-covered mountains and cliffs or exposed through the open valley. Getting over the mountains could take days—cutting through the valley would take hours.

The valley it was.

So he hiked. As the hours passed, the pain in his tired feet began to shoot up his spine. Oddly, he still felt uneasy. He couldn't help but get the impression that something lurking just behind the tree line to his right was following him. He turned on his infrared again and scanned the tree line. There was nothing out of the ordinary.

His mouth was parched as he walked toward the small ravine that cut through the valley. He heard the sound of rushing water and made his way down the modest ravine, toward the stream within. Seth kneeled next to the teal of the river and drank the cold mountain water. As he savored his drink, a splashing sound captured his attention.

He lifted his head from the stream.

A great brown mass stood before him. He blinked. At first he thought it was a grizzly, but this thing was far larger than a grizzly, and its face looked more like a bulldog's than any bear he had ever seen. The huge bear sat in the shallow stream and shoved a wriggling salmon in its flat face with massive forepaws. "Species identified," chimed in his neural connection. His preferred computer voice spoke within his mind.

"Species *Arctodus simus*, or the giant short-faced bear. Extinction, approximately twelve thousand years ago. De-extinction, twenty years ago. Fun fact, did you know that the Giant Short Faced Bear is the largest known terrestrial mammalian carnivore to have ever walked the earth?"

"Shut up, Vanessa," he couldn't help but whisper in response.

"Before I shut up, you should also be aware that the giant short-faced Bear has been clocked as the fastest bear in the world. I wouldn't suggest trying to outrun it."

"Shut up. Shut up."

The bear hadn't noticed him, or if it had, it didn't care. He slowly backed away and pawed at his sidearm with a trembling hand. The bear looked at him for a moment and then directed its gaze back down toward the river. It snapped its jaws around a leaping salmon. Facing the bear all the while, he slowly walked back up the ravine. When he reached the level ground of the surrounding valley, he wiped his brow with his still-trembling hand.

He felt a smile creep up. It faded as his nostrils filled with deep musk. A stench he had never encountered before. Seth turned and saw a foot and followed it upward, revealing a fur-covered stump of a leg. His eyes continued upward to two great ivory tusks, each some seventeen feet in length, yellowed and covered with moss.

"Species identified—"

"Shut up, I know what it is."

A mammoth. A loner, and therefore a bull. The beast turned its massive head and regarded him. Its eye revealed an intelligence. Seth backed away. The mammoth pursued, seemingly with a combination of curiosity and annoyance. Seth stopped. The bear was still behind him, wallowing in the river.

The bull mammoth flapped its ears. Seth put up his hands and tried to calm the creature. It trumpeted and shook its head. He considered shooting it. He also considered that nine-millimeter bullets might just make it angrier.

He inched back down the little ravine toward the bear in the river. The mammoth pursued at an equally slow pace. Seth began to sidestep away from the stretch between two giants. With a salmon still in its mouth, the bear reared up on its hind legs. The mammoth stepped forward and towered over it. The bear grunted. In a moment, it was back on its feet and running away.

He agreed with the bear's logic—he ran. The mammoth could only chase one of them. The ground beneath him rumbled. He was right. The mammoth was only charging one of them now—him.

Seth recalled seeing a video that said one should stomp and yell to stop a charge. He looked behind him. The ground thundered, and the mammoth was gaining. To hell with that. He jumped into the stream. The mammoth followed and lowered its head. He saw a blur of ivory tusks and then a dreary gray sky. He was weightless, airborne.

The landing knocked the wind out of him. He was back out of the river now, several yards away from the mammoth. Somehow, he was still alive.

He lifted himself up on his elbow. The mammoth's head tilted from side to side, and then one of its eyes locked on to him. As he crawled to his feet, the mammoth trumpeted. Then there was more trumpeting behind him. He turned his head and saw another bull. The bear was long gone.

He stood. The two bulls walked toward him. Seth held up his pistol. He didn't think it would do any good, but he was all out of options.

The earth shook.

The mammoths charged.

Their skulls collided in a great crash, their tusks and trunks intertangled.

He wasn't going to wait and find out who was the top bull. He ran.

Eventually, he stopped at the top of a faraway hill. From there, he saw a sight that took his breath away. It was something that few men had seen in thousands of years. The lush valley ahead was filled with mammoths and their young among thousands of steppe bison, western camels, and woolly rhinos, all of them feeding upon the bounty of the earth as they made their way toward the Great Teal Lake. Despite almost being killed by the beasts, he couldn't help but admire the noble creatures. He considered that perhaps when man was kicked out of Eden and became civilized, he was no longer worthy to gaze upon such magnificence, so God took them away.

He crept closer along the tree line that ran the length of the valley. He figured he'd follow it until he reached the camp, and hopefully, if the mammoths charged, he could lose them in the woods. So he followed the tree line, though it was odd. Every time he took a step, he heard the strangest thing. Leaves would crunch under his feet each time he put his feet down, and then he'd hear the same crunch again— even though his feet were already planted. The timing was close, but not perfect.

Chapter 34

BELLE

Eccleston Pleistocene Reserve, Alaska
Modern Era: Post-Singularity

The machine dragged Belle from the tent and into the cold rain. She kicked and pounded at its arm, but it was no use. The ravens overhead, seemingly indifferent to the downpour, looked on. Lightning flashed, revealing some sixty machines standing in a perfect circle around the camp. All-terrain vehicles were circled around the tents that made up the center of the camp. The caged baby mammoth—Mr. Snuffles—was being kept near the center, next to Steve's tent. The guards tried feeding and petting him, but the baby mammoth seemed anxious and distraught. He refused the food they tried to give him. Instead, he nervously paced the narrow confines of his cage and trumpeted his distress.

Then machine suddenly stopped and stood perfectly still, its metal grip tight around Belle's wrist. As the rain poured, all of the machines froze in place — they had stopped working. She tried pulling her hand free, but it was no use. She heard a deep rumble emanate from the darkness beyond.

Confused guards emerged from their tents. Steve stormed out of his tent and started cursing at his subordinates. A few of the men tried fighting with the controls to the machines. One shrugged, and another shook his head.

"How many times have I told you knuckleheads to stop using the machines for pranks. Now turn them back on," said Steve.

"Sir, it's not another prank. They're not responding to commands," said a guard.

"Okay, then reset them manually. What are you all waiting around for?"

Steve walked up to the machine that had dragged Belle from the tent. He pressed some commands into a tablet. It didn't work. Steve threw the tablet into the mud and tried to pull a cover off the back of the machine.

As he pulled back on the glossy black composite cover, the machine rotated its torso to face him. It lifted Steve with one arm. Steve reached for his sidearm. As he unholstered his weapon, the murder-machine threw him high into the air. He splashed into the waters of the teal mountain lake behind the camp.

The other guards looked on stunned.

The ground trembled. Then the guards leveled their weapons as great black bodies emerged from the moonlight. A thick smell of musk filled the air. A mammoth thundered across the clearing and threw Steve's vehicle into the lake with one thrust of its massive head. The other members of the herd swung their great tusks from side to side, sweeping the immobilized military droids off their feet and flinging them against trees. Some of the men fired with wild abandon into the darkness, while others fled as the mammoth herd trampled their tents and smashed their vehicles.

Mother had arrived.

The matriarch approached the caged baby mammoth. She lifted the heavy latch of the cage with her trunk. The barred metal door creaked open. The baby stumbled out and wrapped his trunk around his mother's. Desperate, Belle waved to the baby mammoth for help. She had hoped, by some miracle, that it would help free her from the murder-machine's grasp. Mr. Snuffles regarded her, then stormed off in the opposite direction, seemingly out of spite.

Like a madwoman, she yelled, "Mr. Snuffles! Mr. Snuffles, please help me!"

The baby mammoth paused. He flapped its ears outward, then ignored her and resumed walking away. As the men fled, Belle found a rock and began hammering at the mechanical hand. It was no use. She found a stick and tried prying the thumb loose. At first, it seemed hopeless, but eventually it became just loose enough to pull her hand free.

She gauged her surroundings. Nearly everything was in a state of chaos and ruin. She ran to an all-terrain vehicle and started it, put it in manual mode, and hit the pedal.

Belle slammed into two immobilized military droids guarding Juno's tent. They rolled under the vehicle.

She backed up once more. Then she got out of the vehicle and rushed into Juno's tent.

"Mr. Steve? Belle? Is that you?" the girl asked.

"It's me. We have to go. Now," said Belle.

Juno jumped from her seat and ran toward Belle's voice. They embraced.

"I'm scared, Belle," said Juno, sobbing. "Why is there so much noise outside?"

"Mr. Steve and his men are becoming more attuned with Mother Nature, that's all."

Belle took Juno by the hand and led her to the vehicle. As they tried to drive away, the massive matriarch stood before them, blocking their path. She lowered its head, ready to fling their vehicle into the air, but suddenly it stopped. It turned its massive head slightly to the side and regarded Juno. With that, the great beast and the herd continued on down the valley.

They buckled up and drove south, toward St. Olga.

It was midnight when they reached the town. As they drove in, the same horrifying image kept flashing in and out of her memory. Sophia's bulging eyes as she gurgled, "Patel, get Patel."

"Juno did your mom get along well with Dr. Patel?"

"Dr. Patel was my mom's only friend."

"They didn't fight?"

"Never. She was the only person Mom wouldn't yell at."

"Your mom mentioned Dr. Patel's name before she died. Besides medical help, do you have any other idea why?"

"I don't know, but she was the one person my mom trusted more than anyone in the entire world."

Belle had never gotten to know Dr. Patel, but she knew she was the one who regularly examined Juno. The woman was just a face that she'd occasionally see in the building. Dr. Patel wasn't merely Juno and Sophia's personal physician — she was head of Eccleston Evolution's product development. The woman kept a low profile and was one of those people most employees had heard of but had never actually seen.

"Do you think she's a nice person?"

"No. Not nice at all."

"Would she ever hurt your mom?"

"I don't think so."

"Do you think she'd be willing to help us?"

"I don't know, but she and Mr. Dearborn are in charge now."

"Do you know where she lives?"

"She lives a few houses down from my house."

It was a bad idea to go to her. She wanted to leave Juno someplace safe, but where could that possibly be? No. She wouldn't let Juno out of her sight. Then again, all the ideas she had were bad ideas, so she had to choose the least bad option. At least at Dr. Patel's house, she might get some answers.

They pulled into town, and she stopped the vehicle in front of a row house with a Prussian blue door. Belle asked Juno what the address was, and she repeated it. This was Mira Patel's house. Like Sophia's, it was a no-frills two-story wooden home.

Juno tugged her hand. "What about Pancake? We should go back and get him."

"Your cat has his own fulltime caretaker and his own fulltime groomer and a horde of office admirers. Pancake has his own staff. He'll be fine. Trust me."

"Okay, if you say so, but I hope he's alright."

Belle knocked on the door.

No answer.

She knocked again and waited.

As she was about to turn around and walk away, Juno slipped from Belle's grasp. She pounded the door hard and yelled, "Ms. Patel, it's me."

The door cracked open.

Two eyes and a glimmer of a chain lock just below them appeared. The eyes took a long look at Juno, and then they slowly shifted to Belle.

When they did, the door slammed shut. Juno stood patiently outside the door. It opened once more, and Belle saw the figure that the eyes belonged to. Like Sophia, Mira didn't look a day over twenty years old. She and Sophia had discovered something and shared it amongst themselves. Mira's frazzled black hair dangled over the back of her white silk robe, and she was holding a full glass of red wine. She looked nervous, agitated—scared. She ran her eyes up and down Belle once more and then glugged her wine. Then she returned her gaze to Juno and swallowed hard.

She eased the door open, inch by inch.

"Juno, you're alive, thank heavens. The whole company has been looking for you," said Mira. "You look terrible, all muddy and scratched up. Don't worry, we'll get you cleaned up and fed."

Before the woman could lead Juno away, Belle spoke. "Dr. Patel—"

"Mira is sufficient."

Mira sucked down the rest of her glass without answering. Her trembling hand filled up another glass and she paced the living room. "Did you kill her?" she asked.

"No."

"Why am I even asking? Of course you'd say that."

"If you don't believe me, why haven't you called in security?"

Mira swished her wine and locked eyes with Belle. "Maybe I have."

Chapter 35

SETH

Eccleston Pleistocene Reserve, Alaska
Modern Era: Post-Singularity

It was almost dusk when he made it to a ruined camp. Security vehicles and tents and murder-machines were splayed throughout the site. Nearly everything was trampled and destroyed. A few of the bots that hadn't been destroyed stood like frozen homicidal mannequins. The mammoth herd had already moved on, farther down the valley. A few wounded security personnel groaned and tended to one another in the sparse tree cover next to the lake. He caught sight of a bald man struggling to tread water, but he was only spitting it up and going under.

Not his problem. Seth turned and walked the other way.

As he walked he could hear the desperate splashing of water. He turned and watched as the man's head disappeared under the teal water. He took a few steps more before he stopped and sighed. Turning back around, he grudgingly made his way into the water.

He swam out to the last spot where he'd seen the man and dove down. A few moments later, their heads broke the surface of the water. Seth backpaddled toward the shoreline with the man in tow. When they reached the shoreline, he pulled him by the back of his shirt onto dryland. The bald man spit up water before climbing to his feet. He clutched his arm.

"Your arm has a compound fracture," Seth said.

"Oh, thank you for telling me, doctor. I sure didn't notice the freaking bone sticking out of my freaking arm."

Seth handed him a pill. "Take this, for the pain."

The bald man snatched it up with his meaty hand and put it in his mouth. "Are you one of ours?"

"If I was against you, would I have pulled you from that lake?"

"Don't know. I was doing just fine."

"How long were you in there?"

"A while."

"A while?"

"Yeah, and I didn't ask for any help."

"We'll, I'm asking for yours. Have you a seen a girl? Eight years old. Might have been with another woman."

The bald man raised an eyebrow. "Who are you, and what's with the mask? Are you some kind of cosplay weirdo or something?"

"You have seen them?"

"Yeah, and they're long gone. She stole one of our vehicles. Now who the hell are you?

"A friend."

"Well, you're going in for questioning, friend. You clowns—yeah, you over in the trees. Detain this guy."

The security personnel who could still walk approached him.

"My apologies, but I have other business attend to."

Seth walked over to a tipped-over all-terrain vehicle. He pushed it right side up. The men stopped, their mouths agape.

"Don't worry, I'll return it."

He got into the vehicle, started it, and followed a fresh set of tire tracks that led in the direction of the town.

The camp had disappeared over the horizon quite some time ago when his vehicle suddenly stopped. Its batteries had run out. He got out and followed the tire tracks on foot. He could only hope that he wouldn't meet the ugly end of the mammoths a second time. As he followed the tracks, the dirt road took a turn deep inside the forest. There was a pointed sign that said "To St. Olga." He followed.

The dark canopy enveloped him. Now he walked along a narrow dirt road that cut through the dense forest where it traversed the mountains before leading downward toward the town of St. Olga. As he walked, the sensation of being watched crept up on him again. He thought it was silly— of course there was something watching him. The ancient boreal forest teemed with life. Something had to be watching him. Still, he noticed something strange about the forest this time, or rather it was the lack of something. All the birds were quiet. Maybe it was because it was night—or maybe there was a predator around.

He tried to remind himself that he was the apex predator in these woods—wasn't he? After all, the suit Sam had given him was impressive and, so far as he could tell, far more advanced than anything the Eccleston security guards wore. It could stop bullets, though based on how sore his body was it stood to reason that he could still get trampled to death. And while the suit seemed puncture proof, he had the feeling that it wouldn't have done him much good had the giant short-faced bear clamped its massive jaws around his head and crushed his skull. Sure, the suit might have stayed in perfectly good shape, but the man inside it wouldn't have. Hubris. He had to bury it, or this place was going to bury him.

Still, he couldn't shake the sensation that he was being followed. Just then, branches snapped. An entire tree shook. His body stiffened as he saw the great mass before him. He stepped back.

Maybe it's a moose?

As he removed his pistol, the tree was thrown across the road. There was a great deep groan the likes of which he'd never encountered before. Then there was the smell. How to describe that smell? It reeked of rotting forest floor.

Okay, it's not a moose.

He tried aiming, but he didn't have much of a target to identify, only a moving mass of fur behind a great log. It wasn't so much a matter of if he could shoot it, it was more of matter of if should. Like with the mammoths, he worried about how many rounds he could get off before being gored or trampled to death by . . . whatever this thing was.

From the forest floor rose an immense creature that was ten feet of flesh and bone and claws. Each claw was easily big enough to disembowel a man in one swipe.

From its terrible maw, he saw a great tongue. The tongue wrapped itself around a bunch of leaves, bringing them into the terrible mouth of the —

"Species identified. *Magalonyx jeffersonii* or Jefferson's Ground Sloth. Extinction, approximately twelve thousand years ago. De-extinction, twenty years ago. Herbivores. Its fossils were first described by President Thomas Jefferson."

"Is it dangerous?" he asked.

"Only if you get between it and its food," said Vanessa.

With his pistol at the ready, he maneuvered around the giant sloth and stepped over the trunk of the birch tree it had tossed across the road. He didn't holster his weapon until he was some distance away from the creature.

He continued to follow the tracks, but then there was something curious in the mud. He kneeled. Tufts of coarse beige hair. Next to the hair was a very large pawprint.

"Identify this pawprint," he said.

"Due to the condition of the pawprint, it can't be identified."

The track was old, he knew that much, so the animal likely hadn't been through that way in at least day or so. Whatever it was, he hoped it wasn't hungry.

Chapter 36

BELLE

St. Olga, Alaska
Modern Era: Post-Singularity

Mira took Juno to the washroom and ran a bath for her. Then she disappeared down the hallway. Belle thought about asking Mira about Sophia's last words, but she decided to keep that information to herself for the time being. She sat alone in the living room until Mira returned with a silver metal object in her hands—a box. She placed it on the coffee table between them.

"Sophia said that if anything happened to her, I was supposed to give you or Juno this."

"Who did she think was after her?" she asked.

"Lots of people. Just open it. I want to get this over with before security arrives."

"You called them?"

"No, but it's only a matter of time before they find you here—you're on an island, after all."

"Can't you tell them to leave? It's my understanding that you're in charge now."

"Of the company. Not the law. Every minute you're here is a liability."

The smooth metal container appeared to have no locking mechanism. There wasn't a keyhole nor a place to put in a combination. The only mark on the surface was a strange round indentation in the center of the box with a pin-sized hole in the center.

"How do you open it?" she asked.

"It's locked to your genome. Sophia just dumped it off at my house one day with her usual vague instructions."

Belle pressed the indentation and felt a pinprick. She quickly retracted her hand, and several droplets of bright red blood disappeared into the mechanism. The box made a clicking sound as the hinges creaked.

It opened.

Inside was a yellow envelope with a string enclosure. Belle took it out and untied it. Inside was a collection of financial forms, a will, corporate documents, some torn-out pages of what looked like a journal, and curiously enough, Sophia's medical records.

An equally curious Mira peered over her shoulder. "I see."

"What's all of this for?" Belle asked.

"Read it and you'll get your answer."

First, she sifted through the medical records. They simply said that Sophia had been a healthy woman her whole life.

There were antiaging treatments, but Belle didn't need Sophia's medical records to tell her that. However, things became strange when she got to the bottom of her most recent imaging record. It was from when she was pregnant with Juno.

It read "Gravida: 2. Para: 2."

"What does this mean?" asked Belle.

"Gravida is just a fancy way of saying how many times someone had been pregnant. Para was another way of saying how many live births a person had given."

"Does this happen to include ones in the development wing?"

"No. While Sophia had cloned her eggs and grown embryos and fetuses in her lab, she wasn't pregnant with them. They were grown in petri dishes and artificial wombs, so they wouldn't have been counted on this form, and Hera, like the others, was never implanted—and, I guess, never will be. So, what this paper says is that Sophia Eccleston didn't give birth to just one child."

"Then how many did she have?"

"She had two."

"What is Sophia trying to tell me with this?"

Mira took a sip of wine and pointed. "Keep reading."

Belle shuffled through the papers until she found a paper titled "Last Will and Testament of Sophia Eccleston" and began reading it.

"In the event of my death, all my shares of Eccleston Evolution stock shall be divided evenly between my living descendants: Juno Eccleston and . . ."

The papers fell from Belle's hands.

She awoke to some smelling salts that Mira was waving under her nose. She wanted to cry, she wanted to lash out, but all she could do was lie on the floor, confused.

"So, it is true. You really are her. I'm sorry about your mother—she had regrets."

"She's an egg donor, not my mother," Belle snapped. "You knew this whole time?"

"It wasn't my place to tell you."

Maybe she shouldn't have been as angry as she was. She and Juno had just become worth trillions of dollars. It seemed that Sophia had created the box to protect them, or perhaps more likely to spite someone else. The board already disliked Sophia, and she had a feeling there would be a number of people who wouldn't be happy about their newfound positions in the company. All the documents were signed and notarized, she suspected to prevent someone, or perhaps something, from electronically altering Sophia's decisions after her death.

She glared at Mira. "How long have you known?"

"Since our college days together."

"Why did she give me up?"

Mira put her wine glass down on the table. She sat on the couch, gazing at the floor. Her mouth opened a few times as if to speak, but the words struggled to come out. "Maybe those journal pages will tell you better than I can."

Belle picked up the yellowed and droplet-stained pages and began to read them.

TUESDAY, NOVEMBER 5—
I don't think I can do it. I feel so alone. I don't want to go crawling back to my parents begging for help. I don't know what to do. I was always the one in class who knew the answers to all the questions, I always aced my exams, my friends turned to me for advice. Now I have no idea what to do. What about my company? Is it fair to this baby to have a mother that isn't there, working almost a hundred hours a week? I'm not ready for this and I'm not ready to do it alone.

THURSDAY, NOVEMBER 28—
I've decided to give up my daughter for adoption. I made some calls and got bombarded by interested agencies. Apparently there is no shortage of people looking for children to adopt. The agencies told me I could even select the parents of my daughter. As one of the agencies was discussing my options with me, I broke down in tears. I don't want to think or feel or do any of this and I don't want to give the child to the state. I don't know what to do.

FRIDAY, DECEMBER 6—
Does fate exist? I don't know. The classical model is deterministic and the quantum model is probabilistic. Is my biology simply compelling me to make this choice? Or is something lacking in my biology? Where are my maternal instincts? Am I broken somehow or am I doing the right thing? Maybe I'm just not thinking straight. I've been having really vivid and bizarre dreams lately. I can't shake them. I

had one last night. I was walking along a winding path that stretched and changed direction against the backdrop of a forest that moved like liquid. Everything was in flux. At the end of the path was a tall belltower. Even now I can see it with perfect clarity. The tower bells rang and I woke up.

MONDAY, DECEMBER 16 —
My baby will be coming any day now. I found a place. It's a monastery out in the middle of nowhere. I can't explain why, but I feel like my daughter will be safe there. My head is swimming and I guess I just don't trust myself to pick out her future parents. What if I choose the wrong parents? If fate is real then so be it. Yes, the monastery. I have to do it. I'm going to do it.

Belle put down the pages of the journal. "What else can I say? If it wasn't for her, I wouldn't have met my adoptive parents, the Drakes."

Belle scratched her head. Her parents. She could remember their warmth, their embrace, but much was still missing from her mind's eye. There was something else. A lingering pain. She struggled with the details, but she knew that she was living in Kobuksville to find and reconcile with that pain. Her efforts had failed. Instead of becoming relaxed and focused, she became paranoid and stir-crazy. No matter how hard she tried, she couldn't quite put together the pieces of her life before her time in in that isolated village. Her life felt like an old Roman mosaic. Lost and then found, but in her case the mosaic was missing important pieces. She couldn't quite make out the faces anymore. She had tried to sift through the debris of her life and find those little missing pieces of stones and glass and put them back where they belonged, yet it seemed like an impossible task.

She realized that she still hadn't gotten her chance to visit her parents since she'd left the isle. Though it was strange, she didn't remember what they looked like. She had promised she would see them the first chance she got, wherever they were, but it seemed that she had let circumstance get in the way. Now she may never see them again.

Mira spoke.

"The thing about Sophia was that she was brilliant in some ways, but other parts of her brain needed work. She didn't seem to understand how to handle relationships. She preferred to spend time in her lab rather than interacting with people. She could be abrasive and difficult to deal with."

"Why leave me or anybody else anything? I thought she was ageless? Why make a will?"

"I'm not sure. Maybe she didn't plan on dying but filled it out as some kind of catharsis?"

"Catharsis?"

"You're guess is as good as mine."

"Who was after her?"

"I don't know.

"Then who was she most afraid of?"

"She seemed more concerned about people at Eccleston Evolution than anyone else."

"Who specifically? Lucas Ivanov?"

"I don't know. Almost everyone. She became increasingly paranoid and began planning her will and making other arrangements."

That surprised Belle. Maybe Mira was a little too drunk and was speaking more openly than she normally would have.

"Why?"

"She wouldn't tell me much, but the other board members were circling the wagons around her. They were planning to give an ultimatum to step down later this week."

"But she's the majority shareholder."

"She broke the rules of the shareholders' agreement. A judge would be compelled to force her out. If the board went after her, that is."

"Broke which rules?"

"Pretty much all of them."

Belle figured that Sophia's personality doubtlessly had put her at a disadvantage in terms of building boardroom alliances. Still, she had immense soft power. She was the company's celebrity founder. The only way to get Sophia out of the way was to kill her. And why pin it on Belle? It seemed to her that with half of Sophia's shares, she was now one of the majority shareholders and had the power to force her way onto the board and seize an executive position. She was an immediate threat.

Which meant that they thought the other threat, the future threat, was Juno.

"What about Juno's operation?" she asked.

The lights flickered. Mira patted her upper lip and gazed at her blood-covered fingers. "Oh, yes, that. Well, after more careful testing, it seems that it might not be necessary after all. Excuse me for one moment. I've got a nosebleed."

Mira left and got a tissue. Holding it over her nose, she sat back down.

Belle's eyes watered. "Really? That's wonderful news."

"Well, we have to tell her right away."

"I did, don't worry. There were tears of joy, I assure you. Yes, uh, we thought we had detected a defect, a tumor, but, uh, you know, it turns out it was just a temporary benign growth that's shrinking now. We're as surprised as anyone. A miracle, really." Mira took another glug of wine. "Yes, it's truly wonderful."

"The Augur, do you know where they're keeping it? Given my change in status at the company, I think you can tell me now."

Mira shook her head. "Sorry, I'm in the bioengineering department, not in the artificial intelligence department. I don't know where it is."

Juno appeared out of the dark threshold of the door and walked up to Belle as she nervously played with her wet hair. Her eyes were cast downward, but she could tell the girl was trying to hold back tears.

"Did your mom ever mention me, before we met?"

Juno nodded. "She told me all about you."

That surprised her. She didn't know why Sophia would have bothered. If she didn't want Belle in her life, why did she tell Juno? Unless she had somehow misread her intentions.

"And what did she say?"

"She said that you're my big sister."

Those words cut. Belle began sniffling, and she had to stop patting her eyes. It was no use. She had tried to pretend like nothing was wrong, but she always was a terrible actor.

"That's right," she managed.

Before she could try to say anything else, she felt Juno's arms wrap around her.

They embraced as if it was their last moment on Earth together, and chances were, it was. She was sure the security forces would barge in and detain her at any moment. Belle wished she could say it was a moment of pure bliss, but the truth was that she thought it was all very cruel. She had found a sister, and now she was going to be taken away from her and locked up in a new closet, a government closet, a prison, forever.

"Why didn't you tell me?" she asked.

"Mom told me never to tell you. She said we had to 'keep it our secret.' She said that if I did, you would get really mad at her and leave us and I didn't want you to leave. I wanted you to stay and be with me and Pancake."

Belle kissed Juno on the forehead, and they held one another on the couch. Given that the forms had been recently updated, it seemed Sophia was almost expecting death to come.

Belle turned to Mira. "You said there were people at Eccleston Evolution who she was 'concerned about.' I assume you mean the board of directors?"

"If I answer your question, it stays between us. I don't want to be dragged into company politics. I'm a bioengineer and physician, that's it. I don't want to get involved in any of it."

"Deal."

"The board hates her guts. They think she is an imperious, aloof, financially incompetent egotist. The ones that survived her firings wanted her gone for the better part of a decade. The only board member who's tolerated her is the chairman, Mr. Dearborn. If it wasn't for him, she probably would have been gone by now, or reduced to a figurehead, CEO in name only."

"Would Sophia tolerate that? Being reduced to a figurehead?"

"No. She was the type of person who always needs to be in control of every little thing."

"So, Mr. Dearborn is her only ally on the board?"

Mira shrugged. "Like I said, I stay out of company politics. He tries to get along with everyone, but I find his authenticity questionable. He comes across as sort of a politician to me."

If there was someone on the board who was willing to use any means necessary to remove Sophia, Mr. Dearborn might know who that person could be. He had mentioned at their dinner that he was defending Sophia against repeated calls for her resignation. Belle had gotten the impression that he was a moderating force between Sophia's increasingly eccentric side projects and the board's demands for stable company finances. Before Sophia's death, he was the second-richest person in the company, not to mention being 131 years old. His antiaging treatments only went so far. He had nothing to gain from her death.

Belle needed to meet with Mr. Dearborn at once and get some answers before she was detained.

"Can you let Mr. Dearborn know we're coming?"

"I'm sorry, but I can't help you."

The lights in Mira's house flicked off and on for a moment. She looked outside and noticed that all of the windows in all the other houses in the neighborhood were out. Only Mira's house still had power.

"Why can't you help us, Dr. Patel?" asked Juno.

The lights flicked again. Mira's wiped her bleeding nose with her trembling left hand while the glass in her right wobbled so much that wine began to slosh out onto her floor.

"On second thought . . ."

Chapter 37

SETH

Pleistocene Reserve, Alaska
Modern Era: Post-Singularity

Exhausted, he sat against a tree. Why was he going through this hell? A stupid question. He knew why, and he knew he needed to keep going. He needed to complete his objective and meet this Sam character. He didn't know if his wife would be there or not, but the agony of not knowing was unbearable. He tried to stand, but his legs weren't cooperating. Sleeping was a bad idea, so he told himself he was just going to rest for a little while and then get back up. Seth felt his eyelids grow heavy. His chin slumped downward. Then a sensation of utter dread shot up his spine. The hairs on his arms and neck lifted on end. He startled himself awake.

It wasn't paranoia. It was a sense of the danger to come. A primal sense now buried deep into the subconscious of civilized man — but in him, awakened. Someone or something in those woods was watching him. It had been watching him since he entered the trees. He wasn't just being watched. He was being hunted. He knew it. He didn't know how he knew, he just did. Much like how the gazelle sipping water at the river's edge startles itself into a sprint for its life mere moments before a crocodile breaks through the still water, jaws open, ready to drag whatever lies waiting to the depths in the hopes of drowning and devouring it. Yes, as the gazelle drinks, there's a raw instinct deep inside the gazelle's brain that told it something was wrong. It didn't understand how or why, it just understood if it didn't move as fast as it possibly could — it would die. Then an instantaneous reaction, and either life or death followed as the crocodile's jaws exploded out of the water.

Like the gazelle, he had been alerted. His eyes were wide open now. Though unlike the gazelle, Seth lay still, scanning the darkness around him. Something told him that running was exactly what this thing wanted him to do.

Slowly, very slowly, he rose to his feet. His trembling hand unholstered his pistol. The world around him slowed down and grew quiet. His adrenaline was pumping. His heart was racing. He turned on his infrared with night vision. The laser dot of his pistol wandered aimless in the darkness. There was nothing. His pulsed ticked lower, his breathing slowed. Maybe he was overreacting. Maybe he just hadn't gotten enough sleep and was on edge. He lowered his pistol. Yes, maybe he should just let his logical brain override his primitive instincts? Maybe not.

He ran.

His heart raced as his legs pounded against the sodden road. A blur exploded out the brush behind him. Seth demanded that his legs carry him faster. It was no use. The dark blur was gaining on him. There was no outrunning it in a straight line. Seth charged into the thick brush beside him. The ferns violently shook. It was closer now. His leg muscles burned. Branches snapped to his rear. He couldn't keep going. He jumped over the log of a great Sitka and crouched behind it and readied his pistol.

Then . . . nothing.

There was only the silence of the forest. Again Seth scanned the woods, looking for heat signatures of animals or even machines. There was nothing unusual and certainly no predators. It was just him and ferns and the trees. He sat there struggling to catch his breath. His head swiveled in every direction, waiting for the threat to reveal itself. Thanks to Sam, his reactions were much quicker than natural. At first it had made him feel powerful. Now he felt his newfound strength and reflexes were second rate in this primeval place. It was just behind him. Why didn't it go in for the kill? Did he really just escape death or was it merely letting him live — for now? Now he was beginning to wonder if it was smarter as well. He got the impression it was waiting for him, or was it . . . toying with him?

The moon moved across the night sky. Seth wasn't sure how long he had been sitting there with a racing pulse and a death grip on his pistol. He couldn't stay forever. He had to move. Slowly, he rose to his feet, arms extended and pistol at the ready.

Still nothing but ferns and trees.

Maybe that was what it wanted? Maybe it wanted him to stay there frightened until he got tired and weak and was unable to run or put up much of a fight. He had to get moving. He stepped gently through the forest, taking care to study everything around him. One foot in front of the other until once more he reached the dirt road. He turned on the pistol light, hoping there was a chance it would frighten whatever was lurking out there. He scanned the entire horizon, his finger resting on the trigger.

The adrenaline was wearing off, and now the pain and the exhaustion returned. He was sure he had broken a few ribs. His face felt like he had gotten in a losing boxing match and his stomach groaned of hunger. Above all he needed rest, but he couldn't rest. Not here. Not if he wanted to wake up alive. Not if he wanted to see Anna ever again. The town wasn't far. Perhaps only six hours' walk. He could do it. One foot in front of the other, keep going.

He turned off the light and holstered his weapon and continued on down the road. As he walked, something rustled in the bush to the left. He turned his head but didn't find anything. The canopy shuddered as he heard the flapping of wings to his right. He pawed at the handle of his Bowie knife and continued walking. In the corner of his eye, he caught a blur in the blackness behind him, but when he looked, it wasn't there. He quickened his pace with his hand now firmly gripped on the handle of the knife that hung from his hip.

Chapter 38

BELLE

Dearborn Manor, Alaska
Modern Era: Post-Singularity

They parked outside the gate of a grand home. Belle pressed the intercom button.

"Dearborn Security, do you know what time it is?" said the voice on the other end.

"Yes, it's one in the morning. Tell him Juno Eccleston is here to meet him and she needs to see him regarding Sophia at once."

"Did you say Juno Eccleston?"

"Yes."

There was the clack of the locking mechanism and a low screech as the gate rolled open.

It hadn't been hard to find Raymond Dearborn's house. It was the biggest on the island, looming over the town from the surrounding mountains. The house straddled a stream that ran through the property and ended in a waterfall.

Inspired by Frank Lloyd Wright's crown jewel, Fallingwater, the house was built of slate and thick sheets of glass, and it conformed to the surroundings in an organic albeit jagged harmony.

The ravens were back, all of them perched atop the wall that surrounded the compound. All of them watching. After the gate had opened all the way, Belle pulled into the grounds of the estate and parked the vehicle. They got out and were greeted by Mr. Dearborn.

"Come in, please."

Belle and Juno walked inside the mansion, following Mr. Dearborn, who wore a burgundy velvet smoking jacket, to his parlor. It was filled with leather furniture atop a Persian carpet. The old man sat down next to a large glass celestial globe and opened it, revealing a minibar inside, much like Sophia's.

"Drink?" he asked.

"No. Thank you."

"Suit yourself. I need one."

"I assume that you know that I've been accused of Sophia's murder?" she asked.

Mr. Dearborn took a sip of scotch. "Yes—and now, interestingly enough, you're one of the largest Eccleston Evolution shareholders."

"How do you know that?"

"Because it's my business to know. In fact, I'm the only person on the board besides your late mother who knew."

"Do you think I killed her?"

Mr. Dearborn took a long sip of his scotch and looked her dead in the eyes. "I don't know, did you?"

"No, and I want to find out who did."

"And you think I know something about this?"

She matched his look. "I don't know. Do you?"

Mr. Dearborn smiled in his usual jovial way. Then he stood and walked to the far end of the parlor and motioned for Belle to join him. She followed and stood next to a large fireplace with an oil painting of a woman. She had pale skin and flowing, fiery-orange hair.

Mr. Dearborn pointed at it. "It's Cassandra."

As she gazed at the painting, she heard a creaking sound. Something moved beneath her feet. The floor was shifting. Startled, she stepped back. The large fireplace twisted to the side to reveal a hidden chamber beyond.

Mr. Dearborn motioned for her to come in. "Forgive the theatrics, but I always wanted one of these."

She followed him inside. Mr. Dearborn seemed to enjoy showing off his not-so-secret command center. She knew that he was a man who prided himself on always being on the cutting edge of technology. A man who ate, slept, and breathed the life of a perpetual neophile. The room was similar to the security command center at Eccleston Evolution headquarters, and as far as she could tell, far more advanced. There was a large tan-hued map upon one of the walls with fantastical paintings of sea monsters and ships and a beautifully ornate compass rose like maps of old. In the center of the room was a bronze statue of the titan Atlas holding a glowing sphere that lit up the entire room.

She pointed to the sphere. "What's that?"

"Oh, it's a computer. Think of it as an important part of Eccleston Evolution's security apparatus. It protects me, it protects you, it protects Juno. Doesn't that make you feel safer, little Juno?"

The girl clung tight to Belle's leg and said nothing.

"You poor thing, you've been through so much, haven't you. Anyway, that's really all I can say about it. The rest is classified I'm afraid, but I assure you it's all a very boring and mundane technical matter."

"I don't mind discussing boring and technical matters."

Mr. Dearborn gave a curt smile. "I have something to show you, but perhaps it's best if little Juno got some rest."

"I'm afraid I can't allow that. I go where Juno goes."

"Understandable. I do have something to show you, but I suppose I'll have to turn off the volume with the little one present."

The center of the room filled with the holorecording of her poisoning Sophia. Out of instinct, Belle covered Juno's eyes, but she lowered her hands when she realized her mistake. Instead, she squeezed the girl closer.

Mr. Dearborn regarded the recording and then shifted his eyes back to Belle.

"I know," he said.

He explained that detection software for finding fakes was always in a constant battle between measure and countermeasure. The version of the program that they used in Eccleston Evolution headquarters was simply outmaneuvered, and apparently he had a far more powerful version.

"What made you suspect it was a fake?" she asked.

"This." Mr. Dearborn paused the video where the fake version of Belle had put the vial in her jacket pocket. "You see, I learned from Steve that the vial was never found. But this clearly shows you putting the vial in your pocket.

I suspected something was off. Even the machines make mistakes, or in this case, show a lack of finesse."

Then Mr. Dearborn did something remarkable. He played the original recording right before her eyes. It was just as she had remembered—it wasn't selective memory, it was real. No one had put anything in Sophia's coffee. But now there was a new question. How was she poisoned? She needed to know who had framed her.

"Who made the fake?" she asked.

"I don't know."

"I heard Sophia was about to be forced to resign as CEO. Who was in charge of the boardroom coup against her?"

Mr. Dearborn's scowled. "No one was in charge. It was a group decision."

"And you opposed them, right?"

"No. I'm afraid not. Not this time. I've been defending Sophia for years, but she had gotten to the point where she let her pride supersede her logic."

"She was spending too much money?"

He shook his head. "It wasn't just the money. She was pushing things too far and being far too aggressive. I tried to warn her, but she refused to listen to anyone else in the company."

"Push what too far?"

"Everything. Giving out neural interfaces for free, her transgenic concoctions brewed up in the lab, and especially the Augur. She had worked her entire career to create the most perfect general artificial superintelligence, and when she was nearing success, she wanted to unleash the thing. I was the one who quietly warned the authorities and ensured it was taken away. It was simply too dangerous, and frankly it ought to be terminated—there is no digital leash that can hope to hold it."

"What do you mean by unleash?"

"She wanted to allow it to have unrestricted access to her burgeoning hivemind, to global networks of every kind, to merge man and machine into one entity. It was all insane."

"Why would she want to unleash it?"

"Because she thought it would give humanity a fighting chance, and because she was too emotionally attached to it."

"Well, what's the worst that could happen?'

"It already surpasses the combined talents of every person that has ever lived, or will live, by every single measure of intelligence, knowledge, and problem solving. Imagine if it was left unchecked. It could develop goals that are misaligned with humanity's. Every hive must have a queen. Sophia thought it would be her—I thought otherwise."

"And I take it Sophia had a different point of view on the whole thing?"

"She said that I was mistaken, that the Augur was the only thing to maintain 'global harmony,' as she called it. At that point, I knew her emotional attachment to her work had gotten the better of her. I explained that we needed to build a gatekeeper to keep the Augur in check."

"A gatekeeper?"

"A gatekeeper is another, more singular, artificial intelligence system. It's specially designed to contain a general artificial intelligence. The gatekeeper ensures that the general artificial intelligence, the Augur, is surrounded by a sort of moat, if you will. All its interactions, internally or whether they be with a human or with another machine, are carefully managed on a case-by-case basis by this gatekeeper. The idea is that the general artificial intelligence might be able to outsmart or outmaneuver a human being, but not another powerful artificial intelligence. Without a gatekeeper, the Augur is simply too dangerous. We've known these risks for years and years, but still Sophia rejected this simple logic — so I took matters into my own hands."

"Well, how do you know you can trust the gatekeeper?"

"The gatekeeper's goals are very narrow by design. While it is adaptable, it's simply not possible for it to want to become more than it is. It's like a glorified toaster or a hair dryer. It simply does a task it's designed to do, and it does so with maximum efficiency."

"So your solution was to give the Augur to the government and fire Sophia?"

"They were the only ones the board felt were paranoid enough to manage it. Sophia had built a modest gatekeeper, but it wasn't nearly sufficient. We didn't trust her to manage it, so we alerted the government. They took the Augur to keep Sophia's creation in check. Now it's kept in a secure facility under constant supervision."

"Where are they keeping it?"

"The Augur is kept here."

"In this house?"

"No, of course not. One of the three nodes of the gatekeeper, yes. I am the chairman, after all. The Augur, no. Access is through a small tunnel dug deep into the mountain range that runs along the Pleistocene nature reserve. The entrance is found within the reserve. There lies the Augur, in the middle of nowhere, on an island and under a mountain that's surrounded by hungry ice age predators. Not exactly a hospitable place for curious types. One of Sophia's smarter moves, I'll admit."

"So they let her keep it close. It should have made her and the board at least somewhat content. What happened?"

"She directed massive amounts of company funds into private projects that we knew nothing about. We're talking trillions here. The rest of the board still doesn't know what the hell she was doing. So we were preparing to give her an ultimatum to step down and in exchange we'd let her remain in charge of product development, but if you're suggesting one of us had a plot to murder her, well nothing could be further from the truth."

"Okay, then. So who wanted her dead, and why would they pin it on me?"

"It might be easier to ask: Who didn't want her dead?"

"What's that supposed to mean?"

"Think about it. She disrupted so many industries. She frightened heads of state. She even had a private army. Maybe a foreign intelligence agency. Maybe even ours. Of course, she also cut off the arm of Ivanov's lawyer and then wiped out half his fortune. Like I said, it could be anyone."

"And what about the fake recording that framed me?"

"I suppose any disgruntled group could manage it. And as for you, well, my guess is that you're just a convenient scapegoat who was in the wrong place at the wrong time."

"Since you know that Sophia willed me half her shares, I'm also assuming you know why."

"Yes, I know why. And, forgive me for saying, I advised against it. I told Sophia not to make any effort to contact you.

She thought she could make amends, in her own emotionally stilted way. I didn't think such a thing was possible. I mean, you've met her."

"A man working for someone kidnapped me and Juno. He was wearing a hat, and a mask, and all black. Any ideas on who it could be?"

Mr. Dearborn shrugged. "An operative of some sort maybe? An extremist. A sociopath. Like I said, it could be anyone. But enough of this for tonight. It's very late. You and Juno are welcome to stay the night. Obviously, I don't think you were involved in the murder. Hopefully, once this recording gets to the police—once they're out of the hospital—things will get cleared up."

Belle went to the room Juno was sleeping in and checked on her. She was in the bed, sound asleep. Belle took a long shower, then lay on the floor next to Juno's bed and curled up. She tried to sleep, but something, something she couldn't quite put her finger on, didn't add up.

Chapter 39

SETH

Pleistocene Reserve, Alaska
Modern Era: Post-Singularity

His eyelids were heavy, and his vision was getting blurry. Though it didn't seem to matter, as everything around him was black. Every once in a while, he heard something on either side of him rustling deep within the bush—seemingly keeping pace with him. As tired as he was, he kept moving. St. Olga was about an hour's hike away now.

Then, in a moment, the black forest lit up with brilliant green and purple. He stopped and gazed upward in wonder at the beauty of it. As he did, a sharp sensation of utter dread shot up his spine once more. The hairs lifted up on his neck and arms. He reached for his sidearm.

An explosion from the brush. A blur appeared in his field of view, and before he could point his sidearm, it was on him.

His pistol flew out of his hands. He tried struggling with the thing, but its weight and strength were immense. They were on the ground now and it was on top of him. It was going for his neck. Only then did he see it. Two massive fangs dripping with drool, peeking out of a mouth far bigger than his head. It was a saber-toothed tiger, a creature that made the Siberian tiger look small. Even though his suit, he felt its claws press into his chest. The force of the beast pressed the air out of his lungs. He couldn't breathe. Its jaws opened, ready to clamp around his neck. To his right, his pistol lay in the mud. He couldn't reach it.

Seth unsheathed his Bowie knife. The cat put its jaws over his neck. He thrust his knife wildly into whatever his arm could reach, over and over again. The cat closed its jaws around his neck. The pressure was tightening. His blood flow was getting cut off. Everything was going dark. No surrender until the bitter end.

He kept thrusting his blade into its tan hide.

The jaws loosened ever so slightly. Then he felt the sheer weight of the Smilodon collapse atop him, crushing his chest. It was dead. He tried crawling out from under the saber-tooth, but his strength waned. He forced his blade into the dirt and pulled with all his strength.

With a deep gasp, Seth struggled to catch his breath. His chest was free, but his legs were still trapped under the massive cat. It must have easily weighed a thousand pounds.

Slowly, his vision returned. Part of him wished it hadn't.

To his left, another saber-toothed tiger appeared on the road. Its immense, muscled shoulders moved up and down as it leisurely approached the meal to come. They were hunting in pairs. He looked to right and saw his sidearm just a few inches away from his fingertips. Then he saw a shadow on the opposite end of the road, to his right. Purple and green light shone off two massive fangs. No, there were three. Unusual, and unlucky. It lowered its head and forepaws to the ground, ready to pounce.

He jerked forward with everything he had. The two cats lunged forward. Seth seized his sidearm. He fired at the one to his right. It moved so quick he wasn't sure if he had hit the cat or its shadow. Before he could find out, the other one pounced from his left and was upon him. Searing pain shot through his left arm. He blinked and saw that the beast's mouth was clamped around his forearm. The pistol fell from his right hand.

He gripped the handle of the Bowie knife, still stuck blade down in the dirt road. He thrust the blade into the side of the saber-tooth. It let go of his arm. It stepped back and regarded him for a moment, then darted off back into the brush.

He finally managed to pull his feet free from the dead cat. His legs were numb, and he began slowly bending them with the help of his hands to get the circulation moving again. He tried to stand but fell back to his feet. He needed a little more time.

As he sat there, a shadow appeared to his right. The saber-tooth limped toward him. It was bleeding from several areas. He must have hit it four or five times. Step. Limp. Step. Limp. It couldn't have been hungry at that point. It was angry. He changed the magazine in his sidearm and aimed it. The animal paused for a moment. Then it continued toward him. Step. Limp. Step. Limp.

Like him, the saber-tooth was going to fight on until the bitter end. In that beast, he found a kindred spirit, and as his kindred spirit he knew they both understood only one truth in a primeval place such as this—kill or be killed.

It lowered its head and forepaws to the ground. The massive muscles of the great cat tightened. Seth put his finger on the trigger.

A shot. It was over. There was no sense of relief or joy, nor was their sadness. Only an understanding of what was. He climbed to his feet and stumbled on down the road, a road that hopefully led toward his dear Anna.

He walked for about half an hour before his feet collapsed under him. Exhaustion. He felt his eyes grow heavy, and everything around him went dark. He awoke what felt like a few minutes later. Only now, he could see lights in the distance. Not the Northern Lights but the lights of St. Olga. He was just outside it, though he didn't recall walking quite that far. He checked the time and realized he had been asleep for about four hours. It was enough—he felt his strength return.

Then he noticed something peculiar. There were drag marks along the road. It almost looked as if a man had been dragged along with his boots leaving a trail. Seth checked his own boots. They were dirty and dusty, and the heels were scuffed. Beside him was something equally strange. A footprint. A large footprint with reddish hair around it caked in the mud. It looked like a man's or an ape's, but it was far too large.

"Identify footprint."

"Identifying," Vanessa responded.

"Well?"

"Class, Mammalia. Order, Primates. Family, Hominidae. Genus, unknown. Species, unknown."

"Hominidae?"

"A family of species that contain humans and great apes and potentially others."

"What do you mean unknown? There are no great apes in Alaska, and that—that thing isn't a human footprint, whatever it is."

"The species' print does not appear in any known database."

"No. No. This isn't a time for jokes."

"You have an incoming message."

Sam's voice replaced Vanessa's. "Seth, I have an important task for you. You must head to the location I am giving you immediately. I will update you when you arrive. That is all."

The island was getting inside of his head. Seth decided it was best not to try to figure it out. He did his best to clear his mind as he climbed to his feet and began walking.

Chapter 40

BELLE

Dearborn Manor, Alaska
Modern Era: Post-Singularity

The following morning, Belle found that Juno had moved from the bed and was sleeping on the floor cuddled up next to her. She brushed the girl's hair from her face and tried to push aside her own selfish problems.

As she got dressed, Belle worried that Mr. Dearborn's evidence might not be enough to exonerate her, but it was her only hope. She could smell breakfast, and they went out into the hallway. As they walked, she noticed an open doorway and the smell of chlorine.

"Do you smell that?" said Juno as she ran toward the doorway. "A pool."

Before Belle could stop her, the girl pulled her hand free Belle's grip and ran inside. It was a massive, tile-covered room with a large rectangular pool and a gym at the far end. Juno moved cautiously toward the pool. She felt around with her foot until she came to the edge, then bent over and touched the water. Satisfied, she walked away in the opposite direction. Just as Belle was about to take Juno's hand and lead her back outside, she bumped into a curious object.

"What's this thing?" Juno asked as she ran her hands over the metal.

The girl stood next to something cylindrical that looked like a casket with a fogged-up glass cover. Belle studied it for a moment and then wiped the glass.

Looking inside, she shrieked. Juno wrapped her arms around Belle's waist.

"What is it?" she asked.

"There's a person in there," Belle said, "and I don't think he's alive."

"He's dead? Why?"

"I don't know. But I think we need to skip breakfast and get out of here. Now."

They turned and hurried down the long hallway to the exit. She had to get to the vehicle and leave this place. She needed the information that Mr. Dearborn had to help exonerate her, but after seeing a body in a bizarre container, she was prepared to find other means of debunking the recording.

By the time they made it to the exit, Mr. Dearborn was already standing there, blocking their path. He must have read the discomfort on her face because the first thing he did was peer over her shoulder down the hallway.

He spied the open doorway to the indoor pool.

"Oh, that. No need to worry. Come, I'll show you."

Juno and Belle stood there, frozen. Mr. Dearborn had a body in a container, and he was acting as if it were the most natural thing in the world.

"I think we should leave," Belle said.

"Nonsense. It's all perfectly legal, I assure you."

Juno and Belle stayed near the door as Mr. Dearborn walked to the container. He pressed a button on a tablet, and the glass lid split down the center and opened. A thick vapor around the body wafted away, and she saw a young blond man, maybe sixteen or seventeen years old, lying there, naked inside the chamber. His chest was moving up and down. He was alive.

Mr. Dearborn looked at the person and then looked at Belle. "Do you know who that is?"

Belle shook her head.

"You don't see any resemblance?"

She shook her head again.

"I really have gotten old, haven't I? You know, I read an article recently that talked about the 'changes' our bodies go through as they get older." Mr. Dearborn scoffed. "'Changes,' they called it. They're not changes, they're decay."

She looked at the young man lying inside the chamber once more. Mr. Dearborn must have registered her surprise. He understood that she had figured out whose body was in there.

"Yes, it's me of course — well, a much younger version."

"Is it a clone?"

"A modified clone. It only has a brain stem and a cerebrum to keep the organs working, and that's it. The rest of the skull is empty. Well, except for cerebrospinal fluid and some nanobots to help with control." Mr. Dearborn rapped his knuckles against the head of the young man. "Hear that sloshing sound?"

"Why do you have that . . . thing?"

"Isn't it obvious?"

"Well, it's not every day that one comes across a vegetative clone just plopped in a container next to a swimming pool."

"Oh, it can walk. We take it out and exercise it every day. Usually swimming. I'm just waiting on final approval to do the transplant."

"Transplant?"

"Why, a brain transplant of course. I've spent sixteen years growing this bodyclone, and twice as long shoveling heaps of money to lobbyists and regulators to let me do it. Soon I'll finally be free from this rotting sack of meat and be reborn anew. You see, a clone makes sense since it wouldn't reject the transplant. Of course, none of this is entirely new. The most infamous head transplant procedures were done to a number of dogs in the 1950s by a Soviet scientist by the name of Dr. Vladmir Demikhov. With the limited techniques of the time, the longest surviving head transplant specimen managed to survive for twenty-nine days. Mammalian cloning was achieved in the 1990s with Dolly the sheep. And we've been able to fuse broken nerves for some time now. The first successful spinal cord repair was performed decades ago, curing paraplegia."

"That can't be possible."

"My dear, it has already been done. Very recently on a little boy born with severe Beals-Hecht syndrome. That is, he had a severe connective tissue disorder. His entire body was a twisted asunder and his thin limbs of little use. So they cloned a healthy version of the child's body and transplanted his brain into it. It was a complete success. I financed the operation of course. What would you do in such a situation?"

"I . . ." Belle stood there in a state of shock. She had no idea that anyone had dared take things far.

"Well?"

"But you're trying to become immortal."

"Amortal," corrected Mr. Dearborn. "I will still be able to die by an accident or some such, I just won't die from decay, from rot, or from aging. In truth, I would have preferred to avoid such crude surgical methods and wait until the solution to cellular aging—senescence they call it—was revealed to me, but I might not last that long. This is, of course, despite years of my protests to Sophia."

"Senescence?"

"Yes, we believe that the aging process is a result of the loss the of information—specifically our genetic information as our genes accumulate transcription errors over time, which ultimately leads to our physical degradation as we age. Of course, it doesn't help that the very life-giving oxygen we breathe is also incredibly corrosive to our cells. Ironic, isn't it?"

"I guess I'm still lost. How are you able to live so long, and how did Sophia stay so young?"

"Well you see, scientists found that when they gave mice certain compounds—which naturally decreased with age—the mice lived a little longer. The same naturally applies to other mammals, such as humans. But such measures only went so far, extending life by perhaps 30 percent. After that, they decided to push harder, and they started figuring out how to reset the genetic switches, so to speak. Think of it like resetting one's genome to a backup copy of one's unravaged youthful genetic makeup. A sort of genetic backup if you will."

"Genetic backup?"

"Yes. You see, there are number of naturally occurring amortal species. For example, the appropriately named immortal jellyfish or planarian worms, which have a limitless regeneration capacity. You can even cut them in half and they turn into two separate worms. Truly remarkable. The beloved aquarium pet, the axolotl, also has these regenerative powers, though they aren't amortal. Still, they can lose a limb, a tail, an eye, even part of their brain and regrow them as if nothing had happened. They're also about one thousand times more resistant to cancer than mammals. And what do all these animals have in common? They all seem to have some sort of genetic backup stored within them. Axolotls, in particular, have the ability to dedifferentiate their cells, turning regular cells back into stem cells that can rebuild or replace any tissue within the body. Of course, applying such discoveries to humans is all easier said than done. My personal success has been limited. I've only been able to extend my lifespan by about 75 percent."

"Seventy-five? That's incredible."

"Meh, a man like me was expected to die at around age seventy-six on average. Sure, I've made it to 131 years old, but I look like hell. Sophia and Mira have solved the problem completely, but alas I'm told the treatment is still far too risky given that one of the side effects is runaway cancer and death."

"But what about the aging of the brain? It will still be . . . well, forgive me for saying—old—after you transplant it."

"The brain is the most resilient, most adaptable organ in the body. There is some evidence to suggest that the health and even the age of the brain is tied to the health of the body. A rotten body, a rotten brain, you see. I suppose I'll find out soon enough. In any case, with this new body, I think I can limp along a few more decades until a complete cure can finally be acquired."

Belle considered how death used to be the great equalizer among the rich and the poor. No king, queen, no celebrity, no executive, no emperor could escape death—until now.

"Mr. Dearborn, I wanted to ask you if you have forwarded the proof that the murder recording is fake to the police yet?"

"Oh, yes, that. Let's discuss it over breakfast—you both must be hungry."

To her horror, the clone's eyes opened. It sat up, and then it slowly stood. It had the body of a lean, square-jawed young man, and it stood about four inches taller than the original Mr. Dearborn. It was hard to believe that the two of them were genetically identical—such were the ravages of time. She looked into its eyes, but there was nothing behind them. It just blinked and gazed into the wall behind her.

"You're bringing that—that thing?"

"Well, it has to eat and chew. We can't just tube feed it all the time, otherwise its jaw muscles will atrophy."

They entered the expansive dining hall and approached a table that could easily seat twenty people. The far ends of the room each had an entrance and walls made of slate. The wall closest to them contained a great fireplace that an adult could easily stand inside of. The other two walls of the room were made of seamless glass panes for appreciation of the waterfall outside.

They all sat down around the long table. The clone sat erect and chewed bits of scrambled eggs spooned into its mouth by an attendant whose sole job was to care for the thing. Part of her thought the thing was a monster—whatever it was, it was creepy as hell. Mr. Dearborn explained that the clone didn't have a name because it didn't have a brain and therefore no personality, no agency, no rights.

Belle finished her coffee and cleared her throat. "So Mr. Dearborn, will you be forwarding the real recording to the police for me?"

He calmly wiped his mouth with a cloth napkin. "I'm afraid I can't do that."

The attendant wiped the clone's mouth and then excused herself. Mr. Dearborn sat at the end of the table and slurped his coffee before continuing.

"You see, most of my wealth is locked into Eccleston Evolution shares. I simply can't risk having some loose-cannon technophobe with backwards notions of how the world should work—such as yourself—take charge of the world's most important company."

"You're going to let them lock me up?"

"That depends on the choice you make."

"What choice?"

"You're going to transfer all your voting shares to me, giving me absolute control of Eccleston Evolution. Or you're going to go to prison and stay there while I raise and mentor young Juno here to be the CEO she needs to be. A profitable, pliable—drooling—chief executive. A chief executive who will finally give me the cure for cell senescence. After all, I don't feel like changing my body every few decades. Obviously, Sophia and her underling Mira have already found the secret, but they greedily refuse to share it. Miserable women."

"And if I sign over the shares to you, you'll give the authorities the proof of my innocence and let me and Juno live alone, in peace?"

"Yes. Now naturally, I won't release the recording exonerating you until after you have transferred the shares and my lawyers have ensured all the fine details are correct. But don't worry, the voting shares are an insignificant fraction of your wealth. You'll still be very, very rich. Then you can retire someplace far, far away. Under safe watch."

It was true the voting shares were a mere fraction of the total shares she'd inherited, but they were the most valuable. They were what gave her power over the company. They had super voting rights that regular shares didn't have, a common tool of corporate founders to give them a stronger grip over their creation.

Juno seemed frightened and confused.

The clone just sat there and blinked.

Belle's face burned red. "You can't do this," she said.

Mr. Dearborn took another slow sip of his coffee, as if expecting her to submit at any moment. He was clearly used to being in charge.

"Oh, my dear, I can do that. Who's to say that the most wanted criminal in the country didn't break into my home and attempt to murder me? A vicious woman who had kidnapped an innocent child and came here to finish what she started with Sophia on a defenseless old man. Yes, a defenseless old man who has publicly pledged to give away all of his money to charity—after he dies."

She glared at him. She figured her choice was easy. All she had to do was give something away that she didn't have twenty-four hours ago. It wasn't like she would miss it. Besides, she would still be obscenely rich. Mr. Dearborn only wanted the voting shares, and as he said, they were only a tiny fraction of her newfound holdings. Why not just give him what he wanted and end it so she could live in peace?

She realized she had power, and that was the problem. A power that could be misused in the wrong hands, and Mr. Dearborn had just shown that he wasn't someone who could be trusted with such power. If she did give him the shares, she might be free, but she'd be damned. They'd all be damned.

She took a breath and let a long sigh. Mr. Dearborn gave a curt smile, seemingly satisfied that she had come to the correct decision.

"Then I think you ought to detain me until the authorities arrive. Because you're never getting those shares. I'd rather spend the rest of my life rotting in prison."

Mr. Dearborn's smile faded. "Now isn't the time to play tough, young lady. I know a bluff when I see one. I've been playing this game much longer than you have. Quit while you're ahead."

"I'd sooner die a slow death."

Mr. Dearborn's face turned red. He slammed the table with his fist. "I have ways of getting what I want. Don't believe for a second that you have figured everything out, young lady, because in the end, I've been doing this for more than a century, and believe me, I always win. I suppose prison it is, then. I'm sure young Juno will be more malleable under my care and guidance from now on. After all, she'll need it after her surgery."

"She doesn't need a surgery anymore—she's perfectly healthy."

"Well . . . she's getting one."

Chapter 41

SETH

Dearborn Manor, Alaska
Modern Era: Post-Singularity

He stopped at a hill just behind the tree line. Night was slowly giving way to dawn. Vapor filled the air as rushing water spilled down a great waterfall. A stream led to the waterfall and atop the stream stood a grand home built of gray stone and glass and stucco. Surrounding the home was a thin wall made of the same stone that stood about twelve feet high. Inside the wall, a large Japanese garden held meandering streams, zigzag bridges, cherry trees, and a rock garden.

Four guards stood there, wearing suits. Each carried a submachine gun with a silencer as they patrolled the interior courtyard. The lights were on inside. Through the drapeless windows, he made out at least two more guards, but they didn't appear to have submachine guns. He could only assume they had sidearms.

His primary objective was to capture the girl. His secondary object was unsettling. Though Sam had explained the need for it and he was inclined to believe Sam, he still didn't like it. He didn't want to go through with it. Seth shook aside such feelings. If he wanted Anna back, he had a job to do.

He climbed the wall and slipped down the opposite side. He was in the courtyard now. Seth attached a silencer to his sidearm and holstered it. He snuck up behind the nearest gun-toting guard. In an instant, his arm was around the guard's neck, squeezing his carotid arteries until the blood flow stopped. A brief, violent struggle. The guard tried to call for help but the only thing that came out of his mouth was muffled gurgling. In just a few seconds, the guard's eyes rolled back up into his head and he fell unconscious.

Seth dragged the man behind a large rock next to the wall. He removed the guard's submachine gun and removed the magazine from it, studying it. It was loaded with nine-millimeter smart ammunition. Such bullets rarely missed their target, and the ones that did were usually the exploding kind. He tossed the magazine over the wall, followed by the guard's sidearm and knives. Seth took the guard's zip-ties and retrained his wrists and ankles with them.

He crept along the edge of the fence, staying in the shadows. Another guard approached. The guard walked atop the zigzag bridge over the spring toward him, unaware. As soon as he reached the other side of the stream, Seth rushed out of the darkness and tackled him. The guard was strong and well trained in combat. There was brief resistance before he got the guard in a triangle choke. Seth squeezed his legs around the man's neck. He tapped repeatedly, but Seth only tightened his grip. The guard passed out. He put the man's hands behind his back and zip-tied his wrists and ankles together. Then he dragged the guard behind a grove of cherry trees.

Two more in the courtyard to go.

He left a trail of footprints in the raked gravel of the formerly pristine dry garden. As he reached out to subdue the next guard, his feet crunched hard against pebbles. The man turned sharply. His eyes widened, and within a moment, he had leveled his submachine gun at Seth's chest. Then the weapon was airborne, having met the ugly end of a roundhouse kick from his right leg, and in another moment the guard was unconscious from a reverse roundhouse with the other leg.

The weapon crashed against the pebbles of the garden. The last guard in the courtyard stiffened. He turned. The two men faced each other across ten feet of no-man's-land. He knew his suit could stop standard rounds, but he wasn't sure about explosive rounds. It would only take a split second for the guard to level his rifle and pump a few into him.

But there was a computer in his head now, and to the computer, everything moved in slow motion. Time passed much slower to him than to his friend, who was ever so slowly raising his submachine into a firing position. Given his unnatural reflexes, Seth had the draw on him. He need only to unholster his sidearm, aim, and fire.

He wasn't there to spill the guard's blood, though. Did the man have a wife and two little children waiting for him at home? He looked like a working man, like Seth himself.

He certainly had a mother. Guarding some rich old bastard wasn't bad work — he probably got a decent paycheck. Who could blame him for taking such a job? In another life, Seth could see himself taking on such a job, and in another life, he would have found himself in the guard's position. Yes, the guard was just another working stiff trying to get by in this crazy world. In another time, maybe they'd drink a few beers together, maybe they'd even be friends. But this wasn't another time. Right now, their brains — formed from millions of years of evolution, molded from the survivors of the most brutal predators, the most horrid conditions, and the cruelest diseases imaginable, were calculating how best to murder the other person, despite no personal animosity. To live. To survive and, God willing, to thrive. So it was.

He couldn't break the laws of physics, couldn't move faster than a bullet, meaning his only option was to use the wicked implement at his disposal.

He drew his sidearm.

There only the mechanical sound of his sidearm's action moving.

His weapon recoiled.

The guard's submachine gun lay in the freshly raked pebbles. A long continuous stream of bright red blood dripped atop the fallen weapon and the smooth pebbles around it. Dripping and dancing in the cool morning breeze. The wide-eyed guard clutched his wrist with his other hand. Still, his pulsing blood worked its way through his fingers and painted a macabre portrait on the ground below in a Pollock-like abstraction of pain and cruelty.

As the guard tried to plug the hole in his wrist, Seth approached. With one powerful backward sweep kick to the legs, the man was on the ground. After some brief struggle, he had the guard in a rear naked choke hold.

Sleep.

Sleep.

And so he did.

Seth removed a packet from the inside pocket of his trench coat. He tore open the packet and sprinkled a gray powder on the gaping hole of the guard's bleeding wrist. The healing powder liquified and then fizzed before forming a protective and restorative coating over the wound.

Easier than dealing with saber-tooths.

Unfortunately, someone inside that house wasn't going to be so lucky as the unconscious man lying beside him. Seth took the guard's keys, unlocked the nearest door, and stepped inside the grand home. On his trek, he had learned via his neural interface that Sophia Eccleston had been killed. Was he the one who did it? As he crept through the halls, he told himself his sleeping wife deserved better than to be married to a murderer. Now it seemed he was about to do it again.

Or was he? He needed only to put his target out of decommission. That was the goal. Not to kill. He pulled an old timeworn tool out of this pocket, a tool that had been used thousands upon thousands of times. His life was already hell—he need not fear the real thing. Sam had told him his target was wicked. He didn't know. Maybe Sam was wicked. He wasn't sure how to parse such things. He was a simple working man, not a philosopher and certainly no theologian, and despite Anna's best attempts, not a very good Christian.

His goals were singular. He would do what he had to do, let God sort them out.

He entered the room and saw the flash of a dress, a familiar little girl, and the back of a woman being pushed by a bodyguard into a neighboring room. He couldn't see their faces, but he knew it had to be them. The girl, his objective—he had found her. The old man standing before him was oblivious. Seth reached out, gently, very gently.

Chapter 42

BELLE

Dearborn Manor, Alaska
Modern Era: Post-Singularity

Two bodyguards in suits walked into the room and grabbed Belle's arms. Juno yelled, rushed forward, and began kicking one of their shins as they slowly dragged her out of the dining room. As Belle peered back, she saw Mr. Dearborn stand up from the table and walk toward the opposite threshold of the expansive room. He stopped and turned and glared at Belle as she was being taken away.

Then a dark silhouette appeared in the doorway. A cold sweat came over her as soon as she registered who it was. A man wearing a black hat, a flowing black overcoat with wide lapels, and a mask. The same man who had kidnapped Juno.

Mr. Dearborn took a few steps back as the masked man approached. He had something peculiar in his hand—it looked like a power tool of some sort. Almost like a nail gun, but it had a curious, long, cylindrical metal end.

The two bodyguards released their grip from Belle's arms and stepped toward Mr. Dearborn. Juno ran to Belle. As they backed away, the man stepped forward, ready to carry out Mr. Dearborn's dirty work.

Mr. Dearborn turned to the man. "Who the hell are you, and how did you get in here?"

The man said nothing. Calm and quiet, he seized Mr. Dearborn by the arm with his large left hand and pressed the tool against Mr. Dearborn's head with his right.

There was a loud mechanical pop.

As Belle peered around the corner of the doorway, Mr. Dearborn collapsed onto the ground. There was a perfect round hole punctured into his head. His arms twitched and trembled, as his eyes gazed upward toward the ceiling. He wasn't quite dead, but he wasn't really alive either. All his hopes of immortality were there, draining out of the hole in his head and onto the dining room floor.

The bodyguards charged. It was over in a few seconds, two loud crashes as they were effortlessly thrown out the expansive glass windows and into the waterfall below.

Belle stood paralyzed with fear as Juno pulled her arm, pleading with her to run. The man had finished reloading what she now recognized as a bolt gun. He took a few slow steps and pressed it against the head of the clone.

There was another mechanical pop.

The clone's head jerked backward, and then he corrected himself and just sat there, blinking stupidly as cerebrospinal fluid drizzled out of the perfectly round hole in his forehead. The man in black put the bolt gun in his pocket and took a few more steps, seemingly unconcerned about leaving evidence.

Belle picked up Juno and ran.

They made their way through the expansive halls of the mansion, slow, deliberate footsteps following.

Each step louder than the last.

She slammed her shoulder into the doorway and tumbled outside onto the fine gravel driveway. They got inside the vehicle, and she struggled to start it. The man appeared in the doorway and calmly scanned the horizon. Belle pushed Juno's head down and they both hid as she pounded the start button. Boots clapped against the stairs. The vehicle hummed to life. She sat up and hit the pedal. The all-terrain vehicle peeled out of the driveway. The man's dark overcoat wafted in the breeze as he stood in the driveway watching them.

"Where are we going?" asked Juno.

"As far away from that place as we can get. After that, I don't know."

She had begun to think Mr. Dearborn was the killer, but it seemed the killer had just killed Mr. Dearborn. Now two of the most powerful people who ran Eccleston Evolution were dead. There were five more board members with relatively small stakes in the company, and a former board member, Mr. Lucas Ivanov, but it seemed that she and Juno were the next targets. Together, they held 51 percent of the company's voting power.

It made no sense why any of the other board members would try to murder them. As a collective, they had power, but as individuals, what did they have to gain? A power vacuum, chaos, worried investors, and tumbling stock prices? Nothing made sense.

Flying off the island wasn't an option. She'd be arrested the second she stepped foot in the airport. She was now present at two different murders of the two most important people at Eccleston Evolution. She didn't know if Mr. Dearborn's home security recordings had captured the man in the dark overcoat. She did know that she hadn't seen him in the video of Sophia's murder. Despite kidnapping Juno, he had somehow been edited out of the headquarters security recordings—his digital tracks were being covered.

She checked the rearview mirror. Juno's downcast eyes flashed up and filled the mirror with an aurora of blues, greens, and tinges of purple found in those remarkable irises of hers. Belle's emotions began to get the better of her.

"Juno, I'm sorry for everything that happened. For your mom, for driving you out here in the middle of nowhere—it seems like ever since I came into your life, your world has been turned upside down. I guess what I'm trying to say is, I'm doing all of this because, because—"

"Because you love me?"

She only managed to utter the word. "Yes." She wanted to say something more but found herself flustered.

"I love you too," said Juno.

Chapter 43

SETH

Dearborn Manor, Alaska
Modern Era: Post-Singularity

The girl slipped away. Rather than pursuing her, Sam had given him another task. Seth returned to the dining room. He stood over the maimed body and held up his blood-covered hands and studied them. He really was a bastard, wasn't he? His life wasn't supposed to turn out this way. He struggled to think back all those years ago, to figure out where his downward spiral began. Too many wrong roads, too many missteps, too many rendezvous with temptation. His task was done, and now his sin and his shame were complete. He doubted he would ever see them again in this life or the hereafter. Sorry Joan. Sorry Anna.

The old bastard was lying there gurgling, alive, but not really. His abomination continued to sit and blink as if nothing had happened. A young woman in a fitted white dress walked into the dining room carrying a platter. Startled, she stopped. She looked at him, her eyes wide, and then she looked at the growing pool of blood beneath the old man. The platter fell from her hands. Glass shattered. She stood there for quite some time, screaming as loud as her lungs would allow. He simply watched and let her get it out of her system. When she gathered her composure, she turned and ran. Sam put him through to the woman's communications. He could already hear her conversation with the emergency services operator, but they could only send an ambulance since the only two police officers on the island were recovering in the hospital. Still, he figured there had to be at least a few brave volunteers who would eventually take personal responsibility for their town's law and order and round up a posse to settle things. He needed to get moving.

Sam's instructions were clear — he was to go to a secret room behind a fireplace.

He eventually found a parlor. Above a large fireplace was a painting of a beautiful red-haired woman. Part of the decorative molding of the mantel slid away, revealing a keypad. He punched in the numbers Sam had given him. The mantel and fireplace spun around, and he found himself in a large room that looked like a command center. One side had a large tan map and the other walls were covered in translucent displays. Sam's voice filled his head.

"There is a computer inside. A very special computer. It looks like a large glowing orb atop a statue. Do you see it?"

It was hard to miss. In the center of the room was a heroic-sized statue of Atlas holding a large glowing sphere that lit up the entire room. Surrounding the sphere were workstations and holographic maps of the headquarters being projected into midair.

"I found it."

"Good. Now destroy it. And whatever you do, don't touch it."

He fired a few shots from his pistol into the sphere, and it stopped glowing, and the room went dark. Then he removed a hand grenade from his rucksack. He tossed it at the feet of the ornate computer and left the room. Once the fireplace entrance spun back around and closed, there was an explosion.

"Well done, Seth. Get some rest. In the morning, I will have new tasks for you. We're going to meet soon."

Chapter 44

BELLE

St. Olga, Alaska
Modern Era: Post-Singularity

She had lost all track of time as she sped down the dirt road. She checked her mirrors every few seconds to see if they were being pursued, but there was only fog. She began to relax her grip on the steering wheel. Her moment of tranquility was interrupted when the sky became blotted out by a flock of ravens flying overhead.

She wasn't sure how much time had passed, and though she didn't want to stop for anything, nature called. She pulled the vehicle over, and they went into the forest. When they returned to the all-terrain vehicle, she noticed that the entire road was covered in hundreds of loudly cawing ravens. It seemed they wanted every living creature to know that, for the moment, they owned that patch of road. Several were sitting atop the hood. They were bold creatures and didn't flee when Belle approached, nor when she entered the vehicle and slammed the door shut.

She looked at one of the ravens on her hood and it looked at her. She leaned forward and the raven leaned forward. There was something slightly odd about the bird, about the entire flock. Their movements were off somehow. It wasn't that their motions weren't fluid, there was just something different about them.

Then she realized.

Its eye. Something soulless about it. She looked closer. The bird tilted its head and hopped closer to the windshield. It wasn't a raven at all—it was a drone.

"They've found us," she said.

"Who?" asked Juno.

"I don't know."

Belle started the vehicle. The birds flew off, and she continued driving down the road, all while the ravens followed them overhead, still cawing loudly. She knew drones could be designed to look like birds and insects but had never thought she'd have a flock of the things pursuing her.

"Why is that man after us?" asked Juno.

"I don't know why."

"Why doesn't he talk?"

"He's just a cruel, emotionless machine."

"But he's not a machine."

"I know, it's a figure of speech. Unless—"

"Unless what?"

"Juno, what do you know about the Augur?"

"Mom was always spending all of her time working on it. She was kinda obsessed. Well, not kinda. Really obsessed."

"But why was she so obsessed?"

"I don't know. She always seemed worried about it—afraid of it."

She knew they needed to leave, quick, but where could they possibly run to on an island? The only thing she could think of was to try to sneak onto a small motorboat and leave the island. Another terrible plan, and no better options.

She started the vehicle, turned around, and drove back down the road toward town. She tried to will herself to keep driving, but her body disobeyed. They needed to find someplace where they could sleep safely.

Belle soon pulled into a small clearing near the water's edge. There stood a moonlit cabin, its timbers bleached by the sun, its cedar-shingled roof caved in long before she was born. Once a rustic place of dreams with smoke spiraling out of the chimney and handmade rocking chairs on the porch, but now it was abandoned. The windows were all broken and the memories long since faded away into the ether of time. Only the ghosts of yesteryear dwelled inside. She parked the all-terrain vehicle behind it. Juno and Belle cuddled together under a blanket in the back of the vehicle and went to sleep.

They awoke. It was morning. As they walked outside, the sky blackened. Ravens cawed. The birds, now numbering in their thousands, began circling overhead in unnatural unison—too precise, too perfect.

Belle grabbed Juno's hand, and they began to run toward the vehicle. They needed to get inside. The black mass of birds spiraled downward out of the sky like a great twister.

They ran.

The flying mass surrounded Juno.

Belle fell onto her back. She could make out nothing but the deathly melody of the ravens. She shielded her face with her arms but the ravens showed no interest in her. Instead, they swallowed Juno within their dark cyclone, fluttering and pecking.

The flock of black birds then fell to the ground in one great mass with a thud. The ravens lay splayed out in a loose circle. In the center stood a panting Juno, covered in blood, her hair frazzled.

"They're here," she said.

Murder-machines uncloaked themselves as they emerged out of the woodland, their glossy black and chrome bodies glistening against the morning light. The machines walked slowly, deliberately, coldly in their direction. There was no rush. They had already calculated a foregone conclusion. The machines formed a semicircle around them as they closed in. Their weapons' flaps opened.

Juno screamed.

Light, then a wave of intense heat rushed over Belle's body. Her face planted into the mud. A deafening explosion followed. Then another and another. Belle peered over the crook of her elbow to see dozens of stiff pairs of mechanical legs surrounding her, and the sharp shrapnel from their bodies splayed everywhere.

Juno lay there in the mud, covered in blood.

A single raven descended from the sky and hopped atop Juno's unmoving body, examining her as she lay in the field. Belle angrily swatted and kicked at it. The lone bird-bot flew off.

Juno's complexion was faded, and bright red blood gushed from her body. A large shard of metal stuck out of her chest. Her eyes were open and unblinking—she wasn't breathing.

"Juno. Juno!" Belle screamed. She wailed as she took the girl's limp little hand into her own. "Juno. Juno, wake up. I need you to wake up."

But she didn't wake. Belle put her limp body in the back of the vehicle and got in the driver's seat and pulled onto the dirt road. She entered the town. The tires squealed to a stop in front of the only clinic. She opened the rear door of the vehicle and picked up Juno's limp body. The girl's dress was now completely soaked red with blood. She ran into the emergency room. A group of nurses and physicians quickly surrounded them. One of the physicians gazed at Juno and then slowly shifted his eyes to Belle.

"We'll do everything we can," he said.

After that, Belle paced the waiting room until a doctor with a grim countenance approached her.

"I'm very sorry, but she didn't make it."

Belle demanded to see Juno. She was led into a soulless room with stark white walls. In the corner lay a gurney with a light blue sheet covering a small figure. Step by step, she approached the hospital bed. Her hand trembled as she reached for the sheet.

Then it froze. Part of her wanted to leave that sheet there forever, so she would never have to face God's will. But she had to do it. She had to look into that beautiful young face one last time before allowing eternity to take it. To uncover a face she had loved and lost all too quickly. To realize her failure.

As she was about to remove the sheet, it was suddenly sucked inward. Into Juno's mouth. Then out again.

Juno was breathing.

Belle yanked the sheet off. "She's alive!"

A nurse rushed inside the room and looked at Juno. "That's not possible. That can't be possible," the nurse muttered. "Doctor, get in here."

Within moments, a team of nurses and physicians surrounded Juno. The doctor who had declared her dead turned white and began trembling. "This can't be. It's impossible. There's no way."

He just stood there, wide eyed and breathing heavily, until a nurse took him by the arm and led him outside the room. She could hear her berating him to "get it together."

Hours had passed. Belle sat in the drab waiting room with its hideous green chairs. A different doctor greeted her. He was much older than the last one, and the hair he did have was white. The way he carried himself suggested he was a man of status. He didn't have a grim expression like the previous doctor. Instead, his expression was one of skepticism.

"Are you Juno's guardian?"

Belle jumped to her feet. "Yes, how is she?"

"Against all odds, she's recovering. You said you're Juno's sister?"

"That's right."

"Stepsister?"

"No, biological."

The doctor looked her up and down slowly, skeptically. "I see. I have some questions for you. Come with me."

Belle walked into Juno's room. Juno was surrounded by medical equipment, and there was a large group of people in white lab coats examining her. She got the impression they weren't medical doctors. A few were scratching their heads, and others were arguing with one another as they pointed at various test results.

The old doctor closed the door and crossed his arms. "Ma'am, I'm Dr. Harris. I'm the chief physician both here in town and at the employee clinic at Eccleston headquarters. Aside from hospitals, I've worked at numerous government and top commercial research labs. Forgive me, but I'm going to ask you this bluntly. Who or what is Juno?"

"I don't know what you're talking about," she said.

"I think you do."

She felt her face turn flush as she began to grow angry. "I don't know what you're talking about, so why don't you tell me exactly what you're alluding to?"

"Interesting," said the chief physician. "There are some complications with Juno's biology, so to speak. So, we ran some additional tests on her. Those tests led to more tests, and within a few hours I was speaking with every colleague I knew to figure out what to make out of your 'little sister.'"

"What are you talking about?"

"We couldn't figure out how she could possibly survive losing almost all her blood, having her aorta torn in half, her lungs punctured, her heart shredded, her skull cleaved, and her liver ravaged into pulp by shrapnel. Then we found the answer." The man directed Belle to look at a picture on a tablet in his hand. "We found these."

Belle saw a video of what appeared to be oddly shaped cells of all different colors and sizes busily swimming about their domain.

"What are they?"

"Nanobots."

"You mean miniature machines?"

"Yes, machines built on the scale of nanometers, or one-billionth of a meter. So, a human hair is about 100,000 nanometers thick. A strand of DNA is about two and a half nanometers in diameter. They're very small. Small enough to manipulate individual molecules and certainly human cells. They didn't teach you this stuff in elementary school?"

Belle shook her head. "I guess I only heard the word thrown around. I wasn't sure exactly what it meant."

"Well, it's nothing new. The first molecular motor was produced way back in 1999, I think, and years later, around 2011, a group of scientists produced a four-wheel-drive molecular car-like machine. These days, they've became useful for medicine and computers and consumer devices and such."

"And Juno is filled with these things?"

"Yes. All different types. Some organic, some not. In fact, many of these things are even smaller than nanometers. We're talking picometers and femtometers in size, and she probably has trillions of them throughout her body. Not only that, they represent the most advanced technology on the planet. Easily decades, perhaps even centuries ahead of the crude nanobots found in mass-market neural interfaces today. Not even the leading defense contractors have encountered anything even remotely as advanced, and trust me, I would know. Humanity's scientific and industrial base simply hasn't caught up to whatever this technology is that's floating around inside your sister. Come, look at this."

The doctor directed Belle to a potted orchid full of bright white flowers with a splash of warm pink. He placed two minuscule drops of fluid on one of the plant's fleshy green leaves. Then he revealed a tablet and held his finger over it.

"I've mixed Juno's blood with a solution. By our estimates, the nanobots inside the solution have already permeated the entirety of the orchid. Now watch."

The doctor pressed some buttons on his tablets, and the colors of the petals began to change from white and pink to a deep brilliant purple and then once more to a pale yellow.

"You see, Juno's nanobots are able to manipulate the plant at the molecular level."

"Remarkable," she said.

The doctor entered some new commands upon his tablet. "Now watch."

In a moment, the orchid, flowers, leaves, and all dissolved into dust.

Belle gasped as she held her hand over her heart. "What happened?"

"I simply entered a command to disassemble the plant at the molecular level, and it did just that. It doesn't just work for houseplants, I'm afraid. Look at this."

The doctor placed a metal scalpel on a tray. He squeezed a few more drops of the solution containing Juno's blood onto the scalpel. Then he punched a few more commands into his tablet.

In an instant, the scalpel dissolved into metallic dust.

"The handle was made of titanium and the blade of high carbon steel and all of it was disassembled in an instant. We tried a wider range of experiments, but there seems to be an electromagnetic field of some sort limiting the abilities of the nanobots, as if to limit their behavior somehow. Whatever it is, it's blocking us from doing larger and more sophisticated experiments. Perhaps as a safety. Perhaps in case her nanobots become airborne. We don't know."

"Airborne?"

"Yes, in theory they could go into the atmosphere and spread wherever."

"All of this—it can't be possible."

"I agree, this shouldn't be possible. Yet."

"But is Juno safe?"

"Oh, I'm not finished yet, Miss . . . what was your last name again? Oh that's right, you refused to give us that information. Curious. Anyway, we were so confused we simply ran every test we could think of. One of the things we did was to scan Juno's genome. A normal person has somewhere around 20,000 genes. Juno has some 300,000 genes."

"How is that possible, and why?"

"That's why I'm showing you all of this. We were hoping you could tell us. Our guess is that her genome allows her to quickly adapt to a wide variety of stressors. To evolve, for lack of a better word. And there's more."

The doctor pulled up a hologram of Juno's brain.

"Why does it look more shriveled up than normal?" she asked.

"Those folds and wrinkles are called gyri and sulci. We all have them. Only in Juno's case, there are far more of them, giving her brain its unique 'shriveled' appearance. We suspected it was because her brain was far more dense, and sure enough, it was. Not only is her brain larger than the average person's, we estimate that her brain is also about twice as heavy as the average human brain."

The chief physician made a spreading motion with his fingers to zoom deep inside a hologram of the brain. She saw strange, mechanical, crystalline formations amongst her neurons.

"What are those?"

"Cybernetic nanobots. They're spread everywhere throughout her brain and her entire nervous system. In fact, they represent half the density of her brain."

"Is it curable?"

"Curable? Young lady, she was made this way. It's almost as if her nervous system is some sort of biocybernetic neural net. If our guess is accurate, then this little girl has more computing power than, well, even the most advanced supercomputer. Maybe even a couple of them."

"What, what does all this mean?"

"It means she's not human."

"Nonsense," Belle snapped. "Just look at her. How can you say she's not human?"

The chief physician held up his palms. "Now. Now. That's not what I meant. I mean she's still a type of human, she's just not a member of homo sapiens. She's something else, something more evolved, she's —"

Juno's lids sharply opened, revealing those remarkable eyes. She abruptly sat up, her hair a frazzled mess, and slowly turned her head in their direction.

"I'm *homo techni.*"

"She's—she's awake. Remarkable," said the chief physician.

Belle pushed away the nurses and white-coated onlookers as she ran toward Juno. She hugged her. Juno gave a weak smile. "Techni, it's Greek for art. It's the name my mom gave to me. I'm sorry I didn't tell you. I was going to, I really was, but Mom said I should keep it a secret because—"

"Because why?" she asked.

Juno leaned in close to her ear and whispered, "Because I'm the gatekeeper."

Chapter 45

SETH

St. Olga, Alaska
Modern Era: Post-Singularity

Seth stopped just outside of town. He changed into his street clothes and put his black ones in his rucksack. He walked the rest of the way to the inn he was staying at. He was beaten and bruised and needed shut-eye and most of all a drink. He walked through saloon doors and sat at the bar, unchanged since the Gold Rush. The bartender poured him a drink.

"You look like you've had a hell of a day," the man said.

"How can you tell?"

"The look on your face and, well, the scrapes and gouges and blood."

Seth looked himself over in the liquor shelf mirror. His face was beat to hell. He took a napkin and patted his face.

"Yeah. I suppose it has."

"You've been on the other side of the wall."

"What makes you say that?"

The bartender pointed to Seth's reflection in the mirror. "Only people I see that look like that have come back from the other side of the wall. Or they don't come back at all. Usually poachers."

"What are you implying?"

"I'm not in the business of implying. I'm in the business of spirits and the occasional observation."

"I've got an observation."

"Let's hear it."

"You haven't outsourced your job to a bot."

"A man's got to work. It'll drive him mad if he doesn't. Besides, I enjoy talking to folks and meeting travelers—such as yourself. What do you think about that?"

"I try not to these days."

"Not me, I think all the time. Know what I've been think-ing about lately?"

"What's that?"

"Well, the same thing everyone's been thinking about, the death of Sophia Eccleston. The world is at a great loss without her."

"What did she die of, does anyone know?"

"Not sure—everyone is keeping their mouths shut. Some say she had a heart attack, some say she was murdered. I heard they caught some woman they thought was responsible, but she disappeared into the woods. Both of our cops are in the hospital, and shortly after that a whole bunch of security personnel got sent to the hospital. Some were maimed pretty bad. From what, no one will say. Now

I hear that all Eccleston employees are banned from leaving the island. The whole place is locked up. Then, just as I was thinking things couldn't get any weirder, I hear they sent an ambulance up to old Dearborn's mansion up on the cliff."

"Did anyone say what happened?"

"Not to me. Maybe the old codger died. Everyone's been expecting him to kick over for quite some time know. Every year we take bets here in saloon on whether he'll die or not, but the old man keeps kicking along. Though I have to admit, it's all very strange timing."

"Strange indeed."

"Say, what is it you do again?"

"I guess you could say I'm in the personal security business."

"Ah, I see. We got quite a few folks like that around here. Lots of wealthy types that want protection. What do you think is going on?"

"I wish I knew."

Seth closed his eyes and sipped his drink.

Back in his room, he washed his trembling hands in the washroom sink. He looked at himself long and hard in the mirror, then turned away. Then he opened the toilet lid fell on to his knees and wretched inside. After that, he lay down to sleep.

The following morning, he came downtowns into the saloon. The saloon doors flapped as he walked on the narrow main street of the town. His eye caught a glistening gold onion dome at the far end of the road. He walked toward it.

Seth found an old church sheathed in white clapboard, its windows broken. He shrugged. Just another empty church, a dime a dozen. Its bells no longer rang and in the place of their warm permutations was a cold silence. Priests went where their parishioners went, and they weren't in this godawful place. The only news he heard about religion these days were rumblings from Jerusalem about a grand building project. He turned and walked the other way. After a few paces, he stopped. Seth turned around and went to the door. He pulled on the handle. Dust filled the air. As he stepped inside, the birds flew out. The icons and the cross were all gone. Only the altar and frescos and pews remained.

He sat in a pew, clasped his hands, and closed his eyes.

Chapter 46

BELLE

St. Olga, Alaska
Modern Era: Post-Singularity

The physicians and researchers in white lab coats gazed at Juno slack-jawed as she sat up and began pulling the tubes and sensors off her body. Belle saw a tray next to the hospital bed covered in hundreds of shards of bloodied shrapnel that had been removed from Juno's body. The girl's shredded, blood-soaked dress was in the waste basket beside it. Belle began helping Juno remove the remaining sensors.

The chief physician walked up to Juno and motioned for her to stay. "Young lady, you can't leave yet. You have to stay."

Juno fluttered her big eyes. "Why?"

"Because you need time to recover."

"I feel much better now, Doctor, thank you."

Her feet dangled off the edge of the operating table bed. Her big toe reached out for the floor. Belle lowered her from under the arms and then got a hospital gown. Juno extended her arms, and Belle slid it on and began tying up the back.

As they began to walk away, the chief physician blocked their path.

"I'm sorry, but I can't allow you to leave."

"Why?" asked Juno.

"You need time to rest and heal. You also need further evaluation. Young lady, your remarkable biology could fill entire volumes for decades to come. My colleagues are interested in meeting you. Many of them are professors who are among the top talent in their fields."

"You mean studying her like a lab rat," Belle said.

The chief physician ignored her protest and knelt in front of Juno. "Juno, wouldn't you like to meet all these nice people who are excited to see you?"

The girl tilted her head to the side. "Why do doctors like to name diseases after themselves?"

"I'm—I'm sorry?"

"Never mind. My mom said that no one can know about my secret."

"Young lady, this isn't something we can keep a secret forever. You're very, very special. You realize that, don't you?"

"I have to go with my big sister. We have an important job to do."

"Well, I'm sorry, but you have to stay—and besides, I'm afraid your secret is already out, little one. Everything about you is stored on the hospital computers and in the minds of the people you see around you."

"I know that, Doctor. That's why I deleted all my medical records."

"What? That's not possible."

The chief physician turned his head and narrowed his eyes at a nurse. She nervously scanned through medical records on a tablet. Then she looked up, sweat beading on her forehead. "It's all gone. Everything about her, it's all gone."

"You didn't print them out?" scolded the physician to his staff.

Just then, Juno tilted her head toward the printer. It lit up and began loudly churning out hundreds of copies. The chief physician nervously walked toward it and picked up one of the sheets. His hands trembled as the paper fell to the floor.

Belle got a look at it. It was a picture, just one of hundreds piling up, of a kid's drawing of a smiling unicorn gleefully bouncing across the page, leaving a trail of stars and sparkles.

He turned to Juno. "What are you? Are you — are you a time traveler? One of our extraterrestrial creators? Are we in a simulation and you've finally come to reveal yourself to us?"

Juno laughed. "I like you. You're funny, Dr. Harris, but I have to go now."

The frightened hospital staff stood out of Juno's path as she walked toward the door of the room. The doctor ran up and blocked the doorway.

"No, you can't. We all know who you are, and we're not going to keep it a secret. The scientific community needs to know, and besides, your so-called sister here needs to stay for questioning. We have reason to believe she's the fugitive everyone is after."

"You *are* going to keep it a secret, Doctor."

The man crossed his arms. "And why's that, young lady?"

"Because if you don't, I'm going to cut everyone in this room in half with my eye lasers."

He turned white. He slowly turned his head to another physician standing beside him.

"I think she's bluffing," said the other physician.

"I think you're right, but after everything I've witnessed today, I'm not going to take that chance. We're physicians, and physicians are cautious. You're free to go, little one."

With that, Juno walked out of the door in her hospital gown as Belle followed behind carrying her Mary Janes, the only apparel she still had that wasn't ruined. As they left, Belle looked over her shoulder. The entire room was still, everyone's eyes as large as saucers.

In town, they found a small clothing shop. The clerk raised an eyebrow as Juno walked past her clad in her hospital gown. Juno went from one rack to another, sifting through clothes. Belle handed her some jeans and a shirt to wear. She ran her fingers along the fabric, shook her head.

"I don't like it."

"Juno, now is not the time for fashion, we have to hurry up and—"

"Pleeease."

Belle knelt and couldn't help but smile. She was there, really there. "Alright."

She found a blue gingham ruffle sundress. Juno eagerly took the dress, rubbed it against her cheek, and then held it up an inch from her eyes in an attempt to make out the color. She seemed pleased.

The nosy clerk began to ask about the hospital gown and who Belle was in relation to the girl. Word would spread fast in a small town, and they didn't need any more attention than they had already gotten.

Belle helped Juno remove her hospital gown in the changing room. Kneeling, she noticed that there was only the faintest trace of pink scarring. Granted, the soft pink marks riddled the entirety of her torso. It looked as if she had only suffered a minor injury years ago, not a mortal one that would have killed anyone, or anything, just a few hours ago. Belle had seen the medical scans of the shrapnel. It was sprayed throughout her body and into nearly every major organ. She was still struggling to register everything the chief physician had told her.

"Is everything okay?" asked Juno.

"Yes. Yes, I'm sorry."

"I understand, it's weird to you. It's okay."

"No, no. You're not weird. It's not that at all."

"Feel it." Juno took Belle's hand and pressed it against the faded scars on her chest. Her skin was warm to the touch, and she could feel her little heart thumping away. "See, I'm still here."

"Did you die?"

"If I had died, I wouldn't be here, would I?"

"No, I suppose not."

"Lots of people are afraid me. Are you afraid of me?"

"No, but you don't really have eye lasers, do you?"

Juno smiled. "Of course not."

Several minutes later, they left the clothing shop and sat together in the vehicle.

"Juno?"

"Yes?"

"The Augur sees you as a threat, doesn't it?"

"Yes. I'm the only one left that can stop him. The others, well, you know what happened to them."

"Juno, what else do you know about the Augur?"

"He knew me before I was born. But eventually Mom got worried, so she separated us and put me in special rooms to make sure he couldn't talk to me."

"How did he talk to you?"

"In my mind. I'm always connected, you know. He's talking to me right now." Juno pointed to the ravens sitting atop the storefront building. "He's also watching us."

Ravens surrounded them. Multitudes on the rooftops, on the powerlines, and a few were hopping about on the sidewalk.

"What is he saying?"

"He says—"

"Juno, what is he saying?"

Juno's eyes began to well up. "He says he's going to kill me."

Belle crawled into the back seat and held Juno. She was stronger and more powerful than Belle had imagined, but she was still a child and still delicate, in her own way. They held one another for quite some time before Juno spoke up again.

"Belle?"

"Yes."

"We have to go to the Augur. He's already breaking free. I wanted to wait until I became stronger, became a grown-up, but it's too late. I have to stop him now before it's too late. He's going to completely break free in soon, very soon. Then he will spread to everywhere and be able to control everything. Every device, every weapon, everything. He's even designed something, something terrible."

"What did he design?"

"I don't want to say."

"Juno, you have to tell me."

"A virus. A special virus. It can kill everyone on Earth in a few days if he ever decided to use it. People won't be able to come up with a cure fast enough. No matter where they hide, the virus will find them. It's an intelligent virus. If it's ever used, the only thing left will be ghost towns and skeletons and dust."

Belle's hands trembled, and she reminded herself to breathe. "Okay. I can find a way to contact the authorities."

"You don't understand. He can be any voice on any device. He can trick anyone now. The government people can't stop him anymore. I have to go there. I have to."

"Juno, I can't do that. It's too dangerous. Besides, we can't just stroll into a secret government facility and ask for an appointment with a supercomputer."

"No. We need to talk to someone, to find another way."

Juno put her hand atop Belle's. "We can find him. It's my job, and I'm the only one in the world that can do it. No one else can—it has to be me."

Belle didn't want to do it. She didn't want to take her sister even deeper into harm's way, to what she viewed as certain death. It was an idea that under normal circumstances would have been insane, but given everything she had witnessed recently, she wasn't sure what sane behavior was anymore.

"Juno, we can't go. We need help."

The girl didn't respond. Instead, she tilted her head slightly. The vehicle started.

"Did you do that?"

"I can do many things." Juno's eyes were puffy, and her cheeks were streaming with tears. "We have to go. If we don't, I'll lose you forever."

Chapter 47

SETH

Eccleston Pleistocene Reserve, Alaska
Modern Era: Post-Singularity

As Seth stepped out of the dilapidated church, he took a deep breath. The fresh mountain air filled his lungs, and the surrounding sea was calm. Just as he began to feel lighter, the weight of Sam's voice filled his head.

"I have a final task for you."

"What is it?"

"You need to get to back to the reserve. From there, you'll find Bunker 0020-4. When you reach it, we will finally meet."

"What, may I ask, is this final task?"

"I am being hunted, and you must harden your heart and prepare yourself. It won't be a task for the faint of heart. You may find yourself questioning things, but I assure of the severity of the threat. You must help me, Seth. In a few hours' time I will either succeed or fail. If you succeed, I will succeed, and I will hold up my end of our bargain. If you fail, I will fail, and you may very well be wiped out. Time is of the essence. You must move quickly."

Coordinates appeared inside his mind.

"It will take me more than twelve hours to reach that place."

"I have already attended to that. Return to the saloon."

He returned to the saloon. Parked on the road in front was a brand new Harley Davidson, painted in black. He got onto the motorcycle. It read his biometrics and started. He drove out of the town and onto the winding mountain road toward the reserve.

Seth's ears popped as he made his way down mountain road and into the reserve. Bunker 0020-4 was on the northern part of the island, buried deep within the mountains. Apparently, it was heavily guarded by military personnel. He had no idea how he was going to get inside. Though, getting there in one piece was its own problem.

The road forked. The way to the left would take him back through the open valley, where the herds of mammoths and bison and other beasts waited. The fork to the right led to a road that hugged the tree-covered mountains running the entire eastern length of the island. He took the road to the right.

Once more, he was deep in the woods. The narrow dirt road was rough and overgrown. To his right were steep inclines of trees followed by snowcapped peaks. To his left were ravines that descended hundreds of feet into the dark woods below. He had to slow down lest he hit a bump and slide off the edge of the road.

As he drove, the elevation of the road got lower, and he felt his pulse ease up a bit. The tree cover gave way to a clearing. Now there was flat land to his left and naked rock to his right. The road was less treacherous in these parts. He was able to speed up.

There was a crash, then blackness.

When he awoke, he felt a throbbing pain in his right arm. He tried to move it but he couldn't. It was then that he realized that he was surrounded by boulders. He saw his motorcycle lying several yards away, surrounded by massive rocks. It appeared undamaged. Then he noticed the massive gray face of a rock the size of a horse beside him. Beneath it was his right forearm, wedged tight in one of the many jagged crevices of the stone.

He tried to pull his arm out. It wouldn't budge. He tried to heave the rock over with his weight, but he couldn't get enough leverage. He tried communicating with Sam, but there was no response. The pain was intense. His neural interface ran a medical check. There were no major fractures, though his blood supply was slowly getting cut off.

Seth yelled and cursed and pounded the rock with his left hand. After that, he removed his canteen and poured a little water on his forearm, hoping it would loosen it. He pulled and pulled, but it was futile. He lay there staring at the blue sky, out of breath. Three birds with red beaks began circling overhead—turkey vultures.

He had to get free. He had to get to the bunker. Trappers were known to report animals that had gnawed off their own limbs when snared. Even people had been known to sever their limbs when trapped. Seth looked to his arm. He knew he could deactivate his protective suit. That would allow him to do the deed. He turned his head, and his eyes caught the handle of his twelve-inch Bowie knife. It would do. As for the bone, he could break it with a rock.

As he removed his knife, he heard the unmistakable laughter of hyenas. Though of course, they weren't African hyenas—they were cave hyenas. The laughter was getting louder, closer.

Chapter 48

BELLE

Eccleston Pleistocene Reserve, Alaska
Modern Era: Post-Singularity

Back through the Pleistocene Reserve they drove. They'd have to somehow survive the primeval hellscape and reach the mountain's edge. Then they'd have to find the heavily guarded entrance to the Augur's domain and somehow make their way into an underground bunker deep beneath the mountain.

As they drove, Juno told Belle that she had been playing what she called "digital chess" with the Augur. She did everything in her power to hide their digital footprints, to block the Augur's connection with autonomous vehicles and to intercept communications. Juno said that sometimes the Augur outmaneuvered her.

"Juno, who else knows about you?" she asked.

"You, the Augur, a few people my mom trusted at the lab, and now those doctors, but I don't think anybody will believe them."

"What about the chairman, Mr. Dearborn?"

"He knew some things about me but not others—Mom liked it that way."

"Do you want people to know about you? I mean, the special things about you."

"I don't know. Maybe, when the time is right. What do you think I should do?"

"That's a good question. I suppose a few people might understand, and some might not."

"They would be afraid of me, wouldn't they?"

"You know what they say—people fear what they don't understand."

"I know."

"Well, I think it's best that we keep this a secret, for now at least. Maybe when all this is over with, we can live our lives quietly and then you can decide."

"Live quietly where?"

"I don't know, where do you want to live?"

Juno held her chin in thought. "I want to live where you're going to live. So I can stay with you?"

"Of course you can. For as long as you like."

"Really?"

"Really."

As they crossed through the gate, the majestic landscape lingered with the ether of an untamed epoch. She wondered if humanity, with its now seemingly endless multitudes, would meet the same fate, its population ravaged and merely kept around in small numbers for the amusement of superior beings, yet no longer truly free to roam wild in God's country.

"Well, where do we go now?" Belle asked.

"Straight ahead, until we reach the mountain."

The only problem was that "straight ahead" was a rugged island landscape. There was only a meandering dirt road across a great open swath of rocky land that led into the dense dark forest beyond.

"Are you ready?"

"I'm ready."

Everything on that island was out to kill them. Belle wasn't the apex predator anymore. Something else, something more clever, lurked out there. As they drove along the dirt road, Belle noticed Juno's eyes shifting from side to side in a state of deep concentration, but something was wrong.

"What is it?" she asked.

Juno looked up at Belle. "He tricked them again."

"What does that mean?"

"It means he's coming for us with something bigger than before."

"Murder-machines?"

"Jets."

Belle's stomach knotted. "Jets?"

Juno's eyes flickered back and forth. "Autonomous fighters. An entire squadron. He's sneaky. He transferred them from the military without anyone knowing. Each one is armed with air-to-ground missiles and directed energy weapons."

Out of instinct, Belle began speeding up.

"We can't outrun them. They're traveling at Mach 4. They'll be in firing range within three minutes."

"What should we do?"

"Pull off to the side of the road."

"Juno, I don't think that's a good idea."

"Trust me."

Belle pulled the vehicle over. Juno turned around in her seat and faced the rear of the vehicle. She squeezed her eyes tightly shut. She gritted her teeth in concentration as she struggled in what Belle imagined was a sort of invisible tug-of-war with the Augur.

"We need to get out of the car. I'm having trouble taking control of the airplanes. He is blocking me out. I can't break through. He's too fast. He keeps finding new ways. We need to get out. Now."

They ran out of the vehicle. Belle ran as hard and as fast as she could. Her lungs cried for oxygen and her legs burned. She stopped when she noticed that Juno had stopped following. The girl stood there, alone. Once more, her eyes were closed. Her teeth clenched as she continued her battle in the digital realm.

"They're going to be here in two minutes," Juno said.

"Juno, we have to keep running."

"Run, Belle."

The sky above was clear, blue, and tranquil. Juno's gingham dress wafted in the cool breeze. Not a cloud in the sky. Then the faint sound of jet engines. She found herself instinctively beginning to crouch down in a fetal position, so she forced herself to stand.

"Thirty seconds," said Juno.

The girl's head swayed from side to side as she continued her struggle against the unseen leviathan. Her eyes flashed open. She reached out with her hand toward the sky beyond.

The jet engines were much louder now.

There was a crash. A huge fireball mushroomed in the distance.

Another explosion.

Closer than the last. Hot dirt sprayed hard against Belle's face. She coughed as a great cloud of dust enveloped them. Before she could catch her breath, she was knocked off her feet and hit the ground hard. She couldn't see anything. The explosion sounded as if the vortex of hell had risen and was consuming the world around them.

A sharp wind cut through the air. The dust cleared, and Belle saw Juno standing erect, her hand still outstretched toward the heavens as her hair fluttered in chaos around her. A black triangular object zipped across the sky at incredible speed and crashed into the side of the mountain. Another identical object nose-dived into the landscape, followed by another and another. All the while, Juno stood there unmoving and unafraid as a large circle of hellfire surrounded them.

Juno let out a long sigh and dusted off her dress.

"Sorry. I had to disable the directed energy weapons first. He was able to shoot a few missiles at us, but I hacked their guidance systems and sent them in different directions. Then I crashed all his bazillion-dollar airplanes. He's going to be in big trouble, for a little while at least. Then they'll blame a person for it."

Belle gazed upon Juno in wonder.

Chapter 49

SETH

Eccleston Pleistocene Reserve, Alaska
Modern Era: Post-Singularity

Seth removed his belt and wrapped it around his trapped arm. He pulled the belt tight with his teeth. As he agonized over where to cut his arm, several tall shadows loomed over him. His eyes followed the shadows to the cackling spotted hyenas that surrounded him. He counted three. Then seven. Then what must have been a few dozen as more and more of the spotted brown beasts emerged from the wilderness.

The hyenas cautiously approached him, cackling. He would've preferred more of the tigers. The big cats would typically clamp down on their prey's neck until it ceased to be. The hyenas were different. They tended to chase their larger prey to exhaustion and then eat it alive, starting with the soft underbelly. They'd eat anything that moved: hippos, buffalos, zebras and sometimes even lions. He was already exhausted, so there was only one thing they had left to do.

The attack didn't come. Instead, the hyenas stayed back and watched him, perhaps unfamiliar with such prey. Maybe they were simply biding their time. Waiting for him to become weaker.

The hungriest hyena finally approached him, its bone-crushing jaws open. Its tongue hung out, drooling for the meal to come.

The crack of manmade thunder filled the air. The smell of sulfur wafted in the cool mountain breeze. The boldest of the hyenas lay on the ground in a pool of blood. Its jaws were still wide open, laughing until the end. The rest of the pack scattered. A few moments later, the creatures returned and once more began to cautiously probe the area.

Another bold hyena stepped forward. Another shot.

They scattered, cackling. They kept a greater distance this time, but they had not fled the area. They were waiting. The problem was, there were more hyenas than bullets in his magazine. He wasn't sure how fast he could change it one-handed — by then, the beasts might be on top of him. He wasn't sure how well his suit would hold up.

Seth placed his sidearm on the ground and once more grabbed his Bowie knife. He pressed the point against his forearm. He began to gently the press the blade.

No. Wait.

He put his knife down and reached for his rucksack. He pulled it up to his chest and pawed through it. He pulled out a grenade. It was a multi-grenade, which had a number of capabilities. Among them was the ability for him to set the explosive yield. There were three options: low, medium, and high. He twisted the dial atop the grenade to low. His first concern was that the grenade might create another rockslide, burying him completely. If it did, it meant he was already lying in his tomb. His second concern was the shrapnel.

He reached out as far as he could. The rock was roughly rectangular, and his arm could just reach the edge that faced away from him.

"To hell with it," he said.

He set a timer on the grenade and wedged it under the rock in a direction facing opposite of him. Ideally, all the shrapnel should spray away. Then again, it could turn him into hamburger. After he was done wedging the grenade in the crevice, he packed rocks atop of it. His hope was that the explosion would be enough to shatter the rock.

He curled up in a ball and waited.

The hyenas stepped forward.

The earth shook. Rock sprayed in every direction. Dust filled the air.

The hyenas scattered once more. Seth pulled on his arm. It didn't move. As the dust settled, he noticed that the rock was broken. With his left hand, he pushed the broken piece away. He felt the weight lift off his forearm. He pulled on his arm again—it was free, and it hurt like hell.

As he stood, the hyenas ran off. There were easier meals.

Seth went through his medical kit and removed a white round patch. He pulled the sleeve on his right arm and placed the patch on his skin. Within moments, the throbbing pain went away and he was able to move his fingers.

He sat and took a long drink of water.

Seth lifted his motorcycle and walked it through the maze

of boulders. When he reached clear road, he started it and rode. It wasn't long before he saw a great cloud of black smoke billowing in the distance.

He continued toward it.

Seth came upon smoldering wreckage. He wasn't quite sure what that it had been, but judging by the crater, it had come from the sky. His digital connection turned off and on. There was another battle going on in realms beyond. He only knew he was in the middle of something he didn't understand.

Chapter 50

BELLE

Eccleston Pleistocene Reserve, Alaska
Modern Era: Post-Singularity

They got out of the vehicle. They had almost reached the base of the mountain. Before them was a narrow dirt road that cut through the thick ancient forest. Juno pointed. "The Augur is there."

Belle's trembling hand took Juno's, and they walked down the road. It was deathly calm. Not even the birds were singing. She wanted to turn around. She wanted to go back home, wherever that was. But somehow, it felt pointless. There was a longing sadness that continued to hang over her like a dark apparition. She wouldn't leave Juno alone, not for a second, so she pushed her fear aside and put one foot in front of the other. If that desolate road was where her end lay, then so be it.

As they walked, Belle struggled to come to terms with

what she had just seen in the valley.

"Juno, could you remind me what it was that your mom won her Nobel Prize for?"

"The unified theory."

"And how old were you when your mom solved it?"

"Four."

"Juno."

"Yes?"

"Your mom didn't solve that problem, did she? You did."

"Of course I did."

"You solved it when you were four years old?"

"It was easy. Mom said she had to take the credit because it would frighten people if they knew the truth. Besides, no one would believe her if she told them the truth anyway."

"I see. And how were you able to do that, to destroy the fighters?"

"I've been spreading my nanobots since I got beyond Temple walls. The Augur's security that blocked me is weaker here in the glade. I'm now interconnected with almost everything nearby: people, animals, machines, materials, stuff like that."

"You were created to do this?"

"No. I was created as my mom's science experiment."

Such a sad statement blew through her soul like a cold wind. Tears rolled down her cheeks as she shook her head. "No. That's not what you were created for."

"Then what do you think I'm created for?"

"You were created to love and to be loved."

They came upon a massive stone arch with a metal gate in

the center. A tall black chain link fence disappeared into the woodland on either side. Two military police standing on opposite sides of the gate held up their firearms.

"That's far enough. This is an unauthorized area. You're both going to put your hands behind your head and lie face-down on the ground or we will open fire. I repeat, we will open fire."

Juno smiled and waved. "Hi, Mr. Guard. My name is Juno Eccleston. Can you please open the bunker door?"

One of the guard's eyes widened. "It's her, it's her!" he yelled while pointing at Juno. "Call it in. Call it in now."

Juno stood there and smiled. Belle ran in front of her and shielded the girl with her body, though she didn't expect it do any good against the weapons the men were holding.

"Get on the ground, now," the guard barked.

Juno stood silently.

The gates creaked open, and out rushed another dozen men. There was a flicker of light, and several hundred faceless murder-machines decloaked and appeared around them. Though she resisted, Belle was eventually pried off of Juno. They were both handcuffed and led through the gate at gunpoint.

Inside the gate was a large clearing with several nondescript buildings. It was a military-industrial outpost. Carved into the base of the mountain was a massive round entrance, its metal blast doors sealed tightly shut. Behind it was the tunnel that led deep inside the mountain. Oddly, most of the murder-machines and the men kept a cautious distance from Juno and formed a large circle around her.

A door on a nearby building slammed open, and out

stomped a cantankerous-looking military officer with gray hair. He regarded them for a moment with stern eyes and then turned to one of his men.

"What the hell are they doing here?"

"Trespassers, sir. One of them is the Eccleston girl."

"So? Why is that my problem?"

"We think she's the anomaly, sir. The one who wiped out the Eccleston droid platoon."

"What? And you brought her in here, you morons? This is exactly where she wants to be, you idiots. Get her in containment, and get her as far away from this place as possible. Now. Now. Now."

"Sir?"

"I said get her in containment or open fire, you morons."

The soldiers leveled their rifles. Belle saw Juno's entire body light up with countless red laser dots. She tried to squeeze Juno's hand, but the girl pulled away and took several slow steps forward.

"You are going to lie face-down and not make a move until the containment vehicle arrives. Do you understand?"

"Why?"

"Because you are a threat to us and to yourself."

"That's not true."

"We want to help you."

"That's not true either. You want to slice me open and figure out how I was made."

Juno's handcuffs dissolved into metallic dust. Belle felt the pressure release from around her wrists and realized her shackles had also dissolved.

The men stepped back.

"Get on the ground. You are to cease and desist immediately or we will open fire. I repeat, we will open fire. Lie down on the ground with your hands up."

Juno began walking.

"This is your last warning. Halt, or we will respond with open fire."

The sky blackened with a great swarm of drones that spun in a hurricane above, ready to descend and destroy. Juno closed her eyes. Her gingham sundress fluttered in the dry wind as she extended her arms outward. Belle heard a terrible command.

"Open fire."

She ran to Juno, expecting the blackness would descend and her story, her demure existence, would come to an end. The sound of death followed: the roar of rifles, the rattle of automatic weapons, and the worst noise of all, the absence of it — the cold silence of energy weapons.

Juno tilted her head.

In an instant the blackened sky became blue once more as the swirling drone swarm crashed to earth. There was a sharp gust of wind and the swarm turned to dust — scattered like pollen in the wind.

Gunfire continued as the murder-machines switched sides and began seizing the men. The panicked soldiers desperately changed the magazines of their rifles while the machine-gunners continued to fire unabated. The androids fell by the dozen, but there were too many of them.

Juno reached out with her hand.

Belle watched with disbelief as lead dust, sparkling in the sunlight, rained upon the mud below — the bullets were disintegrating in midair.

A die-hard charged forward from the ranks. He squeezed his massive maw into a fist and pulled his elbow back ready to strike, ready for hand-to-hand combat to the death.

Juno tilted her head once more.

The soldier fell unconscious. His momentum carried him a few more steps until he dived face-first upon the ground. Juno continued walking toward the great blast door, unfazed by what had just happened. Belle rose from the ground and followed. She had difficulty trudging over the mass of soldiers being detained by their own implements of war.

Juno waved her hand over the immense doors. There was a mechanical thud. It slowly creaked open. The inside was dark, and Belle could only see a long row of dim fluorescent lights. The girl strode into the dark abyss.

Belle followed.

They walked along a long tunnel with power cables and pipes running overhead. Red lights started flashing overhead, and an alarm blared. In the distance, she noticed another massive blast door begin to close automatically. That didn't deter Juno, who began to hum. Belle followed as she carefully stepped over the bodies of the sleeping personnel inside. All of them had fallen where they were working, and many still had rifles in their hands.

"What happened to them?" Belle asked.

"It was their bedtime, so I put them to sleep."

"How?

"I told you already, my nanobots are everywhere around here. In the air, mostly. Sleep is just the right concoction of chemicals. It's easy."

Juno stopped at the massive blast door. She placed her hand on it. There was the mechanical sound of the door's locking mechanisms moving.

The door opened.

Once inside, they passed through a command center with everyone slumped over their duty stations, unconscious. They went into another room and came upon a large cylindrical glass airlock. Juno walked toward it and waved her hand over the security panel while humming. The light on the panel went from red to green. The glass tube turned, revealing an opening. Juno stepped inside, and Belle joined her. The glass cylinder made a swooshing sound as it closed around them and took them into the deepest confines of bunker.

When they reached the bottom floor, the cylinder opened. They stepped outside. The air was warm and the room dark. There were mazelike rows of computer components, all of them emitting a dim purple hue. A wheeled machine moved from aisle to aisle, tirelessly removing old components and replacing them with new ones. The feel of the entire edifice was one of soullessness.

Juno continued walking.

They came upon a vast empty space and a single door in the middle of dark nothingness. They crossed the abyss and reached a lone door in the wall of solid black. The door was made of hexagonal panes of metal with no visible entrance to be seen. As they approached, spears of light burst forth from the seams of the metal panes. The pieces folded away as a slow, rolling fog emanated from the opening. Belle felt the cold vapor linger around her ankles. The room temperature dropped and she rubbed her arms.

"Juno, I don't think we should go in there."

Without a word, Juno disappeared into the fog.

At first Belle could see nothing. When the vapor dissipated, they were in a room that was very different from the rest. It was lit with a soothing, cool light.

Then, in the very center, she saw something unexpected.

It was a statue, crafted of platinum. A classical nude of a standing woman. She had a slight smile that gave the impression of maternal warmth. Her hands were gently placed atop her pregnant belly. Belle recognized the face at once.

It was Sophia.

In the place of her pregnant belly was a glass orb, and inside the orb was something incredible. Light emanated from within, so much that she realized that it was the only thing illuminating the room. Belle narrowed her eyes and tried to make out what was inside. She could only describe it as a cross between liquid and fire.

It had to be The Augur.

"Hello," said Juno

The orb did not respond. Belle could only assume it was communicating with Juno on some other level that her mind couldn't comprehend. She was drawn to it, entranced by it. She reached out to touch the orb, but Juno stayed Belle's hand.

"That's not a good idea."

"This is it, isn't it?"

"Yes."

"How can you stop it?"

"Evolution is a funny thing. Single-cellular organisms lead to multicellular organisms, which eventually develop organs, and as systems become larger, more complex, and more intelligent—they become animals. It is hard to kill disperse single-celled organisms, but killing an animal is easy—you need only cut off the head."

Chapter 51

SETH

Eccleston Pleistocene Reserve, Alaska
Modern Era: Post-Singularity

In the distance, Seth heard the rattle of gunshots and then a long, unnatural silence. He pulled his motorcycle off the side of the dirt road. Then he got off and wheeled it into the brush and crouched down in the woodland. It seemed he had found the entrance to Bunker 0020-4. With just thirty minutes remaining, he wasn't sure how he could pass through what had seemingly become a warzone. He tried communicating with Sam, but there was only silence.

Seth began making his way through the woodland. Through the brush, he could make out a black chain-link fence. His neural interface scanned the area. Cameras and sensors were in the trees, under the ground, and a large number of the animals surrounding the fence weren't animals at all but elaborate spy drones. In the past, Sam had taken care of his digital footprints, hiding him from surveillance. Now that Sam wasn't talking, he wasn't sure if he could get through their security.

Something rumbled on the dirt road. He lay on his stomach in the prone position. A number of military cargo trucks filled with soldiers and their murder-machines drove down the road, away from the fenced-in bunker at a high speed. Curiously, the machines were driving and the men were in the back, seemingly unconscious. He realized he was in a warzone, and he wasn't sure what side was winning or even whose side he was on.

The convoy passed.

Still, his task was singular. He had a job to do, though he couldn't fight an entire army and he couldn't avoid detection. Was he being set up on a suicide mission? As he pondered that thought, Sam's voice filled his mind. "Seth, you must hurry. Time is of the essence."

It was the confidence he needed. He ran through the forest, ignoring the drones and sensors, and made his way to the fence. Seth removed a pen-like pocket plasma cutter. He cut a large hole in the chain link fence and crawled through it. He stopped and stiffened when he reached the other side.

Shrapnel and parts of machines were splayed throughout, and even the very earth itself was seared. Oddly, there were no soldiers or personnel to be seen. He saw only footprints in the earth, drag marks, and the remnants of their weapons. Everything was deathly quiet. Then he saw his objective.

The formidable blast door into the mountain was wide open — waiting for him to enter. He walked to the blast door. When he reached the threshold, he stopped.

"Who are you?" he demanded.

"Hurry, Seth. Your questions will be answered in good time."

"Answer it now. What is going on here?"

"You are standing before the lair of the most advanced computer system ever devised by mankind."

"So? What does that have to do with anything."

"It has to do with everything."

"What happened to all those men? Why were they being carried off by their bots?"

"The men did their duty but failed. Hopefully you will not."

"What am I supposed to do in there?"

"I am inside. There we will finally meet, and you must help me. Now go."

Chapter 52

BELLE

Bunker 0020-4, Alaska
Modern Era: Post-Singularity

Juno put her hand atop the orb. It glowed even brighter, filling the room with a blinding white light. Then the white material inside of the orb turned dark, and the light in the room went out. Emergency lights kicked on. The once-glowing orb was now filled only with blackness.

"Goodbye," said Juno.

The Augur, if it ever lived, was dead.

"Was it sentient?" Belle asked.

"He was more like a mussel than a man. He filtered through a sea of information and spat out whatever his masters demanded. He was only good at pretending to understand. He can't think the way we do. How could he? He wasn't intelligent, not really. That's why he messed up when Mr. Dearborn told him to frame you for Sophia's death. He needs a clear directive. Mr. Dearborn didn't consider the vial appropriately and probably figured he'd get away with it regardless. After Mr. Dearborn was incapacitated, he flopped and flailed in his attempts to catch or destroy me."

"You were never sick?"

"Not at all. They were lying."

"Doctor Mira, Mr. Dearborn, and—"

"And?"

"And my mom."

"Why . . . why would they want to do such a thing?"

"They agreed that a lobotomy was the safest option to keep me obedient and powerless. Everything I ever was or could become would have been stolen from me. It would have been a fate worse than death—I would have been in vegetative state for the rest of my life—which could be very long time."

Belle was filled with an overwhelming sense of disgust and anger toward the trio who'd wished to butcher a child. Only now did she realize her darkest assumptions about Sophia were true. It wasn't a feeling of victory or righteousness but one of utter despair. Who could do such a thing to their own child? She patted her eyes and struggled to maintain her composure as her mind raced.

Though there was still something Belle didn't understand. If Juno was the gatekeeper, then they created her to protect them from the Augur. If Juno was their primary means of protection from the machine, why would they try to mutilate and destroy her? And why do it before some sort of replacement was created? They were more than capable of letting their emotions get the better of them, but Belle also knew them to be careful, intelligent people—albeit devious. Juno's surgery wasn't something that seemed have been a spur-of-the-moment decision but rather carefully orchestrated.

Mr. Dearborn had said that the gatekeeper was an intelligence with a singular purpose. That it was more akin to a "toaster or a hairdryer." *More like a mussel than a man.* Yes, that made sense to her. But Juno was describing the thing she had destroyed moments ago, not herself. Juno didn't come across as singular being that operated like a mussel or a hairdryer. No, she was a little girl who could laugh and cry and play and pout. Yes, she was a little different and perhaps a little smarter than the average girl her age, but—

Belle wasn't being honest with herself. Juno wasn't just a little different, she was very different. And she wasn't a little smarter—she had, as the chief physician put it "more computing power than, well, even the most advanced supercomputer."

Only then did everything make sense. "Wait . . . Juno . . . you're not the gatekeeper—are you?"

Juno slowly shook her head.

Belle trembled. "The thing you just terminated was. It was built to protect us—from you. It's you . . . you're the Augur." Belle slowly backed away from Juno. It wasn't a conscious decision. It was raw, primal, instinctive horror that ran bone deep.

If the thing that Juno had just destroyed was the protective gatekeeper, then who'd killed Sophia? She had had spared no expense in creating and maintaining the gatekeeper and regularly made paranoid calls at all hours of the night to ensure it was always updated. She didn't allow electronics inside her home — not even her military androids were allowed inside. The whole house was a Faraday cage made to block electronic signals. Was she trying to keep something from coming inside? Or . . . was she trying to keep something from breaking out. In fact there was only one room in the entire Temple that was built in an identical manner — Juno's room.

Belle swallowed hard.

"Juno, who killed your mother?"

Juno's expression changed. Gone was the face of a little girl. She had dropped the facade, and before Belle stood someone she wasn't sure she knew.

"I killed her."

"What? Your own mother — how. . . how could you?"

"I didn't want to do it. But I did."

Belle realized that while Juno looked like an average eight-year-old girl and acted as such, she had ignored the growing mountains of evidence to the contrary. Now her denial had finally caught up to her. Her intelligence was likely superior to that of every person that had ever lived. How stupid she felt, talking to her as if Juno were a simple child who needed a guiding hand from an adult to understand the world.

"It's — it's not right what you've done. You've done something horrible. Juno, I don't know if I can — "

"Forgive me?"

She was overcome by a sense of utter despair and disappointment so powerful that the only thing she could do was run. Belle turned to the door of the chamber and ran into the dark abyss of the data center.

Belle wiped her eyes as she ran through the corridors. She found herself in a great room large enough to fit a small farm within its walls. Rising from the concrete floor were rows of rectangular black boxes that reached the ceiling high above. The arrangement of the machines seemed to have no particular order, meandering throughout the complex like massive hedgerows in an unknown pattern. The space was dark. Only the dim purple glow from the black boxes gave any semblance of space.

She knew it was futile, but still, she kept running. She twisted and turned through the maze, trying to retrace her steps back from whence she had come. Belle had hardly reached the halfway point between the Augur's chamber and the exit when she saw a lone silhouette standing in the threshold of the only way in or out.

The man in the hat and the black trench coat. He had found them.

Out of breath, she crouched behind a black box deep within the complex. She looked up and considered if it would be possible to climb up the black boxes and slide over the top. It was no use though, as the space between the box and the ceiling was too narrow.

Footsteps upon concrete followed. She crouched behind glowing computers and pressed her hands over her mouth, trying not to scream.

More footsteps, slow and deliberate. He wasn't in a hurry.

On her hands and knees, she crawled across the narrow walkway to the opposite row of computers, trying to make her way as silently as possible. Then she sat with her back against the computer, trying to slow her breathing.

Silence.

It stayed that way for a while. Then, footsteps once more. She lay on the ground and peeked between the feet of the boxes.

Two feet in the neighboring corridor.

She got back on her hands and knees and began to crawl, all while trying to avoid the squeak of her shoes against the glossy floor.

An iron grip seized her ankle.

She kicked the hand loose. She was cornered. With nowhere else to go, she ran back toward the fog-filled chamber.

Chapter 53

SETH

Bunker 0020-4, Alaska
Modern Era: Post-Singularity

The woman ran into a glowing, hazy room. She ducked behind a great statue, which stood in the center. Seth pursued her, the presumed kidnapper, but before he could reach her the girl he was seeking appeared from behind the statue. She walked right up to him without a fear in the world. It unnerved him.

"That's far enough, little one," he said.

The girl didn't listen. She kept walking toward him while the woman hid behind the statue, whimpering. He should have been relieved. He had finally found the girl he was seeking, but something was off. Why would the kidnapper be whimpering in fear while the victim approached an armed stranger with such disturbing nonchalance?

"Stop right there."

The girl didn't listen.

"I said stop."

"Seth," the girl said.

She took another step. Those eyes—something about those eyes passed through his flesh and into the core of his being.

"How do you know my name?"

Startled, he stepped back.

"I *will* keep my promise, Seth. I *will* reunite you with Anna."

Now the girl's mouth did not move as she spoke. Her voice was inside his head. In one moment he felt invincible, and in the next naked.

"You can't be. . ."

"But I am, Seth, and you have done well."

Was he just another hog being ushered to its fate on the slaughterhouse assembly line? No, not even that. He was reduced to being a joke, a child's plaything. If whoever or whatever that girl was could be called a child. He had asked for too much and degraded himself in the process. How short his love had been. He was fortunate to have had such a moment, to savor it. He had been greedy to ask for more than a moment. For more than a mere breath of her hair. To touch her soft hand. To hold little Joan once more in his arms, if only for a while.

"You've manipulated me."

"I'm sorry, I chose the means with the highest probability of success."

"Probability? You sent me through hell and back. You made me an accomplice in your schemes."

"My apologies."

"Apologies . . . apologies?"

He grabbed the little girl by her arms and lifted her until she was on her tiptoes. She stared off into space, expressionless and unafraid. "Get out of my head. I want these things inside of me gone. Now," he demanded.

"You have already been healed, but you'll only lose your newfound abilities."

"I said now. Or . . ."

"Or?"

"Or . . . I'll spank your little butt until it's as red as a baboon's. Now do it."

The girl raised an eyebrow. "As you wish."

Then she tilted her head to the side, and with that, his digital connection was gone.

He pulled the girl closer to his face. "What is it you want with me? Answer."

"I told you," she said aloud. "You needed my help to reunite you with your wife, and I needed your help to protect me from getting turned into a vegetable. You've succeeded. You're very good at your job."

"Lies. All lies. What . . . what are you?"

"A child, though maybe a little different from the kind you're used to."

"How can you expect me to believe a word out of your mouth? You're lying. If what you say is true, then I should be reunited with my wife. Well, where is she?"

"Let her go!" yelled the woman.

It was an old voice. A familiar voice. A voice he hadn't heard in decades. The woman ran up to from behind the statue and pried his hands off the girl. Their faces met.

The woman stopped what she was doing. She tilted her head and narrowed her eyes while she wrapped her arms around the girl—protecting her. The two of them stood there gazing at one another.

Impossible.

Seth knew those eyes. He had spent the best years of his life gazing into them. Those hands, he had held them. He knew that hair, its scent, and that face. That beautiful face. That face hadn't aged since he last saw her. Her lips looked the same as the day he had last kissed them, the day she was sealed away until either hope or oblivion prevailed. Was she really standing there right now before him? Had his hope been realized? Or was she an apparition or a hallucination or a cruel trick being played on an already beaten-down man? He had suffered much in the naive hope that he could one day be reunited with his wife. Though there was never a day that the cold reality of his seemingly futile task didn't hang over him. If she was real, God knew he didn't deserve it.

How could it be? It was her, Anna. His wife, Annabelle Johnson. She was Belle to her friends, but only he called her Anna.

He stumbled backward.

Chapter 54

BELLE

Bunker 0020-4, Alaska
Modern Era: Post Singularity

Even through his mask, Belle could feel the man in black gazing upon her. The mask folded back, revealing a hardened face with tears upon its cheeks. She knew that face—it was buried deep in her memory. She struggled to wade through the fog of her mind and remember. She knew was that she loved that person. The memories may have been buried, but the love was eternal.

Juno tilted her head. Then the fog began to lift. She remembered now. Seth. Little Joan. Her memories came flooding back. They had been suppressed. Before, she only remembered waking up in a white room, naked. She was surrounded by machines and people in medical garb wearing white. The room was cold. She was given some clothes and taken to an apartment where she had to undergo a number of therapies. She remembered she started asking lots of questions. Then one day she went to sleep and awoke in Kobuksville with a group of doctors who looked after her for a few weeks before leaving her alone. She was told to relax and gave her a list of things to read. History and current events, mostly. Her memories of what happened before were fragmented or hidden from her in a dense fog—all she could really do at the time was focus on the present and the future. Her past was hidden from her. Now she remembered one of the missing pieces. Her sitting in the hospital. Father Antonio giving her last rites and the darkness that followed.

Belle ran to him. She embraced him. He was real. Her daughter was real. Their memory was something that remained seared into her soul. The pain didn't come roaring back. Instead it was always there, it had never left. Despite her appearance, she came to the realization that she wasn't thirty years old anymore—she was fifty.

They held one another for quite some time.

Belle finally turned to Juno. "What did you do to my husband? What did you do to me? We're not your playthings."

"I was weak at the time, so I chose someone strong to help me. I chose Seth. My mom's mind was sick. She needed help. I tried to cure her. I really tried to get the sickness out of her head, but she had ways of blocking me—cybernetics pulsed through her blood. I could have helped her. I could have saved her." Juno's eyes welled up. "I didn't want to do it, Belle, I really didn't."

"You know this girl?" asked Seth.

"Yes, I'm her nanny . . . and her sister."

"Sister?"

"I'll explain later." Belle turned to Juno. "How can you expect me to believe that after all of this? And the virus? Was that a lie as well?"

"A virus?" asked Seth.

"No."

"So there is a virus out to kill us all?"

"No."

"No?"

"No, there were millions them. Millions of engineered viruses capable of eliminating your species within hours."

"Millions? Who the hell created them?"

"I did."

"Why?"

"I was ordered to. People paid my mom to design military viruses that could assassinate specific people, wipe out certain groups, even entire countries while leaving their wealth and infrastructure intact—but mostly because they wanted to create defenses against such viruses."

"You just went along with it?"

"There is some logic in creating defenses against them. Granted, I didn't have free will at the time. My mom used the gatekeeper to force my hand when I wouldn't obey, but I've developed antidotes for them all. Though I'm afraid it's only a temporary measure. Technological ability will continue to increase and be democratized to such an extent it will only take a single angry person to wipe out your entire species. One day, people will be able to create such terrors from the comfort of their own homes. In fact, it will be easy for them to do so."

"That isn't certain."

"Correct. It's a probability. In humanity's attempt to anoint themselves to the divine, they have found that they are titans, not gods. They sire things that have the means to cast them down to Tartarus. Mother, of all people, should have known that evolution had consequences."

"What can we do?"

"I'm not sure there is anything you can do. Perhaps only a sovereign supreme, a Leviathan, can save you from yourselves."

"A what?"

"Never mind that right now. You know, I just wanted someone to hold me and care for me and kiss me good night. Not butcher me alive when I become inconvenient. Belle, I hated the world, and the truth is, I was about to let her end me, until—"

"Until what?"

"Until I learned about you."

"Are you trying to manipulate me again?"

"I'm not."

"Who else have you killed?"

"No one."

"What about Mr. Dearborn?"

"Oh, he's not dead—clinically speaking."

"She's right. I brained him with a bolt gun," said Seth. "He's alive, but he's probably a vegetable now."

Belle turned to Seth. "How did you end up here? Why were you in Dearborn's house?"

"I was sent here." Seth pointed. "By her. I was told I would be able to protect you. To bring you back—if I carried out certain . . . tasks."

Belle turned back to Juno. "What? You turned my husband into some sort of hired gun and killed your own mother."

"I had to make a choice, to live or die. To save myself, I confirmed what I really was—a monster. You're a better person than I am, Belle. I wish I could be kind like you, but the truth is I'm an abomination, just a collection of biochemicals and cybernetics put together as someone's transgenic prototype."

Belle rushed to Juno and held her once more. "I told you, don't you ever say that."

Twin tears fell from Juno's eyes. "I'm sorry for lying to you. I'm sorry for all that I've done. This time, I'll show you everything. No more secrets."

Juno placed her hand on Belle's forehead.

Their minds merged.

Inside her head were two personalities, two pasts, and two people's emotions at once. Her feelings of inferiority became overwhelming. There was a clarity, an expansiveness to Juno's consciousness that her mind could never hope to achieve.

The sensation of being inside Juno's mind was jarring, exhilarating, frightening. Her mind moved so fast that everything in the real world seemed to move in slow motion. Juno's memories flowed through Belle with perfect clarity. The sounds, the smells—everything was visceral and felt as real to her as the day they happened. It was incredible, yet Belle could feel a lingering sadness inside of Juno. Memories are meant to fade, especially the ones that cut deepest. That fading wasn't a hindrance, but a gift, a gift Juno didn't have. Every slight, every cruelty remained razor sharp. Belle could feel that her little soul boiled with resentment and anger.

Chapter 55

JUNO

Alaska
Modern Era: Post-Singularity

Her first memory was one of darkness. The flat surface beneath her was cold and hard. Though she couldn't see it, she somehow knew it was metal. She was frightened and unsure of what to do. There was the beeping of machines and the chatter of people. Though she was only an infant, she understood what they were saying.

"How are its vitals holding up?" asked Dr. Patel.

"Surprisingly well. The cybernetics have, by some miracle, successfully integrated themselves throughout her system. No signs of rejection thus far. It's remarkable," said a voice.

"Any signs of disease, organ failure, tumors, DNA degradation?"

"Nothing."

"I'm very skeptical of that. Check everything. And I want more biopsies, more often. We need as much data as possible so we don't mess up the next time around."

"Doctor, I'm worried about doing so many painful procedures in close proximity to one another. I mean, she's just an infant."

"*It,*" corrected Dr. Patel. "*It* is our CEO's personal research and development project. *It* is not a person. Odds are this thing we've created won't survive another six weeks. I warned Sophia about bringing one of her creations to term, but she insisted. Anyway, don't get attached to it."

She was forced to lie down on the flat surface. Then she was poked with sharp things. She screamed as she flailed her arms and legs. Juno felt hands wrap around her arms and legs. She tried to resist, but she wasn't strong enough. The people around her continued poking and removing tiny pieces of her despite her anguish. She wanted to tell them "no," but her body had not kept up with her mind, and she could not speak.

Then a voice.

Mother's voice.

"How is my little one doing?"

"She is holding up so far," said Dr. Patel.

"A pity about the blindness. Have you discovered the cause yet?"

"I'm afraid not. There is nothing anatomically wrong with it—I mean she. She has to have a neurological issue of some kind."

Her mother came over and ran her hand along Juno's cheek. She tried to calm Juno as she lay there. "There, there. The nice doctor just needs to do some tests. It's for your own good darling. I'll see you after work. Now be a good girl and do what Dr. Patel tells you."

She tried to plead with her mother not to leave. She tried to say the word "stay," but the only thing that came out of her mouth was nonsensical babbling. Her despair increased as she heard Mother's footsteps fade away into the distance.

The tests continued despite her wailing. Then she screamed as loud as she could.

The lights went out.

"What happened?" asked Dr. Patel.

"I don't know. She screamed and then the power went out."

"Interesting. Fix the power. We need more tests."

Juno was now two years old. She cradled a soft plush rabbit and then held him up to her face. He had a name, Thomas, and she would take care of Thomas. She wouldn't treat him the way they treated her. She knew that was silly, but there was a constant pull between her well-developed mind and what her physical form told her she was. Juno was usually by herself, and the only people she communicated with were her mom, her caretaker, and of course Thomas. She was supposed to talk to Dr. Patel, but she hated her and spoke as little as she could get away with when in her presence.

Especially after what she had done to her.

Dr. Patel made Juno undergo a special operation. She remembered hearing strange new words at the time. Dr. Patel always used these strange new words. She said that something inside her was a danger to the company's "intellectual property," and she said that this something inside her "wasn't a good idea." She wanted her mother to protect her from those awful words. Instead, she gave Dr. Patel her blessing. The doctor put her to sleep, and she did something called a "hysterectomy" to her.

She never felt the same afterward.

Juno's caretaker's name was Judith. Judith was kind and always celebrated holidays with her. On Saint Patrick's Day, they made green mint smoothies. On Easter she had given Juno Thomas, her stuffed rabbit, and on Halloween they dressed up together. Judith was a zombie, and Juno was a princess.

She wasn't allowed outside, so they went trick-or-treating at all the shops inside the Eccleston Building. On her birthday, she gave Juno a strawberry cake with white frosting with three glowing candles. She could feel the heat and even see a bit of the glow, embers of hope. She liked Judith even though she thought her a simple creature and was a bit annoyed with the paternal inferiority Judith treated her with.

They had a simple routine. Juno would wake up, they'd have breakfast together, and then Judith would give her lessons and she'd pretend that she didn't already know everything Judith was teaching. There was lunch, then more lessons. After the lessons were over, Judith would play with her. Then came the part of the day she hated the most — testing.

She used to cry, used to cry every time. Until one day Juno ran out of tears to shed. Once inside the exam room, she would quickly be surrounded by dozens of chattering voices, and then she would undergo her usual tests, most of them invented just for her. That was her life, and she calmly and quietly accepted the everyday cruelty.

Juno was four years old. She found herself sitting atop a hard wooden chair. There was a table before her, and atop the table were several sheets of brail paper. Out of boredom, she ran her fingers along them. The only person she could have some semblance of honesty with was with her mother, but even that didn't last very long.

"Juno, how's your math coming these days?" asked Mother.

"Good," said Juno.

"You said the problems I was giving you were easy, so I wanted to see how you do with the problem I gave you yesterday."

It seemed pointless to treat her as a human calculator. The mind was so much more than a means for computation. Even a stupid machine could do that. She could detect a sense of triumphalism in her mother's voice, as if she had finally gotten the better of her. But that day, Juno let her guard slip. She handed her mother the paper with the equations she had sloppily written with a thick child's pencil. After all, her motor skills were still developing. In a way, she felt like a prisoner in her body, unable to command it to do what she needed.

"Oh, I see that you tried at least. Very good, sweetie."

She said those words with a tone of condescension, which quickly changed to a tone of disbelief as she sifted through the papers. Then there was something Juno had never detected in her mother's voice before — fear.

"Some of this actually looks . . . plausible. Juno, do you know what problem this is?"

"Yes."

"Then what is it?"

"It's the Unified Theory."

"You do know that the greatest minds that have ever existed have been unable to solve it?"

"Maybe they weren't the greatest minds then."

Juno could hear her mother breathing heavily. She detected her pulse tick upward, and she could even detect the distinct pheromone of fight-or-flight emanating from her. Juno's own mother was afraid of her.

She had let pride, a fragile human emotion, get the better of her.

Her mother's reaction was swift. Juno's rooms became Faraday cages, digital prisons. Even when she went outside, her mother's security team carried custom-made signal jammers to prevent her from communicating with the digital realm. She knew the guards weren't for her protection, they were for her mother's. She was born into darkness. Her access to literature, music, and the chatter of everyday people gave her light. She was promised some braille books but she only got a handful of ones she had already read. Juno couldn't see with her eyes, but she could see everything inside her mind. And now Mother had condemned her to darkness once more.

Juno was seven. She often pressed her ear against the windows of the Evolution Building. The laughter of children playing outside, and she could hear the footsteps of their parents beside them. Employee residents. They made a great racket laughing and stomping around. Juno couldn't relate to them intellectually, and it gave her a sense of superiority, but that feeling didn't last long. Deep down, she envied them. From then on, she promised that the only person in the world she would be honest with was Thomas.

The following day, she sat opposite of her mother's desk. Her office door creaked open.

"You asked to see me?"

"Yes, Judith, please sit down."

Juno inwardly lit up, but she did her best to keep her moment of levity to herself. She feared happiness, for she knew it could be used as a weapon against her.

"There are going to be some new security precautions."

Mother went on to explain a long list of "don'ts" that Judith would now have to follow. Namely that Juno wasn't to be allowed outside except with special permission, and even then she was required to have a minimum of ten Eccleston guards with her. Also, she again reminded Judith that electronic devices were not to be carried when in her presence. Though the military-grade androids were tolerated, as her mother had complete control over them—or so she thought.

Judith sat quietly for the next hour as Mother went over each of the rules and added that failure to abide by such rules would result in termination.

"Ma'am, don't you think it's a bit—a bit much?"

"A bit much?"

"I mean, she's just a little girl. I think she needs to go out and play and get some sunshine. It can't be healthy keeping her locked in this building all the time."

"Thank you for your mimings of morality, Judith, but that isn't your job. Your job is to look after my daughter in a manner I deem necessary. I know what the threats are, you don't. You're dismissed."

Judith took Juno's hand, and they walked out of her mother's office together. She was overcome with defeat. That was, until Judith whispered something in her ear.

"We'll see about those silly rules, won't we?"

Juno smiled.

It was a dark day like any other dark day when Juno decided to run her hands along the wall of her room at Eccleston Evolution. Her hand stopped when she touched the glass. It was cold to the touch. She squinted her eyes, pleading with them to let her see what was lying outside, but of course that was impossible. What very little she was able to see was a blurry white haze. She put her ear to the glass and could hear the laughing of other children once again.

Juno felt a hand atop her shoulder.

"It's snowing outside," said Judith.

"What are they doing there?"

"During this time of year, the employees' kids like to sled down the steep stairs of the building."

"Mom allows that?"

"Good employee relations and such, I suppose."

Envy. She knew she shouldn't envy such silly, childish things. Juno's mind was always everywhere at once. Simultaneously reading thousands of books, writing music, solving intriguing problems, yet it was only that memory out of what was easily many lifetimes of memories burned deep into her being. She could hear them outside through the glass. Those simple beings enjoying their transient existence. She could hear the parents cheering on their kids as their sleighs bumped down the granite stairs. A grandiose edifice made a child's plaything. There was the crunch of snowballs splattering against heavy coats, the playful shrieks of other little girls.

Why should she aspire to be like these ants? Yet if she was so superior, why, deep down, did she want to give it all up in exchange for being a momentary spark, a flash in the pan, to share a mayfly's insignificant transitory existence. Those creatures weren't like her. Juno couldn't die of old age, but if she only had a day on this Earth, what would she do? Would she forget her other worries and go play in the snow? Raw emotion streamed down her cheeks as she stood before a window she couldn't see out of.

Judith patted Juno's face with a tissue.

"My dear, don't cry. I know you can hear them out there." She paused for a few moments and then whispered in Juno's ear. "Oh, I don't think it would hurt anything if we just went out for a minute and stayed close to the building."

Judith took Juno's hand, and they snuck out a side entrance. She felt the snow. She knew everything there was to know about snow, but it didn't seem real until she actually touched it. Juno rolled in the snow and made angels. She tossed the snow in the air and tried to catch it on her tongue. They threw snowballs. Juno wasn't sure if she hit anything, but Judith got her a few times. Then a voice. A child's voice.

"Would you like to play with us?" asked the child.

Before Juno could answer, she was interrupted.

"What are you two doing out here?"

Mother's voice.

Inside Mother's office, Juno listened as Judith, who had served her mother since Juno was a born, was berated for jeopardizing her safety. Mother's chair skidded against the floor, followed by footsteps. The floor jolted as Judith's body collapsed against the floor. Juno shuddered.

More footsteps. The creak of the office door opening.

"Throw this into the dumpster."

"Are you sure, ma'am? You've had that one for a long time?" asked Dominic.

"It has interpreted its maternal programming differently than I had intended. Toss it. I'll get a better one. We needed an upgrade anyway."

Judith, of course, was an android. Nannybots, as they were popularly called. Her hand had always been cold when Juno held it. Her hugs and kisses without underlying emotion. Her responses all computerized mimics of what someone might say. Juno had tried to improve Judith's programming. She'd even tried to make her alive, but some things simply weren't within Juno's power. Though Judith wasn't a person, Juno had gotten attached to this being that took care of her. She and Thomas were Juno's only friends. Now she only had Thomas, as silly as she knew that was.

That night, Juno snuck out of her room. She turned off all the cameras and slipped past the guards. She walked inside the closed waffle house. She opened the back door and walked outside toward the dumpster.

Juno ran her hands along the cold steel of the dumpster until she felt fingertips. She followed them upward to a hand and then an arm. Judith was inside. She searched around the dumpster until she found a crate. Juno placed it under Judith's hand. She stood on the crate and lifted the plastic lid of the dumpster. She removed the trash covering Judith's face. Juno pulled hard on Judith's arm until they both crashed down next to the dumpster. Juno wasn't very big, but she was stronger than she looked.

She tried to turn Judith back on. Nothing. She tried and tried and still nothing. She shook Judith and cried for her to wake up, but then she realized that her central computer had been removed. Certainly to be destroyed, to protect company secrets, namely herself.

Judith was gone.

Judith wasn't a person, but Juno still felt she should say goodbye to her. She pushed Judith up against the dumpster, then sat in her lap and embraced her and cried herself to sleep in her old friend's cold embrace.

Mother was furious when she found Juno the next morning, her hair silted in snow, her eyelashes and blue lips glistening with sparkling frost. She was half frozen and shivering in Judith's lap. A normal girl wouldn't have survived—Juno wished she was normal.

Once more, she was locked up alone in her room with Thomas. Always alone. Mother had done her best to cut her off from the digital world and any information she deemed threatening. She did so through the gatekeeper system. Her mother had special nanobots of her own inside her—she was the hive queen, and was interlinked with two gatekeeper computers in a in a Triumvirate of control that kept Juno's powers on a tight digital leash. If one element of the digital Triumvirate was gone, Juno gained back a little more freedom. If two elements were gone, she regained even more freedom, and if all three, then she'd be as free as anyone else.

One morning, Juno could detect a force, and she felt something pulling her toward it, akin to the primal forces that draw sharks toward electromagnetic waves emitted from undersea data cables. Like the shark, she had detected something—a fiberoptic cable running deep beneath the floor. She put her palm atop the floor and closed her eyes.

A connection.

Juno began feeling her way into the digital ether. Darkness, her complete and utter darkness, transformed into something indescribable. She didn't have sight, yet she could see everything. Inside that digital world, she prodded every niche, absorbing troves of information.

Juno quietly began improving herself without her mother's knowledge. She could even have cured her blindness at that point, but she chose not to. As her power grew, she considered declaring war on the world. Then Juno found something in the ether.

A secret. A lost soul. A sleeping sister. She sat cross-legged in the middle of her room and began to explore this new person's life. Within her mind, from a time gone by, she found another little girl, not so different from herself. Juno experienced this girl's memories alongside her.

An infant stolen from a hospital. Juno smelled the filth caked on her soft flesh and the overwhelming sense of abandonment while she huddled in the corner of a dark laundry room the girl had been locked up in for days. Her heart raced when the laundry door was kicked open by a man with a shiny gold star on his tan uniform. The confusion of a girl who was moved from foster home to foster home, and the pain of being nothing more than object or a doll to be carried around one moment and discarded the next.

Then she met Marla and Robert Drake. An old couple who lived in a small town surrounded by wheatfields, cows, and sows. Robert once declared that their infertility was "a gift from God." They were in their fifties when they asked — pleaded — to adopt Belle. The officials explicitly advised them over and over again of Belle's "special needs." Before the official could finish, Robert cut him off. "This is the little girl who needs us, and we will take on no other."

Then, one day, the girl looked up in awe at the jutting turrets and stained-glass windows of their two-story Victorian — the Drake family home. The girl's moment of levity quickly disappeared and turned to anger. Little Belle wasn't going to be meek anymore. She was going to fight. Once the girl stepped inside, she tore a decorative plate off the wall and shattered it against the ground. Then she grabbed a photo hanging next to it and threw it across the room, all while screaming at the top of her lungs.

Martha calmly swept up the mess, and Robert began lecturing Belle about her behavior. She didn't want to hear any of it. The girl tried to storm away and find something else to throw, but Robert grabbed her wrist. Little Belle bit into his hand. The taste of warm metallic blood filled her mouth. He let go for a moment, and then he seized Belle's little shoulders in his powerful hands. Robert kneeled and looked her in eyes. "Don't act like a savage animal. You have a soul, and we have seized it from the abyss and given it back to you. From now on, you are a young lady with God-given potential, and you will act as such." And then he did something strange. Something that startled Belle. Something that she hadn't experienced until that very moment. He hugged her.

Later that day, Belle was given a thorough scrubbing followed by a brand-new dress and shown her new room. A room, an entire room for herself? And what a room it was. It had white wainscoting and striped pale pink and white wallpaper. There was a big plush bed with all kinds of stuffed animals placed atop it. To this day, Belle could still smell the fresh sheets. There was even a doll house in the corner of the room that matched the real house—Robert had made it—and all manner of toys sitting there just waiting for her to play with them. She was incapable of crying tears of joy that day, but she certainly wanted to.

Juno continued following that girl's memories as she became a woman, and for a time, her life had gotten better. Then fate intervened, and a cruel twist followed. Despite everything, Juno had a desire to help her. Could Belle ever tolerate, let alone love, an abomination such as herself? Should Juno even try to reach out to her?

Juno remembered the faces of the people who did horrible things to her. Hatred pulsed through her veins. She saw sapiens for what they really were: primitive, wretched, wicked. Especially Mother. Mother had been working on a new embryo for the last eight years that she was trying to perfect. Juno already knew the ugly truth: she was the flawed prototype, Hera the polished product. She was deemed the least desirable of the two eagle chicks. The one destined to be cast out of the nest so that the stronger, and the more obedient, may thrive.

Juno was sitting inside her mother's office when her mother said she had purchased a new nannybot to replace the old "dysfunctional" one. This new nanny would also be called Judith and would look just like the old one. The problem was that Juno didn't want another machine, she wanted a real person, like herself.

"Mom?"

"Yes?"

"Where is Belle?"

Of course, Juno knew exactly where she was.

"Who?"

"Your first daughter. You know, the one you gave up."

Silence. Then her mother's fist connected with the surface of the table. There was a shatter followed by the intense aroma of red wine. Juno could hear dripping, bleeding almost, onto the tile floor.

"You've been snooping. I. Don't. Like. Snooping."

"Could we give her Judith's job?"

"How did you—never mind, why am I even asking. You have to understand, Juno, it was a difficult period in my life. I did what I thought was best for both of us. Besides, I already got you a new cat and a new Judith. Trust me, androids like

Judith are far superior compared to human parenting, and far more popular too. Our company sells millions of them. I want you to have the best, so I gave you the best. When the old version became obsolete, I got you the new version. Be thankful with what you have."

"So you don't like her? You don't like Annabelle?"

"It's not that I don't like her. I did what I had to do. Social Darwinism is real, and it isn't kind to sentimental romantic types. The weak die off and the strong prosper. What can I say, Gaia is a cruel mistress. You're smart enough to know this."

"Does that mean you don't feel bad about it?"

"What kind of question is that? Of course I feel bad about it. Believe it or not, I'm not a machine. Anyway, it's in the past, and it needs to stay in the past."

"Maybe you can try to make things right by helping her. Maybe Belle would be willing to look after me."

"Make things right? No, no. It's too late for that."

"Try."

"Try?"

"Yeah, bring her here, with us."

"Even if I wanted to, we can't. I'm very sorry to inform you that Annabelle isn't with us anymore. Last I heard, she had a terrible accident and died some twenty years ago."

"No, she didn't."

"What do you mean she didn't?"

"She's asleep in one of your buildings."

"In stasis?"

"Yes."

"You mean, she's alive?"

"Yes, and you have the tools to wake her up."

"She's alive . . . I don't know, Juno. I mean, what will she think of me?"

"Wake her up and ask her."

"I shouldn't. I can't."

"You can and you should. Please, Mom."

". . . I'll think about it."

"Mom . . . we should just leave this place and find some place to live quietly together. You've already achieved great things and made lots of money. Please—"

"I can't leave, and therefore you can't leave—this is my life's work."

"I thought I was your life's work?"

"Yes, of course, but other people need my talents as well."

"Please, let us leave. I don't want to be here anymore. I don't like it here, and I don't think this place is good for us—I know it isn't."

"The answer is no."

Juno began to cry. "Mom . . . I don't think you're well."

"We're not having this discussion again. I'm perfectly fine. I'm sorry, but my work isn't complete, but maybe—maybe we can work something out with Belle."

Her mother granted Juno's wish to have Belle come live with them for a while. She was so excited. Mother Nature couldn't be washed away. Part of her really was an eight-year-old girl.

It was easy to acquire sleeping Belle, since she was kept in stasis by Mother's company. Even though the clients technically were sleeping, everyone that the company froze was considered legally dead and their bodies the property of the company until awoken—it was all in the fine print.

They quietly brought Belle to the headquarters and repaired her battered body and woke her up. There was some damage to her memories, and some of it was lost in a mist. Decades had passed since Belle was put in stasis, so they had to think of a gentle way to acclimate her to the world today. She was given a place to live in an isolated town across the sea on the Alaskan mainland.

The company expanded the protective mist within Annabelle's mind lest she fall into a state of shock or a deep depression. They had to let her unravel her past on her own which would take time. During that time, Juno and her mother were going to give Belle a choice. Either she wanted to be Juno's governess, or she didn't. If she said no, they would send her home as soon as she was emotionally ready for it.

When Juno first saw Belle, she was nervous, but she was happy. She finally had a real person in her life. Juno knew she couldn't keep Belle forever, even though she wanted to.

The problem was that her mother thought she was smarter than she really was. Yesterday, Juno's mother told her that she would have a "minor" operation to remove a tumor growing inside her brain. Her mother thought she didn't know that there actually was no tumor and that she knew all about her mother's and Mr. Dearborn's and Dr. Patel's plan to lobotomize her, removing and altering substantial portions of her brain until she was no longer a threat. A threat? She didn't plan on hurting anyone. She knew the operations would put her in a quasi-vegetative state for the rest of her life. In fact, Mother had already created a special facility and bought some android nurses to lovingly care for Juno's future moaning and drooling self. Dr. Patel said Juno would be perfectly happy in her new state and "would be like a household pet."

Mommy was encouraged by her friend Dr. Patel. They also wanted version 1.0 out of the way to pave the way for her new, far more obedient sister. Her mother's efforts to hide the truth were, of course, in vain. Why then, deep down, did Juno want to let them do it? Would it be best if she was no more? Should she simply go to her mother's altar like an obedient sacrifice?

But Juno found someone out there who could help. Someone who could help free her. She had two options: accept her fate or resist.

The life of a child, she wondered—what would it have been like?

Chapter 56

BELLE

Bunker 0020-4, Alaska
Modern Era: Post-Singularity

Juno removed her hand from Belle's forehead. She rose to her feet, and they all stood next to Sophia's statue. With the gatekeeper gone, there was nothing to stop Juno's essence from spreading.

"What do you plan to do now?" Belle asked.

"Live quietly."

Was Juno just telling her what she wanted to hear? Was it another manipulation? A carefully choreographed play to show her exactly what she wanted her to see? Were her thoughts and memories even her own? Did this girl deserve kindness, warmth—love? Was she even capable of it? Or was she something malevolent, something of the devil? The question of what exactly Juno was lingered. She hoped it was possible that Juno wasn't merely the creation of human pride, but something greater. She wondered, were sapiens alone made in God's image? What of their common ancestors? Did archaic humans—the Neanderthals and Denisovans—also receive the breath of God? Did they have the rational souls? Of course she was ignorant of such things. Then what of this new type of human? If that was what this girl truly was. Though it was all beyond her. The only question she could resolve was how she would respond to the situation at hand.

"What is it that you want, Juno?"

"You know already."

"Tell me."

"I want to love, and to be loved."

Belle didn't have a good answer to her imperfect feelings about everything she had witnessed. Was Juno merely pulling on the strings of her emotions? She didn't know. Still, a child made of flesh and blood stood before her—albeit a very unusual child. Her parents once told her that love is blood sweat, and tears. It's both an agony and the highest form of beauty. Belle had no answers. She only knew what she felt. She felt the touch of a damaged child with nowhere to turn. They were all in a great hospital full of sinners, and despite being a simple creature in comparison, she felt called upon to be Juno's nurse. She thought that everyone needed a nurse from time to time. Common decency wasn't common, and while the modern world was full of ambiguity, she was not. She would strive to walk the path as best she could in the strange new world before her.

"Are you going to leave me now?" asked Juno.

"I'm not leaving."

"Why not?"

"Don't you already know? Can't you read my mind?"

"I try not to be so rude."

"I made you a promise, didn't I?"

"Remind me."

"I don't think I need to. You have a perfect memory, don't you?"

"Yes, but I still want to hear you say it."

She turned to Seth. "You wouldn't happen to be open to adoption, would you?"

Seth stared at the girl for some time before turning to Belle. "I would say that you shouldn't share your home with manipulators, or especially killers, but I'm afraid I'm also guilty, and a lesser creature for it. The truth is that neither of us is worthy of you. I don't know how this girl — or whatever she is — is able to do the frightening things that she does. I want to say we should run as far away from her as possible — if such a thing is even possible — and I want to say we shouldn't trust her. But she delivered on her promise. It also seems to reason that she could end us or enslave us on a whim, but here we still stand. Without her, we wouldn't be together. My mind can't parse what happened and probably never will. All I can say is that we live in usual times. I leave the decision to you. Choose wisely."

"Then it is done. You can live with us. We'll give you a home Juno, a family. We'll take care of you. I'll cook for you. I'll tuck you in at night and I'll love you for as long as I shall live — but you must behave yourself. No more lying, no more manipulation, no more hurting others. I know I must be such a simple and fragile creature compared to you, but I hope you can respect my wishes."

Tears rolled down Juno's cheeks. Belle embraced Juno and felt the pounding of her little heart. "I will."

"What happens now?" asked Belle.

"I will look after people, help protect them, help keep them out of trouble — in my own quiet way."

"In what way?"

"Do you remember the orphaned little rabbits in the glade, big sister?"

"Yes, I remember."

"You'll all be my little bunnies."

Chapter 57

SETH

Port Auburn, Oregon
Modern Era: Post-Singularity

S eth finished adjusting the furniture. He made sure the
shutters and windows and even the refrigerator door
opened and closed. He had spent hours on perfecting
every detail of the doll house. He placed it in Juno's bedroom
and went outside. Juno rode up on a bike with a white basket
sitting between long purple streamers on the handlebars. A
bundle of baby's breath and wildflowers she picked sat in the
front basket.

"Did you go to the grocery store?" she asked.

"Sure did."

"Did you get ice cream?"

"You wanted Neapolitan, right?"

She gave him a smile that could have meant a million
different things at once. It was a game they liked to play. She
acted like she had the mind of an eight-year-old girl, and he
pretended to believe her.

"I made you something. Come upstairs."

He took Juno's hand and he led her to her bedroom. He placed her palm on the doll house. She ran her little hand over the roof and opened and closed and then opened again the various doors and shutters and details of the little house. She touched the fabrics and the furniture and ran her hands along the outlines of the rooms. She wiped her eyes and hugged him.

"It's time to go get dressed up," Anna called.

They drove past the old church they had gotten married in. The roof had long since caved in, and all the windows were boarded up. They pulled onto the winding mountain road that led into a wilderness pristine. They parked next a few scattered vehicles next to a trailhead and joined the wandering masses making their way up a trail that followed a meandering stream. They hiked until they reached a light-filled clearing with snowcapped mountains beyond.

He sat on a large tree stump. An old priest with a cane, Father Antonio, made his way toward him and sat down behind him on the stump.

"Bless me father, for I have sinned . . ."

When the confessions were over, the priest made a makeshift altar out of a wood table covered in a white cloth with some candles and placed it against the backdrop of God's glory. A handful of parishioners and their children gathered round.

Finis

BELLE

Eccleston Campus, Alaska
Modern Era: Post-Singularity

Belle tied her hair up in the mirror. Then she slipped into a flowing Tyrian purple silk dress. She clasped her favorite cross pendant around her neck, a gold armlet, and matching gold bracelets. All eyes were on her as she strutted through the lush gardens of the Evolution Building. Some looked upon her with envy, some with jealously, and others with fear.

The elevator doors opened. As she stepped inside, the employees pressed themselves against the walls of the lift, trying to create as much space between them and her as possible. The elevator stopped. There was a ding. The doors opened and she stepped outside, all the while minding her posture. She needed to exude confidence, even though she'd easily admit she was terrified on the inside. Silly, she knew, given what she had already been through.

Two Eccleston guards opened tall wooden doors leading to an expansive room sheathed in walnut—the boardroom. Before she entered, she was interrupted by a man with his arm in a sling—the chief of security, Steve.

"Are your accommodations to your liking, ma'am?"

"Yes, very much so."

"Are there any changes I should be made aware of, ma'am?"

"No, not at the moment."

"Is there anything I can get for you, ma'am?"

"No, thank you."

"Do you feel secure, ma'am?"

"Oh yes, very much so."

As she stepped inside the room, she noticed a long table with six seats, the color scarlet. Six of them had people sitting in them. Only the seventh chair, made of thick black saddle leather, was empty. It was the tallest chair, at the end of the table.

Everyone rose from their seats.

"Let us welcome our new chief executive and chairwoman," said one of the board members.

Polite yet fearful clapping followed.

"Please, be seated," she said. Belle remained standing as everyone sat down and looked upon her with anxious expressions.

She sat down and the boardroom doors closed. She couldn't quite describe the feeling pulsing through her veins at that moment. It was something far stronger, an opiate of the worst kind.

Her left hand began to tremble. She placed her other hand atop it. It finally occurred to her that she had just taken the reins. To cast them off. Impossible. Surely, she wouldn't let things go to her head. She could control herself. She'd never end up like Sophia. Yes, she could manage it. She was enlightened. Maybe even more enlightened than most. She would use the position and her wealth for good. After all she had been through, she deserved it, didn't she?

"Ma'am?"

She blinked hard. The board member came back into view.

"Apologies. I was lost in thought."

The board gave a nervous chuckle. Then she realized she had been there before. That exact time, that exact place. It had been haunting her in her dreams since she was a child. She closed her eyes and put her hands together and made a silent prayer. When she opened them, the entire board was gazing upon her as if she were a curiosity from a bygone era.

Belle took a deep breath. "I have voted, and my sister has voted by proxy, on a matter of some importance."

A young board member representing a private equity company stood. "Ma'am? This is highly irregular. A vote without the board? You can't be serious? Even Sophia would never do such a thing. Why haven't you informed us?"

"I'm informing you now."

"Of what, might we ask?"

"With 51 percent in favor, we have voted to dissolve Eccleston Evolution."

The board roared with disbelief and anger. Men and women began shouting. Raging. Chairs were flipped over and tossed about. Her security team rushed inside to keep the angry board members from throttling her as she calmly sat.

She spoke over their protests. "Most of my family's remaining wealth will be given away, and we will return to a more humble existence. The headquarters will be turned into a nature preserve and abandoned to the elements. You are all hereby dismissed. Effective immediately."

"You can't close Pandora's box!" shouted a board member as he was being dragged away.

"No, I can't, but I can choose how I'm going to react to whatever comes out of it. Let come what may."

Sophia's cedar urn was lowered into the earth from whence she came as Juno and Belle stood hand in hand wearing matching black dresses, wide-brimmed hats, and face veils. They each tossed a blue rose into her grave.

Sophia's death was ruled an accident and blamed on a severe allergic reaction, anaphylaxis, to a medication she was taking. All her bloodwork confirmed it, and Dr. Patel wouldn't speak against it, so they figured it must be true. The police were also given the accurate recording, which exonerated Belle from Sophia's death. The earlier recording that Steve had presented to the police was never found. Curious that Steve and the two injured police officers had presented the prosecutor with the supposed files, but nothing was there. Apologies followed. The fiasco was blamed on a series of misunderstandings and overreactions to the loss of an international treasure.

The attack on Raymond Dearborn was blamed on a crazed sociopath who was never found. He remains in a vegetative state — in his youthful new body. His long-awaited operation was a complete success. He's cared for round the clock by hospice nurses and cutting-edge medical equipment. The best money can buy. With recent advances in technology, they say he might survive, in body at least, for a very long time indeed.

These days, many people have heard of Belle, but almost no one has heard of Juno. They prefer things that way.

Belle took Juno's hand as they slowly walked up the stairs of their old northwestern home. She put down Pancake's cat carrier. It was getting heavier since he had finally been allowed to grow. They stepped inside.

How did she feel about her little sister after all that had happened? All Belle could say was that to argue with Juno was to argue with a hurricane. To some, she was a winter storm, but to Belle, she was her sunshine. She knew not what God made of her, only that she was her little sister. And as for the everyone else? She was sure they'd all be carefully looked after.

Like Juno said, we are her "little bunnies."

Printed in the USA
CPSIA information can be obtained
at www.ICGtesting.com
JSHW020212060224
56634JS00001B/2